REVELATIONS

REVELATIONS

THE ANCIENT ONES TRILOGY
BOOK III

❧

CASSANDRA L. THOMPSON

QUILL & CROW PUBLISHING HOUSE

CLEVELAND

Revelations by Cassandra L. Thompson.
Book Three of The Ancient Ones Trilogy.
Published by Quill & Crow Publishing House.

Cover Design by Fay Lane.

Printed in the United States of America.

Cataloging-in-Publication Data is on file with the Library of Congress.

ISBN: 978-1-958228-05-0
ISBN: 978-1-958228-04-3 (ebook)

Author's Website: http://cassandralthompson.carrd.co

For my

L.

Foreword

The Ancient Ones is a story twenty years in the making. From the initial idea at fifteen, to the moment I got the courage to finish it in my thirties, the entire process has been an incredible journey. I knew in the back of my mind, I wouldn't be able to stop with just one book, and no sooner did I finish The Ancient Ones and send it for editing, did Lucius creep back into my mind.

Within one year, Book Two and Three were finished, and I am so excited to give readers a completed trilogy that is exactly the type of story I have always wanted to read. I can't believe I'm closing the book, so to speak, on something that has profoundly changed my life. I hope you were able to find something of yourself in at least one of my characters, and hopefully see the overlying message I was trying to impart.

There is so much more to the world than what we see on the surface, and things run deeper than what we are taught. Some angels are actually demons, and some demons turn out to be heroes. If you have made it this far, I sincerely thank you for giving this trilogy a chance, and I hope its resolution leaves you satisfied. We begin our tale right at the point where we left off, but in case you need a quick reminder, allow me to assist.

Book One tells the story of an ancient immortal named David, the last of his kind, who is in the midst of an existential crisis. The year is 1857 and David has just bought an old abandoned house called Lardone Manor, once a countryside cathedral. After a particularly long depressive slump, he heads to his favorite Limehouse pub where he meets a brash, unapologetic lady of the night who is dying of consumption. After taking him along for a taste of her self-destruction, she convinces him to tell her his story.

David reveals he was born in Ancient Gaul, the son of a Druid Elder. Julius Caesar invades their tribe, kidnapping him to be sold as a slave. On the harrowing passage home, he is comforted by a mysterious woman who protects him from harm. After a particularly gruesome arrival at the Roman Port, he realizes she is The Morrigan, a Celtic war goddess who has decided to look after him. In the Roman forum, he finds a young slave girl named Gaia who takes him under her wing and into the forced employ of a winemaker named Eridus. She gives him his Roman name, Davius.

Eventually, Davius falls in love with her, convinced that one day he will earn enough money from his paintings to buy their freedom and get married. But strange things start to occur, including nightmares of a hideous, bloodthirsty dragon. Eventually, he meets a strange man named Lucius, who seems to be a world traveling philosopher. He hires Davius to paint for him and the two become fast friends. He is warned by the apparition of a boar that he should steer clear of Lucius, that he is not all he seems.

Davius learns Eridus wants to marry Gaia and panics. He looks to his new friend for help and finds out he is a reincarnated dark god, brought to the earth flawed, therefore becoming the world's first immortal blood drinker. Lucius wants Davius to join him, but Davius flees in terror. He returns to the villa to learn Eridus knows he's been sleeping with Gaia. He sells her off to an abusive slave owner named Nirus and beats Davius half to death.

Davius wakes up to discover Lucius has rescued him and killed Eridus. Lucius encourages him to use his inherent Druidic power to rescue Gaia. Davius realizes he has command of the wind—he can create windstorms and channel its energy. Unfortunately, Gaia dies and Davius vows to avenge her death. He decides to become a creature like Lucius to do so.

Five years later, in Ancient Greece, the boar that once warned him returns, revealing that he is a liminal being named Libraean. He reveals more about Lucius's past, including the fact that Gaia was pregnant with Davius's child at the time of her death. Davius decides it's time to avenge her death. He decides to summon the Morrigan for help, unknowingly igniting a war between him and Lucius for her attention. She says she will help, but only if they make her one of them. Lucius doesn't think it will work, but Davius insists it will.

Davius is approached by a strange council of creatures who tell him they want him to bring back Morrigan. He meets Anubis, and they fill him with power to help him. Davius succeeds in killing Nirus and brings Morrigan to life. The problem is, she decided Nirus's wicked daughter, Delicia, would be her vessel and instead of taking her over, the two souls braid together, making her half-Delicia, half-Morrigan to become an entity called Morgana.

Jump to 15th century Wallachia. Davius (now called David) lives with

Lucius and Morgana in a Romanian castle. Lucius has stolen the identity of the Wallachian prince, Vladimir Dracula, and presides over a court of self-created nemorti and revenants. Tension is at an all-time high: David and Lucius are at odds, compounded by Morgana slowly losing her grip on reality and bouncing back between Delicia and the Morrigan. Delicia seems content with Lucius as her lover, but Morrigan and David have a special connection that neither one of them quite understands. She begs Lucius and David to kill her so she can be a free goddess once more, but neither one of them are willing—they love her too much.

At a feast, Lucius brings in a prisoner for entertainment, who turns out to be a hideous lycanthrope. He terrorizes the entire court, forcing David to take Morgana's blood so he can shapeshift into a wolf and stop him. Her dying wish is for him to follow the wolf to a witch named Hekate. He obeys, discovering a group of otherworldly beings called the Council (the creatures from before), who inform him they are responsible for all magical workings in the world and they need his help to stop Lucius, who is upsetting the balance on earth. He meets Dragos, one half of a pair of healer twins, and he discovers the true identity of the beast, a reincarnated Viking god who goes by the name of Danulf. He learns there is an Insurgence rising up against Lucius made of human subjects and escaped nemorti.

Eventually, Lucius's knights catch up with David and Danulf in the Carpathian Mountains as they travel to find Hekate. Lucius ties him up outside to die in the sun, but Danulf saves him at the last moment, and delivers him to Hekate, a pregnant healer/witch who holds the secrets to his past.

As she heals his wounds, she reveals that all of them—Lucius, David, Morrigan—were once part of a quartet of Egyptian gods who existed at the beginning of time, reincarnated on earth with no memories of their past lives. She reveals that Lucius and Morrigan were once husband and wife (named Set and Nephthys), but David (Osiris) slept with Morrigan, impregnating her with his sons (gods Anubis and Horus). Morrigan flees, letting her sister, Isis, raise her sons as her own in order to protect them from Set. He still manages to find out, and murders Osiris.

The sisters, Isis and Nephthys, decide to bring back Osiris from the dead. Anubis and Horus, now grown adults, assist, knowing they have to use Set's blood to revive him. The plan fails—Horus kills Set, but not before Set plucks out Horus's eye, therefore cursing his reincarnation, and

Osiris comes back wrong, biting Nephthys's neck and forcing Isis to stab him in the heart.

Nephthys and Osiris (Morrigan and David) go to the Upperrealms (heaven), Set (Lucius) is banished to Tartarus (hell) with Anubis guarding him. Isis frees her soul and puts her body and magic in an acadia tree. Horus reincarnates as Libraean.

With this new knowledge, David is ready to end Lucius for good, and freely joins the Insurgence. Anubis and Libraean contact him beforehand and Libraean gives him the last bit of power so David is strong enough to defeat him. After a brutal war, which includes the deaths of Dragos, Hekate, and Danulf, and one last embrace with Morrigan in spirit form, David evokes the power of all the elements and slays Lucius, who had become the horrible creature from his dreams.

Throughout the story, David and his companion (the prostitute from the tavern) arrive and talk at Lardone Manor, but towards the end, David learns her death is coming quickly. She still wants to hear his story, and after he finishes, he is content to hold her in his arms until she passes. At the last moment, and with the help of some very ornery crows, he realizes she is the Morrigan incarnated. He runs to find Libraean, who has also been alive this whole time, living in the secret vaults underneath his cemetery. Libraean turns her into a blood drinker and they happily reunite...until there is a knock at the door. It is Danulf, surprisingly still alive, come to tell them Lucius has returned.

Liminality picks up where The Ancient Ones ends in Victorian London, 1857. David, having just brought his lover, Morrigan, back to life with the help of his companion, Libraean, opens his door to reveal his friend, Danulf, still alive after he believed him to be dead for centuries. He tells him that Lucius, his detestable brother last seen masquerading as the mad Wallachian prince Vlad Dracula, has returned to Earth after David killed him.

Danulf, now called Dan, explains that Lucius was reborn in 1740 to a family of French aristocrats, and was raised by a vampiress named Angelique and her brother, Ares, who just so happens to be Dragos resurrected. Lucius switched bodies with King Louis XVI until the French Revolution, then went into hiding.

After they all take time to rest and feed (which includes Morrigan and David getting a chance to reunite properly) they reconvene and Dan explains his story in depth, beginning the day the young Viking realized he was a lycanthrope. He tells David what he saw at the conclusion of the Night War was not real. He was not dead—the wolf part of him, a Norse monster named Fenrir, remained alive and ravaged the earth for centuries, while the other half of him was stuck in the astral plane. His two halves were restored when Fenrir found a young, feral girl in the woods, after it killed her mother and the pack of wolves she considered family.

The young girl, named Cahira, turned out to be a very powerful witch, who carved ancient runes into his chest so he would be under her command. She brings back Dan's soul, and informs him that a dream instructed her to find a creature named David, and now that her mother and pack are dead, he must keep her safe.

The two embark on a journey out of the Carpathian Mountains, through the Bohemian Forest, and into France. Over time, they develop a strong bond that transcends the magic he is bound to her by. He ends his tale in France, where he and Cahira head into Paris, believing they are going to find David. Dan trails off from his story visibly distressed, but not before he tells the others what he learned: something is killing all the gods and their realms. The vampires decide they must head to France to find Lucius.

Meanwhile, Libraean, tired and still upset by the revelation that David's manservant, Jacob, has been his reincarnated ex-lover this entire time, goes to his room. He ends up having a conversation with one of the ghosts of David's manor, a young man named Philip Lardone, who confirms that all the realms besides the Christian Heaven and Hell (Tartarus) have been destroyed.

Upon Phillip Lardone's advice, David and Libraean head into London to request the services of a medium that can access Morrigan's repressed memories, in the hopes they will uncover the key to the problem with the realms. While they're gone, a mysterious stranger appears, claiming to be looking for David. Morrigan invites him in before realizing she's speaking to the reincarnated Lucius. The others return, and Lucius insists he has no memory of his former life. He claims his name is Louis, and that he fled those who turned him into a vampire and tried to make him king for their own purposes. The vampires decide to put him in the vaults until they can determine his truthfulness.

The medium David and Libraean recruited agrees to hypnotize Morrigan and access her memories. They discover that after she and Lucius died in 15th century Romania, he rose out of Tartarus and settled back in the Underworld. He summoned Morrigan, who was drifting listlessly between realms, claiming he was trying to protect her from a goddess named Discordia. They end up rekindling their love until something summons her back to Earth. Before they can access the rest of her memories, Morrigan pulls out of her trance in shock to see David, who is heartbroken. He leaves the manor and heads into town to anesthetize.

After a week of chasing the dragon and nearly killing the owner of the opium den, David wakes up in a hazy stupor with an arrow pointed at his face. It is Cahira, who takes him back to her cabin, where she tells him her story and the rest of what happened between her and Dan. She explains that when she and Dan reached Paris, they met a vampiress named Angelique who was grooming a young boy named Louis (Lucius) to be a vampire and take over the throne of King Louis. They discovered she had an entire "galere" of vampires and chaos gods she presided over, including a vampiress named Sandrine. Cahira and Sandrine are curiously drawn to each other, and Sandrine reveals Angelique intends on stealing Cahira's power. In the midst of this, Cahira discovers Dan in bed with another woman and realizes their relationship can no longer continue as it had before.

Meanwhile, back at the manor, Libraean and Jacob make peace. Dan, who reveals he was tricked into thinking he was sleeping with Cahira in Paris, drowns his sorrows in scotch, while Morrigan has locked herself in David's parlor, refusing to speak, sleep, or eat. With no sign of David for a full week, and Morrigan's memories still hidden, Libraean and Jacob decide to ask Lucius to look after her. Attempting to lift her spirits, Lucius takes her into town under the guise of two married aristocrats, where they drink absinthe and dance…before someone from Morrigan's past sets off Lucius, who goes into a rage and lights the entire ballroom on fire.

David heads home to tell the others he's spoken to Cahira and they all must go to see Anubis where he has reincarnated in Africa, since he knows the secret to why the realms are being destroyed. He finds Morrigan and Lucius have gone missing, and goes with Dan to collect them. David throws Lucius back into the vaults and after an impassioned conversation, David is hit by one of Morrigan's repressed violent memories, which knocks him unconscious.

With David down, Morrigan takes command, sending Dan to fetch Cahira so they can still journey to Africa. She lets Lucius out of the vaults, and tells him to drink her blood so he can see the memories she uncovered. Lucius now remembers their entire past and agrees they need to go to Anubis. But before they can do so, they are attacked by an army of daemons sent by Angelique. Lucius and Morrigan end up killing them all, much to the surprise of Cahira, who stumbles upon the aftermath. Eventually, Dan and Cahira reconnect and prepare her ship for their journey. She reveals Sandrine has been her traveling companion over the many years they were apart, and soon the group, including an unconscious David, are headed towards Calais to access Lucius's ship which will take them to Africa.

On route, Lucius reveals that while he can remember everything else, he is missing memories from his initial banishment to Tartarus until the time he rose to Earth as Lucius the vampyre. Concerned, Morrigan asks Cahira for help pulling out both their memories. Cahira resumes where the medium left off with Morrigan first, and they are shocked to learn that Morrigan was the adopted mother who raised Cahira in the woods before she was killed by Fenrir: After the pregnant witch Hekate died in Romania, Morrigan delivered her baby to the Sagittari for protection. It was that young man, the last of the Paduri clan, that summoned her from Lucius's arms in the Underworld. His ghost tells her he was tricked by a demoness who grew pregnant with his child before killing him and taking the baby. Morrigan rescues the baby and decides to raise her, knowing it was Lucius and her sister's granddaughter and that she would need protection. That child was Cahira.

When her death at Fenrir's hands brings her back to the Underworld, she finds it in flames, with Lucius near death. She discovers an angry chaos goddess named Discordia, who turns out to be the one responsible for destroying the realms and killing the gods. While she breaks Morrigan's bones, she gleefully admits she killed Isis in the ancient days and pretended to be Persephone to trick Lucius into coming to Earth. She was also Hekate in Romania and technically Cahira's birth mother. She then murders Morrigan and Lucius, then rises to Earth as Angelique so she can make sure to kill their human reincarnations.

Morrigan comes back to consciousness, but before they can wrap their minds around all the revelations, another monster sent by Angelique attacks them. It is a hydra, and it cannot be killed. Dan sacrifices himself to pull it down into Tartarus. Cahira is destroyed, the ship is now falling apart, and then suddenly, David wakes up. That is where our final tale begins.

Hope you enjoy Book III of The Ancient Ones Trilogy, Revelations.

Dreadfully Yours,
Cassandra L. Thompson

PART ONE

Before he even opened his eyes, he heard them. Twittering interrupted by squawks and croons, an avian chorus conducted by the steady, piercing shriek of a falcon. He could tell it was midmorning just by the way they sang, even without the sun rays that settled on his skin, the scent of thawing earth in his nose, or the rustle of leaves tickling his ears. A strong flap of wings struck right above him and he bolted upright, yet his eyes did not settle on a crow as he expected, but the falcon, who studied him with suspicious black eyes.

"Good morning," a voice came from behind him.

He spun in alarm. Thick, oppressive jasmine immediately accosted him, its familiarity disarming him as he observed a ghost from his past. Radiant against the azure sky, she moved across the grass towards him, her rose-gold hair lifting in the breeze.

David blinked, trying to bring rationality into his mind. This felt too real to be a dream—it had to be another realm, one that managed to be spared in the Purging. Or had he finally died? Could it be that he was in Heaven? Or had he landed himself in Tartarus, and this was simply a cruel trick of the mind?

"Shhh," Gaia whispered as she drew closer. She looked exactly as she had when he left her in his youth, her heart-shaped face dusted with sunspots, her lips full, blonde lashes rimming eyes the color of spring. "I know it is a lot to bear, but you are safe here. This is my realm."

The longer he peered at her, the more he felt as if the past millennia hadn't transpired at all, and he was once again a young Druid boy standing in verdurous grasses with his first love. The urge to hold her overcame him, a yearning to breathe in her fragrant hair and touch her skin, although he'd left Morrigan only moments before. "Your realm?" he managed.

Gaia smiled, the act bringing a sparkle into her eyes. Their shade matched the flora surrounding her. "Do you remember this place?" Her voice married the pitch of the songbirds.

He looked around him at the verdant plains, the cloudless sky, and the lush trees that seemed to have no end. He felt peace, contentment even, and that was when the realization dawned on him. He stood in a realm that perfectly resembled the ancient hills of Gaul. "Where are we?" he asked in wonderment.

"We have much to discuss."

He looked down to see he was dressed in a tunic similar to hers, blinding white in the sun. His bare feet sunk pleasantly into the earth, the grass snaking between his toes. He felt her hand slip into his. He'd forgotten how small her hands were, how nicely they fit together. The act itself grounded him, his disorientation subsiding.

"Come," she beckoned. "I will show you my home." She led him through the unkempt plains as his mind continued to piece together his reality. The last soul he'd spoken Gaia's name to was Anubis, back when he lived in Wallachia, centuries ago. The death god had assured him her soul was safe in the Underworld, but since that time, the realms had been destroyed. So where were they now?

"You think too much." She laughed as though she could hear his thoughts. "I will explain everything to you, I promise."

A forest heavy with oaks and yews loomed up ahead, and she guided him through it to a winding creek. She didn't hesitate to cross it, balancing on the scattered stones until she reached the other side. He hurried to keep up, nearly colliding with her when she stopped in front of a mammoth oak tree who proudly dwarfed the saplings surrounding it. Its thick bark bore warts like an ancient elder, its arms so long, they weaved through the clouds. She gestured for him to follow her through its open mouth.

David wasn't sure what to expect, but it was not the cozy abode he found nestled inside the warm, fragrant wood. Thin vines streaked the walls, plants sprouting at every corner. The sudden realization hit him—she was exactly where he'd left her, so many eons ago.

He followed her up a set of mossy wood steps into an open space warmed by the sunlight filtering through the cracks in the wood. She settled down into a cluster of leaves, inviting him to join her. Butterflies flitted back and forth between the jasmine blossoms that dotted the vines, their dewdrops glistening in the light. Her eyes followed as he sank down next to her, waiting for him to settle before she spoke. "So, my long lost love. Where do we begin?"

CHAPTER ONE

❧ THE SURVIVORS ❧

THE ATLANTIC OCEAN, 1857
MORRIGAN

MORRIGAN STOOD SILENTLY IN FRONT OF DAVID as he observed the disastrous deck, slick with rain and gore. Broken wood, torn sails, and pieces of rotting hydra lay scattered around them. David scratched at his head as the ocean misted his face, dampening the confused expression behind his tousled auburn hair. His gentle green eyes met hers. "How long was I gone?"

Morrigan's throat had gone dry, but she forced herself to make words. "We are on Cahira's ship, headed towards Africa."

"Cahira…" David's brow furrowed as he tried to remember. His attention flickered away. "And who are you?"

Morrigan remembered Lucius stood at her side, apparently also shocked into silence. He recovered, however, replying before she could, "My name is Louis." He swept past her to reach out his hand in an amicable greeting. "You have been out for quite some time now. How much do you remember?"

David took it, though a frown settled on his lips. His eyes drifted back to Morrigan. "My last memory is broken glass. Everything before that is hazy."

The image of when he'd fallen, shattering the beautiful stained-glass windows that circled them in a tornado of sorrow, uncomfortably wedged its way into Morrigan's consciousness. Sorrow gnawed at her stomach.

"Perhaps we should let you rest before we dive deeper into an explanation,"

Lucius suggested. He placed his hand gently on David's back, guiding him to the ship's hold.

David acquiesced, using Lucius's arm to steady himself as he took several uneasy steps forward. In any other circumstance, the interaction would have been unusually endearing, but Morrigan had trouble grasping onto her bearings. She licked lips parched from seawater, grateful Lucius had stepped in. She'd been so swept up by everything happening that seeing David again rendered her stunned.

She gazed wistfully at the rippling sapphire ocean, picturing the hideous, multi-headed creature and the werewolf it had just swallowed. Her chest squeezed with regret, the remnants of Cahira's pain still clinging to her like spiderwebs. She'd hoped for a chance to know her daughter as a grown woman, but the opportunity had been shattered by Morrigan's decision to hold her back while Cahira's lover jumped to his death. Morrigan felt very much like the broken ship, in pieces, and she was too exhausted to pick them up. She let out a deep sigh, stepping around the carnage to follow Lucius and David down the broken ladder.

A few inches of seawater remained in the hold, and anything that hadn't been bolted down now bobbed freely with each rock and sway. She maneuvered her heavy skirts through the mire as she approached the cramped sitting area. David sat on the table, rubbing at his temples, as Lucius shoved open the door to Libraean and Jacob's room. Water poured in and swept away the candles and chalk that had been arranged to summon the portal, while simultaneously releasing both herbal smoke and Libraean, who ran to David in relief. Jacob followed suit, the two older men cradling him in their arms like their long-lost prodigal son.

Though elated, the elderly human appeared drained, alarmingly slender in the dim light. Still, he managed to give David a warm smile from beneath his tired eyes. "It is good to see you, sir, but I'm afraid I'm feeling a bit more tired than usual."

David cupped his narrow shoulder. "By all means, please rest. We can talk more in the morning."

Jacob nodded gratefully, patting his hand and giving Libraean a quick kiss on the cheek before plodding back to their room. Lucius secured the door behind him.

David looked at Libraean. "My friend, what is happening?"

"In case anyone has forgotten," Lucius interrupted before he could reply, "we are in the middle of the ocean on a ship that is standing still, vulnerable not only to the dangers at sea, but whatever else Angelique decides to throw at us. Perhaps we should decide our next course of action before regaling him with our latest escapades."

Sandrine abruptly resurfaced from the captain's quarters, securing the door behind her with a forceful push.

"How is she?" Morrigan asked.

"Naturally, Cahira is furious with you," Sandrine replied coolly. Though Morrigan was tall, she seemed taller, her mound of coiled hair grazing the ceiling of the cabin. She wore thick trousers tucked into dark men's boots, but her shirt was light and flowing against her sepia-toned skin. "It's better that she rests without additional upset. We might be away from land, but there are still plenty of ways an earth goddess can ruin our journey if angered. And Louis is correct, our ship is badly injured. We must figure out how to move it before it sinks to the bottom of the ocean. I would survive, but I'm sure the rest of you would prefer to reach land."

"We could fly," Lucius suggested.

"But what about our things?" Libraean objected. "And surely Jacob wouldn't be able to handle that sort of travel. He hasn't seemed well since we set sail." He glanced at their cabin door as if reminded of his worry.

"I may be able to repair the masts and sails to the point where they can catch wind again," Sandrine told them. "But we would still have to rely on it to go forward. The ship already holds so much water, I don't know how long we will be able to wait for it to pick up."

"I need to eat," David abruptly interjected.

Lucius wordlessly ducked into his room and produced a bottle of animal blood which he thrust in David's direction.

He took it gratefully, taking several large gulps before addressing Sandrine. "Have I met you before?" he asked with blood-stained teeth.

She didn't respond immediately, taking a moment to study him. "My name is Sandrine. I am a friend of Cahira's."

"Sandrine, after I have eaten, I can help with the wind," he said. "I've just woken from a long slumber, but if you'd like to try to mend the sails now while I regain my strength, I can assist you in getting the ship moving shortly."

Sandrine nodded.

"I'll help with the sails," Lucius offered, surprising them all. Morrigan caught a hint of sadness in his amber-colored eyes. "I need the air," he explained to her quietly.

Cahira burst out of the captain's quarters. She dove at Morrigan, her face twisted by fury. "How could you?" she hissed.

Thankfully, Sandrine moved to intervene in one fluid motion, successfully blocking the attack before it unfolded. Lucius came immediately to Morrigan's side, folding his arms as if waiting to defend her.

Morrigan's stomach twisted at the raw pain streaked across Cahira's face, suddenly overwhelmed by everything around her. She focused on the ocean water that swirled around her ankles, listening to the soft waves as they lapped against the boat. "Please forgive me," she managed. "He told me it was the only way."

"You shouldn't have listened," Cahira spat. From behind Sandrine's strong arms, her eyes appeared entirely black with rage, no hint of the golden brown that usually warmed them. "I overheard your conversation—you chose your lover's life over his."

Sandrine's deep, syrupy voice slid through the commotion, diffusing the tension with its tone. "Cahira, this is not the time. We must reach land and you must control your temper."

Cahira's eyes remained locked on Morrigan's, despite her friend's words of reason. Morrigan could still see the feisty girl she once loved hidden behind the womanly visage, hardened by time and riddled with grief. Cahira let out a sound of frustration, shaking herself free from Sandrine's grasp and heading back up the ladder to the deck.

Morrigan deflated, trying to quell the emotion that threatened to break her. She caught the aroma of heavy spice, and looked up to see Lucius had crept closer to her during the exchange. She knew it took everything in him not to comfort her, and that thought proved enough to steady her sway. Out of the corner of her eye, she noticed David observing their unspoken interaction with curiosity.

"Let us mend what we can," Sandrine unknowingly intervened, motioning for Lucius to follow her back on deck.

David took another sip from the bottle he held, watching them disappear above deck before turning his gaze Morrigan's way. "What was that all about?"

She swallowed, uncertain where to begin.

"We should let Morrigan rest," Libraean's voice mercifully broke in. The way he looked at her, with nothing but genuine kindness, pulled the rising sobs in her chest that much closer to the surface. "Our lady has been fighting many battles while you slept. I will fill you in on everything."

"Of course." David rose to his feet. She froze as he came up to her, pulling her into an embrace as he planted a swift kiss on her forehead.

She bolted to her room as soon as he released her, terrified she'd collapse before she reached the bed. She managed to land just in time, and whatever was holding her together dismantled into a hundred tiny pieces. She shut her eyes, focusing on the sound of the ocean until she fell asleep, her face coated in inky black tears.

DAVID

"Where are we?"

The foliage around Gaia stirred, a fluttering moth finding respite in her hair. She tucked a lock behind her ear before taking a deep breath. "After my death," she began, "my soul lived quite happily in the Underworld for more years than I can recall. Upon its destruction, souls found themselves floating either to a place called Heaven, gathered by creatures called angels, or cast into Hell, the realm once called Tartarus. A few souls were told they did not belong in either place—for they were neither good nor bad—so they were ushered into the astral plane to live amongst the humans as ghosts. It was a confusing time for all. The angels told me I could stay in Heaven since I was apparently pure of spirit, but in my own realm because I am part goddess. So I chose a place that looked like home." She paused to admire the breathing plantlife around her, a trace smile on her lips.

"Am I dead?" David asked, suddenly alarmed.

"You are a traveler of the realms, Davius," she reminded him, sending a shiver up his back as she brought forth his ancient name. "You can come and go as you please. Whether you decide to stay here is up to you."

David noticed a hummingbird had found its way in, its tiny wings fluttering as it sipped from a blossom. "Do not mistake my question for complaint, but why did you bring me to this place?"

"The Holy Watchers who reside in Heaven wish to speak with you."

David's heart sank. "So you are meant to manipulate me."

A few petals had trickled down from the flower nursed by the tiny bird, and as it flitted back from whence it came, the bud fell completely from its vine. Gaia rescued it, twirling the stem between her fingertips. "I do not know their intentions. All I know is the kindness they offered me. I lived here undisturbed for eons before they came. They told me they wanted to contact you and asked if I would help. Forgive me, but even after all these years…" She glanced up at him shyly. "I did want to see you again."

Relief flooded David, followed by a happy warmth that crawled into his cheeks. He realized it had been so long since he felt authentic, effortless happiness. "I can't say it's not wonderful to see you again."

She beamed. "I was hoping you hadn't forgotten about me."

"How could I forget you?" David sputtered. "You are the reason I have a conscience, the reason I…" He grew quiet, the memory of Morrigan settling over him like a dark cloud. "Because of her," he remembered.

A look of sadness crossed over Gaia's eyes, but she managed a loving smile. "You do not have to speak of her if it brings you pain."

"I am cursed with the heart of a romantic fool," he sighed.

"But that is what makes you such a wonderful artist," she pointed out. "Your eyes see things that others cannot."

David looked up at her in surprise. "My word, I'd forgotten…"

"You no longer paint?"

"There are many things I no longer do," he admitted.

"Painting was your favorite pastime! What do you do instead?"

David considered the question for a moment before he answered. "Brood," he said earnestly before letting out a laugh.

She joined him for a moment, the sound filling the chamber with merriment. Then she leaned forward to take his hands, her face somber. Her eyes poured into his. "I am so deeply sorry your life turned out the way it did. I wish I could have helped you. I would have, had I known, but once I entered the Underworld, I drank from the River Lethe and forgot who I was. When I entered Heaven, my memories returned, but I quickly discovered you had long moved on."

"So you know about my past and the seemingly endless struggle with my brother."

"I learned everything," she confirmed. "It was heartbreaking to watch—not the discovery that you love another woman, but that you've been so unhappy for so long. I thought many times you'd step out into the sun."

David was quiet.

Gaia leaned back, folding her hands in her lap with a sigh. "I wonder if you and your brother were even meant to split at the dawn of time. Perhaps that is the reason she loves you both, constantly torn. Maybe even the Great

She was intended to be one soul. There was just never an opportunity for discord between sisters. Isis's soul was split so soon, but both you and Lucius loved her at different points in time as well."

David considered her words. It was hard to imagine she'd been there through it all. "So you see all that transpires on earth?" he asked.

"Well, I do not spy, if that is what you ask," she replied with a playful smile. "I can only see your life, and I only listen when important things come to pass. I suppose that even though I am content in this realm, I feel I should look out for you."

David smiled.

"And I still hold a piece of Isis's soul, so I have her memories as well, like pictures floating by. I'm sure Sandrine must feel the same way."

"Sandrine?" David looked at her, confused. "Cahira's friend from Paris?"

Gaia searched his eyes. "I thought you knew."

"Isn't Cahira connected to Isis, which is why she can command the earth? Imperium de Terra, as Libraean calls it."

"Cahira inherited Isis's powers, not her soul," Gaia corrected him.

David was taken aback. "How does Sandrine have it?"

"Lucius was not the first creature to try to siphon the magic out of the acacia tree Isis once inhabited," she explained. "Long before that, a shaman from Egypt stole a branch. He took it all the way to Africa, claiming a voice told him to bring her spirit there. Although it was never recorded in human records, there was once a cult near the Kingdom of Dahomey that worshiped Isis. They channeled her spirit out of the branch, attempting to funnel it into a young girl strong enough to bear it. Unfortunately, they failed numerous times, and gave up as each girl went mad. Centuries later, a priestess decided to revive the old ways and found a girl to try the ancient practice on again. Miraculously, it worked. The soul piece needed a body strong enough to house it—and found it in the reincarnated goddess Medusa."

"I had no idea," David murmured. "All this time, we thought it was Cahira."

"Of course, before any of this, Discordia stole Isis's power, and she and Lucius created Cahira's bloodline. Her power comes from them, which is why it's so volatile. Sandrine is strong in her own right, but gained a bit of heka from Isis's soul. Fortunately, the two have naturally found each other, Sandrine acting as a buffer for Cahira's darker impulses."

"Does she know who she is?" David asked. "Does Cahira know?"

Before she could reply, a tiny voice broke in. "Mama?"

David jumped to his feet. He spun to behold a small boy with bouncy blonde curls and bright green eyes. He nearly fell to his knees as the child brushed past him, settling into Gaia's arms before he looked up at him. This can't be real.

"Lucius told me you weren't with child," David managed to whisper, his entire body trembling. "He said Libraean was deceived, that it was not true."

Gaia merely smiled, running her fingers through the boy's sandy blonde locks as he pressed into her. He apprehended David with curious eyes, a muted shade of green. "Who are you?" he asked.

Gaia spoke into his ear. "That is your ater."

David's flesh prickled at the Gaulish word, even more so when the child gazed at him shyly behind blonde lashes like his mother. "Hello."

"Hello," David whispered.

"Do you want to see my treehouse?"

"Isn't this a treehouse?"

"No, I mean my treehouse," the child clarified.

Gaia met David's eyes. "We can talk more later. Enjoy your time with him. He shifts in age, but he chose to meet you as a child. I would take advantage."

The boy stood, smiling up at David as he grabbed his hand. "Come, this way."

CHAPTER TWO

❧ The Morning Star ☙

The Atlantic Ocean, 1857
Lucius

THOUGH IT WAS STILL DARK, HE COULD SMELL THE RISING SUN. The heat it brought to the wind warned of its arrival, carrying a stale, smoky taste only those outside in the early hours could pick up. That is, if they weren't swept away by the peaking radiance of the glistening stars above.

Lucius sighed, still unable to reconcile all that had transpired over the last hour. He watched the woman that was supposedly his granddaughter stomp her way around the deck, offering him a glimpse of himself as if holding a mirror.

Sandrine slid beside him, the exact image of the creature he'd known as a child, her presence an eerie reminder of the true nature of immortality. He could remember pieces of his many lives before this one, but it was unfathomable to picture an eternity in the same body when living inside one that had seen barely a century turn.

She studied him with her bright mosaic eyes, the shades of green and flecks of gold all the more brilliant in the moonlight. "So. You escaped her clutches after all."

Lucius looked away as he thought of Angelique, still infuriated by the fresh knowledge of her true identity. There was a brief time when he thought he loved her, a wayward boy manipulated into believing she was his savior. He'd been convinced she was the woman he'd seen in his dreams, the man-ifestation of a young girl with sparkling blue eyes and hair that matched the ravens swirling around her. He tried not to think of the actual woman that fit that description, who laid alone in bed beneath his feet. Instead, he recalled the deception that helped him escape from Angelique's control, replaying the murder of his keeper, Kali, and how he ended her life with a satisfying crack of the neck. "I did have some help," he reminded Sandrine.

She smiled. "I was happy to hear you made contact with Thoth. He goes by Thomas now."

Lucius turned back towards Cahira, who was now angrily skewering hydra parts with her sword and tossing them over the edge. "Does she know your true history?"

"The time for revelations will come," Sandrine dismissed, leaving his side to approach Cahira. She was immediately met with combative, wildly gesturing arms. Their inaudible conversation ended with an audible growl as the earth witch relented, stomping his way with a scowl.

Although she was much shorter than him, she had an enormous presence, and he was momentarily taken aback by how similar her eyes were to his, blazing golden orbs struggling to stay within their confines. The clipped horns that betrayed her liminal nature were hidden behind her wild, chestnut curls, a splash of freckles across her nose. His mind flashed to the moment he'd met his other descendants, Hekate and Dragos, a fleeting moment that pulled nothing out of him at the time. He longed for such emotionless moments now. He once convinced himself that immortality robbed creatures of empathy, that it was the antidote to the curse of human emotion, but feelings plagued him in this life more than ever before. Perhaps he'd come back wrong this time. Perhaps he was now like David. He frowned, reminded of his discomfort with his brother and Morrigan's close proximity below deck.

"Come on, Gramps, you're coming with me," Cahira broke in as she brushed past him.

He blinked in surprise before chuckling to himself. He decided he liked her.

One of the masts had split during their attack but still managed to hang on by a few strands of rope. She unwound the broken bits, the jagged tears in her linen shirt exposing her muscles as she worked. "In the last few hours," she began through gritted teeth, "I've discovered my mother was a demon, my father was a centaur, the woman who raised me was a goddess, and the only creature I have ever loved now sits at the bottom of the sea. It is taking everything in me not to destroy the entire world right now, and

I would appreciate it if you could just follow my orders right now. Do we have an accord?" She looked up at him with a raised eyebrow, her visage a perfect combination of him and Morrigan.

Yes, he definitely liked her.

He lifted up the mast with a grunt, pushing it upwards into place and holding it steady. She seemed surprised he had the strength to do so but didn't hesitate, quickly gathering the fresh rope and twisting it around the column so it would stay in place. Eventually, she made her way up the other mast to the top, performing a near impossible balancing act as she tied, knotted, and pulled them into submission.

"You don't speak much, do you?" she finally remarked as she worked upside down, her long hair hanging like a curtain below her determined face.

"I have long learned not to provoke a woman in the midst of a rage," Lucius told her, continuing to keep the mast still as she wrapped.

"Well, don't expect me to forgive her any time soon," Cahira muttered as she flipped herself forward, landing easily on her feet. "You can let go now; it should be steady."

Lucius released his grasp, looking up to observe the impromptu repair held firm. He noticed the stars had reached their brightest moment against the dark, velvety sky and took a moment to admire them. "She has always loved very deeply," he told Cahira softly. "I don't imagine you're an exception."

"She held me against my will while my partner chose martyrdom," Cahira deadpanned, bringing his eyes back down to her. "That is not love, that is betrayal."

Lucius sighed. "I suppose you could see it that way."

Cahira drew closer, staring up at him with angry amber eyes. "I will forgive her when you bring him back."

Lucius blinked. "Whatever gave you the idea I could do that?"

"Oh please. You are the strongest amongst us. No matter how many times anyone has tried to kill you, you still manage to live on. I know you offered to open up Tartarus when that creature attacked us, but she refused to let you die, sacrificing Dan instead. Tartarus was once your realm, and if anyone can open it, it's you."

Lucius crossed his arms. "If you think I would take my own life to retrieve your petit copain, you are gravely mistaken."

She looked confused. "That's not what I meant at all. We all must be together to save the realms. However, we are headed to meet Anubis, who commands the spirit world. Between you, him, and I, I think we can manage to open up the gates of hell. Unless you are afraid."

Lucius laughed, amused despite himself. "You are aware that neither David nor Libraean would agree to something so unpredictable. Morrigan may not even acquiesce."

"Well, they don't have to know, now do they?"

Sandrine appeared behind her, examining the mast. "Will it hold?" she asked.

"It will get us there," Cahira replied.

Lucius felt a shift in the air, realizing David had joined them. The mere sight of him filled Lucius with dread, reminding him of the promise he'd made to himself not to feed the flames of his resentment. Nevertheless, his temperature rose, drawing a curious glance from Cahira, who seemed to sense it.

"Should we start now?" David asked, carefully avoiding Lucius's glare. He looked better than when they first met in London, his cheeks fuller, his forest green eyes free of the shadows that had lingered beneath them.

"Yes." Cahira resumed her haughty, authoritative tone. "Sandrine will steer, and I will help you summon the wind. I absorbed some of your power a few days ago when I drank your blood."

"You drank his blood?" Lucius repeated in surprise.

"He was my captive, and I needed to be sure he was who he said he was," Cahira explained. "The best way to learn a creature's secrets is to drink its blood."

"Interesting," Lucius commented, finally able to meet David in the eye. He was pleased to observe hostility flashing back his way, to notice the slightest twitch in his facial muscles. David was beginning to remember him. "I'll leave you to it," Lucius said cheerfully, abandoning them abruptly as he headed back down into the hold.

As soon as his feet hit the watery cabin floor, he was struck with the overwhelming urge to go to Morrigan, her scent lingering in the air, calling to him. That was the one aspect of his life that had always been constant: his love for her. He once viewed it as obsession—an irrational, volatile urge to possess her and have her beside him at all times. It was something he'd tried to fight, but fell for repeatedly, a torment like no other. Yet something had shifted. He was an intelligent man, and he knew what he felt was still not the healthiest love, but obsession had tempered itself. He assumed it was his period of introspection in the Underworld, although he was still surprised it kept its hold. Even as he discovered her again, piecing together memories from their past and becoming something entirely new, he was able to maintain a respective distance, honoring the independence she cherished. At least for now.

He noticed Libraean sitting at the table, despite the cold ocean water that swirled around his feet. His gray hair lay rumpled around his ears, and he rubbed at darkened eyes. "Where is she?" Lucius asked him.

"Resting," the elderly liminal replied, placing his glasses back on his nose. The thick frames blurred both his clear blue eye and the dead one Lucius once plucked from his skull. "I'll have you know, I told David everything that transpired in his absence…except what happened in the Underworld."

Lucius raised an eyebrow. "Do you think it wise to deceive him?"

Libraean scowled, pointing at him with an angry, gnarled finger. "Don't you dare imply I have anything less than his best interest at heart. It's not wise to upset him so soon after his revival, so it would do us all good if you could put this blasted love affair behind you until we reach Africa."

Lucius prepared to retort, but thought of Morrigan alone and broken-hearted in her bed. Again, the urge to go to her washed over him, but he gritted his teeth, forcing himself still. He realized that as intense his dislike for David, his unwillingness to upset her overruled. "Agreed." He gave a curt nod and left a very surprised Libraean behind him. "If anyone needs me, I'll be in the lower hold."

"Wait."

Lucius paused. He turned to observe pain in the old man's face that he hadn't noticed before, hanging onto the corners of his eyes. Lucius frowned, crossing his arms. "What is it?"

"Jacob," Libraean replied simply. He rose to his feet. "He desires words with you."

"Well, tell him to come out here."

"I'm afraid that's not possible right now," Libraean sighed as shuffled back to his room.

Thoroughly confused, Lucius's curiosity pushed him to follow.

The room was a mess, a swirling pool of chipped wood, soaked parchment, and dead candles swishing around their feet. The human lay in bed under a heap of blankets, his eyes closed, his leathered skin sunken at the cheeks. Lucius could hear his heartbeat thumping weakly in his chest, its faintness alarming.

"He hasn't seemed right to me since we left London," Libraean explained.

"He had a low rumbling cough in his chest, which he assured me was common for him in the cold. Regardless, I had my suspicions and begged him to rest. As soon as David went up to help Cahira, he collapsed. I put him to bed, but he kept repeating how important it was that he speak to you."

Lucius peered at the human, examining his pallor while maintaining a respectful distance, not wanting to tempt his pallet. He was still a blood drinker, after all, and though he didn't dislike the man, he was reaching his limit of tempering instincts. He noted the beads of sweat collecting in the wrinkles of the human's forehead, though the room was quite cold. "He has a fever," Lucius deduced. He shook his head. "It was foolish to bring a human on this ship at the dawn of winter. Has it been so long that you've forgotten that mortals grow ill?"

"Would you have left Morrigan?" Libraean snapped, moving to sit beside his bedridden lover.

Lucius did not respond.

Libraean fell next to him, sweeping away a few stray white hairs out of his eyes. "Gabriel, I have brought him to you. Say what you need to before I lose my temper."

The old man coughed, weakly prying open his eyes. They were dry and shot with blood. "Lucifer?"

Libraean stared at him blankly. "No, it's Lucius, David's brother. You wanted me to bring him here—you insisted that you had something to tell him."

"Leave us," Jacob told him, resting his hand on his arm.

"Absolutely not," Libraean protested. "He is a predator—he will surely kill you."

Jacob shook his head, revealing a sweat-soaked pillow. "No, he won't drink blood tainted with sickness."

Libraean shot Lucius a look that dripped with loathing. "How positively chivalrous of him."

"Libraean, please," Jacob pleaded, the exertion causing him to cough. It was a thick, wet sound as if his lungs were teeming with fluid.

Lucius frowned. The old man was clearly dying. It would be a slow, feverish death quite similar to the sensation of drowning, a very unpleasant way to pass. "I will not harm him," he promised.

"You had better not," Libraean growled as he rose to his feet, glaring at him with his variant eyes. "Or I will kill you myself."

Lucius did not reply, simply watched him storm out, and rose to shut the door behind him. "You should take off some of those blankets to draw down the fever," he told Jacob, turning upright the floating stool that accompanied the desk so he could sit across from him.

"I am dying and I want to die warm." Jacob whispered his reply, folding his hands across his chest. "I know I'm dying because Jesus has already visited me."

"Is that right," Lucius said flatly.

"Yes," the old man croaked. "He will be taking me to his Heaven, a serene haven for souls to rest. But first, I must deliver you a message."

Lucius raised his eyebrow.

"I have your memories, the ones you are missing."

He was stunned. "How could you have my memories?"

"They are not just yours." Jacob's voice shook. "There are others who have witnessed what I am about to reveal to you, including the One who is omniscient. These memories come from them. You must take my blood and remember."

"Absolutely not." Lucius rose to his feet. "The halfling will have my head. They are all looking for an excuse to be rid of me, and killing you would provide them with just that."

"Lucius, please." He could tell the man struggled to breathe. "It is merciful to end a creature's suffering, not cruel. The rest of them do not understand these things, but you do."

Lucius could not argue. He knew the man would suffer miserably over the next few days, his death inevitable. It was cruel to stand by and watch his agony, but he doubted any of the do-gooding immortals he was occupying space with would have the heart to do it. Especially not David. And he did want the memories back that he'd lost, convinced they had more information on his past with Discordia. He winced, however, when he envisioned Morrigan reacting to the news that he'd killed one of them. Would she believe it was the man's own wishes or would she assume the worst?

"Take it from my arm," Jacob whispered. "They won't know."

Lucius sighed. "Don't you want your lover here when you pass?" he asked.

"I will find him again in another life, in another realm. I have never done well with goodbyes." Jacob lifted up his arm, trembling so hard, Lucius took it to steady him.

He searched the man's soft blue eyes, observing nothing but steel resolve. He had seen the look reflected in the eyes of many—he was ready to die. Lucius took a deep, tentative breath. She had to believe in him now—he'd proven himself to her time and time again. The others couldn't hate him more than they already did, and perhaps Cahira would understand. She seemed to burn with the same temper that swam in his veins, the type that knew hard decisions often had to be made. Perhaps she would even help convince them.

He looked down at the weak, blue vein barely circulating blood, robbed of precious air as the human labored to keep his organs alive. It was merciful what Lucius did—saving him from the hell that is drowning in one's own lungs. He focused on the huge blank spot in his mind, eager to have his earliest memories restored. Then he pictured Morrigan's sky blue eyes before he closed his and bit.

Tartarus, Ancient World

THE ENTIRE REALM WAS A SWELTERING LANDSCAPE of volcanic rock and lava, but it wasn't the heat that bothered him. It was the silence. The loneliness. An entire world devoid of mental stimulation, one he could not escape from. He knew he would grow mad from it, though he tried to stay busy etching everything he'd ever learned into the mountainside with a jagged piece of stone. Soon the surrounding rocks were all covered in hieroglyphics, depicting the story of how he arrived at the cursed place to begin with, the characters mocking him from where he sat miserably on the ground.

Eventually, he built himself a home out of the very mountains that encircled him. It took time to finish, for he had no tools, but all he had was time, and he was desperate for any distraction. He could not bear it when his mind drifted to memories of her, visions of building their home while she looked on, designing and perfecting alongside him. A painful longing would follow, as if something physically pulled at his insides, only to be quickly replaced by rage. Ire was useless to him now—there was nothing to unleash it upon, only miles of monotonous rock and rivers of fire.

It was during one of these occasions, when she cruelly popped in his head, that he remembered his dog.

In the early days, while the young gods concerned themselves with humans, he found solace in beasts. He created his own, designing companions to pass the time while she was away. He put birds in the gardens, snakes in the forests, and wolves in the woods. Of course they weren't perfect mirror images of those that roamed the Earth, but they were uniquely his. Crawling, inverted beasts of the Underworld.

A part of him hoped she'd enjoy them, perhaps even coaxing her to stay. But when he introduced her to his new three-headed companion, she merely smiled, running her fingers through his black fur briefly before darting off to another one of her appointments, engagements…affairs.

Despite not receiving the reaction he hoped for, he grew quite fond of Cerberus, appreciating his glowing red eyes and trio of curious heads that never seemed to look the same way at the same time. The beast quickly became his faithful companion, guarding the Underworld while he was away.

"If I could create the Underworld and my own creatures," he thought aloud as he paced his new volcanic home, "then what prevents me from doing it here? Manifestation is simply the result of mind control, and I have the same mind in this realm as any other." It sounded logical enough, though he would be a liar to deny he was beginning to feel quite mad.

Nevertheless, he began.

He sat on the throne he'd fashioned out of cool, hardened lava, remaining motionless as he imagined Cerberus—his wiry fur, the curved claws that ended each muscular paw, the narrow slope of his teeth. He focused until he could see a clear picture of him in his mind's eye, as if he stood patiently before him. He sat for so long in concentration that he lost all track of time, and it wasn't until he heard a loud and sudden pop that his eyes burst open.

To his dismay, what stood before him was not a furry canine creature, or anything like he'd ever seen. Instead, it looked like the skeleton of an overgrown rodent with bulbous, gelatinous eyes and bat wings. Leathery scales attempted to wrap its frame like skin, but they barely covered bones that appeared to be scorched by flames. It peered at him curiously, ejecting a loud and high-pitched chirp.

Set sighed. "Well, it's a start."

From that moment forward, he manifested each day, filling the entire realm with beasts wonderfully grotesque and obscene. He took great pleasure in naming them, the process sating his need for mental exertion. His favorites were dragons, gigantic scaled lizards that breathed fire, so large they brought shame to the tallest volcanoes. They soared around the sulfuric skies, kicking up tornados of ash as they flew. He grinned when he imagined them rising to Earth, setting their destructive fires on the humans who turned against him. He pictured Osiris standing amongst their burnt remains, agonized by their loss. Such joy the image brought him.

All in all, he was content ruling the frightening new realm he'd unintentionally birthed. It was better than nothing, and at least now, he had loyal company and creatures to serve him.

Until one day, an angel appeared.

It took him immediately by surprise, for he knew there was no way he'd created such a being. It gave every indication of being human, save for the feathered wings that stretched behind it, with wavy brown hair that swept a brilliant white toga. The creature carried both sword and shield, a smug look of self-righteousness plastered across a face neither handsome nor homely. His eyes shone a muted shade of hazel as it stared.

"Can I help you?" Set deadpanned.

The being observed his surroundings, eyeing the agitated volcanos and clouds of ash as a few spidery demons twittered past. "This is an interesting realm," he remarked.

"I was banished here and I made do." It felt strange to speak words aloud, as communication with beasts was conducted solely through the mind. "Now please tell me why you are disturbing me or I will unleash upon you one of the creatures you currently gape at."

"My name is Michael," the being replied quickly. "I am a Holy Watcher, an angel who lives in the Upperrealms. I serve the God of Light."

Set snorted. "My brother?"

Michael shook his head. "A different God, one who cares for His people."

The information took Set aback. "So the humans are creating new gods?"

"God always was and always is," Michael deflected.

Set sighed. After all this time, his solitude had been broken by a blinded subordinate. He briefly wondered if the angel's sudden appearance was just another means to torture him. "You still have not told me why you are here."

"The Holy One has caught wind of what you created down here, and would like to adopt this realm for His own purposes."

Set struggled to contain derisive laughter. "You cannot be serious."

"Human beings grow more corrupt as time passes," the creature continued, unfazed. "We need a place to house wicked souls so they cannot return to Earth. This is the perfect place—a horrific inferno with an endless supply of monsters."

Set frowned. "And what about me?"

"We have a proposition. Years past, the Holy One gathered an army of angels to cast out wicked souls on Earth in order to save His people. As a creature who once waged many successful battles alongside the humans, we thought perhaps you would consider joining our cause."

Set snorted. "I do not join causes, nor do I wish to serve some god I have never met. Especially one who has to send one of his sycophants to recruit me."

"If you do join us and allow us to take over this realm, then I will personally reveal to you the whereabouts of both your brother and your wife."

Set stiffened, his old resentment instantly rekindled. "So she succeeded in bringing him back to life."

"In a way, yes," the angel replied. "I know exactly where they are. You can do with them whatever you wish, as long as you help us first."

Set felt his jaw tighten. After all this time, they were still together. He allowed his mind to pull up her image, fantasizing about the look in her celestial blue eyes when he finally murdered his brother—her lover—right before her. He would make her see what she had done to him, make her feel his pain. His revenge would be sated at last, a perfect end to his torment. He glanced back at the being, who patiently awaited his decision.

"Alright," Set agreed, rising from his throne. "I will join you. But how will you pull me from this place? I was banished here."

The angel did not respond and in an instant, they were somewhere else. Set cried out despite himself, shrinking back and shielding his eyes from a blinding light. "Where are we?" he demanded.

"This is Heaven, where the Holy One and his angels live. This is your new home."

"Why is it so terribly bright here?" Set complained, forced to squint at the creature from underneath the shadow of his arm.

Michael laughed. "Come, I will introduce you to my brothers. I think I shall call you Lucifer. The name means 'bright, shining one.'"

Set scowled. "If living here means I have to withstand your horrible jokes, I'd much rather rot in my realm."

"Oh, come now, it is a perfectly fine name. I can't exactly tell the others you were once an Egyptian deity." Michael stopped to study him. "We will have to alter your appearance a bit as well." He waved his hand, giving Set human hands to replace his claws and smooth, human skin instead of jackal fur.

Set reached up to touch shorn hair, realizing his headdress was gone. He now wore a toga similar to Michael's, his feet wrapped in sandals, and his own set of wings nestled neatly between his shoulder blades. He flapped them curiously, deciding he enjoyed the sensation. Perhaps this wouldn't be so bad, he thought.

His eyes finally adjusted to the light, offering him the ability to see the vast aerial realm stretched out before him. Its landscape appeared to be constructed entirely of immaculate clouds against a vernal blue sky, besmirched only by the marble building directly ahead, also a hideous blinding white, but gilt-edged with towering columns.

"This way." Michael guided him forward.

Set looked down at his feet, surprised he could walk down the nebulous pathway without falling through. He followed Michael to the front entrance, up the stairs, and through the domed archway. He was met with lofty ceilings like any other palace, but this one was littered with angels flitting around like common birds, the eye unable to discern what was actual ceiling and what was sky. He caught several of their glances, but they promptly turned back to their business once they saw he was accompanied by Michael.

The apparently high-ranking angel led Set farther down the hall, stopping at an open doorway. This room housed an actual ceiling of gold-streaked marble and was oddly circular, three angels sitting patiently behind a long desk. Set observed a fourth seat unoccupied, assuming it was the one belonging to Michael. Each creature rose as they walked in.

"Good morning, brothers," Michael greeted them. "I have retrieved the Egyptian pharaoh."

Set raised an eyebrow, prepared to correct him, but was interrupted by fluttering wings as they flew down from their high table to greet him with amiable handshakes and smiles.

"These are my brothers, Uriel, Gabriel, and Raphael." Michael introduced him. "Uriel, Raphael, and I are the oldest angels in the Kingdom of Heaven, presiding over the congregation since the beginning. Gabriel has just joined us—a younger brother, if you will."

The angel he called Gabriel was shorter than his brothers and much slighter, with such a lovely, youthful face it appeared genderless. Wide blue eyes sat above a small nose and pink lips, bouncy blonde hair curling around his shoulders. "It is good to meet you," he said warmly, as he took Set's hand. "What is your name?"

Michael promptly responded for him. "This is Lucifer."

Set shot him a scathing look, but Gabriel nodded, searching his face with gentle eyes. "Yes, I can see that. His skin is so pale, he appears iridescent. Bright, like a star."

"We are glad you have decided to join us," the one named Uriel cut in. His dusty brown hair was longer than the rest, his eyes a sable green. "We needed someone of your strength and talent to lead the Watchers."

Set raised an eyebrow. "What exactly am I doing?"

Michael led him by the shoulders. "Come, let us sit."

The chamber filled with the sound of fluttering feathers as the angels settled around the high table, folding their wings behind them. Michael retrieved a chair, which he placed on the opposite side of where they all were seated.

Set reluctantly sat, irritated by the position of the chairs. "I thought I would be speaking with your god."

Raphael, the only angel who hadn't spoken yet, chuckled as he leaned forward, crossing his hands on the table. "God speaks to no one but us. He is not corporeal, he is transcendent, and does not speak in words that humans or creatures can understand. Therefore, we act as translators on his behalf."

"How convenient."

"As I said before," Michael broke in, "we are the Archangels who watch over the congregation. There are over two thousand angels currently residing behind Heaven's gates. One hundred of them were recruited by us to observe a human settlement in a place called Canaan. They were dispatched several years ago, but it has come to our attention that there has been a... disturbance among them. We have decided to send a hundred more, but we need someone strong enough to lead them. It cannot be any of us, since our work here is imperative. Therefore, we have decided to ask you."

"Why not ask my brother? He is the one who created and led the humans for centuries. He is their beloved leader."

The angels shifted uncomfortably, murmuring amongst themselves.

"God created humans, friend," Raphael finally corrected him, brushing back a lock of his auburn hair. "And your brother is no longer available."

"What do you mean, no longer available?"

Michael shot Raphael a warning look as he spoke to Set. "As part of our agreement, his whereabouts will be revealed to you after you succeed in your mission. But we can tell you that your ancient family died along with you, many years ago."

Set was stunned. "But surely he must still exist."

"Again, he is no longer available," Michael repeated. "That is all the information we can give you. Besides, we do not need someone who has ties to humanity. We need someone strong enough to lead the chosen angels, to properly observe the humans without growing attached to them, and to make the corrections some might not feel comfortable making."

Set paused, quietly studying the angels before him. Their unlined skin and crystalline eyes, forced into kind expressions against an immaculate backdrop, offered him a glimpse into their true nature. They had spent their existence in service of goodness and light, but they'd come to realize more was needed when dealing with the human world. They needed someone wicked. "I understand."

Michael smiled, revealing a set of teeth so large and pearly, they didn't seem real. "Excellent. So can we assume that is an agreement?"

Set sighed. "Yes."

"The Watchers that have already descended are living amongst the humans under the impression that Samyaza is their leader," Raphael informed him. "Continue allowing them to believe this. You are the one who will be secretly in charge and will correspond with Michael, divulging to him all the discoveries you make. The humans must not know we are from Heaven, so we must use human names. Yours will be Azazel."

"You just named me Lucifer."

"That is your angel name," Michael explained impatiently. "You cannot speak an angel's name to humans. Amongst them, you are to be known as Azazel."

Set frowned, growing tired of the creatures and their strange ways. "Let us get on with it."

The angels rose, offering him smiles much too wide and much too brilliant. Masks, Set thought.

"We are so happy to have you with us."

Ancient Phoenicia, 2000 BC

THE NEFARIOUS DARK GOD SET, the impromptu angel Lucifer, and the one-day infamous vampyre known as Lucius, looked up from the tablet he had been studying. There, standing before him, was a child. Her hair was long and curled, with the shiny black luster that only children seem to accomplish and soft brown eyes wide with innocence. "Are you one of them?" she asked him in a small voice.

"You should not be here," Lucius scowled.

"My brother and I were curious," she explained. "But he was too scared to come in."

"Well, he is good to be scared. Where is your mother?" He rose to his feet, looking to see if a woman had accompanied him.

"Why are you so tall? You are not a human, are you?" She didn't look the least bit frightened, affixed in her stance as she looked up at him.

Lucius found himself at a loss. Normally he abhorred being interrupted, no matter what the occasion, but he found it difficult to direct rage at something so tiny.

A woman suddenly rushed in, a little boy in the crook of her arm as she grabbed the little girl with her other one. "Please forgive me," she stammered, struggling to meet his eyes. "They are supposed to be playing with the other children while I work." Unlike her precocious daughter, the mother was afraid, her face partially concealed by her hood, her dress dusty and frayed. Their feet were all bare, the little boy's face streaked with dirt. Again, Lucius felt no anger.

"It is no trouble," he assured her. "I can understand her curiosity over our presence."

"Thank you for understanding," the mother said as she backed away. "I will make sure she does not bother you again."

"It really is no trouble," Lucius repeated. "If they ever wander over, I will send them back your way."

The woman finally met his eyes with a smile, relief melting away her worry. "Thank you, sir. My name is Elissa. This is my son, Abibaal, and my daughter, Ashera."

"Please, call me Azazel," Lucius said, using the name Michael had instructed him to use.

"Bye, Azazel," the little girl said with a wave as her mother gestured them away.

It was two days before she returned. This time, she was shadowed by her little brother, who shyly hung onto her arm. Lucius couldn't help but smile, setting down his writing instrument and crossing his arms as he leaned back in his chair. "You came back."

"My brother and I do not think you are like the rest of them," Ashera said boldly.

Her brother crept closer, and for the first time, Lucius realized they were twins. "Is that right?"

"Yes," she said as she edged in too. "I think you are like Ba'al, but from a land far away."

Lucius blinked, recognizing the name of one of her gods, surprised she'd made such a connection. He found he could not reply, the way her rich brown eyes bored into his making him feel as though she saw right through him.

"Do not worry," she assured him with a smile. "Your secret is safe with us."

Lucius cleared his throat. "Does your brother talk?"

Ashera looked sad. "No, he has not spoken since our father died. He was a shepherd."

"I am sorry to hear that," Lucius said softly, rising from behind his desk. "However, I did promise your mother I would bring you back home if you came here again."

"Alright," Ashera sighed, her little hand slipping into his.

Lucius swallowed the strange emotion that rose in his throat. It faded when he thought of Nephthys, pregnant with children that were not his. He pushed thoughts of her from his mind, leading the children out of his tent and into the blistering sun.

The wind swirled the desert sand around their feet as they walked, and suddenly he wondered if their bare feet burned from the heat. They seemed unaffected, guiding him through the town towards their small hut, furthest from the market. He recognized one of the original Watchers, Armaros, standing near a cart offering various nuts and grains for sale. He waved as the woman next to him looked away with a mischievous smile.

Lucius quickly diverted his eyes, hoping no one else would notice them walking through the town. He preferred solitude as he observed from afar, unwilling to make any acquaintances with Watchers or humans alike. Finally, they reached the children's home. He immediately noticed its wear and tear, the thatched roof nearly gone, the mud brick crumbled and patched with flimsy clay. Ashera lifted the wool rug that covered the doorway, gesturing him inside. The house was small but kept clean and free of clutter, with stacks of blankets at one side and a spindle at the other. Elissa was asleep against the wall, her hands still wrapped in yarn as if she'd drifted away from exhaustion while she worked.

"Hi, Mama, we brought Azazel," the little girl said cheerfully, jolting her mother from slumber.

Again, her eyes were stricken with fear. She looked around her wildly, piecing together what she had done.

"Do not apologize." Lucius held out a hand, stopping her before she could speak. "I needed to stretch my legs."

The children ran to their mother, who held them tightly in her arms, grateful they'd returned. "My husband died several years ago and I must work extra to feed them," she explained tearfully, gesturing to the spinning wheel and piles of wool gathered on the floor. Her hands were raw from the labor, her eyes rimmed with red.

Lucius frowned. "Perhaps I could help you make money." He went over to the low fire burning nearby as he pulled a piece of metal out of his pocket. Elissa and her children watched as he held it in the flames for a short while before grabbing it and twisting it quickly with his fingers. He didn't feel any pain—he'd always liked the warmth—but still he worked fast, lest the metal cool and harden, until it resembled a bracelet.

"See," Ashera whispered. "I told you he was a god."

After it cooled, Lucius handed the bracelet to the awestruck woman.

"I do not think I could do that," she whispered.

Lucius rose to his feet and shrugged. "I could make more for you if you would like. I am easily bored in this world."

"You are not like any of the others," Elissa said quietly.

"That is because I am not one of them," Lucius confirmed before he could help it. He bent down to say goodbye to Ashera and her brother. "I am sure I will see you again soon."

She startled him with a hug, drawing a sound of shocked disapproval from her mother.

Lucius awkwardly left, hurrying out of their hut and back into the parched air. The sun was low in the sky as he headed home, his mind beginning to concoct ways to help her earn money. It wasn't right that the Watchers killed their husbands, regardless of their intentions. It hadn't meant much to him when one of the angels he traveled with explained it, relaying the story of how the Watchers secretly lured the men to their deaths so they could take their place amongst their women. He scarcely took anyone's stories for truth, but if they had killed them, they killed not only husbands, but fathers. That notion was appalling enough to him, but it was particularly senseless if some of the women, like Elissa, hadn't been chosen and left to fend for herself.

"I see you have met Elissa," a teasing voice interrupted his thoughts. He turned to see Armaros leaning against a post.

Lucius scowled. "Is there a particular reason you are watching me?"

The creature laughed behind his dark beard. Most of the Watchers had grown them, attempting to look more human than angelic, covering the impossibly youthful skin common to them all. "You spend so much time alone that your sudden presence in town provokes attention. I think this might be the first time I have seen you walking about. It makes sense it is to the home of the loveliest widow in town."

"If she is so lovely, then why has no one else claimed her?"

Armaros laughed again. "You think no one has tried? She refuses them all. Except for you, that is."

"I am not interested in procreating with humans like the rest of you," Lucius corrected him sharply. "I came here to teach and observe, as was the original purpose here."

"We all came here with the same purpose," Armaros said defensively. "But what were we to do when we saw all of their men had been murdered? They needed our protection and care."

"So, you say," Lucius muttered. "And now you are all trapped here, bound to Earth to care for your children."

"Earth is not so bad." Armaros shrugged.

"Well, I have no interest in taking advantage of human weakness." Lucius informed him as he began to walk away.

"Whatever you say, brother," Armaros chuckled, ducking back into his hut.

Lucius reached his abode, once the home of a Watcher before he retreated with his children to Mount Hermon, a safe haven turned fortification for the Watchers and their offspring, giant humanlike creatures with angel wings. It was a humble dwelling, but one with sturdy walls that offered him quiet solitude. He was looking forward to its sanctuary, startled to discover Michael already waiting for him inside. He'd helped himself to the chair behind Lucius's desk, looking over the tablet he'd carelessly left open. Michael searched his face. "Why study Egyptian texts when this is your job now?"

"You do not control what I do in my spare time," Lucius reminded him coldly.

"Where were you just now?"

"A child wandered into my house. I escorted her home."

Michael seemed satisfied with the answer, rising from the seat. On Earth, he appeared human, his thick ivory wings absent from his muscular back. He still kept his sword nearby, however, the blade laying neatly at his side. "Do you have the reports for this week?"

Lucius went to his shelf and selected a roll of papyrus. "I believe that Armaros has impregnated his human wife and will be moving to the mountains shortly," he informed Michael as he handed him the scroll. "There are only a few original Watchers still left in town. Other than that, the reports are the same. Occasionally, those who have moved to Mount Hermon come into town to visit and make trade. The human settlement continues to expand into a proper village, the humans using what they learn from the Watchers to cultivate the land. They now make furniture with cypress trees exported out of the mountains, make crude weapons from iron, predict the weather to improve their planting, and create their own medicine. All unremarkable actions common to any growing civilization."

"And have you been able to gain passage into their fortification yet?" Michael asked as he unrolled the papyrus to examine what Lucius had recorded. "Do you know what kinds of weapons they possess?"

Lucius sighed. "I have visited the mountains, but I cannot get close enough to observe, since it remains heavily guarded. From my estimations, there are at least seventy Watchers still alive and at least double the number of offspring. It is hard to say how many of the human women still live, but I have heard whispers that they do not survive long after they give birth to the Nephilim."

Michael rolled up the scroll. "What about the mother of the twins? Perhaps you can use her to gain access to the stronghold."

Lucius darkened. "I have no interest in human women. That is not what I have been brought here for."

"As if you are above using manipulation tactics," Michael dryly pointed out. "That is precisely the reason we chose you."

"I have already told you how many there are, so why not attack them now?" Lucius asked. "Your numbers far exceed theirs. My true skill set lies in waging war—let me guide you there, instead of wasting time as an informer."

Michael had stiffened, his lips pressing into a line. "It is my skill set as well, for I am General of Heaven's Great Army. I would like to see the type of creatures we are dealing with before I send hundreds of angels to their deaths."

"I did not mean to upset you." Lucius put up his hands in defense. "I will find a way to breach their fortifications."

"You had better," Michael said with a lingering scowl. "Need I remind you, we pulled you out of Tartarus for our purposes. It would be a pity to have to send you back."

Lucius sighed, suddenly wondering if that wasn't such a bad idea.

Three more days went by before the twins' next visit, and Lucius found he was relieved to see them. This time, they carried across their little arms a sash dyed the most beautiful shade of purple he had ever seen.

"What is this?" he asked, as they proceeded to hand it to him.

"Mama made it for you," Ashera explained. "She traded the bracelet you made her at the market for figs and nuts. We had enough for three dinners! She wanted to say thank you, so she made you this."

"She does not have to thank me," Lucius murmured, though he was touched, examining the fabric in his hands.

"Mama is very proud," Ashera informed him with a knowing tone.

He looked down at the children standing at his feet. "Do you often go without food?"

For the first time, sadness crossed over Ashera's soft doe eyes. Her voice dropped to a whisper. "Sometimes, but do not tell Mama. She works so hard."

Lucius frowned. "Follow me."

He marched the twins into the marketplace, where vendors bargained the last of their wares before the day's end. Ashera kept up with his long stride, but Abi seemed tired, so Lucius scooped him up in one arm as they navigated the carts, filling up a basket with more figs, nuts, wheat, and wrapped slabs of meat. When the basket got too heavy for Ashera to carry, he held her in his other arm, trying to ignore the smirking Watchers as he headed towards Elissa's tent, food and children in tow.

Elissa was so surprised to see them that her hands flew up to her mouth, staring at him with wide eyes. "I cannot accept this!"

Lucius pointed to the sash she'd made for him, which he'd draped across his tunic. "This is far too nice a gift for me to accept, so I had to make sure things were even."

"Then you must join us for dinner," she insisted.

The twins jumped up and down, delighted at the prospect. "Yes, please stay!" Ashera echoed.

Lucius smiled, overcome with the first genuinely pleasant sensation he'd felt for many years. "I would be delighted," he told them.

The days went on in this way, Lucius and Elissa engaging in a battle of generosity, seeing who could out-gift the other. Ashera strolled into his house at will, always followed by Abi, begging him to come over for dinner when the sun set. Elissa's nerves had finally settled, finally able to flex and move her once shriveled hands. She now wore her head held high as she strolled through town, Ashera and Abi healthy and thriving, dressed in clean clothes with proper sandals on their feet.

Lucius continued his observations, though he noticed Michael stopped pressing him to infiltrate the Watchers' stronghold. He didn't feel moved to bring it up for he was adjusting to his new life, any thoughts of Nephthys and his brother fading further and further from his mind as the days passed. He enjoyed spending time with the children, their simple innocence something he'd never gotten the chance to experience in his former life. They managed to surprise him every day with their thoughtfulness and views on the world around them, little minds that absorbed everything he taught them, as they managed to teach him as well.

"Do you love my mother?" Ashera asked him randomly one day.

They were outside, Lucius in the process of building a new cabinet for Elissa to store her fabrics in, sweat dripping down his shirtless back. He almost dropped his tools, unsure of how to respond.

"I would not mind if you were my father," she said when he did not respond.

Lucius wiped his brow, thinking carefully about how to respond. "I care for you children and your mother," he finally said. "And I know this might be hard for you to understand, but I think you both are very wise and I want to be honest with you. Can I be honest with you?"

Ashera quickly nodded, nudging Abi, who promptly mirrored the action.

"I was once married to a woman who hurt me deeply," Lucius explained, trying not to picture her as he spoke. "And as much as I want to forget her, she is still the one I love. There is a part of me that still hopes I will find her again, and until that part of me dies, I should not marry anyone else.

If I did, then I would only be giving that person half of me, which is not fair to anyone."

"I understand." Ashera's eyes were wide and solemn before they shifted to worry. "I just do not want you to leave us."

Lucius knelt down so that he was at their level. He grabbed one of her hands and one of Abi's, staring into their soft brown eyes as he spoke. "I am not going to let anything happen to either of you," he promised. Abi threw himself into his arms in response, squeezing him tightly.

Lucius embraced them both in return before standing upright, squinting to place the sun's location in the sky. He wiped his dirty hands on his tunic. "Come, I am sure your mother will have dinner ready soon and I need to wash up."

"We will meet you there," Ashera told him, grabbing her brother's hand and pulling him back into the village.

It was sunset when Lucius made his way to their hut, the gentle evening breeze a welcome respite from the blistering sun. Elissa lit up when she saw him, the children already settled around the table, prepared to eat. Lucius noticed a bottle of wine next to a dish made of lamb and lentils, with fresh bread nearby. He hadn't realized how hungry he was until he smelled the food, enjoying it and a few cups of wine as Ashera twittered about their day, asking him her nightly round of questions while Abi added the occasional laugh and squeal to the conversation.

"I should have the cabinet done tomorrow," he told Elissa when they finally quieted, curling up by the dwindling fire.

"Wonderful," Elissa smiled, her dark eyes glassy in the firelight. He realized she looked different, her hair swept back from her face, wearing a new set of robes. He smiled, grateful she was adjusting to a better life.

"I should get going," he said with a yawn, realizing the wine was making him drowsy. He helped her tuck the twins into their bed before giving her a quick kiss on the cheek. "Sleep well," he said as he started to duck out of the door.

"Wait." She blocked him in the doorway. "I just wanted to tell you how much it means to me that you take care of us like you do."

He met her eyes and suddenly Ashera's words echoed in his mind. He noticed she was wearing one of the bracelets he'd made for her to sell, and scented water wafted up from her skin. He started to panic. "It is no worry, truly..." he assured her as he tried to exit.

"You are so good to these children," she insisted. "You have no idea what that means to me."

"I am not able to have my own and I appreciate that you let me care for them," he explained. "So there really is no need to thank me, I am equally beneficial—" But before he could finish, she rose up on her tiptoes, cupping his face with her hands and kissing him on the lips.

He broke free in alarm, pulling her hands away from him. "I am so sorry, you do not need to feel obligated to do this—"

Elissa looked confused. "I know—I want to."

Lucius felt himself fumbling for words, wishing he could flee. "I am already married," he blurted out, then immediately wished he hadn't.

Elissa's eyes welled up with tears. "You have a wife?" she cried. "Then why do you visit us, why do you care for us like you do?"

Lucius's stomach twisted with regret. "Please, I never meant to hurt you," he attempted to explain. "We were all sent here to help you, that was my only intention."

"Then why have most of you taken wives, and have children who live in the hills? You have led me to believe you wanted me as your wife—my children love you like a father!"

"I do love your children," Lucius sputtered.

"Get out," she said with gritted teeth. "Get out of my home and do not come back here."

Lucius stormed out of the house, furious at himself for the way he'd handled things. Perhaps he could explain things to her tomorrow when he wasn't dizzy with wine, he thought. He could tell her he'd misspoke, that his wife was long dead to him. She was right to be upset if she thought he was trying to take a second wife while abandoning the first. These things mattered to humans—they mattered to him. He'd have to sort out the misunderstanding.

Lucius entered his home, his mind continuing to race, when he realized Michael was inside waiting for him. "What could you possibly want right now?" he growled.

Michael rose to his feet. "I come bearing good news. As of tomorrow, your job here has ended. The Holy One is sending a great flood to clean out the valley. He has decided there is no place on earth for a race of human and angel hybrids."

Lucius blinked. "It is his decision to murder all these people? Is that not the antithesis of something a god of light would do?"

"They are not people," Michael corrected him. "They are Watchers who chose to defy him with their grotesque offspring."

"There are innocent women and children who also live here."

Michael frowned. "Are you hearing my words? You are free of this place—something you have been complaining about since you arrived. You can either return to Heaven with us or retrieve your wife."

Lucius grew quiet, a whisper of Nephthys in the wind. "You will tell me where she is?"

"As it was promised," he confirmed with a nod. "You have time to pack your things if you choose. The day after tomorrow, the rains will come. I suggest you leave long before then, as I am certain the Watchers will begin to panic once they realize what is happening. I would not want to be caught in the crossfire if I were you. Report back to Heaven before you go and I will give you the exact whereabouts of your wife and your brother." And with nothing more, he disappeared.

Lucius sunk down into the wood chair behind his desk. His mind spun, trying to digest everything he had just been told. His life as Set wriggled its way through, forcing him to remember who he was. He saw Nephthys and Isis standing over Osiris, pooling their magic together to bring him back to life. He saw Anubis's cold, unforgiving eyes, and Horus as he tried to bleed him. He watched himself prepare to immolate them before she turned, her azure eyes full of terror as she screamed, "Set, no! They are my children!" The words had jolted him so hard his knees buckled, for it was in that moment he realized why she had left him. But before he had time to react, Horus leapt up and sliced his throat.

Lucius leaned forward, resting his head in his hands. His mind traveled back to the twins, their sweet faces soothing his anguish. He thought of Elissa, who he didn't love, but perhaps should marry. Now that he was free of his duties, he could take them away and give them a life they deserved. His existence in Egypt was over—this was his life now. He was not Set anymore, he was Lucifer. It was time to stop chasing the ghosts of what was and what could be, and time to accept his place now.

He stood, freshly determined.

He hurried back to her house, noticing a crisp shift in the wind as if the skies had already begun pulling moisture into the clouds. He frowned as he arrived to see Armaros standing in Elissa's doorway. "What are you doing here?" he asked, confused by his presence.

"She does not want to see you again," Armaros said, crossing his arms.

Lucius scowled. "I do not see what business it is of yours."

"She is my wife's dear friend," the Watcher explained. "She asked me to make sure you do not come near her or the twins again."

"This is ridiculous." Lucius snorted. "I need to speak with her immediately."

Armaros reached for the sword he kept against his side. "I do not want to harm one of my brothers, but we cannot force our will onto the humans."

"That is rich coming from you," Lucius scoffed. "And no sword is going to stop me from seeing my children."

"They are not your children, brother. They are hers."

Lucius felt an old anger rise in his chest, as if he'd awoken an ancient flame long put to rest. It tingled in his chest as he struggled to keep it contained. "You fool, hear me. Your god is sending a flood tomorrow to kill all of you. I am here because I intend on getting Elissa and the children out of this place before that happens."

Armaros looked dumbfounded. "How do you know?"

"I have been sent here as a secret informer. Your god does not want a race of human and angel hybrids to exist, and has decided your annihilation is the solution."

"Come with me."

Before Lucius could dip out of the way, Armaros grabbed his arm. He pulled him at a speed Lucius had never experienced before, and it took him a moment to realize the angel had sprouted his wings to fly. In an instant, they arrived at the mountains. Armaros pulled Lucius past the guards, directly into their stronghold.

He was shocked to observe an entire city had been built inside the mountain. Clusters of homes were carved from the interior rock, roads stretching from one corner to the next with a small stream cutting through the center. It wove about a marketplace bustling with creatures. He discovered the Nephilim were not the repulsive giants he had been warned about, but human beings only a foot or so taller than him with angel wings. He could point out their fathers, smoothly preserved by immortality, and older human mothers hobbling about with canes. But he was most surprised to discover that many of the Nephilim were female, gathering wares at the market with their own children, a second generation of the hybrid species.

He looked up to see Samyaza, the original leader of the Watchers, standing before him with his arms crossed. He was a stocky creature with a crop of dusty brown hair, accompanied by several Watchers and Nephilim dressed in warrior attire with iron sheathed at their sides.

"Tell him what you told me," Armaros ordered Lucius with a nudge.

"I will tell you only if you assure me that you will not stand in the way of me seeing Elissa and the twins," Lucius shot back.

Armaros sighed, visibly annoyed. "Fine. Tell him."

Lucius met Samyaza's dark eyes. "Your god is sending a flood to kill you all. It will come the day after tomorrow, so I suggest you find somewhere to flee."

A murmur of distress rose up from the soldiers, gathering the attention of the others. "Is this true?" Samyaza demanded of Armaros.

"He says he was sent as an informer," Armaros told him. "I believe his words. He has never seemed a true Watcher, his actions suspicious. I do not trust him entirely, but I think it unwise not to take his words seriously. Why else did the Holy One send another hundred Watchers down to our village? He does not approve of what we build."

Samyaza turned back to squint at Lucius. "Who are you?"

"I am older than all of you, born of the stars," Lucius replied. "I have no loyalty to any Watchers, in fact, I have long grown tired of this whole charade."

"He is Set," a voice spoke up. Amazed to hear his true name, he turned to see a female Nephilim with rivulets of ebony hair, wearing a headdress of precious stones. A thin veil rolled down her back. She appeared only a few years older than Ashera, but was already quite tall and slender. "He was the Egyptian god of death, war, and destruction."

Samyaza looked from the girl back to Lucius. "She is our Seer, who we have no reason to doubt. Now answer me this—why did the Archangels recruit an old Egyptian god to spy on us?"

"You know why," Armaros said bitterly from beside him.

A crack of thunder boldly interrupted, striking so loud above them that it shook the entire mountain range. Several loosened rocks and stalagmites fell to the ground with a crash.

"You said the rains would come the day after tomorrow!" Samyaza cried out as the entire cave erupted into a panic. He did not wait for Lucius's reply, swept away by the retreating throng of creatures.

Lucius moved to join them, when Armaros grabbed his arm. "You are either with us or against us," he said as he thrust a sword in his hand.

Lucius began to protest before realizing how long it had been since he'd seen combat, a part of him left unsatisfied for years. He looked up, but Armaros had disappeared.

There was another deafening crack and Heaven unleashed its furious rain. Lucius climbed up a winged statue, struggling to see around the flurries of Watchers and Nephilim. He observed most retrieved weapons, prepared to fight, while the others barricaded themselves in their homes. No sooner did he leap down from his perch, was he promptly swept up by the armed throng—male, female, angel, giant—as they raced out to greet the angelic army who descended with the rains. Pandemonium exploded in a clash of steel and water as Lucius pushed through the crowds with his sword. The Nephilim lacked no skill at administering death, tossing the armored angels aside with easy sweeps of their elongated limbs. Lucius wove through the warring bodies, dodging steel and furious blows, until he made it past the battle, only to see the water already collecting in the valley below.

Lucius dropped his sword and broke into a sprint, the rising water fighting against his legs. The village had already been destroyed, the tents and huts swept away, and the last standing structures threatening to follow suit as waves crashed around them. It was then he saw the twins huddled on his roof, struggling to stay planted as surges of water reached up with greedy fists to pull them in.

Wings burst out of his back and unfurled, the sensation of ripping flesh nearly derailing him, but he pushed through the pain to soar through the torrential rain to where they were huddled. He snatched them and pushed himself back into the air, feeling their little hands gripping his skin as he fought the torrents to reach the mountains. He glanced down to see the water continuing to rise rapidly, no longer able to see any sign of life—not even the armies of warring creatures. He squinted through the raindrops until he found a hollowed cave near the apex of the mountain range, and tumbled inside.

The children were hysterical, clinging to him as he tried to set them down. He held them for a moment, trying to calm them down while being struck by his own emotions—a surge of compassion, empathy, and protectiveness he'd never felt before. He hugged them a bit tighter. "I am so sorry," he said helplessly.

Ashera pulled away to look at him, her teeth chattering. The sight of her blue lips snapped him into action and he gently pried Abi's fingers from around his arm. "Hug each other for warmth while I make you a fire," he instructed them, scouring the cave for scraps of wood.

It didn't take long for him to realize it was empty, filled with nothing but rocks and dirty puddles. The rain roared outside, echoing in the hollow chamber. He growled in frustration, not wanting to take them back out into the cold. Tartarus flashed in his mind, but they would be terrified, and he doubted they'd be able to withstand the heat. His mind worked quickly, weighing out his options, considering every possibility. And then, it came to him.

"Close your eyes," he instructed the children, grabbing a nearby rock. "Do not open them, no matter what you hear."

They obeyed as he carved the sharp end into his flesh, pulling his blood to the surface before it trickled down the muscles of his arm. As soon as droplets hit the ground, it trembled. He closed his eyes and pictured Cerberus clear in his mind, recalling the sensation of his fur and his playful brown eyes. He heard the portal open, filling the cave with warmth as a beast lumbered up from the opening crevice. He opened his eyes to his old friend, who looked pleased to see him.

Their reunion was cut short by the loud churning sound he brought with him, a horrible bellow that reverberated through the chamber, forcing the children to cover their ears. Lucius hurried back to them, pulling them back into his arms as the unnatural rip in the fabric of the realms let its protestations be known.

"I must go to stop the noise," he yelled, "but I will return shortly to take you out of here. Cerberus looks frightening, but he is my old friend and he will keep you warm and protect you until I come back."

Ashera looked suspiciously over his shoulder at the three headed dog. "Okay," she called back.

Abi did not look convinced. "I do not want you to go," he whimpered, startling Lucius by speaking more words in that moment than ever before.

"Cerberus will not let any harm come to you while I'm gone," Lucius promised. "Stay close to him and I will come back with food and firewood."

"Do not be gone too long," Ashera demanded.

Lucius was overwhelmed by the desire to stay, but he noticed a demon's tentacles snaking out of the opened crack, causing Cerberus to emit a low growl. He looked back at the twins. "I will come back," he assured them, giving them both a firm kiss on their heads before bracing himself and tumbling into the fiery, gaping hole.

But he was not met with the familiar smells of sulfur and ash as he expected. Instead, he was hit with a cool wind. His eyes stung from a blinding light that accosted him, and he squinted, trying to see what was in front of him. The sinking realization hit him just as his eyes came into focus.

Michael's normally indifferent expression was twisted in anger. A group of angels surrounded him, drenched in sweat and blood as if they'd been fighting, though Michael remained conspicuously clean. "Do you have any idea what you have done?" he sputtered.

"You can be mad at me all you wish, but I regret nothing," Lucius snapped. "Wiping out an entire race over the mistakes of a few is despicable—even I can see that."

"How dare you assume to tell us what is right and what is wrong!" shouted Raphael, quivering with rage. "You are not God—you are an detestable creature from the depths of hell!"

"Then send me back there." Lucius shrugged.

"You will tell us where you stashed the rest of the giants and we will let you leave," Michael said through gritted teeth. "Hopefully we can find them and resolve this before the Holy One finds out."

Lucius snorted. "What makes you think I have any idea?"

Michael peered at him. "You agreed to work for us so I would reveal to you the whereabouts of your wife. I know exactly where she is. She and your brother."

Lucius twitched.

"Tell us where the giants are and I will tell you where Nephthys is."

The sound of her name threw him. It pulled forth memories of happier times, flooding his mind before he could stop them—the feel of her in his arms, the echo of her laughter reverberating throughout the Underworld, the way she spent time with each soul who descended. How her brow furrowed over her bright eyes as she created the layers of their realm with artful vision and strategic design. How she could never be still, a restless energy coursing through her veins—just like in his—satisfied only in their brief moments of bliss before she'd be off again, searching for something else… The way she used his love for her to trick him into capture, how she turned away when they tied him up, preparing to bleed him to save Osiris. How he waited for her to intervene, and his heart-wrenching disbelief when she never did.

The visions ended with the image of the twins, shivering as they waited for him in the cave.

"She has made her choice many times," he told Michael quietly. "I no longer care where she is."

Michael growled in frustration, unsheathing his sword. "Do you not understand that you serve us now?"

Lucius scoffed. "I serve no one."

"I banish you from this realm and all others, you worthless wretch!" Michael spat. "May you be hated and scorned for as long as you live out your days."

The angels advanced, surrounding him as he shielded himself with his arms. He refused to cry out as they took to his wings, ripping until there was nothing left but bloody stumps. Lucius shook with pain, powerless as Michael broke through the throng of celestial beings to drive his sword into his stomach with triumphant glee.

Lucius's jaw dropped. He staggered backwards as the blood gushed between hands that tried to hold the gaping wound together. His dizziness brought back recollections of the first time he died, when the blood from his cut throat splattered the floor as his family looked on. The familiar slipping sensation engulfed him now, but this time, he fell from the towers of the heavenly realm, through the fabric that separated it from Earth, all the way to its desert floor, where he landed with a horrible crack. He wheezed for breath between shattered ribs as the ground beneath him trembled, finally splitting open to swallow him. He plummeted through layers of rock, squeezing his eyes shut as the jagged tunnel scraped at his skin as he smacked against the sides. Just when he thought he could bear it no longer, the tunnel narrowed, and he was met with the sensation of being squeezed before he was finally expelled with a loud pop.

Yet again, he did not land in the fiery halls of Tartarus as expected, but lay panting in a realm that was shadowy, dark...and oddly familiar. He bolted upright. He was in the Underworld.

His eyes adjusted to the visage of Anubis looming above him, and he quickly realized his broken body had been mercifully restored. The death god cocked his head to the side as he studied him, the midnight fur of his jackal visage bringing out the brilliance of his blue eyes.

"Who are you?" he asked. "You are not human." He looked exactly as Lucius remembered him—an impressive human physique with gold and lapis lazuli necklaces across his muscular chest and gold cuffs at his wrists, his entire face obscured, save for his eyes. Eyes that shone like his mother's.

Lucius's mind worked quickly, and he winced as he climbed to his feet. While his bones were no longer broken and the wound in his stomach healed, his back still throbbed where they had torn out his wings, the sores painfully fresh under his tunic. "I am a death god," he lied, "created by the Greeks."

Miraculously, Anubis believed him. "Ah, I have been waiting for more gods to arrive." He thrust out a muscular arm to assist him.

On his feet, Lucius surveyed his surroundings. They stood in what appeared to be a colossal cave, similar to the realm he once occupied, but far more bleak and dismal. It presented itself like an inverted version of the warm and lively Nephilim grotto, the ceilings covered in stalactite that hung over a glassy, caliginous lake.

"The place where we stand is the original Underworld, a landing place for souls," Anubis explained. "From here, I either guide them down the shore to my realm—the Egyptian Duat—so their souls can be weighed, or I direct them to the east to Kur, the death realm ruled by Queen Ereshkigal. Beyond the lake lies a vast amount of unclaimed space, if you are interested in creating your own realm there."

Lucius peered at him, amazed Anubis was unable to recognize him. He looked down at his hands, and realized he was still wearing the visage Michael had created for him, save for his torn, bloody wings. "Yes, that would be fine, thank you," he said.

"I realize this seems a bit odd," Anubis said with a sigh. "My uncle and my mother once ran this entire operation, but it has been left in my hands. I have been trying to make room for all of us down here so we can live in peace, like they managed to do in the Upperrealms."

"The Upperrealms?"

Anubis nodded. "Once my mother and father died, they ascended to a realm far away from my uncle. He murdered my father and was imprisoned in Tartarus, the infernal realm beyond this one. Since that time, the humans have devised new gods and goddesses. Ereshkigal, the Sumerian goddess, landed here just as confused as you were, but we were able to make arrangements that suited her. I have been waiting for more gods since then, as the human population has been rapidly expanding."

Lucius nodded, trying to keep his facial expression calm as the revelation settled in on him. So that was where Nephthys and Osiris were. Together in another realm they'd created for themselves. The thought of it made him shake with rage and he swallowed, reminding himself that he needed to find a way back to the twins. "Well, I appreciate your hospitality," he managed.

"Of course. But you must excuse me, this job does not offer me very much time for anything else. The rules of the Netherworld simply state that if you are meant to be here, you can bend it to your liking. I only ask that you respect our boundaries. I am the first being anyone sees, but I will send any Greek souls across the river to your realm."

"Thank you again," Lucius said.

Anubis nodded and faded into the shadows.

Once alone, Lucius let out a roar of frustration. He peered across the placid river stretching out before him with a scowl. Of course he could bend the realm—he was the one who built it—but he had to find a way to leave without raising suspicion. It felt like only an hour since he'd left the twins, and he hoped with all his might it hadn't been any longer.

He shifted his focus to the surface of the lake, funneling energy until he saw a boat materialize out of the murky gloom. It was paddled by an old man with a dirty beard so long it grazed its hull.

As soon as the tip of the boat reached the shore, Lucius approached. The man's eyes were hollow, black voids contained in a weathered, expressionless face.

"I need your assistance," Lucius said, undeterred. "I must find a way to leave this place, but I will need a realm built in my absence. In it, I will need a palace erected with enough space for children. It must be black—not a single piece should be described as white or bright. In return, I will name you gatekeeper and for each soul that crosses your river, you can keep the toll."

The old man's face remained blank, but he nodded. He used his oar to push the boat away from shore, turning it until he was headed back from whence he came.

Lucius waited until he faded into shadow before folding into a seated position. He took a deep, steadying breath and pulled Cerberus's visage into his mind's eye, picturing the cave he'd left them in.

"Summon me," he whispered, pushing his voice into the void so one might hear him. He pictured their dark, innocent eyes, Ashera's twinkling laugh, Abi's cherubic arms as they wrapped around him. He pictured Cerberus keeping them warm, recalling the tickle of his fur and the way his heads cocked in curious unison. Summon me.

Remarkably, the sensation of being pulled followed. His body trembled as he dissolved, his spirit called back to earth. Once there, he attempted to stand but was so disoriented he could only steady his breathing and rub at his eyes until he felt corporeal again. His cleared vision revealed nothing but an empty, echoing cave.

"Ashera? Cerberus?" he called, rising to his feet. He hurried to the mouth of the cave, only to greet an ocean that stretched endlessly, no sign of the valley nor the hills that once lay below it. He whipped back around to see Cerberus curled up against the cave wall, completely still. He ran over, crouching down to rouse him. His heart leapt against his chest thinking he was dead, but six eyes finally wrenched open to look in his direction. They were listless within protruding eye sockets, the outline of his skeleton visible under his fur. He realized he'd been gone much longer than he had hoped. "I am so sorry, my friend," Lucius murmured in despair. "I did not know they would keep me so long. Are they here?" He searched around for any clue of the twins, even a bone, but the cave was devastatingly bare. He looked down at the sea, trying not to imagine the worst scenario. Perhaps someone rescued them, he thought. Perhaps they found a way to escape. Perhaps.

He swallowed hard, trying not to fall apart as he resumed his place beside Cerberus, stroking his back. At least his oldest friend was still alive. "Come on, let us go home," he said softly.

They returned to the same part of the Underworld he had left behind, but there was no jackal-faced god waiting to greet him. This time, Lucius remained splayed out across the charcoal sand where he landed, motionless as he listened to the gentle lapping of the river. Cerberus curled up neatly beside him as an intuitive understanding passed between them that neither was in a place to be disturbed.

Lucius wasn't sure how long he lay there despondent. At some point, he felt Cerberus rise up to find food, settling back down next to him without a sound. His mind had slowed to the point of numb stagnation, ceasing its unending race, knowing there was nothing left to solve, nothing to plot, nothing to push his way through. He had never felt sorrow so fresh and deep that he could not think, but it had come, an unyielding king who immobilized his limbs with iron shackles, bleeding his hopes out of him with scalding pokers. Lucius was its willing captive, for somewhere inside, he knew he didn't deserve the life he'd gotten a fleeting glimpse of, that his existence was one of unrelenting sorrow, and that's all it would ever be.

He was content to remain on the Underworld floor indefinitely until one day, he heard a gentle wave upset the lake. A growl picked up in his dog's trio of throats, rousing his mind from its miserable slumber. "It is just the old man I left to set up the realm," he murmured to Cerberus.

"Not quite," a female voice corrected him.

Lucius bolted upright, his mind fully awake. He observed someone sailing towards him, but it was not the man he'd left behind, but a woman with slick white hair and strange red eyes that matched the scarlet toga wrapped around her generous curves.

"Who are you?" Lucius demanded. "What have you done with the old man?"

"The old man is Charon, and he is the one who will bring souls across the river Styx to your realm," the woman explained as she climbed daintily off the boat, one foot at a time.

"Is that right," Lucius said flatly. "And who might you be?"

"My name is Minthe," she said with a smile and a mock curtsey, the action rippling the fabric of her dress. "You left Charon behind to create, and he created the woman you see before you. Fortunately, my soul has already existed for quite some time, simply waiting for the right form. A few years from now, the Greek people will become civilized and write stories about the Olympian Gods, including Hades, the King of the Underworld. I just so happen to have the gift of foresight, and I have saved us all a lot of trouble by creating it ahead of time. You are now Hades, and I'm to accompany you to your new kingdom."

"Hades?" Lucius scoffed. "Well, I suppose of all the names I have been saddled with lately, that one is not too intolerable."

"I think what you mean to say is 'thank you,'" Minthe said, extending a hand to help him up. "There is no way Charon could have created an entire realm alone."

"My dear, I am not in a position to thank anyone, let alone appreciate the current prison I have found myself in." Lucius stood up by himself, his lanky frame towering over hers.

"Then let me guide you to your home so you can rest," Minthe offered, unruffled by his hostility. She gently took his arm.

Cerberus let out an indignant sound, reminding Lucius of his presence. He had risen up into his full size, his heads sweeping the cavernous roof. "Look about the realm for me, will you?" Lucius asked. "I would like to be sure there aren't any more unexpected guests. There will be fresh meat for your troubles."

The three-headed beast bobbed its heads before lumbering off to inspect the tenebrous realm.

As soon as Lucius boarded the tiny boat with his unrequested tour guide, it moved by itself, slicing through the long body of water. He stared at his new reflection in the inky ripples, blinking only when he thought he saw pale, bobbing limbs of bodies trapped beneath the surface.

"This is the river Styx," Minthe explained. "It flows out into four smaller rivers: Acheron, the river of sorrow, Phlegethon, the river of fire—which separates us from Tartarus—Cocytus, the river of lamentation, and Lethe, the river of oblivion—my river," she added proudly. "Your palace is separated from the realms of the dead in a place called Elysium. No one can access it but you."

Lucius stared at her.

"What is the matter?"

He turned his gaze towards the angular structure he assumed was his palace as it crept into view. "For a moment, you reminded me of my former wife," he said softly.

"I am going to take that as a compliment," she said as she followed his gaze. "Women are natural creators. It is what we do best."

Lucius was silent. The urge to rest suddenly overwhelmed him.

"Here we are."

The palace was a colossal, rigid structure, several stories high with a single dome. Constructed with polished black stone, it glistened even without any discernible light source, even its wooden adornments painted black. The sheer size of it fostered intimidation, but it was made even more so by the towering pointed gates guarded its facade. They had done well, he decided, as she led him through them, climbing the marbled steps into the echoing main hall.

Lucius froze in his tracks. He squeezed his eyes shut against the assault of painful visions of children running past, filling the hollow chamber with their laughter. He thought of them shivering as they starved alone in the cave and his chest seized up with despair. The world began to spin and he dropped to his knees, ignoring Minthe's worried voice as he reached back to King Sorrow, begging him to take him back to the dungeon. Just kill me, he pleaded. And then, oblivion.

He woke to the rumbling snores of a beast nestled at his feet. He groggily sat up, grateful to see Cerberus had returned, shrunk back down to normal size. A fire crackled nearby in what he assumed was his bedroom, the flames white against smooth black marble etched into patterns depicting death's many faces. He threw off his sheets, yawning as he looked around for clothing. But before he could progress forward, the events of what led him there returned with a vengeance and he fell back miserably onto the bed. I should have just let them drown rather than starve with false hope, he thought morosely. Perhaps that would have been the most painless way to go.

Like a bolt of lightning, a thought struck. If they had died, Anubis would have known, for it was he who met the souls before sending them to their prospective places. It was that thought that catapulted him out of bed. He threw on a robe and tore down the winding stairs to the main floor of the palace.

Minthe was already there, waiting for him with a stack of papyrus in her arms. She blinked in surprise at his hastiness. Her hair hung neatly down her back and she looked fresh faced with a new set of scarlet robes. "Where are you off to in such a state?"

Lucius scowled. "Why are you in my home? I thought you said you lived near the Lethe River."

"You have rested and now we must go over the plans for the realm," she explained, lifting up the bundle. "You will begin to receive souls soon, and we have nowhere to put them."

"I must speak with Anubis immediately. Can you contact him?"

Minthe frowned. "There is an unspoken pact between us all to respect the boundaries of the realms."

"I do not care about any of that," Lucius snapped. "And quite frankly, I do not care for this ruse either. Tell me how I can reach Anubis."

Minthe put her free hand to her hip. "Do you want Anubis to discover you are really Set, so he can banish you back into the depths of Tartarus?" she challenged. "You are aware that this time, no one will help you escape,"

Lucius peered at her. "How do you know who I am?"

"I already told you, I have the gift of sight." She sighed impatiently. "If you do not at least act like the Greek God of the Dead, eventually those who want you gone will find out."

Lucius let out an exasperated sigh. "Alright, I will play this game. But first, I must locate the twins I left behind. Can you find them for me?"

Minthe brightened. The action pulled life into her face which, he noticed for the first time, was actually quite lovely. Familiar, almost. "That I can do. But you must construct a plan for deceased souls while I am gone. It should be easy for you—you once ruled over the entire Netherworld."

Nephthys's whisper drifted into his consciousness, pulling at the space where the twins had taken residence. He wasn't sure he could handle both of them tearing at him at once.

Minthe squinted up at him, her unusually hued eyes searching his. "What tortures you so?" she murmured.

Lucius drew away from her with a growl, irritated to be caught in a weak moment. "Are you going to find out or stare at me?"

She shoved the papers into his arms. "I will be back tonight. You have an office down the hall. Have the plans drawn up by then." She turned on her heel and promptly disappeared.

Lucius looked around the obsidian palace, its emptiness suffocating. He left the stack of papers on a nearby table and flew out the door. The air that met him was cool and damp, droplets from the hanging rock formations hitting the gray earth beneath him in a steady tempo. A smoky charcoal fog skimmed the surface of the lake, snaking its way around the distant mountains. He broke into a stride, following the stony bank until he came upon a field, waves of grain oddly placed in the inhospitable realm, dancing as if a breeze trickled through it.

There was a soul sitting not far from where he stood, a nearly transparent woman who looked at him with wide, weeping eyes. "This is the place for those who love and are not loved in return," she said wistfully, her hair fluttering in the absent wind.

"Then I belong here," he muttered.

"Do not speak of this to Minthe, but you can see those you once loved in my tears." She gestured around her, where a pool had collected.

Lucius stepped back, no part of him wanting to see Nephthys. "I will keep that in mind," he said. "What is your name?"

"Cyane," the woman said miserably. "I was Persephone's lover until… until…" She burst once more into sobs, pouring down her cheeks into fat droplets that splashed down around her.

Lucius backed away until he was headed back to the palace shore. He looked down to see a jar of her tears had miraculously found its way into his hands. He set it down near a rock, making a mental note to create his own pool with them, when he was ready. He headed back into his palace and, for the first time, noticed the throne she'd put at the end of a columned hall. He sighed. No part of him wanted to play king. Not anymore.

He turned instead into the office, surprised to see Minthe already there. Although he was growing annoyed by her unannounced appearances, he was glad to see her. "Well?" he demanded.

Her face was solemn. "They are in Heaven, safe and at peace with their mother."

Lucius sunk down into a nearby chair, defeated. "I failed them," he murmured as the news settled in.

Minthe knelt down to be at his level, resting her hand reassuringly on his knee. She seemed pleased he did not push her away. "I am sorry that this brings you such pain. I was hoping to bring you some better news."

Lucius sighed. "I have long accepted that my life is one of suffering, though a part of me hoped it was going to change."

Minthe rose and glided to a table at the other side of the room. She retrieved a decanter and a goblet, filling it with wine before setting the cup on his desk. "What if I told you there was a way to forget—a way for you to be rid of the afflictions that haunt you?"

Lucius reached for the goblet and gulped down the wine, pleased by its complexity. "I would tell you I am not interested."

She wrinkled her nose with displeasure. "Whatever do you mean?"

He paused before taking another sip. "There is a part of me that would love nothing more than to forget my wife and what she did," he explained. "To forget her betrayal, to forget I ever loved such a wicked creature. To be freed of the wretch who bore children with my own brother—children she hid from me when she abandoned me. I would also love to forget the pain of finally having children in my life, only to know that, despite my best efforts, I let them die." He met her eyes. "But they all make me what I am. I am honored to have loved so hard that it broke me so deeply. The pain is worth it to me. I do not wish to ever forget it."

Minthe looked at him with wide, scarlet eyes. "I had no idea."

Lucius looked away, embarrassed to have revealed so much. He swiftly finished his drink, setting it back down on the desk.

"Well," Minthe sighed, as she slipped down into the seat across from him, "I hope that if you remember this part going forward, you will forgive me."

Lucius was confused by her words until it dawned on him. He grabbed the cup. "What have you done?"

"One sip from the River Lethe and all of your painful memories disappear," she explained with a shrug.

He threw the cup across the room, jumping to his feet. "How dare you?"

"You might want to hold onto your pain like some kind of martyr, but you have a realm to run—a realm I helped you create and am now a part of. Nothing will be gained by you moping around, whining about human children. Soon, you will be thanking me."

Something inside him snapped, releasing a rage he had kept tightly leashed since he held his brother's head underneath the water as he thrashed, waiting until he floated limply to the surface so he could drag him onto the shore and chop his body into pieces with his sword. It washed over him like a scalding flame, blurring his vision, his blood screaming in his veins as his hands promptly caught fire. The unassuming white flames in the nearby hearth burst to life, devouring his desk in an easy sweep as it began to hunt for wood and cloth, grabbing hold of any curtain and furnishing it could find.

He lost sight of the insufferable nymph in the chaos, the soothing sound of a crackling inferno filling his ears as he let all his built-up anguish ignite the world around him. He walked calmly out of the palace as it turned into an untamed pyre and settled down on the shore by the placid lake, watching the bright, violent sparks behind him reflected in the water. It looked like a majestic painting, swirls of red and orange dancing on its surface.

Strangely enough, the fire in the water made him feel better.

THE ATLANTIC OCEAN, 1857

LUCIUS FOUND HIMSELF STARING AT THE DECEASED OLD MAN as the vision of flames faded from his mind. He blinked, taking a moment to fully return to the present, letting the sounds of the rickety ship lumbering through the ocean guide him back.

The old man looked serene in death. His labored breathing had ceased, his chest still beneath folded hands wearing skin that looked like glass. Lucius wondered if he'd ever been saddened by the visual of death, or if he'd always been mystified by its peculiar beauty. Death had been a part of him since inception, a natural transition that so many feared and not many appreciated. He had been lost in the blood memories, but he knew at some point, the man's soul had been released from its prison of flesh and took its place with the deity he held the most dear. Lucius found it quite moving to witness the end to a creature's suffering, met with the promise of something new.

Lucius rose to his feet, and quietly exited the room. He was immediately accosted by Morrigan's scent, temporarily disarming him. He managed to push past the room where she slept and into the dank, lower hold, though his mind screamed to check on her. The trunks bobbed and swirled in the inches of seawater still trapped in the lowest level of the ship, but he found a heavy chest that had remained planted through it all. He seated himself upon it, folding each spindly leg into a cross-legged position. The blissful dark and quiet proved ideal for contemplation, especially after the blinding succession of memories that just re-entered his consciousness.

He exhaled, letting his mind put together the pieces of his fractured timeline. He had no doubt that Minthe was Discordia, that she had consistently taken on whatever guise necessary to provoke his compliance. He pulled her forward in his mind's eye, wearing Isis's skin. He envisioned her on the fateful night she brought him to life as a deplorable dragon, screeching spells into the air as she siphoned him into the strongest identity he ever had: Lucius, the vampyre. It was she who had created the first immortal creature; it was she who started the chain reaction of unbridled chaos that was his life. But why? Why did she consistently target him—from Minthe to Isis to Hekate to Angelique—perpetually twisting his mind in whatever way she deemed fit? Was it simply an illogical motive, driven by pure thirst for discord, as her name would suggest? And furthermore—he thought with a wave of anger—how was she able to best him over and over again?

And then, the revelation hit him so strongly, it almost knocked him from where he perched.

Morrigan.

She was his weakness, and Discordia was somehow tied to her.

He nearly bolted to his feet to wake her, but the fresh human blood running through his veins decided to pull another memory to the surface—the continuation of Hades. It was as if he stood witness to his younger self, and he relaxed as the vision took hold.

Hades scratched fervently with his quill behind a polished stone desk, then paused to lift the parchment and blow on the wet ink. Satisfied it was dry, he tucked it in the stack that had accumulated nearby. Hades looked content—happy even. Was this when his memories were taken?

Lucius watched Minthe appear in the doorway, leaning seductively against its frame to accentuate her crimson wrapped curves. He noticed she had taken extra care to smooth her flaxen locks, her lips stained like wine. "Were you able to finish?" she asked him.

Hades gestured with his eyes towards the stack of parchment. "Of course I did. I have been managing the Underworld since its inception."

"I am surprised you remember." She slid into his office, and headed towards the pile.

Hades frowned. "What do you mean by that?"

"Oh, nothing," she said lightly. She flipped through the pages, scanning the notes he had made. "I cannot believe how much the realm has grown over these past years," she remarked. "I will make sure Thanatos receives these. His recent employment has proven such a fruitful addition." She moved to leave, but he rose from his desk.

"Wait—"

She turned as casually as she could muster, a smile pulling at the corners of her mouth. "Yes?"

"I wanted to tell you how much I appreciate all the work you have been doing here lately," Hades said. "It would mean the world to me if you could join me for dinner tonight. My way of saying thank you."

Minthe blinked, then beamed, a soft, rising pink blemishing her pale skin. "Of course. I would love to."

"Good," he said as he resumed his place behind his desk. "I will be returning to the palace shortly. Get the paperwork to Thanatos and then you may head over."

"I am looking forward to it."

The vision shifted, taking Lucius back to Hades's fully restored palace. He and Minthe laughed over bottles of wine, ignoring the elaborate spread of food that covered the dining table, dozens of slender black candles waning at the center. Hades's face showed no sign of disdain—he seemed rather drunk, to be frank—and eventually, he rose to his feet and swept the table clear with his arm. The silver dishes clattered to the floor as he hoisted Minthe on top of it, kissing her fervently as her bare legs coiled around his back.

Lucius turned away in disgust, but not before he caught the glint of a blade in the dwindling candlelight. Hades's free hand had been searching behind her in mid-embrace, his fingers finally landing on a carving knife. He gripped it tightly and without any hesitation, plunged it into her liver.

Minthe's ruby eyes widened with confusion as he stepped back, blood sputtering from her mouth as she reached down to feel the blade lodged between her ribs. Her hands shook as they came back coated in heavy crimson.

Hades crossed his arms across his chest. "Apparently," he said with a smirk, "you had no idea what sort of god you were dealing with."

Minthe stared at him in shock, unable to speak as she slumped from the table to the ground, gasping and gurgling.

"I am not sure exactly what happens when a god kills another god," he told her as he crouched down to where she lay. "But you are no longer welcome here. Whether it is a grand facade or not, I am the king of this realm, and trying to trick me into forgetting my memories was an amateur mistake. I built this realm—your rivers have no power over me."

Minthe coughed up a fresh splash of blood, coating the marble as the life drained from her eyes.

"And though I do thank you for your assistance," Hades continued as he stood, "your services are no longer required in the Underworld."

She made a weak attempt to reach out to him, but he briskly exited the room.

"Thanatos," he called. "It is finished."

"Who are you talking to?"

Back in the present, Lucius looked up to see Morrigan standing on the stairs.

PART TWO

THE BOY LED HIM OUT OF THE ANCIENT OAK and back into the forest, guiding him across a bridge that swayed as they crossed. "My name is Aengus," the child said over his shoulder.

"My name is..." David faltered.

"I know who you are," Aengus pulled him onward until they reached a smaller treehouse, multi-tiered and woven with ladders and nets. David was distracted by the intricate design, wondering how a small child had managed to build such a thing, when he discovered the boy had shifted into a young man, and a near identical image of himself stared back at him.

Aengus had the same jaw, the same nose, the same rusted curls that sprang around his forehead in defiance. But his skin was alive, real blood coursing through his veins, bringing life to his cells, color into his cheeks, and light into eyes green like his mother's. David looked down at his hands, reminded that his own glowing skin was only an illusion, that as soon as he woke, he would once again be walking death.

"You don't have to be a blood drinker anymore if you don't want to," his son told him with a shrug.

David's heart sank. "Again, I have the terrible feeling you are both meant to be a trick." He smiled sadly.

Aengus chuckled. "Not a trick. But they did ask us if we would help them." The young man leaned against the bark of his tree, crossing his arms. "We really are the souls of your lost family," he assured him.

David let out a deep sigh. "When do I get to meet these Watchers?"

"I can take you now," Aengus suggested, straightening.

Gaia abruptly appeared around the bend, wearing worry clearly on her face. "You will bring him back, right?" she asked her son. David was struck by how similar the apples of their cheeks were, the mirroring slope of their lips as they spoke to each other. "It has not been long enough of a visit."

"I will come back," David promised her. When the look of panic didn't budge, he walked over to where she stood and without any hesitation, took her into his arms. She felt so soft and warm, so unapologetically human. She seemed to melt against him as if she also witnessed the memories from long ago that filled his mind, threatening to consume his reality. He recalled his life before his transformation clearly for the first time in centuries, the one that existed in the sunlight. Where he didn't have to try to be moral—he just simply was. His mind reached back even farther to the days as Isis's husband, when he played the righteous king, the father of humanity. The time before he was forced to live apart from humans, to control his murderous instincts around them. When life was simple.

Gaia pulled away gradually, as if appreciating the moment of nostalgia. "I will hold you to that promise," she warned him.

Aengus led him out of the forest and down the hill to a lake, where a small rowboat had been tied to a post. They climbed inside and David watched quietly as the soul that was supposedly his son row until the current picked them up. He threw David a smile as he put the oar on his lap, letting it carry them as the river opened to a wide expanse that seemed to stretch on into oblivion. A bright, but very dense fog obscured any hope of sight, until an enormous shape broke its way through. Aengus didn't seem bothered, and as they grew closer, David realized it was a towering building made entirely of white marble. It reminded David of the architecture in Rome, except that it had no embellishments nor details beyond the two Doric columns that held up its square facade, its door gated like a crypt. His son pulled their boat to shore, holding it steady so he could climb out.

"Go ahead," Aengus told him, nodding towards the steps. "I will be waiting here when you return."

David was hesitant, but he climbed them, surprised the gates creaked open as if they anticipated his arrival. Upon entrance, he was even more surprised to discover the inside of the building was circular, defying reality, his footsteps amplified by the domed roof. The entire space was bare, save for a long table situated at the farthest end. Three men sat behind it, watching him with calm, expressionless faces.

One rose, ivory wings rustling behind him as he moved. Although David was accustomed to the youthful visage of immortals on Earth, these creatures were different. Each feature appeared exaggerated to an unsettling perfection; teeth too white, skin too smooth, eyes too big.

"Welcome, David," the standing creature said cordially. "Please, do sit."

David noticed a chair had appeared behind him, but he did not take it. "Who are you?"

"My name is Michael," the standing creature with muddy eyes and hair replied. "These are my brothers, Raphael and Uriel. We are the Holy

Watchers, the Guardians of Heaven's gates. Where once a Council stood to take care of all that transpires in the spiritual world, we now stand in its place."

David frowned. "I knew the members of the original Council. What has become of them?"

"Please sit," Michael repeated.

David complied, but kept him locked in a stare, waiting for an answer.

The creature sighed, moving to the front of the table. He was dressed like a man from ancient times, a white tunic wrapped around his overly muscular frame, a pair of sandals strapped to his feet. "The Council was destroyed by a goddess named Discordia," he explained. "We have graciously stepped in and now act in their place."

"Discordia?" The name sounded familiar, but David could not place it.

"She is an old Greek goddess, the goddess of chaos and strife. Ignored by worshippers and historians alike, she has been able to wage war covertly against the rest of the pagan gods, murdering most of you and destroying your realms. We did not wish to interfere, but she is causing too much trouble for us to ignore her any longer."

David studied the being, trying to penetrate his impassive brown eyes. "You mean to convince me there is an unknown goddess who simply decided to wreak havoc upon us?"

"Your brother knew her quite intimately," the creature named Raphael broke in.

David sighed. "Of course he does."

"We brought you here because we have a proposition for you," Michael continued. "The creature who calls himself Lucius has consistently given us problems since the beginning of days. We once offered him a chance to join us, around the time you and your … ahem, lover ascended to your own realm. But he betrayed us, as I've heard he has also done to you. As many times as anyone has tried, no one seems able to successfully kill him. Our only hope has been to keep him banished to Tartarus, but once again, he has found a way out. You are the only one who manages to consistently put him in his place. If you can take care of Lucius for us, we will take care of Discordia for you. And you are welcome to have the realm we gave your first wife so that you may rest with her and your child for eternity."

David couldn't believe what he was hearing. "You want me to murder a creature who hasn't done any wrong?"

Michael looked surprised. "You and I both know what he is capable of."

"Well yes, my brother is nefarious at best, but in his current life, he hasn't done anything to warrant his execution."

"He has killed countless humans over the last hundred years," Michael reminded him with a raised eyebrow. "Just because it is not on the scale of what he has done before does not make it any less wicked."

"I have killed humans," David pointed out.

Michael crossed his arms. "I am certainly not saying your actions are commendable. You are a natural sinner, just like the humans. But once your conscience was returned to you, you stopped. The handful of humans you fed upon over the last millennia were those who yearned for death—you were merciful in your actions. If you repent and agree to serve the Holy One by taking care of Lucifer, you will be forgiven and welcomed into Heaven."

David squinted. "What did you call him?"

"You must be tired of life as a demonic immortal," the last creature, Uriel, interjected. "Forced to live in the darkness and feed on the blood of the living to survive. What sort of life is that? You were once a great king who stood proudly in the sun."

David glowered at him. "You seem to forget, I am not alone. I have an entire family on Earth I would be leaving behind."

Michael revealed a glimpse of his grotesquely large teeth with a forced smile. "We have already promised Libraean a natural death. We allowed our brother Gabriel to reunite with him, and have arranged a place for them here when they both pass. Your friends Cahira and Dan are content to live out their lives eternally on Earth together—once they also reunite, of course."

"There are other gods…"

"Surely you don't mean Morrigan."

David was quiet.

"I think you and I can both agree that the dark goddess belongs in the Netherrealms with her husband." Michael snorted.

David felt a prickle of anger. "Do not presume to tell me what I feel," he warned him.

Michael sighed.

"Show him, Michael," Raphael hissed.

"I do not need to be shown anything," David told him coldly. "I already know she has made her decision. That does not mean I hate her, or even him for that matter. You, creatures who supposedly serve a God of Light, are trying to convince me to murder my own brother and the woman I love, then abandon my Earth-bound son and any other poor lost god who has managed to reincarnate unscathed."

Raphael jumped to his feet, struggling to maintain the calm facade of his brothers. "You seem to think you have a choice. Your realms are gone. If you do not help us, eventually Discordia will succeed in killing you all. Then you will cease to exist. At least if you agree to work with us, you will have a place to rest."

David rose. "I will take my chances. Thank you for your time."

He marched out and, as soon as the blinding sunlight hit, he saw not his son waiting on the shore, but Isis. Waves of ancient memories threatened to surface, pulling at the emotions in his chest. He forced them away, still not entirely convinced anything he saw was real. Like Gaia, she had taken her earliest form, a true Egyptian goddess dripping with gold, her blinding green eyes framed by straight black hair that swept her waist. "I had a feeling you would not comply."

"Last we spoke, you were Hekate." David crossed his arms. "You wanted to send Lucius and Morrigan to the Underworld then, just as the Watchers do."

She came closer, her appearance shifting until her eyes had cooled to a soft jade, her skin fading, and her hair shriveling up into strawberry blonde curls. His rigidness softened at the sight of her.

"That was not me," Gaia said softly. "That was Discordia. Isis and Gaia are the same soul. You were Isis's companion at the dawn of time and you found me eons later as Gaia. Our love was pure and true. I agreed to work with the Watchers to bring you here, but the decision is yours to make. It doesn't change the fact that I know in my heart you belong here with me and our son." She took his hands, staring up at him with pleading eyes.

David realized the tower had disappeared behind him, leaving them alone on the island. "I would love nothing more than to stay here with you, but I cannot leave everyone else behind."

"Why do you always have to play the hero?" She dropped his hands to put hers on her hips. "I know you better than to think it's pride. Is it because of your guilt?"

David frowned. "I don't know what you mean," he said, trying to turn away.

"That is why," she realized. "You regret falling in love with her—it is why you feel you must constantly repent. You blame yourself for creating Lucius. Had it not been for you, Set would have never spiraled downward—he would have never killed you, taking us all down with him. He would have never become a blood drinker."

Her words hit him so hard, he fell to his knees, his old familiar misery beginning to press on his chest.

She sank down to join him in the sand. He could see the sunset in her eyes. "You blame yourself for all of it," she continued, "which is why you feel you must constantly keep Lucius in line, protecting humanity from him and whatever else may befall it." She abruptly grew quiet. "Do you blame yourself for my death?" she whispered.

"Of course I do."

"Oh, Davius." She lifted his face, cupping it with her hands. "You cannot live the rest of your existence in martyrdom. Lucius and Morrigan certainly don't."

"Yes, they seem to constantly rise above things, don't they?" He sighed. "Somehow I've become very lost."

Gaia stood, brushing off her skirts. She stuck out her hand. "Then allow me to find you."

He looked up to see tears had gathered in her eyes, and was struck by how beautiful human tears could be, glistening water instead of the inky black that poured from the eyes of vampyres. Maybe it was time to rest, to give up the useless fight against his own misery. Maybe it was time to cease being a creature of night.

"Can you stay one night with us before you go back?" A child's voice came from behind them. David turned to see Aengus had shifted back into the form he was in when David first arrived, looking up at him with innocent eyes.

"Time stops while you are in the heavenly realms," Gaia assured him. "I know that even though what I say is true, you will not give up your guilt so easily. You can rest assured, however, that those you left behind will not even realize you are gone. You can go back to the shattered glass."

David frowned as he saw Morrigan and himself in his foyer, the stained glass above erupting with his anger. His pain. He looked back at Gaia, admiring the way the light shimmered in her hair. "I can stay one night."

CHAPTER THREE

❧ The Fractured She ❧

Atlantic Ocean, 1857
Cahira

Cahira stood at the helm of the ship, finally able to bear her anger quietly and focus on the task at hand. She watched pinpricks of light flicker in the distance, the French port growing closer as each moment ticked by. The wind had picked up enough that David no longer had to funnel it beneath the sails, but he didn't seem in a hurry to return below deck. Instead, he leaned against the stern as if searching for the indiscernible line that marked black sky from black ocean, plumes from his cigarette drifting into the air.

She kept her distance, empathetic to his situation. Lost love was something she now could understand, and she struggled not to imagine Dan in the painful grips of an infernal realm. She concentrated instead on her plan, knowing that with her power combined with Lucius and Anubis, former guardians of the Underworld, they would be able to set him free. She just had to stay patient and get them safely to Africa.

"How are you, little witch?" Sandrine surfaced from the shadows, sliding up beside her.

Cahira winced. She still hated the nickname, though today, she welcomed the nudge from their past. "Numb," she replied honestly.

Sandrine looked reflective in the scant moonlight that revealed her smooth, unaged face. It seemed locked in perfection compared to Cahira's, which had gradually lined, gray hairs snaking through her brunette waves. She squeezed her eyes shut against a wave of pain, remembering her conversations with Dan of immortality. She never expected he would be the first to go.

A cold hand on her shoulder pulled her free.

"I wish I had words for you, Cahira," Sandrine said softly. "I know too well the path of the warrior is not easy."

Touched by the brief display of vulnerability, Cahira softened, resting her hand on Sandrine's for only a moment before they both stabilized, invoking their shared resilience. They stood for a moment in silence, listening to the lapping waves.

Though their bond seemed instant, it had grown stronger over the years. The past decades were marked by a whirlwind of adventure as the duo wiped out scores of demons while artfully dodging Angelique's own hunt for their souls. Some days, Cahira wondered where she ended and where Sandrine began, the synergy between them mirroring that of twins more than different souls from different eras. But they never questioned it, just as they never questioned when it was time for silence or when it was time to speak.

"Morning approaches. Shouldn't you be retiring?" Cahira asked.

Sandrine pointed up at the swirling plumes of charcoal that finally managed to obscure the moon. "Morrigan ensured cloudy skies for our arrival. You should get some sleep."

Cahira snorted. "I am not sharing a room with that woman right now."

"As upset with her as you are, she is the woman who raised you," Sandrine reminded her.

A tremor of rage threatened Cahira's resolve. "I'm not in a forgiving place yet."

"I think he shares a similar temperament," Sandrine remarked, nodding towards David, who had yet to abandon his post at the ship's edge.

Cahira followed her eyes. "That is no concern of mine."

Sandrine slid her a look. "You have searched your entire life for him, and now you cannot be bothered to make pleasantries? You both lost someone dear to you. That is how civilized beings cope, is it not? By communicating with one another?"

Cahira scowled. "There are days I cherish your friendship and there are other times when it drives me mad."

Sandrine smiled. "Besides, we're nearly at port. He should warn the others." She gently took the wheel.

Cahira sighed and relented. She headed towards David, making sure her footsteps were loud enough for him to hear her approach. He didn't turn, his gaze fixed on the rolling waves as they sputtered out from behind the moving ship.

"We should be there within the hour," she said in greeting.

"Thank you." He broke his gaze to give her a small smile, the wind tossing auburn curls around his forehead. "I was thinking about Dan."

Cahira's face fell, overwhelmed by the urge to retreat.

"I'm sorry, I'm not trying to upset you," David quickly said. "He was a cherished friend in the short amount of time I knew him. I know it pales in comparison to the time you two spent together, but I did think I'd be on this journey with him."

She softened, but only slightly. "No need to apologize. I abandoned him a long time ago—it's only fair that it be my turn to be abandoned." Before he could disagree, she added, "I should probably inform you that I plan to bring him back. Don't attempt to persuade me otherwise."

David looked surprised. "But the realms are gone. Once a god dies, we cease to exist."

"The hydra took him down to Tartarus with it," she pointed out. "I'm certain he is there."

"Will you be sending Lucius down there to retrieve him?" David half-joked, his voice light but his eyes weary.

"Ah, so you were told about their reconciliation," Cahira deduced, recalling her first happening upon Morrigan and Lucius, wrapped in a passionate embrace.

David sighed, tossing his cigarette into the ocean. "Libraean insists he told me everything, but I'm not a fool. I know he omitted things to spare me heartache. He means well."

"You are better off without her," Cahira assured him. "When we arrive in Calais, it will give us all some well-deserved distance."

"I gather you still haven't forgiven her."

"Why should I?" she scoffed. "I heard her speak to him before it happened, on the line that animals communicate—like telepathy except only beasts and shape shifting gods can use it," she explained quickly. "Lucius offered to kill himself to take down the hydra, but Morrigan refused. Yet as soon as Dan offered to launch himself into the belly of the beast, she agreed without batting an eye. She selfishly chose her lover over mine."

David looked dismayed at the revelation, resuming his absent gaze towards the dark horizon. He was quiet for a long pause, and Cahira wondered if she misspoke.

Eventually he turned to her, his handsome face melting with sadness. "We don't know if Lucius's death would have been enough. From what I remember, it takes the death of a wicked creature, and one with the power to open portals to send a creature to Tartarus. He might have been able to send himself there, but I don't know how he would have brought the hydra down with him. As noble as Lucius wanted to be, it was another poor decision on his part. Perhaps Morrigan knew that—she is far more intelligent than given credit for."

Cahira snorted. "Why are you sticking up for her? Didn't she just break your heart?"

David looked down at his hands. Cahira noticed they were unlined, the unsettling reminder that he was not human sending a shiver across her skin.

"I cannot hate someone I once loved," he told her. "That flame does not go out so easily. I don't even hate Lucius, and he has ruined my life on more than one occasion."

"I warned you once that love makes you weak," Cahira playfully remarked.

He let out a small chuckle. "Then you are just as weak as I am."

Cahira snorted, though he was right. She mirrored his stance, folding over the side of the ship beside him. Though it was seasonably cold, the ocean spray felt good on her face, like the kiss of snow. "I had finally gotten up the nerve to tell him, after far too many years." She reached up to the nape of her neck and pulled her multi-colored braid forward to show him.

"Is that his hair braided with yours?"

She nodded sadly. "It was the only way I could show him how I felt, before the words could come. But then ..." she trailed off, thinking of Paris. "It is what I will use to bring him back."

She felt David's eyes searching her face. "Do you really think you will be able to?" he asked.

"Dan did not die a regular death," she explained. "There's no telling that he died before the hydra was cast into Tartarus. He could have survived it—I turned him into the wolf right as he descended. His soul could be trapped down there right now, waiting for us to rescue him. I don't think I could forgive myself if I don't at least try to bring him back."

David considered her words. "I'm not inclined to try and stop you, but how will you manage it? There aren't many with the powers of resurrection, and even for those who do wield it, their targets often come back quite wrong." He gave her a look that meant he was referring to himself.

"Isis's blood runs in my veins, David," she insisted, "and I will have Anubis and Lucius at my disposal."

"Well, I'll never argue with anyone sending Lucius away."

The ship creaked, startling them. They turned to see Libraean, who managed to make his way up the stairs onto the deck. He lumbered over to where they stood with the mild limp that still lingered despite his restoration from being hunchbacked and hooved. As he grew closer, David straightened his posture, visibly concerned. "Libraean, what is it?"

Cahira was accosted by the creature's pain, hearing the thoughts he made no attempt to shield. Another death, another broken heart. She winced as she watched David hurry alongside him to the cabins, unable to follow herself. There were too many creatures now with fresh pain and she wasn't sure she could withstand the onslaught.

Cahira cursed under her breath and followed reluctantly. She lingered near the ladder, listening to the quiet sobs of the old liminal, his thoughts like whispers in her mind. I have long accepted being away from him and I knew the day would come again. I'm glad to have resolved things before he passed, but I will miss him so.

She couldn't hear David's thoughts, but his low voice rose up from the cabin. "He was a kind soul. He will be missed by all."

Then it was quiet, as if the two men comforted each other. Their dynamic struck her as odd, the elderly man who played the father David never had, although in actuality, he was his son. She had a hard time envisioning the golden child that was Horus, written about in the mythology books she once feverishly read. Yet every so often, when the old liminal looked her way, she heard the call of a peregrine falcon and saw its reflection in his strong, blue eye.

Though she had to admit, it was no stranger than the tall, raven-haired woman sleeping nearby who turned out to be the one who raised her. Nothing about her life—or any of theirs—followed any sense of normalcy. They were cursed to look like the humans around them but forced to bear the heaviness of immortality, to know that, even though they seemed mortal, they couldn't partake in simple human pleasures. Most of them did not eat real food, none of them could bear children, and many could not see the sun. And yet, they still fought for the preservation of Earth and man, though no human was the wiser and instead prayed to a God with no face and no name.

Her nose picked up the scent of fresh pine, sharp like in the winter woods. She stiffened as a cold breeze drifted across the part of her neck that her braided hair exposed, pulling the soft hairs to attention. She closed her eyes as the sob rose in her throat, for it suddenly felt like he held her, his warmth combating the winter chill.

"I just wish you were here," she said softly to no one, or someone, and the response was snowflake kisses that landed on her eyelids and melted on her lips.

She licked them, brushing a hand across her eyes and clearing her throat before she descended the ladder, letting them know they'd arrived.

Port of Calais, 1857
Sandrine

Sandrine moved through the city, strategically hidden by shadow. The old French port was like any other, save for the remains of a medieval fortress that once stood at her shores, its obstinate, weathered sandstone withstanding years of pummeling ocean air and waves. The modern city was erected just beyond it, made up of tall hotels and offices with shops underneath, a central square, and several chateaus that bordered the outlying woods. The buildings closest to shore, however, were forced to work around the old feudal design, shabby buildings packed next to each other holding taverns intended for merchant sailors and rooms for quick board. It was here that the lower class lingered, the layout offering plenty of opportunities for one to go unnoticed. Slumbering beggars nestled in her crooks and crevices, while the occasional sordid rendezvous took place in her narrow alleys. Sandrine stumbled upon one such occurrence now, and patiently waited until the skinny girl scurried away with her meager earnings before she approached the filthy sailor buttoning up his trousers. She didn't give him the opportunity to finish the slur he attempted to fling at her before she pushed his head so far to the side that his neck cracked, the bones breaking through the skin so she didn't even have to bite to take her fill of his blood. She waited until she felt his heart stop before she released him, his body hitting the ground like a sack of potatoes.

Satisfied, she dabbed her lips with the handkerchief kept in the back pocket of her trousers and exited the city towards a neglected edge of shore. She slipped her tired feet out of her boots as she approached the water, enjoying the icy waves that ran over her bare skin. She closed her eyes, wishing she still sailed. Though they had only just arrived, she longed to move along the rocking waves once more, leading her ship into the great black beyond under a cloudless night sky.

Her mind fluttered to Cahira, amusement pulling at the edges of her mouth. She'd hated sailing at first, a true earth witch with stubborn land-legs and a stomach that rebelled at the motion. But she transcended the obstacle over time—like she always did—and now shared Sandrine's lust for adventure upon the sea.

Sandrine wondered how she was getting along with the others. She imagined it was only a matter of time before she joined her. If anyone knew how difficult it was to be a lone wolf amongst the crowd, it was Sandrine. It was the main reason she stood barefoot in the snow-crusted sand while the rest settled into their temporary lodging.

Sandrine looked down at the foamy water at her feet, reminded of when they reunited in the Bohemian Forest. To think she almost decided against searching for her.

To say her trip had been harrowing was an egregious understatement, and she was barely able to maneuver her way through the tall brush, wildly unlike the plains she just left behind. Though weak, she was grateful to be starving; it helped her pick out Cahira's scent almost immediately.

Sandrine vividly remembered the look on her face when she froze instinctively, prepared to grab an arrow and shoot. Yet as soon as Cahira's warm eyes found recognition in hers, she dropped her bow and ran to greet her.

Sandrine stiffened, shocked by the uncharacteristic display of affection. She relaxed however when Cahira pulled away, letting her see the childish joy spread across her freckled, still very human skin, as if she'd just been reunited with a long lost sister. "Come to my home," she said. "Let me see if we can get you something to eat."

Sandrine nodded, grateful for the gesture. Cahira's scent was starting to churn up her hunger.

Not far from where they met was a moss-covered hill, hidden by clusters of shrubs and plants and protected by a creek they crossed to get there. Cahira lifted a curtain of ivy to reach the wooden front door, which she opened for Sandrine.

She was pleasantly surprised by its coziness, observing the slabs of pine that made the walls and floor, the cabinets Cahira had built for drying herbs and storing tools, the kitchen table strewn with weapons, and her various potions. She was alarmed to see an old wolf perched on a netted bed hanging from the wall, but the animal barely acknowledged her presence.

The master warned me of your arrival. The animal's voice jolted Sandrine in her mind.

Geri, my hunt was interrupted—do you mind fetching supper? Cahira asked hopefully.

Geri jumped down from her perch in wordless acquiescence, landing easily on the floor and heading out the door. Cahira hurried to clear the table, putting her knives and arrows back in their respective places in the cabinets. She pulled out a chair for Sandrine before lighting the candles around the house so she could shut the front door.

"So you've abandoned your search for David already?" Sandrine asked when she joined her at the table.

Cahira sighed. "I have not abandoned the plan. I'm just not sure where I should be looking anymore. I've heard nothing from the spirit world since I left Paris. I was beginning to think maybe it was all some trick of Angelique's to bring me to France."

Geri interrupted them with a scratch at the door. Cahira complied, letting the wolf in with her prize. "That was fast," she remarked as she gingerly removed the wild bird carcass out of her mouth and patted her head. The wolf climbed back up to bed to wait for Cahira to prepare their meal.

"Actually, that's why I'm here," Sandrine resumed their conversation. "I just returned from Africa, where I met a reincarnated god named Anubis— the one I told you about in France."

"Oh?" Cahira chopped off the head of the bird, squeezing the blood into a cup for Sandrine and handing it to her quickly before it grew cold. She returned to the preparing table to defeather and gut the rest.

"Yes," Sandrine replied, taking an appreciative sip from her cup. The warmth soothed her aching limbs. "Anubis believes David is still alive and residing somewhere in Europe. No one can find him, however, because he lives with one of his reincarnated sons, a liminal being called Libraean, who put a protection spell over them both."

"I don't suppose he knows how to break it."

"No, he does not," Sandrine confirmed, taking another careful sip before she cleared her throat. "Cahira, there are several pieces of my story I never told you."

Cahira paused, turning to offer her full attention.

"When we first met," she began, "I told you the story of how I arrived in France to meet Angelique. As you may have already guessed, that was the story she wanted me to tell you to gain your trust. In reality, I was not a child when I came over on the slave ships, but a grown Hangbe Warrior." She cleared her throat again, apprehensive at sharing so much of herself. But she knew it was right—Cahira was to be trusted. The sea had told her so.

"The Hangbe Warriors were a band of women soldiers created to protect Queen Hangbe of Dahomey from the men who wanted her throne. Our training was a brutal endeavor, designed to sculpt us into perfect instruments of death. Yet one of her brothers still managed to poison the queen in 1718. No one believed it was him, but I knew better. He became king and wanted to assume command of the Warriors, but I fled, jumping aboard a slave ship headed to France. I was young, obstinate, and foolish then, and somehow I thought a life of forced servitude would be better than fighting for a corrupt king in my own homeland."

Cahira had stopped preparing their food, joining her at the table to listen with rapt attention.

Sandrine continued. "The ship did succumb to smallpox during our voyage, as I told you before, and I used this opportunity to escape. I'd been hearing the ocean calling to me since I boarded, and when I jumped into the cold waters, I met the Greek God, Poseidon. He helped me ashore and revealed my true nature to me—that I was the reincarnated goddess Medusa, once his lover. He assumed I'd want to pick back up where we'd left off centuries ago, but I was unwilling—not only had I sworn off men as a Hangbe Warrior, but my memories were trapped. He was nothing more to me than any other man." The blood had gone cold, but she took the last sip, wishing there was something stronger mixed in. Oh, how she hated speaking of Poseidon.

"He insisted I try, revealing there was a sorceress named Angelique who could help unlock them for me. Again, I was quite headstrong back then and driven by my curiosity, so I left him and headed to Paris. There, I met our dear Angelique who—as you may have guessed—turned me into a vampire against my will."

"And that was when you met me, in Paris," Cahira said.

Sandrine nodded. "When you and I parted, I thought Lesplaies and I were returning to Africa against Angelique's wishes, but it turns out, it was all a part of their plan. Long before I met you, when I was a young vampire, I accompanied Lesplaies to the Kingdom of Hueda, which had become one of the busiest slave ports. On our journey, he admitted that Angelique made a deal with the king to take over the French slave trade, but he believed her intention was to stop it once and for all. I was skeptical, of course, but I said nothing, assuming we were on the same side. As soon as we arrived, Lesplaies unleashed one of the worst plagues I had ever seen onto a colony of white men settled nearby, taking the entire African village along with it."

She took a deep breath. "It was utter chaos. Humans dying in the streets with no one to bury them. The bodies were thrown into the French compound, which eventually was burned to the ground. The loss of so many lives left Hueda easy prey for King Agaja, Queen Hangbe's brother and latest Dahomian monarch, who swept in and took over the port for himself."

Cahira rose, rustling around until she produced a pipe. She used the candle to light it, filling the room with herbal smoke. She wordlessly offered it to Sandrine.

"No thank you," Sandrine said before continuing. "In the midst of the pandemonium, I realized that the plague was just a cover for Lesplaies's true motive—to weaken a reincarnated god named Anubis so he could take him back to France for Angelique, who wanted to consume his power. He bade me to prepare the ship so we could leave immediately with the sickly Anubis in tow. He had been feeding him drops of his blood so he stayed alive, but weak enough with sickness that he could not fight against his capture. But an old spirit came to me, revealing who Anubis really was. I turned him into a vampire so he would not die from his fever, then snuck him off the boat.

"Lesplaies never found out that I was the one who freed him, but Angelique was highly suspicious. On our second voyage—the one we embarked on after I met you—Lesplaies was meant to let another plague loose onto the Kingdom of Dahomey, for reasons I do not know. This time, I killed him before he had the chance. I met Anubis when I arrived on shore, who remembered me fondly, but warned me not to set foot in town. While Anubis was favored by the African gods, killing one of them, as I had just done, was unacceptable. I was forced to leave. Since then, Angelique has been hunting me, just like she hunts you. She can no longer access Anubis or find you, but she is not giving up. Her demons still crawl about, wreaking havoc on the world as they search for us."

Cahira took a long drag from her pipe and sat quietly, waiting for Sandrine to continue.

Sandrine looked down at her cup. "I have long understood that creatures like us depend on humans to live but, over time, I seem to have grown a sort of empathy I never had before. I think there might be more to us creatures than a destructive existence. Perhaps we reincarnated to help preserve the balance between the light and the dark."

Cahira grinned through a cloud of smoke. "So you've become one of the good guys."

Sandrine felt her face grow hot. She grabbed Cahira's pipe. "I don't know what I am, but I plan on traveling the world and when I run into one of her wretched gods or demons, I'm going to kill them with my bare hands. I came here because I was hoping you'd want to join me."

Cahira lit up. "Of course I will," she said immediately.

Sandrine melted with relief, pulling the smoke from the shouldering herbs into her lungs. A curious blend filled her mouth, and she was surprised how tantalizing the flavor proved. "What is this?"

Cahira laughed. "A blend of medicinal herbs and tobacco. You will sleep well."

No sooner had she spoken, did Sandrine's exhaustion finally break through.

Cahira gently took the pipe back from her. "Your home is mine," she said. "I will prepare Geri and my dinner while you rest. We will make our traveling plans when you rise."

"Still chasing women that don't love you back?" A male voice burst through her memories, bringing her back to the present, her feet still plunged in the cold, wet sand.

The moonlight caught on the metal beading of his locks and beard, and his silver capped teeth glimmered as he mischievously grinned.

Sandrine was not pleased to see him, though she had expected he might resurface. "I haven't seen you in years and that's the first thing you say to me? I thought you'd have learned by now that I don't anger easily."

Poseidon shrugged, causing his jewelry to jingle like a set of keys. "One day I'll succeed in riling you up."

"I am not chasing Cahira—she is like a sister to me," she informed him. "I don't have time for romantic entanglements. Now how do I know that you are really you and not one of Angelique's illusions?"

Before she could dart out of the way, he grabbed her face and kissed her quickly on the lips. She didn't react, though she was jolted by memory. Instead, she crossed her arms and waited until he was finished, maintaining her indifference. "That proves nothing."

"We can try something else," he suggested with a metallic grin.

"That has never worked out well for either of us," Sandrine reminded him with a sigh. She tried not to envision them swept up in the heat of passion in Athena's temple as it was swallowed by sea, floating dreamily afterwards as schools of fish fluttered by, the entire island submerged.

"Unlike myself, who is tethered to the sea with no realm for anyone to destroy, Athena is dead," the old god pointed out. "I can still feel the Olympians whose souls have remained, which is actually why I decided to approach you. Though it was hard for me not to intervene when I felt the hydra entering into my sea."

"You did the right thing," she assured him. "There is a reason we chose not to intervene in each other's lives."

He grunted, letting her know he was still unhappy with the arrangement.

"Must I remind you that Athena murdered me when she found out about us and nearly ripped apart the entire pantheon in her quest for revenge? And that when I finally came back to life, you were so desperate I remember you, that you sent me to a chaos goddess who turned me into an abominable creature—the creature I am today? My reasons for not swooning into your arms are valid. Besides, there is nothing quite like immortality to quell human instincts. I could live out the rest of my days without ever having to take a lover."

Poseidon scowled, his black eyes glinting like polished obsidian. "I shouldn't have come."

Sandrine merely lifted her shoulders, blatantly unaffected.

He put his hands on his hips and stared at her, as if waiting for a break in her resolve. "Fine," he growled when he didn't receive it. "Discordia knows you are all here. Ares is on his way to kidnap Cahira and she's hired an army of sirens to attack the harbor. You have a few moments, at most."

"Are you planning on joining the fight?"

He showed his back to her as he slid back into the ocean. "We have an accord not to intervene," he called over his shoulder.

She sighed, watching the water swallow its king. Though she had managed to convince both of them she was no longer interested, a small piece of her wanted to rip off his jacket the second he was near, fill her mouth with the briny taste of his, and feel the coarseness of his locks running over her bare skin. But she didn't enjoy being vulnerable, and her walls served her well. Love, lust, whatever it was, only served to dismantle her.

In response, she abruptly shifted into Medusa, the hiss of her snakes calming her with their presence. *She is sending sirens*, she told Cahira. *I am waiting on the shore.*

She shifted back, knowing Medusa's gaze was useless against females. It was the only part of her legend that was true; Athena was so overcome with jealousy that she'd cursed Sandrine to lose control over her power—any man who looked into her eyes would be turned to stone, but never a female. The memory poked at Sandrine's resolve, waking up the pieces of fury she often pulled forward in battle. It was an old skill taught to her by Queen Hangbe, who trained her warriors by way of torture to never let their emotions get the best of them. She asserted that the key to true strength was in its proper channeling.

Sandrine kept her rage in a small box within her mind, one she opened only when she had to fight something stronger than she was, a secret weapon carefully guarded after years of practice. Etched on the front of the box was the image of Athena, as a reminder of the years she had faithfully adored her and was met with nothing but scorn, only to finally fall in love with someone else who truly loved her back and have it ripped away from her. Not because Athena loved her, but because she was exerting her dominance. Sandrine took the key and unlocked it when she saw the siren heads bobbing up from the ocean's surface, their shrill cries beginning to stab the quiet air.

She glanced up to see that the moon had disappeared, obscured by heavy black clouds that moved at an unnatural speed. She realized they were no ordinary clouds, but flocks of ravens, signaling that Morrigan and Cahira had come to join her. She was glad that they'd arrived, for she always thought fighting was best shared with others, but a secret part of her knew it didn't matter how many soldiers were alongside her. There was nothing in the world more powerful than her rage, and Pandora's box had already opened up inside her.

Morrigan

S HE WAS SHROUDED IN TOTAL DARKNESS, the only sound the screeching birds above her, demanding that she rise. The scent of raw earth in her nose betrayed her position, laying under layers of cold and heavy mud. She wondered if she was blind until she felt someone gently brush the wet dirt away from her eyelids, and she wrenched them open to behold a man smiling down from above her.

She abruptly rose, sending him toppling backwards from his crouched position, knocking the torch from his hands. As he fumbled for it, she took a minute to take in her surroundings, confirming that she was indeed sitting in a pile of slick brown muck, her naked body covered in it, the night echoing with shrill crickets and the song of distant wolves.

The man was able to right his torch before it went out, revealing his features in its glow. She could see the outline of his thick auburn beard and wild hair, with bright green eyes that flashed underneath his brown, hooded cloak. "Do not be afraid. I came into the world just like you. 'Tis unsettling at first, but ya adjust."

She stared at him blankly, trying to understand what he was telling her, his accent strange to her ears. A single crow loudly interrupted their exchange, drifting down to land on her bare shoulder.

"Never seen crows at night," the man remarked.

"I think," she tried to speak, her voice hoarse from lack of use. "I think... they belong to me."

"Amazin'." He climbed to his feet and extended his arm to help her stand.

She took it, her legs shaking as she used them, but able to hold as she observed the man's height and stockiness, admiring the length of his beard. He had grown quiet, staring at her with his jaw slack, when she remembered she wasn't wearing clothing. "Did you bring that for me?" she asked, pointing to the cloak he'd tied with twine to his waist.

"Oh!" He fumbled, handing her the garment. "Forgive me, they dinna tell me you were a woman when they sent me to fetch ya."

She smiled, slipping the cloak over her head as her companion crow found a nearby branch to settle upon. "Who are they?"

"Yer family, the Tuatha De Danann," the man explained. "Yer a goddess—a descendent of Danu."

"Who are you?"

"Ah, forgive me manners. They call me Daghda."

Morrigan bolted upright in her bed, panting. The dream faded as her room came into focus, snowflakes trickling in through the windows she'd left open. The panic subsided as she realized that she was only dreaming. She threw off her sheets and grabbed her robe, stepping out onto the balcony. She saw vapor as she took several steadying breaths, the frosty air nipping at her skin as she gazed up at the night sky. Since they arrived in France, she hadn't been able to sleep, though the gentle snowfall that persisted since the day of their arrival had proven quite tranquil. She couldn't recall dreaming after she became immortal, but they had become so vivid she had trouble discerning their authenticity. She had a sinking feeling it had something to do with David being so close by.

Her last solid rest was when she awakened groggily on the ship to discover Jacob had passed, but before she could wrap her mind around it, Cahira announced they had reached France. Her bewilderment had only increased when they stepped off the boat at a private port in Calais, where Lucius was greeted by a handful of well-groomed lawyers whom he had apparently given warning to ahead of time. They stood patiently in the building snow until they all unboarded, with strange dark eyes and very light hair, before ushering them around with indifferent efficiency, unloading what was salvageable of their luggage and hurrying them into the carriages they'd provided. No one amongst their entourage made a comment except for David, who caught her eyes as they climbed aboard separate coaches, giving her a sideways smile accompanied by a shrug. "You can always depend on Lucius to take care of things in style."

She knew he was right. Although Lucius rode with her in contemplative silence, gently clasping her hand, the second they arrived at the chateau he owned under a different name, he began ordering around the help that awaited them like a natural marquis. Within moments, he'd appointed a man responsible for acquiring a hearse to transport Jacob's coffin, a man to make funeral arrangements, one to guide each guest to their rooms, another to call about his ship and crew, and still more to order clothing and supplies for each one of them to travel. At one point, she wondered if he even remembered she was there, until a tiny slip of a human approached Morrigan to guide her to her chambers.

"Put her to the west," he instructed him.

Morrigan slid him a look when she realized David had been shown the eastern rooms. He responded with a playful wink before turning back to continue his arrangements.

She'd let them all believe she needed more rest, but she wanted to do anything but sleep. Instead, she lay motionless on the bed, staring up at its rose-colored tester and the chandelier that seemed wasted in the perpetual state of darkness she kept her room in. She still heard Libraean's weeping through the walls, still felt the smoldering hatred burning off Cahira, and was lost in awkward sorrow when David was near. She knew deep down she was avoiding Lucius, which he seemed to sense and respect, but she missed him around her. She couldn't believe how easily they'd fallen together in this life, such a stark difference between times in the past when all it seemed they did was fight. Even so, it seemed blatantly insensitive to focus on that when the rest of the house was in mourning, each one of them bearing their own respective burdens whilst nestled in their rooms. Although she loved all who slept behind its walls, she longed to be freed from the collective weight of sadness.

She hurried back into her room and rummaged until she found the feathery black coat Lucius had delivered to her. She marched back to the balcony through the giant windowed doors and hurdled herself off it, landing with a gentle thump on the enclosed porch below. She startled when she realized someone was already standing there with their back turned, before she recognized Cahira's combative stance.

"Please don't go," Morrigan said quickly before she had the chance to avoid her.

Cahira crossed her arms as she faced her. "I cannot help the anger I feel," she said. Her hair was loose around her shoulders, snowflakes catching on her hair and fur-lined coat. "You cannot expect me to forget what has happened so that you might find peace."

Morrigan folded her hands at her waist. "I understand."

Cahira sighed, turning her gaze back out into the distance. The snow wasn't heavy enough to fully stick, swirling instead around the fallen leaves that cluttered the distant forest floor, the wind shaking the bony, twisted branches of its trees. "I know why you did what you did," she continued, her tone softening ever so slightly. "You were forced to make a quick decision. Had it been me, I likely would have done the same. However, you might have raised me as a child, but Dan picked up where you left off. He was everything to me for a very long time. It might have taken a hundred years for me to finally accept how I felt, but I did come to love him. I finally told him, after all that time, and then he was taken from me. You have to understand my fury."

"I do," Morrigan said quietly, once again swept up by emotion.

Cahira shifted her golden-brown eyes back towards her, their radiance suddenly so similar to Lucius's that Morrigan took a step backwards. "Then you will understand why I intend to bring him back."

Morrigan almost protested, biting her lip to stay quiet.

"You, David, and Lucius have been running into each other in different bodies for eons. Dan was once a god himself—I am certain his soul still exists and will reincarnate, but I'm not waiting that long. I'm going to open up hell and pull him out."

Morrigan couldn't help herself. "Lucius was once impatient trying to retrieve Isis from her tree and it didn't fare well for either of them. It's actually the reason you have a piece of her soul. Do you want to potentially sever Dan's soul in that way, after the lifetime he spent as a split entity, tied to that horrible wolf?"

"I'm not Lucius," Cahira argued. "You know as well as I do that I have more power than any band of Druids. I also have you, Lucius, and Anubis with me—the original Underworld triumvirate. If there is anyone who can bring someone back from the dead, it's one of you."

"Just because you can do something, doesn't mean you should," Morrigan insisted. "Death is a transition, one that Dan chose of his own free will. Truly loving someone means letting them make that choice for themselves, regardless of our own desires."

"You can cease with the maternal advice now," Cahira said coldly. "I am no longer the young child you once knew—I technically have been on this earth longer than you. And I'm honestly not surprised to hear you won't help me—in fact, I anticipated it."

Morrigan sighed. "I'm sorry I bothered you. I was just restless and needed air." She turned to head back into the house.

"Do you feel up for a fight?"

Morrigan blinked. "I'm sorry?"

"Do you feel like fighting? We're about to be attacked. Sandrine just warned me."

It took Morrigan a moment to comprehend what she said, but Cahira took off without waiting, heading into the slumbering port city towards the water. Morrigan darted after her, weaving through the twisting alleys to meet Sandrine on the beach. As they grew closer, Morrigan noticed the heads rising out of the ocean and immediately summoned her crows. The shimmering onyx birds fluttered in as if they'd been perched in impatient anticipation for her call. She threw off her cloak and caught the knife Cahira tossed in her direction.

The emerging sirens had chosen to wear human-like legs, though they were still covered in oily scales, armed with weapons made of sea shells and bones, their fingernails sharpened into points. They'd also shed the guises they used to lure mortal men to their dens for feeding. Their eyes, piscine and oily black, sat above mouths filled with rows of tiny fangs, with two slits where their noses should be and gills slashed along their necks. They advanced and Morrigan's inert adrenaline came rushing in, sweeping away her melancholy as it reminded her that her natural instincts for combat were just as strong as her whirlpool of emotions. She relinquished total control, joyous as she rushed into the throng of grotesque creatures.

There was no pause, no distinction between the screeching crows dominating the sky and the harpy-like screams rising out of the sirens of the sea. They held up impressively against the three strongest warriors the Earth had ever borne, nicking and barbing Morrigan's skin as she twisted to avoid the skillful thrusts of their weaponry. She managed to behead a few as her crows swooped down to pull at their gooey, aquatic skin. Sandrine's arms bore a few angry gashes as well, but her sword continued to send sliced appendages to the ground, the severed pieces flopping like fish kept out of water. Morrigan was unable to find Cahira until the sirens finally began to retreat, clearing enough space that she could see her silhouette marching towards another creature all together as it headed towards them through the mist. Morrigan moved to assist, but Sandrine stopped her with her arm.

"That is the creature who once killed Dan," she told her. "She wants this one for herself—it will do her good."

Morrigan frowned, for the advancing creature was large enough to give her pause, hideously misshapen as it lumbered forward. But she acquiesced, pirouetting her way through the rest of the sirens until the last one retreated under the surface of the water. It was apparent they didn't care enough about Discordia's war to risk total annihilation, slinking back into the depths of the ocean lest they lose more of their tribe. She took a few moments to collect her energy, before joining Sandrine and trudging back up the shore. Cahira remained out of sight but again, Sandrine shook her head when Morrigan started to speak. "She is quite capable on her own," she promised as she wiped the siren slime from her healing arms.

The snow picked up around them as Morrigan bid her crows a regretful farewell, watching as they became nothing more than black clouds in the night sky.

They were both startled by a loud thump at their feet. Morrigan looked down to see a severed head rolling across the bank. Remarkably, it appeared as if it had been chopped off once before its final severing, a fresh, angry gash expelling black blood from its rancid flesh, cut veins sprawling out onto the sand like the tentacles of a jellyfish.

Cahira jumped down from the cliff above to join them, completely drenched in vampyre blood, her eyes so wide with exhilaration Morrigan had no doubt of her paternity.

"What is that?" Morrigan asked, pointing to the head.

"Ares, the Greek god of war, also known as Dragos to David and Dan in fifteenth century Wallachia," Cahira explained, skewering the head with her sword so she could lift it up for Morrigan to see.

Morrigan wasn't sure if she could call what stared back at her a face, rather a swollen patchwork of putrid flesh holding dead eyes shot through with crimson.

"Angelique brought him back to life after Dan hacked him to pieces," Cahira explained. "He is the one who has been creating other blood drinkers and demons around the world. He was technically my uncle." She admired the head with a sigh. "But not anymore." She marched down to the shoreline and tossed the head into the water with a flip of her sword. "Take this back to her," she yelled to the sirens. "Let her know I'm still not impressed!"

Sandrine crept up behind her, placing a neutral hand on her shoulder. "Perhaps we should go back and tell the others."

Morrigan could see the internal war brimming behind Cahira's stoic expression, a drive and rebelliousness not often sated, even when she stood victorious after battle. She swallowed, for she saw both Lucius and herself reflected in Cahira's temperament...but she wondered how much of it was from Discordia. After all, Cahira shared her blood as well. Fortunately, Cahira softened with Sandrine's touch and nodded before she headed back up from the shoreline. It was apparent Sandrine had the same calming effect on Cahira's rage as Morrigan did with Lucius, which Morrigan was grateful for. Though a small tinge of jealousy wiggled into her heart, a longing to have such a bond with the child she now remembered.

Cahira strode past, surprising her by patting her shoulder. "Good fight."

Morrigan smiled, grateful for the small gesture. She tucked the borrowed knife into her boot and retrieved her cloak from the cluster of rocks. She winced as she wrapped it around the battered frame her body still worked to heal. The snow finally reached a steady fall, collecting in little drifts around the beach, and she followed the footprints that her daughter and her companion left as they deserted the frigid beach, side by side.

Lucius almost knocked her from her feet the moment she entered the chateau. "Where were you?" he demanded, trying not to appear frantic.

"Angelique sent sirens," Cahira explained as she fell onto one of the newly upholstered couches. She pulled off her water-logged boots, seemingly oblivious to the mud they dripped onto the cream-colored rug.

David and Libraean joined them, apparently having heard the commotion from their rooms. Libraean wore a pair of silk pajamas as though he'd just awoken, while David wore his standard frown, wrinkling the skin between his eyebrows. The tension in the room squeezed at Morrigan's chest.

"Are you certain it was Angelique?" David asked Cahira.

"I would have brought you Ares's head, but I threw it into the ocean after them," she replied.

David looked shocked. "You killed him?"

Morrigan turned towards Lucius, startled by the intensity of his stare. "We need to leave as soon as we can," she told him.

"But we haven't even buried Jacob," Libraean protested from across the room.

Lucius sighed, running his fingers through his wavy black locks. Morrigan observed from his unkempt appearance that he'd also been attempting to rest.

"That, and we're in the midst of a winter storm. My lawyers have amassed a crew who understand the delicate nature of what we are, but they are not convinced a safe passage can be had right now."

"Can't we man the ship ourselves?" Cahira protested.

"It is much too large for six to manage, even if they all happen to be supernatural."

"Then we can take my ship."

Sandrine interjected. "Cahira, your ship is in ruins. I have sailed to Africa several times and it requires a sturdy vessel to get us there safely. The southern ocean is unpredictable. Although the climate grows warmer the further we descend, it's not the easiest time to sail."

"Then what are we supposed to do, wait until Angelique throws another army at our feet? A stronger one perhaps?" Cahira said hotly.

"Wait—" David interrupted in a voice louder than usual, the authoritative tone echoing throughout the parlor. "Cahira, you might be a liminal, but you are essentially a human, and your adrenaline is so high the entire room can hear the blood rushing through your veins."

"It's true," Morrigan softly confirmed.

"You should take a minute to pull yourself together," he told her.

Cahira stared at him, speechless.

"And Libraean is right," he continued to the rest of them. "We are not leaving until we properly bury Jacob, in a churchyard, as he would have wanted it. Lucius?"

"I planned to tell you all before I discovered the ladies were missing—I received word that the service is scheduled for tomorrow morning," he replied. "We're fortunate I have influence in this town."

"Good." David nodded. "Then we can plan on being here for at least one more day. Morrigan, are you able to control the snow like you do the rain? I could try to blow away the clouds, but I fear I would just end up creating a cyclone of snowflakes."

"It is not the same as with the rain," she replied, avoiding direct eye contact with him. "It requires much more effort. If you'd like, I can try the night after tomorrow, after Jacob is in the ground."

He nodded. "Alright, then can we leave here two nights from now, with Morrigan containing the snow until we hit warmer temperatures." David looked up at Lucius amicably to confirm, even though Morrigan could see his jaw tense.

"Yes," Lucius said simply, without betraying a single emotion in his face.

David didn't seem to notice. He turned back to Cahira who had been watching him distrustfully since he'd asked her to calm down. "Do you think you can put up some sort of shield around us, like you did when you prevented Angelique from finding you before?"

"I hid my scent from her, then barely used my power unless I had to," she explained. "We would all have to stop using any power to achieve the same effect, and you would have to stop sending out your scent."

It was Libraean's turn to interject, appearing thoroughly confused. "What scent? How do we do that?"

"All creatures on earth—animals, humans, creatures—involuntarily emit pheromones," Lucius explained. "Since we have all long adjusted to having heightened senses, we forget how strong our sense of smell truly is. It's how we hunt so well, and how we know when the others are near, long before we see or hear them. The pheromones of unnatural creatures are especially strong because we are, essentially, both human and animal—perfect sentient predators."

"Chamomile," Libraean whispered. He looked up nervously when he realized they all looked at him. "Jacob smelled of chamomile," he explained, sorrow softening his voice.

The room went quiet. Unbearably so to Morrigan as she contemplated how much she enjoyed the scent of hawthorn and tobacco, just as much as she enjoyed the smell of bonfires and cloves. "How do we stop emitting them so Discordia cannot detect us?" she asked Cahira, who appeared lost in her own recollection of desirable scent.

"We all must stay calm," she sighed, looking at Morrigan, then David, then Lucius. "Meaning we should stay separated until Jacob's funeral. Since I suspect emotions will rise there, Sandrine and I can keep watch over the house while you're away. Then we will get through the next day, and set sail right before Morrigan has to call on her power to control the storm."

The room plunged into silence once more.

Lucius was the first to speak, breezing past them all as he headed up the stairwell. "I'll be in my library if anyone needs me."

"I'm going to take this opportunity to rest," Libraean decided, shuffling back towards the direction of his room.

Sandrine looked at Cahira. "I agree with what David said earlier—humans need to rest. I'll guard the parameter while you do."

Cahira rolled her eyes. "Fine," she mumbled, grabbing her boots and sending another spray of mud across the marble as she headed up to her room.

Morrigan could feel David's eyes on her as Sandrine quietly withdrew with a nod. "Goodnight," Morrigan murmured to him before he had the chance to speak, climbing up the stairwell after Lucius.

"I've been thinking about Ireland."

Morrigan froze.

"Did you think about him then?" David asked her quietly. The fireplace gave a startling pop.

She refused to look at him, not waiting to see his expression. "We aren't supposed to let our emotions rise," she reminded him.

"I am not like him," he continued, edging closer to the stairs.

She could see his soft, imploring eyes in her mind, could envision the way his hair fell into them as he spoke.

"I have never chased you nor demanded anything from you," he said. "I don't even want to convince you to be mine—if you wanted to, you would be. But I do think you would offer me some closure after all we've been through together. I want to know if Ireland was real, or if you pined for him back then."

Morrigan stared up at the dark corridor ahead of her. "Ireland was real," she told him. But he never once left the back of my mind, she thought as she hurried up the stairs to her room.

Thankfully he did not follow, leaving her alone to walk down the hallway to her room. It was quiet, a few long candles still casting their shadows across the floor. She moved so that her footsteps were inaudible, passing door after door until she hesitated by one, the room she knew he was in. She paused, imagining him sitting in front of the fire, closer to it than anyone else could ever be comfortably, a book spread open across his lap. She could see the midnight blue wallpaper and shelves around him, picture the expression on his face as he embarked on the sacred exchange between writer and reader—agreeing with some, disagreeing with most—and either throwing the book across the room in disgust or placing it lovingly on the shelf with the others, as if it were a precious artifact to be studied later. She imagined he was reading anything he could find that would be distracting—certainly not anything that would draw out his anger—but nothing so light that it bored him. In fact, she realized that since David's return to consciousness, Lucius had been remarkably calm, uncharacteristically so, even when it came to her. It was odd, for as much as she hated his possessiveness, its absence was equally unsettling.

She let her fingers rest against the mahogany wood, bidding him a silent goodnight when suddenly she smelled him, feeling his heat permeating the door. She startled, wondering if she should hurry back to her room.

"Cedarwood," he said softly through the door.

"What?"

"Fresh cedarwood that has just been cut, the autumn woods right before it rains. The sad sweetness of fallen leaves as they wait for winter, the creek before the first frost."

She couldn't help but smile, her cheeks warm. "We shouldn't be talking," she whispered through the door.

"I just thought you should know," he murmured. "I didn't tell you enough when we were married… How much I adore you. I would offer to write you poems, but I'm an awful poet and we both know how much I love to talk… I just wanted you to know that to me, you smell like home."

Morrigan felt emotion building in her stomach. "If I don't go soon, I'm going to tear this door off the hinges."

She could hear him chuckle.

She pressed her lips against the door, imagining it was his face. "Dragon's blood, summer bonfires, and cloves," she told the door, and then, before she did anything she was going to regret, she hurried down the corridor, barricading herself into her room.

CHAPTER FOUR

❦ THE HISTORY ❦

THE ATLANTIC OCEAN, 1858
LIBRAEAN

LIBRAEAN STARED AT THE BLANK PIECE OF PARCHMENT sitting in front of him, waiting for the words to come.

It had been a week since they boarded Lucius's ship, one of the latest in traveling innovations that utilized steam. Originally built as a merchant steamer, Lucius had it entirely restructured with passenger comfort in mind. Their perpetually gracious host, despite his typical air of annoyance, had provided them all with fresh clothing to travel with, even though he had to argue loudly with Cahira: "All this money has been stolen from filthy rich bureaucrats—half of it is rightfully mine, but half is Angelique's and you're goddamn right she should pay for our excursion! Now take the damn clothes and stop your complaining. I bought you knives, as well."

The rest accepted his generosity, for they knew money was irrelevant, but to pretend to be human, one had to play the part. Libraean had been long accustomed to Lucius's penchant for opulence and grandeur, and did not waste the mental exertion on how he managed to acquire such a vessel. The upper decks had been furnished to mimic any other aristocratic establishment, boasting a sleek dining hall, library, common room, and several covered porches. The second deck held a dozen passenger rooms and sitting areas, with the furthest end intended for cargo. The crew lodged in steerage, a group of silent professionals hired by Lucius's lawyers who seemed to understand they were not sailing with ordinary humans and kept themselves completely isolated.

Libraean had been lost since they put Jacob in the ground. The four immortals had ridden in silence to the chapel, a crumbling edifice that once belonged to the fortress that defined the city. It was in a better state than its crumbling predecessor, though ivy relentlessly climbed its mossy stones. A lawyer named Jonathan Harrow had made the arrangements, even filling the grave digger's pockets with extra coins to ensure the grave was dug the full six feet deep.

Libraean felt as if he walked in a dream, grateful for Morrigan's guiding arm as they maneuvered through a graveyard that wore a blanket of white like fresh paint, save for a singular trail of footprints. The gravedigger wiped sweat from his brow, though icicles covered his coat. It was Mr. Harrow who addressed the lumbering priest exiting the church. The terrified fellow crossed himself several times, refusing to look any of them in the eye as he hurried through the service, clearly wanting nothing more than to retreat to the safety of his chapel.

Lucius appeared equally annoyed by his presence, but remained respectfully stoic; David's expression held its own blend of emotions. He patiently waited until Morrigan stepped back, and linked his arm around Libraean's, patting him reassuringly though he was distraught himself. It felt good to have them all there, even Lucius. He hated that his heart hurt so badly at Jacob's loss. He had known their days on Earth would be brief—they'd existed for centuries apart before—but still, he ached. While grateful they had a chance to reconnect, their final separation occurring at a time where there was forgiveness and love rather than hatred, all these logical, rational things had no effect on his mourning. He was utterly, irrevocably devastated.

David squeezed him a bit tighter when the priest finally ended his sermon and abruptly took off. The gravedigger slammed his spade back into the earth. "I'm sorry, my friend," Libraean heard him murmur. He didn't respond, not knowing how to articulate that no one should be sorry for death, that he was not upset that death came for Jacob, he was actually envious, for Jacob had easily achieved what Libraean had always yearned for—natural, well-earned death. It was he who secretly longed to be in the ground, freed from his prison of flesh. But he could never tell David that, the two having an unspoken accord to live out the rest of their days together. Yes, it did pain him to be away from the man he loved. But he knew, in the way that those who often indulge in introspection know, that first and foremost, he was envious.

Mr. Harrow motioned to return to their carriages. Libraean caught sight of Morrigan and Lucius standing inches apart, looking into the grave with the calmness one would expect from two gods of death. The blinding white snow caught on their black cloaks and equally black hair, and they both offered him a look that showed they understood exactly how he felt without having to say it. It was that look that finally dismantled any residual anger he had towards them on behalf of David, melting away like the snow that caught on his shoes.

David hadn't wanted to leave his side since the service, but finally Libraean insisted, explaining that the longer he waited to resume his solitude, the harder it would be for him to return to it. The first few days, he simply slept, wondering if he could just fall away like David could—he was older than him after all, with a far older body—yet he couldn't stop his mind from racing long enough to stay planted in deep slumber.

On the fifth day, he finally pulled out the ink and quill Lucius provided for him, laying them out neatly on the desk in his room before gathering a stack of unmarked paper.

And there he'd sat for an hour, staring at the blank pages.

He threw off his glasses and rubbed his eyes. There was so much more to write, so many more layers to a story he thought he'd known. He had yet to write Cahira's tale, he'd only just met Sandrine, and now, the one who had once been the most loathsome immortal they'd ever known was playing generous host, leading them forward on their adventure with a completely different perspective than had ever occurred to him.

He gazed out the small circular window in his room, noticing the sky grew brighter. He wondered what David was doing, considering taking the stroll down to his room. He decided against it, staring back down at the blank page with fresh determination. He grabbed his quill, dipped it in the ink, and scrawled out, "The Immortals," which he promptly crossed out to write, "The Gods," which he also crossed out and wrote "The Vampyres," before letting out a sound of exasperation, crumpling the paper, and tossing it across the room. He stood up, grabbed his hat, and hobbled down the hall. It didn't matter that he'd easily adjusted to having human feet after centuries of living behooved, his joints still creaked with age. As he headed down the smooth hallways with freshly painted walls, he wondered if he should just give in and buy himself a cane. He had a feeling Jacob would have approved.

He gave a swift warning knock before he entered the stately library and annexed study, knowing the person inside would most likely apprehend him with a raised eyebrow. Instead, Lucius hopped right to his feet as if he was waiting for him, grabbing a stack of books from the nearby desk. "I had Mr. Harrow make sure the library was stocked before we left, but there are a few titles he couldn't grab in time," Lucius explained as he breezed past him out the door. "Come on, I don't expect you to carry these with that limp of yours."

Libraean took a moment to wrap his mind around their odd interaction before hobbling after him down the hall. Lucius strode into his bedroom, setting the books down on his desk with a thump. He frowned when he noticed the crumpled parchment on the floor. "You will get there again," he told him softly. "Grief persists in waves, but normality does return."

Libraean squinted up at him. "You're different."

"Am I?"

"Is it Morrigan?" Libraean pressed, searching Lucius's gold eyes over the rim of his glasses.

He noticed something flash in them at the mention of her name, but Lucius chose to deflect rather than respond. "You have the record of our individual histories, the lives that have led us up to where we are now. But you have nothing that describes what we are. We've become a species in our own right, and it doesn't appear that we will be going anywhere anytime soon. Even if Angelique succeeds in killing us, there will still be immortals left walking the earth. You are the Earth's record keeper, and it is high time for another installation."

Libraean walked over to his desk to examine the books he'd given him—volumes of folklore and mythology, scientific speculation on blood fevers, and theories of the supernatural. He was stunned, wondering if Lucius had somehow read his mind.

Lucius opened up the book on top, pulling out a small, printed pamphlet that had been nestled inside. Clearing his throat, he read:

> *"But first, on earth as vampire sent,*
> *Thy corpse shall from its tomb be rent,*
> *Then ghostly haunt they native place,*
> *And suck the blood of all thy race,*

There from thy daughter, sister, wife,
At midnight drain the stream of life,
Yet loathe the banquet which perforce,
Must feed thy livid living corpse;
Thy victims ere they yet expire,
Shall know thy demon for their sire,
As cursing thee, thou cursing them,
Thy flowers are withered on the stem."

He replaced the pamphlet, closed the book, and set it back on the stack gently. "Despite our best kept efforts to remain hidden, the humans see us—they know us. Now whether we go down in history as the romantic fantasies of writers like Lord Byron, or in cheap penny dreadfuls, or as the ancient gods responsible for the very world we walk upon is entirely up to you. I'd like to think the world will someday want to know our true origins. Besides, it would be interesting to determine why some of us have no empathy and are brutal killers, while others do."

Libraean was suddenly overwhelmed with emotion, which he swallowed. "Thank you," he said quietly.

He must have noticed the shift in his voice for Lucius quickly resumed his apathetic tone. "Oh, please, we all know I enjoy notoriety, don't thank me for being selfish." But as he exited the room, he patted Libraean gently on the shoulder, saying nothing more as the door swung shut behind him.

Libraean turned back towards the stack of books and his empty parchment. He took his place back behind his desk, moistening the tip of his quill with his tongue and dripping it back in the ink before writing on the top, "The History of Vampyres."

He wasn't sure how long he sat at his desk writing, but when he looked up to see who had arrived at his door, it was night again. Morrigan stood tentatively in his doorway in her perpetual shroud of black, her brilliant eyes shining between waterfalls of raven hair. "Am I disturbing you?" she asked softly.

Libraean looked down to see his wrinkled hands were covered in ink, the well running shallow next to scores of scribbled pages that were scattered all around him, some sticking to his elbows. "I could use a break," he admitted as he straightened up his mess. "Please come in."

She drifted into the room in her weightless, ethereal way; she always managed to move gracefully, even though she was tall and commanding when provoked. There was a faraway look in her eyes as she observed his room, a veil of sadness hanging over her as she took a seat across from his desk, folding her hands in her lap. "How is he?"

Libraean removed his glasses for they had begun to painfully indent his nose. "He seems distant...distracted."

"Is that a typical reaction when he comes out of one of his spells?"

Libraean sighed, suddenly longing for a cup of Jacob's tea. "Usually, he is in better spirits, even getting dressed and going into town. Considering the circumstances, however, I think his temperament is to be expected."

Morrigan nodded. "You must detest me," she said sadly.

"On the contrary," he assured her. "While we are long past any glimmer of a maternal bond, I know your heart is good."

She blinked. "It has been a very long time since I've heard words like those said to me," she murmured. "Will you wait here a moment?"

Libraean nodded, though he was confused. She left for several minutes before surprising him with a tray in her hands, a tea kettle and cup balancing on top next to a tin of herbal tea. "I don't know what kind of tea Jacob used to make you, but the pantry had a few different blends. I used to adore spiced tea as a human."

Libraean stared.

"Oh, forgive me," she laughed as she set down the tray. "I didn't mean to read your thoughts, but you don't put up any guard. Your craving came to me loud and clear. We are shapeshifters, remember, connected in animal thought."

"Oh yes," Libraean chuckled. "Sometimes I forget these things. David has always been telepathic, but I suppose I forget I'm also around other creatures with abilities. Thank you for the tea; that was very kind of you."

"My pleasure," she said as she handed him a cup. The steam drifted into his face, a rich aroma of black tea and citrus wafting up into his nose. He was grateful to have been so far removed from drinking blood that his human cravings were back, his palette longing for things like tea and biscuits. He took a sip, letting the warmth revive his tired bones as she sat back down in the chair.

"If you wish to resume your solitude, please let me know," she said. "This journey feels agonizingly long, and I am infamously restless and lonely."

Libraean smiled. "I've been trying to update my memoirs to alleviate my own such restlessness. As a matter of fact, since you are here, would you mind helping me fill in your book?"

Morrigan flinched. "I've grown to hate recalling the past."

Libraean stood, shuffling to the bookcase nestled in the corner of his room, where he had lined all of his books, including their handbound histories. He pulled out hers, a thick tome covered with a carmine fabric that had already begun to fray, titled "Lilith," with a snake and a crow drawn underneath. "Ah," he pointed out, "but I know you appreciate the keeping of records."

"Touché," she smiled.

Libraean retrieved another glass jar of ink before he took his seat back behind his desk. He poured it into the inkwell and gingerly opened the delicate book, smoothing out the first blank pages. The scent was lovely, swirling with the aroma of his tea. One day, he'd print all his books and bind them in leather.

"Where would you like to begin?" she asked him, a touch of nervousness in her voice.

He smiled. "I would like to begin at the beginning. Do you remember anything at all from the early days?"

Morrigan frowned, but she closed her eyes as if trying to sweep the dust off of memories as old as time. "None of us can remember the true beginning, nor exactly how humans came to be," she began. "I remember flashes of Isis and I as children running through fields, but nothing solid. Philosophers have tried to answer the question of whether humans are born with knowing or if they learn from the environment in which they are born. I cannot answer these questions—I don't think any of us can. Maybe the humans created us, maybe we created them." She looked pensive. "All I know is that one day, they existed, but humanity was so fragile that Isis decided to take care of them. So, she did so with David, who she pulled down from the stars along with Lucius. I don't remember caring for either of them back then, they just didn't matter to me like my sister did. Besides I was always exploring and searching, enamored by all the secrets the earth revealed to me. I had little desire for anything else. Meanwhile, civilizations sprang up around us, which Isis and Osiris took care of. I remember being briefly worried about what would happen to the souls of the humans when their bodies died, but Set was put in charge of them. I had nothing to worry about for years, except protecting my sister from harm. Then one day, the humans began to speak of me as if I was Set's wife and then I just was. I also don't know how we started...when we started..." She trailed off, her porcelain cheeks pulling up a shade of rose.

"Making love?"

Morrigan shifted uncomfortably in her seat. "Yes, making love."

"Breeders," Libraean shook his head with a laugh. "So painfully modest about something so natural."

His playfulness relaxed her, bringing about a grin. "In my defense, you are technically my son, who just so happens to adore David. Talking about making love to his brother seems rather insensitive, no?"

"I see your point," Libraean said pleasantly. "Please continue."

"I have no idea when nor how we began to express our love for each other physically," she continued. "I can't even answer the question of why."

"You didn't know any other way," he offered.

"True," she said, crossing her legs beneath the black ripples of her skirt. "And most importantly, I cannot recall when that stopped being enough."

THE BEGINNING
MORRIGAN

"NEPHTHYS, WHERE HAVE YOU BEEN?"

Morrigan turned to see her sister, hands folded tight with apprehension. She looked every bit a proper queen, gold jewelry and gemstones sparkling against her skin, her bright white tunic wrapped tightly around her curves, revealing slivers of bronze legs as she moved. Her heavily kohled lids made her green eyes impossibly vivid as the wind tossed her straight black hair. Morrigan wondered what she must look like in return: the rambunctious twin, dried mud underneath her toenails and splattered up her legs, sweat clinging to her back even though she'd ripped up her tunic to allow for breeze. She couldn't remember the last time she'd combed her hair, nor the last time she'd scrubbed the dirt from her face. "I was helping the humans finish the harvest before dry season," she explained.

"They found a way to create life," Isis said quickly. "Osiris told me this afternoon. I have been searching for you since."

Morrigan blinked, openly stunned. "How is that possible?"

"Do you remember telling the women stories of you and Set as you helped them wash their clothes in their river?"

"Yes, but we do not create life that way. Only pleasure."

"It is another one of Earth's mysteries," Isis decided. "When the humans perform that act, a child grows inside the woman, just like it happens for the animals."

"Does that mean they do not need us anymore?" Morrigan wondered.

"I think they need us even more now," Isis replied. "Especially their death gods. When the humans begin to steadily procreate, they will populate the Earth faster than ever before. There will be just as many deaths as there will be new births. Perhaps you and Set could reinvest your time back in the Underworld?" A bit of hope clung to her words.

Morrigan frowned at the mention of her arranged husband's name as she thought of the dank lower realm they had been forced to inhabit. It was a suffocating, dismal place that filled her with dread. She much preferred to spend her days running free under the rays of the sun or working amongst the humans in the dirt.

"You never gave it a chance." Isis gently took her hands. They read each other's minds so often that neither of them questioned it when it occurred. "You have been so angry you were forced to have a husband that you let it spill out into the entire realm. Over time, you have come to enjoy his company—why let it upset you still?"

Morrigan sighed as she thought of him, wondering where he'd disappeared to. Unbeknownst to the others, neither one of them spent much time in the Underworld, nor with each other, meeting for the occasional romp before promptly going their separate ways. She did enjoy that part of their interaction, but other than physical pleasure, their connection was nonexistent. "He is away."

Isis shook her head. "Osiris spoke with him earlier. He is in your realm now."

Morrigan sighed again, looking down at her tattered, dusty clothes. "I am taking a bath, then I will join him."

Isis smiled and wrapped her in a hug. The fragrance of lilies drifted up from her hair. "Thank you, sister."

Morrigan waited until she was back at the palace before she walked down to the edge of the Nile, peeling off her clothes along the way. She wasn't worried anyone would see—the humans were unaware of the hidden stretch of river she swam in, bordered by lush palms and flowering bushes. The water was deliciously cool and crisp as she dove into it, soothing her sunburnt skin. She let the current carry her as she floated, thinking of her sister's words and weighing their implications. It wasn't that she hated the Underworld, she just loved the Earth more. It felt as if it was an extension of her own body—the mountains, her curves, the trees, her bones, the water, her blood, the birds, her children. She couldn't imagine life apart from something so integral to her being.

But as much as she adored the colorful light of day, there was something captivating about the night, the way the air suddenly cooled and sharpened, inviting the owls, the bats, and the cobras to come out and play beneath a dome of starlight and silver moon. Perhaps if she looked at the Underworld like it was simply the night to the Earth's day, she could learn to love it in the same way. She swam for a bit longer, procrastinating, until finally she stood in the shallow end, letting the water stream off her body as the fiery rays of the setting sun dried her skin. She closed her eyes, filling her lungs with a few last breaths of fresh air before she would have to return to the stale realm of the dead.

She heard rustling in the leaves. Startled, she whipped around to behold her brother-in-law, Osiris, his eyes wide as he stared. She wasn't sure why she'd never recognized how handsome he was before that moment, but she found herself admiring eyes the same shade as her sister's, and light hair with flecks of gold. Her eyes traced a distinct jaw that managed to construct a face that was strong, innocent, and kind, all at the same time. She realized he was admiring her in similar fashion, his eyes sweeping over her exposed breasts, her stomach, down to her legs. The look in them thrilled her, bringing color into her cheeks as she watched him nervously lick his lips. She smiled and gave a gentle wave of her fingers before disappearing under the water's surface, letting it pull her down into the realm of the Underworld.

She dropped easily to the ground, right in the middle of her neglected bedroom. She squeezed the water out of her hair as she searched for something to wear, sorting through the hundreds of tunics Isis sent her until she settled on one that felt right—a shade of ebony that matched her long waves. Just like the night.

Set was waiting for her in the throne room, slumped over his chair wearing a look of annoyance. He was free of the headdress he'd had fashioned into an intimidating jackal, allowing his own black hair to cascade down his shoulders, pulling out the color of his amber eyes. They brightened when he saw her, though his expression stayed grim. "Did Isis find you?"

"Yes," Morrigan sighed as she approached him. "They want us to recommit to our roles as death gods."

"The audacity," he growled. "Who are they to tell us what we must do—we are their equals."

"It is not their fault," Morrigan said as she tried to push away the vision of Osiris creeping back into her mind. "It was the humans who decided what sort of gods they required."

"Yes, the humans," Set pronounced the last word with open disdain. "The insignificant creatures whom we should have dominion over are the ones who decide our fate."

"It does not have to be so bad," she insisted. "We can create our own home here."

"We?" He raised an eyebrow. "When have you spent more than fleeting moments here?"

"I will help you," she promised. "But if I must rule the dead alongside you, I want a say in how. There will be no more harrowing challenges for them to fight their way through. If they pass the Weighing of the Heart, they will be allowed to rest peacefully until their souls want to return to Earth. I will keep track of it all, but I need to build something to help me organize the records."

Set softened as he listened to her talk. "I will make you whatever you wish," he told her.

"Good," Morrigan said, pleased. "And I want us to have a palace like the one on Earth, but it will be ours, with rivers, lakes, ponds and fountains, painted in colors that match the evening sky with flowers that only bloom when the moon rises. I want it to be like the night." She realized her words were coming into fruition as she spoke them, Set's eyes and hands building in sync with the cadence of her voice. The pressing vision of Osiris slipped out of her mind to be firmly replaced by him, suddenly beautiful to her as he created a world for them, the action pulling forward the smoldering appeal that lay beneath his hard exterior. Although she had always been attracted to him, knowing he could fill her entire body with pleasure, he was even more so now, surprising her by how gentle he looked when separated from his hatred. She bit the inside of her lip, hoping it wouldn't be too long before they finished so she could pull him into her bed.

Perhaps things wouldn't be so bad after all.

Morrigan was miserable.

"You are not leaving," he snarled, crossing his arms as he stood in front of her.

"You cannot control what I do," she argued. Though she had tried to make good on her promise to stay planted, she had grown utterly bored, longing for fresh air and sunshine. She'd managed to keep it at bay, up until the moment he strode into her room to tell her that he was leaving.

"Yes, I can," he told her. "You are my wife and you belong down here with me. I created this entire realm for us—for you. I made it exactly how you wanted—there is simply no reason why you need to go to Earth."

Morrigan laughed in his face. "If you think that is going to convince me to stay, then you are sorely mistaken."

"The humans need me to preside over their wars," he explained hotly. "I cannot just stay down here forever. There needs to be someone here to take care of things while I am gone—that is your job."

"Why is it my role to be left behind? Why can you not stay here and take care of things while I am gone?"

"What do you have to do that is so important," he snorted. "Teach women how to make love to their husbands? Plant flowers?"

Morrigan's anger flared up around her as she glared at him. Every part of her wanted to tear the condescending expression right off his face.

"I have wasted enough time trying to reason with you," Set snapped as he threw on his crown, the vicious jackal glaring back at her with glowing eyes. She noticed his spear at his side. "I will be back soon." He disappeared, leaving her alone to seethe.

Her skin vibrated with anger, rendering her unable to put together thought until she drew in a steadying breath. She marched back to the Records Hall, determined to get her way. How foolish she had been to think he would continue to make the best of things with her, that he wouldn't eventually abandon their duties. She reached the towering documents where the histories of souls were housed and focused her energy until it began to move by itself, shuffling and organizing as if she stood there directing it. *There,* she thought victoriously. *Now I can leave, too.*

She spun around to be greeted by young Cereberus, who cocked his triple heads at her. Although he was Set's animal companion, she'd grown to appreciate his company as well. "I will return," she promised, scratching him behind one set of ears.

He let her slip away and she ran down to the long river that surrounded their palace, diving in without hesitation. She felt the old familiar squeeze of realm travel as it popped her out at the surface of the Nile. She swam to shore, rising to her feet triumphantly before transforming into a kite and taking to the skies.

She'd forgotten how much she enjoyed flying, watching the landscapes roll beneath her as she navigated the sky. She found exactly what she was looking for within moments—a settlement of humans preparing for battle. She found a perch on one of the tents they had erected, observing peasant men readying maces and sharpening arrows before filling their leather quivers. Though the men were aware they were going to die, there was palpable excitement in the air. Morrigan wondered what it would be like to fight alongside them, to run barefoot and shirtless towards the enemy, unleashing a spear.

Her imaginings were interrupted when she sensed Set in one of the tents, her suspicions confirmed when she heard his booming voice over the excited chatter of the army. She flew in closer, hoping no one would notice a lone bird of prey perched unnaturally close to camp.

Set had disguised himself as human, his dark hair free of his jackal headdress and hanging loose down his back. He scowled as he spoke to the men gathered around him, towering over most of them in height. "You long for power and territory, but you lean on peasants to fight your wars. You must organize and train your soldiers."

One of the men scoffed. "We do not have enough men."

"Then cover them with protection before they fight. You sacrifice their bodies to the enemy, then wonder why your numbers are too low to win."

The men murmured amongst themselves, taking in his words. Morrigan softened despite herself. The humans did need him for help. While Osiris and Isis guided them with the basic necessities of life, Set helped them to be strong. Her anger at being abandoned still held firm, but its intensity had cooled. Perhaps she could find some way to manage their unpleasant situation.

She returned to the river, dissolving back into human form as she prepared to head back, when suddenly a sparkle of light caught her eye. Upon closer inspection, she learned it was a bracelet, the silver band dotted with shimmering lapis lazuli stones, brilliant in the sun. Beneath it were a few sheets of papyrus stacked neatly into a pile. Confused, she looked around, wondering who could have left it behind. Then she lifted up the pages to see.

A warm blush crept into her cheeks as the realization dawned on her. They were verses written in ink from Osiris...for her.

Continually asking why
Countless nights
Spent in torture
Time frozen
In hopeless melancholy
But I have come
Called to this place
Pooling water
Also waiting
Hoping
Begging
For a glimpse
The surface breaks
Time accelerates
Swirling anticipation
Your eyes shimmer
In the moonlight
Raven hair flows
Across your shoulders
You see me
With a wave
You're gone
And I know the answer
To my question
The reason
Has always been you

Heart now racing and skin hot, she tucked the pages into the shelf of her tunic. She struggled to keep herself grounded, making sure the pages stayed with her as she descended into the dank Underworld gloom, where she could stow them safely away in her box of jewels. She left the bracelet clasped around her wrist, however, admiring the cool metal against her skin.

She kept it on even when she retired, crawling under her blanket with a smile as she drifted peacefully to sleep.

She awoke to the sensation of Set's fingers trailing up and down her skin, lingering around the dip of her waist and around the curve of her hips. She didn't turn towards him like she always did when he was near, her way of accepting his invitation.

"Forgive me for leaving you." His voice was soft and deep in her ear. "It is not fair that I asked you to stay behind while I left. I did miss you."

Morrigan snatched the blankets back around her body as she flipped over to glare at him. "You are only saying that so I will let you touch me."

"I am not," he said, indignant.

"Leave me alone."

He growled with frustration, jumping out of her bed. "You cannot expect me to stay down here with you and ignore the humans."

She tried not to linger at the sight of his naked body. "Then take me with you," she said.

"I can collect the expired souls myself."

"No, I want to be a part of the battle."

He laughed. "A death goddess fighting in a war? Do you hear yourself? Besides, who will run things down here while we are gone?" He sat back down on her bed and reached out his arms. "Enough with this nonsense, come to me."

Morrigan fumed. "No."

Set let out a sound of exasperation. "You are not coming with me and that is final. Play all the games you want in the meantime." He withdrew, slamming the door shut behind him.

She rolled over, trying to calm her fury as she fingered the bracelet on her wrist. She pictured Osiris's letters, mouthing the words she'd memorized as she imagined his arms around her, holding her as she fell back to sleep.

From that moment on, she crept back up to Earth to find more of Osiris's letters every time Set left her behind. She cradled his words to her heart, dreaming of a life with a true companion who ran freely by her side. Eventually, she replaced them with her own.

Moody charcoal skies
Lacing emerald canopies
Rain your nectar

Down upon me
Drench me sweetly
I am your vineyard
Drink of me
Your goddess
No realm can hold me
Untethered, wild, and free
Make me your Queen
Come to me

Then one night, Set tried yet again to seduce her. He'd filled her room with dozens of white roses spilling out of obsidian vases, leaving bands of silver jewelry set with gleaming white stones to look like the moon near her bedside. Her breath caught in her throat, touched by the gesture, until he slipped his hands around her waist. She shoved him away, furious at herself for falling for his charms.

He threw up his hands in frustration, the fireplace in her room suddenly roaring to life, throwing light against his back. "You are impossible to please!"

"The only one you care about pleasing is yourself," she shot back. "These gifts mean nothing to me."

He snorted. "You accuse me of being selfish, but you and I are exactly the same. You cannot wait for me to leave so you can run away yourself. I saw what you did with the Records Hall. You do not wish to be trapped down here anymore than I do."

"At least I tried," she growled. "I have made my decision—I am tired of trying. The Underworld will carry on fine without me. I am done with this place—I am done with you." She tried to march out the door, but he blocked her, crossing her arms as his height filled the doorway. Her anger reached its boiling point, threatening to explode. Instead, a torrent of water came pouring into her room. Startled, Set jumped back, distracted enough that she could fly past him, skidding down the corridor on her bare feet.

He realized she'd gotten away and ran after her, fire appearing in bursts around her as she shoved open the palace doors, tearing down the shoreline. The river had become a swirling whirlpool, opening its watery vortex as she picked up her pace. She braced to launch herself into it, but before she could, a ring of fire sprang up around her, stopping her in her tracks. The flames prevented her from doing anything other than stand, lest she get burned. She whipped around to see Set with a triumphant smile plastered across his face. "How did you do that?" she hissed between gritted teeth that chattered with her rage.

"I wanted you to stop and the fire listened. The realm must know you are supposed to stay here with me."

Morrigan tried to calm her fury so she could think clearly. She heard the river churning over the sound of the crackling flames of her sweltering cage. She closed her eyes to focus on the sound, imagining the cool river against her skin when she swam. The feeling of gliding through water, weightless and deliciously free. They burst open in surprise when the waves hit her, extinguishing the flames as it swept her up and down into its watery womb. Her heart sang with triumph as it pulled her down until she reached the space that separated the realms.

Her head popped out of the Nile, and she hurried to the river's edge as her eyes adjusted to the brightness. Her nose immediately filled with the smell of living things, of fresh, sparkling nature, soothing her tumultuous emotions. She almost cried out with relief, but forced herself to keep moving, transforming herself into a kite so that she could find a place to hide amongst the humans.

The sensation of flying through the sky alleviated any lingering upset their argument had caused. She knew better than to think their relationship would be anything more than what it was, but she had let hope override her rationality—and she would never let it happen again. She swooped across the village she often visited in her younger days, deciding to land and recharge.

It was nice to see the humans laboring fruitfully, to observe their race thriving. She didn't recognize any of their faces, letting her know the length she'd been absent, but she was still grateful to see them. She felt their eyes on her as she wandered around, but it was quite a different reaction than what she was used to. Many looked away, fear flickering across their faces as they murmured amongst each other, trying to shrink from view.

Dismayed, she headed towards the edge of the village where she observed an older man, sitting on a stone bench in the shade. "Do you know who I am?" she asked him.

He nodded. "You are the great goddess Nephthys."

"Why do the humans look at me with such fear in their eyes?"

"Do not be dismayed by them," he told her. "They only fear you because they fear death. They fear the trials that lay before them in Duat, that their hearts will weigh heavier than the feather of Ma'at. They fear the dark parts of themselves."

"They fear Set," Morrigan realized.

"Though you are his wife, the oldest amongst all gods, remember you are a kind and gracious goddess," the old man assured her. "Your heart is good."

They were interrupted by the sound of screaming.

Morrigan left his side to dart into a nearby hut, observing a woman with a fully pregnant stomach laying on the ground, surrounded by two others. One held her hand, while the other lingered by her spread open legs as she wailed in agony. The women noticed Morrigan's arrival, immediately bowing their heads in fear.

"What is happening?" Morrigan demanded.

"Please, please do not take my baby," the laboring woman managed to gasp.

"Why would I take your baby?"

"You are the goddess of death," another woman responded in a shaky voice. "Your presence here means you have come to collect a soul."

Morrigan didn't have a chance to correct her, for the woman began to scream again, a fresh stream of blood appearing from between her thighs. Morrigan watched in quiet reverence during the entire process, hanging in the shadows as the women held each other during the birth, dampening the wailing mother's forehead with wet cloth, and changing the linens which quickly became saturated with crimson.

After several hours, when Morrigan was certain the woman would die from the pain, she let out a shuddering cry and went limp, the oldest gently lifting her child from her womb. The baby was completely still and white. The older woman sighed, still wrapping it lovingly in blankets. "I am so sorry," she told the mother as she cradled the baby to her bosom.

The mother let out a sound that chilled Morrigan to her core. She turned to flee but before she could go, she heard a tiny cry, realizing the child's spirit was in her arms. She looked back up at the humans in surprise, meeting expressions that dripped with loathing.

"It was not me..." she tried to explain, but the infant's soul was pulling at her, needing her guidance to find its resting place. She flew out of the hut, back through the village, and to the river's edge. The baby's soul gazed up at her adoringly with its tiny dark eyes. She gave it a kiss on its forehead as she lowered it gently into the river, letting it peacefully float away to the Underworld, where she knew it would be safe. Death was a gift, a transition like all others, but humans could not see it. The grieving mother would not see the soul of her child existing in perfect happiness, only knowing the pain of its departure.

Morrigan headed back across the desert on foot, trying to shake the dread that had settled over her. She plodded up to the palace, no longer concerned if Set found her. Any residual anger she felt had been replaced by sorrow. The humans no longer wanted her near them like they once had. They believed she was a monster, a harbinger of death, a goddess to be feared, to be hated. They saw her just as they saw him.

She walked under the towering palace dome to see her sister, who brightened immediately. "Nephthys! You have come for a visit."

She forced a smile. "I have."

"How is the Underworld? You have been gone for so long, I am excited to hear how things have been."

Morrigan didn't have the heart to tell her, remaining quiet as she let her sister guide her deeper into the palace.

Suddenly, Osiris strode in from the gardens. His appearance was like a fresh, rejuvenating breeze, immediately lifting her spirits. She tried to temper her elation at seeing him, wanting to appear composed in front of her sister. She could tell he was lost in a similar battle, his eyes struggling to stay focused on Isis as she spoke.

"Nephthys has graced us with a visit," she told him.

"I heard you and my brother were quarreling," Osiris said softly, finally letting his eyes land on her. Morrigan shivered, although the day was warm.

"Set can be such an intolerable fool," Isis commiserated before Morrigan had the chance to reply.

"You are welcome to stay here as long as you need to," Osiris offered, as casually as he could muster. "This is still your home, after all."

Morrigan struggled to maintain her own facade. "Thank you."

Isis beamed, blissfully unaware of the tension between them. "Come, let us get you some clean clothing. We can share my room, like we used to in the days before."

Morrigan nodded, allowing her to lead her away. Though she had once lived in their palace long ago, she never paid it much attention. As she followed Isis down the halls, she felt as if she was seeing it with new eyes. The walls were impossibly high and painted into bright designs, the ceilings cut into patterns that opened to allow light to stream through. The current sunset pulled reddish orange into the space, glinting against the bronze and gold effects that created the interior. Columns lined each room, interrupted by extravagant arrangements of plants and statues of wild beasts. She imagined Osiris designing it in the same way Set had once constructed their palace under the earth, bringing a smile to her lips.

Isis led her into her bedroom, a chamber that dripped of her sister, from the sheer white fabric that draped the open windows and bed, to the clusters of flowering plants in each corner. Birds drifted in and out at will, twittering as they flitted around the brightly colored blossoms.

"Please get comfortable," she told Morrigan as she removed her headdress, setting it between towers of jewelry that reflected in the polished silver mirror of her vanity. "Tell me what happened between you and Set."

"Sister, I can no longer play goddess of death," Morrigan told her as she folded down to the floor. "The humans detest me now, just as they detest him. I cannot blame them; I can barely stand him myself."

Isis frowned, sinking down next to her. Morrigan liked to see her without all her glittery effects, for it reminded her of the days of old when they both were wild and untamed. She longed for their simplicity; the memories were becoming harder to remember, grains of sand slipping through her fingers.

"I thought you both enjoyed each other," she said.

"My body feeling good is not the same as my heart," Morrigan explained. "There is a disconnect."

"One does not go along with the other?"

"How is it with Osiris? Do you feel connected to him in your heart as well as your body?"

Isis laughed. "Oh no, we do not do those things."

Morrigan was taken aback. "Truly?"

Isis nodded solemnly. "The act that you, the humans, the animals perform—that has never been a part of our relationship. Osiris and I like to create things together, to nurture. That is the root of our bond."

Morrigan frowned, thinking of Set's face as he built their new home, remembering the faint glimmer of hope she'd had in that moment. "The reason I am unhappy with him is because he seems only capable of physical love—there is nothing else in his eyes. That is not enough for me."

Isis gave her a sad smile. "Nothing in this world is enough for you, sister. You are restless by nature."

Morrigan looked away, knowing she was right.

"Let us rest now," Isis suggested. "We can figure things out when the sun rises."

Morrigan nodded. The two burrowed into Isis's soft, pillowy bed and though her twin drifted off easily to sleep, Morrigan found she could not follow. Instead, she slipped from beneath the covers and paced about the room, trying to gather her thoughts. She found herself rifling through her sister's things, wrapping herself in her bright white dresses and covering herself in her jewels. Then she went to Isis's mirror and lined her eyes with her stick of kohl, standing back to admire her reflection. She smiled, wondering if anyone would be able to tell the difference if she ran out to greet the humans or Osiris.

Then a terrible feeling seized her. It hit her that, although they were identical and there was once a time where they couldn't tell where one of them began and the other ended, she would never be Isis. She was never going to be adored by the humans, never freed of the incessant longing for something she could not place, never delivered from her state of perpetual restlessness. She would never be loved like Isis was loved, never be happy like she was.

She frantically ripped the jewels off her body, peeling off Isis's tunic. Out of the corner of her eye, she caught the jade encrusted knife she used to sharpen her makeup and grabbed it, taking her long hair in one hand, the knife in the other. She hacked into her locks with fervor, until chunks of raven waves fell in clumps to the polished stone floors. What was left behind immediately sprang up, light and wild, joyous to finally be free. She stared at her new reflection, and smiled.

Then she bolted, naked, out into the night, cool breeze and moonbeams on her skin as she raced back to her beloved river and dove in. She so was delirious with joy, so lost in the moment, that she didn't realize that Osiris had joined her until she collided with him. He smiled as he waded in front of her, his eyes sweeping over her face.

"Your hair," he said.

She blushed as she ran her fingers through her damp, shortened locks. "I know you thought I was beautiful because I mirrored my sister, but I needed it gone."

He frowned. "Oh no, I mean—well, your physical self is quite beautiful, but I am in love with your soul. The way it pours out of your eyes. The way you are so feral. That has not changed. In fact, I think your hair suits your spirit."

He didn't have much time to finish his last word before she was kissing him, pressing her naked skin up against his. He was surprised at first, but he took her lead, synchronizing his lips to hers as his hands began to shamelessly explore her body. He pulled away with a shiver. "Forgive me, I have never felt like this before."

"I will show you," she whispered, pulling him back to her as the wind rifled the leaves around them.

The Atlantic Ocean, 1858

MORRIGAN BOLTED UPRIGHT OUT OF HER BED, cursing when she realized she'd been caught by yet another dream. This one felt real, as if David had just left the space beside her. She could even smell him, his telltale aroma of burnt tobacco and fresh hawthorn teasing the air. She threw off her blankets in frustration. She'd assumed her conversation with Libraean would sate the nagging feeling that had settled in her stomach since they boarded, perhaps putting a halt to her dreams. But no sooner had she left him to his writing and settled herself into a potentially satisfying slumber, did they return.

She dressed, deciding to stretch her legs. If the dreams would not stop, then she would not slumber. Her supernatural body didn't need it anyway; she only hoped to use sleep to pass the time until they reached their destination. It was becoming clear she needed to find something else to occupy her, something that didn't involve either brother, strategically situated on opposite ends of the ship.

The night air that raked through her hair was warmer than it had been for weeks, a telltale sign they had reached the southern waters. The skies were completely clear, revealing layers of stars often obscured near the smoggy cities. She walked through the covered patio that bordered the ship until she reached the open deck, leaning forward to rest her arms on the edge so she could feel the spray of the ocean. Water never ceased to revive her, soothing her now with its gentle waves. She lingered for a moment before looking up to the stars, just in time to catch one shooting across the speckled expanse.

She closed her eyes against another wave of memories that came forward: the day Daghda had tattooed Morrigan. She ran her fingers over her skin, remembering the conflicting sensation of pain and pleasure as he tapped his inked needle against her flesh. They were both quiet as he worked and once he'd finished, she asked him to lay with her in the dewy grass, the moisture cool against her sore skin. The two of them splayed out under the sky, watching her crows make trails in the fluffy clouds above them.

"I think that is where I came from," he told her, folding his hands on his chest. "The sky."

"I cannot remember where I came from." She tried to think back.

"You came from the mud," he teased.

She stretched her arms out, admiring the settling ink that crossed them. "Do you think I am mad for wanting these?"

"Not at all," he assured her. "Everything about you makes sense to me. If you tell me to carve up your skin like the human warriors, then so be it. I do as you command."

Morrigan laughed as she sat upright. "Then perhaps I should be your mate so I can command you forever."

David sat up to face her, suddenly serious behind his thick auburn beard. "Say the word and I would dedicate myself to you for the rest of our lives."

Morrigan was taken aback, not expecting her playfulness would be taken to heart. "Do you mean it?"

He took her hand in his. "I cannot put it into words, but just as it feels I came from the skies, it feels I have known you before this life. As if we are connected somehow."

Morrigan frowned, finding herself at a loss for words. Since she arrived on earth and was inducted into their clan, she felt drawn to him, a bond developing between them that transcended the camaraderie with the others. There was a flirtatiousness to their interactions that no one could deny, but she'd never stopped to imagine it as something more. She looked up at her crows, suddenly unsure if she wanted to commit herself to another being, to be like the domesticated women around her who she could not relate to.

"I do not say this to try to trap you," he said as if he heard her thoughts, drawing her eyes down to rest in his gaze. "I know you are a bird that needs to fly freely over the hills, who desires her independence above all else. I only want to be yours, demanding nothing in return."

She studied him. "Sometimes I feel as if I have known you before this life, as well," she admitted.

"Then perhaps we were both born of the skies," he said with a grin, bringing a sparkle to the forest that was his eyes.

She couldn't help but smile back. He grabbed her face to kiss her, sending her crows into an uproar. He broke away to laugh. "Even your crows know we are meant to be. Say yes, Morrigan. You can command me for the rest of our lives."

Morrigan melted under his warm hands around her face, suddenly wanting to crawl into his lap and kiss him again. "I can command you for the rest of your life without marrying you," she teased.

David studied her face. "I do know better than to try to get a decision out of you so quickly. Take your time, but if you still cannot decide by the evening of Samhain—the night when I first met you in the mud—then I will let it go and never speak of it again. I will adore you just the same."

She beamed. "Agreed."

The memory of the brilliant daylight sky darkened into starry night, with Morrigan alone beneath it. David of the skies, Lucius of the stars, she of the Earth, and Isis of the creatures of it, she thought to herself. Perhaps they were all destined to be entangled in each other's lives. Or they were meant to be apart.

She hugged her arms, trying to distract herself from long-dead memories by focusing on the present. She shifted her thoughts to Anubis, looking forward to seeing him again. She had been enjoying getting to know Libraean and was grateful Cahira was softening towards her, but she missed Anubis. None of her experiences as a mother were conventional, but of all the children that had come in and out of her life, Anubis was the one tied to her heart. He had been the one who sought her out in the ancient times, a distant but steady presence, no matter the lifetime. She wanted to know him in this one, to learn about his lives both human and immortal, though she'd learned the current state of Africa was far from pleasant. The trading of humans was nothing new for the human race, so quick to force others into servitude and set themselves higher than the rest. But it had taken on devastating proportions. She was glad to learn many had opened their eyes to the cruelty, yet men were not quick to let the things that made them powerful slip out of their hands so easily. They kept their women suppressed and punished those who deviated from their sexual absolutes. It made her proud to know Anubis spent his life fighting against them, for the betterment of humanity, but she felt a twinge of guilt that her own focus had long shifted from the living to the dead. Perhaps the living needed them more than she thought.

When the scent of burning cloves joined her thoughts, it seemed completely natural, until her mind broke free from its stream and she realized what it implied.

She saw only the thick, winding smoke from a cigar and the silhouette of crossed legs a few meters down from where she stood, their owner keeping respectful distance as he quietly rocked in one of the wooden deck chairs.

"How long have you been observing me?" she called to him.

"Since the moment you walked outside," he told her honestly.

She continued facing him as she leaned her arm against the ledge of the ship. "Even though we're supposed to stay away from each other, you somehow always manage to be near," she teased.

"Can you blame me?"

"This trip has proven to be excruciatingly long," she sighed, turning back to peer across the dark waves.

"I agree completely," he said from right beside her.

She slid him a look. His hair was disheveled, fluttering in the wind as he gazed down at her. "You are breaking the rules," she warned, though she was secretly glad he was near.

"Are you really surprised?" He grinned.

"No, but the last thing we need is another hydra attack," she pointed out.

He didn't leave, instead studying her profile. "Something is off with you," he determined.

"I cannot seem to rest."

"Oh?" She saw his concerned expression out of the corner of her eye.

"I've been dreaming about the past," she clarified.

"As have I," he admitted with a sigh. "I believe it is because we are all together, traveling closer to the place from where we originated. The memories have been quite vivid."

She was relieved to hear she wasn't alone, though the thought of Lucius reliving their tumultuous past unnerved her. "We do not have the most pleasant of histories."

"Do you remember anything from the time your soul was tied to Delicia, when you were the vampyre Morgana?" he asked.

She frowned, loathing to recall the centuries she spent battling over the body she shared with a madwoman. "Yes, but it is a hazy recollection at best."

"David claims I lost my mind when I burned down the Library of Alexandria, but I still clung on to my hope for humanity after that. I helped establish the Sorbonne in Paris, remember?"

Morrigan suddenly recalled the freshly paved streets of the burgeoning medieval city and the sounds of church bells echoing from within Gothic cathedrals, drowning out the squawks of the seagulls who lingered above the

Seine River. She could see the Louvre fortress, could picture the enormous domed edifice that would one day become the University of Paris. "The 13th century," she remembered. "You taught astronomy there."

He beamed. "While simultaneously corrupting young minds with my blasphemous ideas," he added. "The rector detested me."

Morrigan continued to piece together that time, when David had left on one of his solo excursions to Italy, leaving her alone with Lucius to ravage the city like the deplorable blood drinkers they once were. She startled when her thoughts ended at their townhouse, realizing the importance of that time in their lives.

"Lucius…" she warned him.

"I'm not trying to seduce you," he promised with a chuckle. "Not yet, anyway. I think I was dreaming of that particular time in our lives because that was the closest I was to remembering who you really were. You swore it was Delicia's aspect that wanted me back then, but in those moments, I felt you trying to find me again."

Morrigan was quiet, unnerved by the revelation. She hadn't realized it then, but he was right. She could almost picture his expression when he walked in the door of their townhouse, surprised to see her waiting for him.

"I thought for sure you'd be traveling with David," he'd remarked.

"Then who would you sleep with while I was gone?" she had replied with a mischievous grin.

He'd been so pleased that he attacked her where she stood, the two of them engaging in what they considered lovemaking back then, ending up naked, breathless, and wearing each other's blood and sweat on the wood floor.

"I hate this city, Lucius," she told him after they caught their breath. "I want fresh air again. And trees."

He leaned on his elbow to study her face. "Both your eyes are blue," he remarked.

She looked away, flustered. "What does that have to do with anything?"

He rolled on top of her, so she was forced to face him. "It means that, in this moment, you are Morrigan. In fact, since we came to Paris, I've noticed you overpower Delicia, depending on what you're doing."

She shoved him off her, furious at what he implied. "You are a fool," she fumed, grabbing for her clothes. "We are braided souls—one cannot overpower the other."

He merely smiled from where he lay on the floor. "Morrigan likes fresh air and trees."

"Morgana likes war," she insisted. "There are wars in Scotland."

"Scotland." He wrinkled his nose. "Is that where you want to go?"

She pulled her underdress over her head. "Well, I know you will never let us return to Ireland after what happened between David and me."

"Ah ha," Lucius flew up where she stood, locking his arms around her waist. "You are Morrigan right now."

"I am hungry," she told him, refusing to acknowledge his assertion. "Let us go kill some supper."

The present Morrigan let the memory fade as a new revelation dawned on her. It was she who had driven herself mad at the end, by constantly forcing Delicia away until she could no longer control the switch of her personalities. It was all her own doing. She shivered, though the air was warm.

Lucius took her long silence as denial. "Wishful thinking, anyway," he said, joining her gaze across the rolling water before his flickered back up to the sky.

She wrestled her thoughts away from that horrible time in her life, joining him in drinking in the night. They stood in comfortable silence, listening to the waves, as close to each other as they could without touching. Finally, Morrigan murmured thoughtfully, "He might own the bright sun and clouds, but you own the night and its stars. Sharing the same space, but never at the same time."

He gave her a defeated smile. "And unfortunately, the Earth needs both light and darkness to thrive."

She started to reply but found she could not argue, and he slid his fingers up under her hair to cup her face. She froze, unable to pull away from his adoring gaze.

"Goodnight, Morrigan," he whispered, running his thumb gently along the line of her jaw as if wishing it was his lips. Then he withdrew, disappearing before either of them could make a decision they would regret.

"Goodnight, Lucius," she sighed, and headed back to her room.

CHAPTER FIVE

❧ The Rebel ❧

The Atlantic Ocean, 1858
Lucius

"I just remember her," he shrugged. "At the risk of sounding like a dreadful romantic, my first memory is seeing eyes as blue as the sky. Then she was gone, like a bolt of lightning that lands right in front of you only to disappear and resurface miles away. She was always running, always hiding. I was intrigued by her immediately, but I never saw much of her until the humans decided to make us their gods of death, forcing us to be together." He looked away, as if lost in thoughts of regret. "Do not misunderstand, I wanted her all the time, but I was filled with rage that transcended all else. It was hard to appreciate anything when I was so blinded by hatred. Even still, I tried."

Lucius saw himself as Set, remembering what it was like to be driven by unbridled toxicity as he stormed into the Egyptian palace, a blaze of fury. "Where is she?" he demanded as soon as he saw Osiris, who sat on his throne as if waiting for him to arrive. As much as he tried to be at peace with his brother, the mere sight of Osiris sent him into a state. He couldn't stand the way he looked down at him, even though they were equals, how he was hailed as the Great One, the beloved Osiris, while he was left behind in the shadows. Seeing him now when he was already incensed did not help.

"You need to leave her be," Osiris told him, rising to his feet.

Lucius scoffed, incredulous at the thought. "How dare you tell me how I should behave with my wife."

Osiris put up both his hands as a signal of peace. "Calm yourself, brother. I know you both have been quarreling, the entire Earth has been in an uproar because of it. You are gods—you affect the humans when you argue. You both created a storm so intense, it flooded a nearby valley—set trees on fire."

"I could care less about the humans!" Lucius spat. "I want my wife back."

The twins suddenly appeared from behind where Osiris stood. Lucius lunged for Nephthys, but Osiris swiftly blocked him. "She does not want to return with you. You must give her time."

Lucius shook with anger, imagining what it would be like to tear his brother limb from limb. "You do not get to speak for her."

"Set, please," Isis's soft voice broke through. "Just leave her be for a while. I am sure she will return in time."

He managed to find Nephthys's eyes between the bodies blocking him from her, but the icy blue orbs were cold and unforgiving. She did not speak, her arms crossed in front of her as she looked away.

Maybe she did just need to calm down, he convinced himself. "I will be back in one day," he growled at Isis and Osiris as he marched out.

"Lucius," Libraean interrupted.

He blinked, snapping out of the memory to see that he'd lit one of the gas lamps completely on fire. He hurried to put it out, sheepishly turning back to the now apprehensive creature sitting across from him. "Perhaps we should discuss something else."

Libraean nodded without hesitation, straightening his glasses as he cleared his throat. "I have enough of the beginning filled in that we can move past it," he agreed.

"You spoke to Morrigan?"

"Yes," he replied, hesitantly, as he turned the pages in Lucius's book. "But what I would like to learn more about is the time between your first days in the realm of Tartarus until you rose up as Lucius the immortal blood drinker. Those make up the bulk of the blank pages in your memoirs."

"Ah," Lucius settled back down in his seat. "I think I can handle speaking about that time in my life." He closed his eyes, unwilling to divulge everything, but letting his mind decide where to begin. There it was—Ireland.

Ancient Ireland, 200 BC

He awoke with a start. Immediately, he reached up to feel his face, his fingertips meeting a prickle of a beard spread along his cheeks. A breeze colder than he'd remembered from his last time on Earth came through the opening of the shabby tent he found himself in. The sound of men conversing drifted in with the smell of freshly dampened dirt and meat cooking over a campfire. He took a moment to let everything sink in. He'd done it—he had taken over the body of a human.

He lifted up his fur blanket to see pale muscular legs dusted with freckles, his shirt streaked with mud and grime. The clothes the man had fought in were hanging up to dry, and underneath them, a variety of weapons and boots were laid sloppily across the earth.

A soldier appeared at the opening of his tent, speaking to him in Gaelic. Lucius tried to focus on the language he'd thoroughly studied but never spoke, realizing the man was telling him there was food ready if he was hungry. He grunted his thanks, observing his voice was now low and graveled. He waited until the man disappeared before rising from his sleeping area and throwing on the clothes. He shivered, realizing the fur he had slept under doubled as a cloak. He grabbed it, as well as the man's sword, before strapping his boots to his feet and withdrawing from his tent.

Although the night was crisp, the many fires crackling around him brought warmth to the camp; some of the men rested in tents, others content to sleep under the stars. They seemed to be enjoying their moment of rest, letting him know the battle recently fought had been won. No one questioned him as he made his way past, heading towards the black woods that hummed not far behind camp. The moon was dark, but the sky was filled with stars, casting their glow onto the barren tree branches. This world was much different than he remembered—the wind robbed of heat, the incessant buzz of mosquitos replaced by the low, throaty hoot of owls, the ground soft and covered in green. He understood why she'd chosen to live there, it was magnificent.

It took a moment for his eyes to adjust to the total darkness as he entered the woods, finding a tree stump to sit on. He slowed down his thoughts, closing his eyes and imagining her, just like he'd summoned Cerberus so many eons ago, focusing on her eyes and the feel of her hair.

"I was wondering when you'd summon me."

Her voice was unmistakable, causing him to jump to his feet. But the woman standing behind him was not the lithe, almond-skinned Nephthys he remembered. Instead, a woman stood before him, petite but rippled with muscle, her pale skin interrupted by dark blue tattoos. Her jet-black hair was short and wild, contained only by the diadem of corvid bones that lay across her forehead. She was dressed in a tunic that had been split into two, revealing her ribs and hip bones, an angry spear in her fist and a black bird perched on her shoulder. She was scowling at him but, in that moment, all the anger he'd felt towards her melted away as he looked into her eyes—for they were the same radiant blue as his wife's.

"You'll be needing to do more than just stare, Cuhullin, if you want my help," she said coldly, reminding Lucius that she was seeing a Celtic warrior, not him.

"Forgive me," Lucius stammered, hoping he wasn't stumbling over the language. "What must I do to earn your favor?"

She snorted. "You do not need my favor. You were so confident in your own strength before, why petition me now? Have you lost faith in yourself?"

"Perhaps," Lucius said carefully. He hadn't realized the body he'd chosen to invade would be a warrior that she disliked, and he deeply regretted the oversight. "I had a vision that I should summon you and ask for your forgiveness," he lied.

"I will bestow my blessings as I see fit," she told him. "Not because you suddenly want to repent for the slight made against me."

Lucius tried another approach. "Where is Daghda, your husband?"

Her face darkened. "Daghda no longer has interest in war."

"Ah, well your blessing means more to me than any other god," he said quickly.

Morrigan narrowed her eyes. "You are a vile human," she chastised him with her finger. "Any human that mocks a crone does not deserve my blessing."

Lucius sighed. "I have a confession I must make."

Morrigan raised a dark eyebrow, the movement rattling her crown of bones.

"I am actually a god trapped in this human's body," he told her. "The human summoned me here to help him win his war, but when I arrived, he used Druid magic to entrap me."

"I thought your eyes looked peculiar," she murmured as she came up closer to him, searching his face.

"Forgive me for the deception, I was not sure if you would be a friend or a foe," Lucius explained, trying not to lose focus as her scent drifted into his nose, a richer, smokier version than he remembered from their days together. His rational mind scolded him, furious at how weak he'd suddenly become in her presence, their tumultuous past gradually fading away the more they spoke.

"Aye, it makes sense that you did," she nodded. "Unfortunately, you are in a detestable body. It belongs to Cuhullin, a hero to the humans. He is Lugh's son, so I cannot be rid of him, but he's offended me many times. I long for the day I can watch him die."

"Then I regret being trapped in such a vessel."

She studied him for a moment, her hand settled on her hip bone. "I will help you," she decided.

"What about the other gods?" he asked.

"I work alone."

He had trouble containing his surprise. "Without your husband?"

Anger caught flame in her eyes. "Somehow you surmised that I am the strongest god nearby, and you summoned me accordingly. I am making the decision to help you, but if you speak any more about the husband I left far behind me, I will gut you like a fish."

Lucius blinked, thoroughly taken aback. Not only had she become more deliciously combative than when he'd known her, but she had left Osiris. His mind spun at the possibilities. Perhaps he could remain in this human's body and be with her again. It wasn't a desirable shell by any means, but he could work around it. He thought about Isis waiting in the Underworld for him to return—perhaps she could figure out a way to bring them back to earth, as Osiris and Nephthys had done. She would chastise him for even considering being with Nephthys again after how much pain she'd caused him, but she'd eventually come around. It's not like he could blame her if she did protest—logically, he knew he was a damned fool but at the moment, he did not care.

"Are you alright?" Morrigan asked.

"Yes," he mumbled. "It just feels strange to be here."

She laughed. "Yes, but it is a wonderful realm, is it not? Do you feel the cold breeze on your skin, the fresh air in your lungs? 'Tis perfect. Come, I will take you to a friend who can help you. You can tell me about yourself as we walk."

"Oh, forgive me. I am Hades, King of the Underworld."

She stopped in her tracks and he watched a shadow cross over her face, as if his words reminded her of something. He held his breath, hoping she wouldn't realize who he really was. Not yet, he thought, just give me a bit more time.

"You are the second creature I have met who spoke to me of this Underworld," she told him. "On the battlefield, after the fight had ended and only the crows were left to feast, I saw the ghost of a man who wanted to know why I had abandoned the Underworld. He was greatly upset, telling me I was supposed to take care of the souls there. I never heard of such a place before, and now in two separate instances, it has been mentioned."

Lucius hoped his face didn't betray his confusion. "I am surprised you are not familiar with the Underworld. I thought all gods have knowledge of the realms."

"No," she admitted as she resumed her pace. "My first memory is when I woke up on Earth, covered in mud."

"You have no memories of your previous lives?"

"I was told it was the Druids who brought us to life," she explained. "It is said that all of us have souls from different realms, and that Daghda and I once lived in one together, centuries ago. Yet I cannot recall any of it."

"Strange," Lucius remarked as they moved deeper into the woods, crunching through sticks and fallen leaves. "Well, the Underworld is quite beautiful in its own right. The work serves me well, but I do miss the feeling of sun on my face."

"You were on Earth before?" She looked up at him.

"Long ago," he admitted. "But only in the desert where there is parched earth and dusty air."

Abruptly, she grabbed his arm. It took everything in him not to scoop her up in response. He couldn't believe he'd spent such a long time away from her and the incessant desire still remained. He tried to replace it with memories of his death in Egypt, recalling his hatred, but it was fruitless. The pain diminished over time.

"I remember the desert," she whispered, her eyes wide. "I remember leafy palms and falcons soaring through the clear skies. How can I remember something I have never seen?"

"Perhaps, once you have taken me to see your friend, you could ask one of your Druids for help?" he gently suggested. "They seem to be the ones who have the magic in this realm."

"Aye…" she murmured, releasing his arm as she walked ahead of him.

"So you knew the man whose body I am in?" he asked, trailing after her.

"Yes, he is a detestable man," she told him with a sneer. "I am a shape-shifter, which is what I use when I need to work amongst the humans. An old woman had her farm ransacked and one of her cows stolen. So, I took on her form and stole the cow back from those who snatched her. Apparently, I was on Cuhullin's land and he chased after me, threatening my life. When I shifted into a raven, he let me go and begged for forgiveness."

"Which you did not give him." Lucius smiled.

"Of course not," Morrigan huffed. "How despicable must you be to steal an old woman's cow, then threaten her when she takes back what is rightfully hers?"

"Well, I would never want to be on your bad side," he said. Then he added before he could help himself, "One would think the humans would be falling over themselves to win the favor of such a beautiful goddess, especially one so deadly."

She halted her march once more. "You should not play with me," she warned him, though her stance had softened. "I have not felt the touch of a man in a very long time."

Lucius met her eyes and his resolve instantly gone, his blood screaming to touch her. Before he could step forward to obey, they were interrupted by a loud rustling in the bushes. He turned to see a giant satyr with a long, scraggly beard and a pair of antlers that arched up out of his skull, seeming to graze the heavens. The creature grinned as soon as his eyes fell on Morrigan, and the old familiar pang of jealousy promptly lit a fire in Lucius's stomach.

"Phantom Queen," the creature greeted her. "What brings you into my woods?"

"I am in need of your skills." Morrigan gestured towards Lucius. "My friend is a Greek god, trapped inside the body of the human who summoned him. Can you help him be free of it?"

The woodland god crossed his arms as he looked him over. "Yes, I can help you, Hades of the Underworld," he addressed him. "I am Cernunnos."

"Cernunnos does not hail from these lands," Morrigan explained, "but he travels through all the woods in the North, keeping watch on all that transpires in the wooded realm."

Lucius kept quiet. He was certain the creature knew who he really was, but for whatever reason, he was not betraying his identity. He knew that meant one of two things—that he was afraid of upsetting Morrigan, or he wanted a favor in return for his silence.

Suddenly her gaze was pulled up to the sky, for her crows had accumulated vociferously above her. "The battle has begun and I am late," she realized.

"I can take things from here," Cernunnos assured her as he took a seat on a nearby boulder, his massive weight sending up a cloud of dust and dried leaves.

Morrigan drew in towards Lucius, so they were standing mere inches apart. "You can find me before you go back, if you'd like," she said with a salacious glint in her eye.

Before he could reply, she abruptly transformed into a crow, departing in a flurry of black feathers. He stared wistfully after her as she disappeared, almost forgetting there was an oversized satyr seated nearby.

"Does she know who you really are?" Cernunnos asked, interrupting his thoughts.

Lucius frowned. "If you know who I really am, why did you tell her I was someone different?"

Cernunnos shrugged. "I want no godly discord in my woods. There is enough of that between the humans. I know all about you. I know that you are a dark god banished to Tartarus by his own wife and brother. I wondered when you would discover there was a tear in the realms and come back. They created it when the Druids brought them here."

"How do you know?"

"I am Lord of the Forest. I see all that transpires on earth."

Lucius crossed his arms. "Well, you may have figured out my identity, but I am only here because I found a way to possess a human."

"Ah." Cernunnos smiled under his bristly beard. "But now you know how to rise up properly."

Lucius was mystified. "Why do you help me?"

Cernunnos shrugged again. "I do not like her husband."

Lucius grinned. "Then I appreciate your aid."

The woodland god rose from where he sat, the effort filling the forest with the sound of creaking trees. "I assume you know how to get back to your realm," he stated as he turned to head back into the darkness. Lucius watched him go, his antlers disturbing the skeletal treetops as he lumbered beneath their branches.

He sighed, resting his hands on his hips. He longed to go after her, but he knew that although he'd find temporary solace and release in her arms, he would be deceiving her by using another man's body, something she would never forgive him for. He wanted to make love to her because she wanted him, not because she was tricked into it, and definitely not with the cumbersome body of some red-haired oaf that stunk of aging dirt with too large of feet. Besides, now there was another way. "I will come back to find you," he whispered up into the night sky. Then, before he could talk himself out of it, he released the human from his clutches, his soul diving back down to the Underworld.

He was surprised to see Isis, dressed as Persephone, waiting for him when he arrived. The Lily of the Nile shade of her dress brought out her eyes as she glared at him. "Where were you?" she asked.

He was so elated that he picked her up, spinning her around the room.

"What has gotten into you?" she laughed.

"I found out a way for us to go back to Earth," he told her excitedly as he set her back down.

Her face fell. "No."

"Isis—she has left him all on her own. She does not remember our past. I have a fresh slate. I can rise up to Earth and serenade her, and if she does remember me, I can show her how much I have changed. There is no doubt she will take me back—she loved me far before he seduced her."

Isis took his hands. "Set, you still do not know for certain that she ever did. Remember the pain you felt—the hatred you had over their betrayal. She is not your answer."

Lucius scowled. "You are wrong."

"I am not wrong," she insisted, even as he pulled away from her. "You told me you wanted to move on and you have. You have built an entire life without her. There is no reason to go backwards."

Lucius stared back at her, observing eyes that seemed that much greener when impassioned. She was not wrong; he'd grown comfortable with his new identity, becoming the much feared but venerated King of the Dead easily. He did enjoy the work, as he enjoyed Isis's platonic companionship, but he would be lying to pretend there wasn't something missing. Seeing her again, even if it was in an entirely different body, as a different person, had made it quite clear what that something was.

"Even if you go back to earth, your memories will be erased," Isis pointed out, arguing with his silence. "That is how the two of them are able to live in bliss, roaming the Earth without a care in the world, oblivious to their true history."

The modern Lucius paused. "You should know the story from there," he said softly.

The Atlantic Ocean, 1858
Libraean

THE CLOCK ON THE MOCK FIREPLACE clicked steadily during the brief silence.

"This is where I need clarification," Libraean told the tall, black haired vampyre seated across from him. "I have written down several versions of what started the Pădurii bloodline. We know Hekate's version was incorrect, but Anubis told David that you convinced Isis to have your children to protect her heka. It makes no sense that you would impregnate Morrigan's sister when your entire reason behind returning to earth was to repair your relationship with her."

Lucius sighed. "I never negated Isis's story because I did care for her as a dear friend. Now that I am aware she was Discordia in disguise, I should set the record straight. Typhon did let me use his body to slip past Anubis and find the tree under the nose of the Council. The acacia drove any man who came too close to it mad, and the man I found worshiping the tree was well beyond the brink of insanity. That particular man, who called himself Erebos, was a raving lunatic in his own right, though we had no idea at the time. His mind was different than Cuhullin's; while I was able to control his mind completely, Erebos's overpowered me. I believe it was because it was so fractured—I kept getting lost."

He frowned, leaning back in his chair. "I did manage to use him to pull Isis—well, Discordia—out of the tree, and we did go back to Erebos's house to rest and make plans for her to restore me fully to life. But we decided to celebrate, drinking heavily with our meal, and I didn't realize how his body would react to alcohol. Besides, she and I made love before and she was Morrigan's twin so… you can use your imagination to arrive at why what occurred did. Isis was mortified the next morning, so we both decided it was something we would never speak of again. Now I know this was all a part of Discordia's plan—she even charmed the memory so that Anubis, then David, would believe the alternate version was real."

"My word." Libraean shook his head in disbelief. "Then she brought you back, disappeared with the child, and you found me. Did you have any recollection of your former life at that point?"

Lucius shook his head. "None whatsoever. Eventually, I did begin to remember bits and pieces of the past, and I found out where she was and that she had my children. Naturally, they were hostile towards me. I discovered that Discordia tried to murder and consume the oldest and her child, but the girl reached out to the Council in time. They are the ones who put her back into the acacia, but told no one. Anubis had created the Council to protect the heka, yet they'd let someone slip past to kill Isis. They feared his wrath. Then you know the rest—I was unaware of the Council's transgressions, so I tried to free who I thought was Isis, giving life to David's ancient girlfriend and killing Discordia so that she would one day come back as Hekate."

"Lucius, do you have a text on Greek mythology handy?" Libraean suddenly asked.

He stood, using his height to retrieve a thick, leather-bound copy that looked a few decades old. He cradled it in his hands, reminding Libraean of what a bibliophile he was, before handing it to him as one might pass a newborn child. Then he sat back down in his chair, resuming his ankle on top of knee position while Libraean delicately turned the pages until he'd found what he was looking for.

"Ah, here." He showed Lucius the handwritten passage. "Erebos was the Greek god of darkness, the child of Chaos."

Lucius scanned it over before meeting his eyes. "Discordia knew exactly what body she was putting me in, one she specifically selected to be the father of her offspring."

"It would also explain why you were so insatiably violent and deranged," Libraean pointed out.

Lucius leaned back in his chair, digesting his words as he crossed his hands along his stomach. "Well, don't go telling anyone that theory. I will lose my notoriety. Besides, I wasn't exactly a saint in my past lives either."

Libraean shook his head with a smile. It faded as he began piecing all the events together, including Lucius's recent admissions. "I cannot believe how artfully we were betrayed."

"Hekate did get her revenge on the Council," Lucius brought up. "Revenge for us all, I suppose. Except now we have a bunch of wayward Watchers in their stead."

Libraean took off his glasses to rub his eyes. "Indeed."

Lucius grew quiet, staring at him with his penetrating amber eyes. "I suppose I owe you an apology for how I treated you back then."

Libraean blinked. "You apologize?"

"It is a rare occurrence, and you should not plan on it happening again," Lucius assured him as he rose from his chair, heading towards the open bottle of spirits he kept in his library. "Brandy?"

Libraean nodded, realizing he was quite parched.

"In any case," Lucius continued, "I'm not entirely convinced it was Morrígan who made it so that we forget our pasts as we come to earth. I think it was Discordia's doing, long before Morrigan and David even concocted their plan with the Druids."

Libraean frowned. "We have nothing to study to prove otherwise— except, perhaps, the humans. They don't remember their past lives when they come back. It could just be the way of the Earth."

Lucius handed him a short glass of tainted brandy before settling back into the leather chair across from him. "I suppose we will never know."

Libraean took a sip, surprised by the pleasant marriage of flavors that hit his tongue. "From what I remember about Celtic myth, Morrigan attempted to seduce Cuhullin and, since he scorned her advances, she wanted his death. To do so, she transformed into various creatures during his battle to defend Ulster from the army of Connaught and Queen Maeve. That account has always bothered me. It sounds nothing like the goddess we know."

"Humans love to distort our history," Lucius agreed. "Which is why it is so imperative that you keep it for us. My guess is the overgrown sack of skin came up with the story as a way to brag. Morrigan is a great beauty. She always was." He grew quiet again, taking a sip from his glass.

"I'm assuming you never told her you visited her in disguise."

"Well, I am just remembering everything again whilst trying to stay away from her, as per our collective agreement."

"We all benefit from the lack of discord," Libraean reassured him. "Though I do appreciate how hard it must be for you."

Lucius said nothing, taking another careful sip.

"What about France?" Libraean changed the subject. "How were you finally able to be rid of Discordia, or Angelique, as she was known to you?"

Lucius perked up. "What do you know of the salons in Paris?"

PARIS, 1760
LUCIUS

CIGARETTE SMOKE WAFTED AROUND THE PARLOR, mixing with the aroma of Bordeaux wine. Lucius scanned the faces of those surrounding him, as well as the numerous portraits hanging on the walls, acting as caricatures of those seated below. He was surprised to see both nobility and bourgeois in attendance, the collection of attendees not nearly as progressive as he had hoped for.

Their salonnière, a refined woman of lingering beauty, despite her gray hair and lined eyes, sat in the center of the room, an air of pretentiousness hanging around her like fog. The name Marie Thérèse Rodet Geoffrin commanded prestige in itself, and an invitation to one of her salons was as prized as any summons to Versailles. Lucius had managed to secure his invite with little effort, though Angelique's noble status would have earned him an easy pass; he didn't want her to know he was there. So he snuck in as a supposed friend of Diderot's, excited to see what the famed salon on the rue Saint-Honore was all about. To his disappointment, the topics being thrown around the room were far less titillating than anticipated. After about an hour of painfully uncontroversial chatter, he slumped in his chair, holding up his chin with his hand as he listened to a man in a freshly powdered wig drone on about how all men should have the right to practice their own religion.

"Or lack of religion," another man chimed in from the back.

The powdered man nodded. "Indeed. One could argue that the natural rights John Locke emphasized were inspired by his desire for religious freedom. He argued that religion cannot be compelled by violent means, that there must be complete separation of church and state."

"Natural rights refer to the human right to freedom," Lucius blurted out before he could help himself. "Stoics argued for natural rights centuries before Locke put ink to paper."

141

The room turned to look his way, causing him to straighten up in his seat.

Madame Geoffrin nodded his way. "Do continue. Marquis de Cardevac is on vacation from his duties as French Ambassador in Sweden," she told the assembly. "He is a friend of Monsieur Diderot."

Lucius cleared his throat, hoping that no one would recognize that he was very much not the person he claimed to be. "Centuries ago, Stoicism claimed that no person could be a slave by nature, that it goes against the very condition of the human soul. Locke only expounded on their assertions, claiming that one cannot surrender their own rights to freedom—it is stolen from them, therefore it is morally reprehensible."

There was a murmur amongst them.

A man seated close to Madame Geoffrin leaned forward. "Even Locke himself declared that enslavement of a lawful captive in times of war would not go against one's natural rights," he pointed out.

"Ah, but we do not take lawful captives through acts of war. We sail to foreign lands in our ships to rape and pillage their lands," Lucius reminded him.

The murmur grew louder, a few of the men grumbling their protestations.

"I believe our conversation is growing heated," Madame Geoffrin said smoothly. "Perhaps we should steer clear of politics in our discussion going forward."

"Isn't any human matter by its very nature political?" Lucius pressed, enjoying their discomfort. "How can we speak of the natural right to freedom and liberty when we enslave our fellow man, when we have a monarch placed on the throne by the 'divine right of kings' who pulls us all down into ruin? How can one divinely be throned if he shares the same soul as we do?"

Lucius smiled as the room erupted.

He hung back as Madame fought to control the crowd, corralling the impassioned voices as many called for an end to the ancien régime. He started to sneak away amongst the chaos, but when he turned the corner, he was stopped by a short gentleman with light hair and eyes. "My name is Arnaud Bisset," the man said quickly before Lucius could dodge him. "There are places where talk of revolutionary politics is welcomed, if you are interested."

Lucius searched his eyes, intrigued.

The man slipped him a small piece of paper. "We meet Friday evenings," he whispered before disappearing back into the crowd. Lucius tucked the paper into the breast pocket of his coat and snuck out the door.

"How was it?" Thoth asked him as soon as he returned home and entered his chambers. Though navy-colored rugs covered the marble floors, the spaciousness of the rooms caused an inevitable echo.

"Careful, Kali is looking for me," Lucius warned him in a low voice, pulling off his fitted coat and loosening his cravat.

"Was your experience that bad?"

Lucius shrugged. "I was invited to another meeting that seems far more promising."

"Ah." Thoth nodded as he took the chair across from where Lucius had slumped and began peeling off his stockings with rueful contempt. Though he enjoyed excess, he hated formal attire, grateful for the hour when he could replace the stifling clothing with nightclothes. He suddenly wondered how he would feel when he was turned into one of Angelique's vampires, if starchy fabrics and lace would make him shudder the same way as before.

"I need to figure out a way to be rid of Kali," Lucius told the apparition across from him.

"I think you've done a remarkable job of avoiding her thus far," Thoth commented. "Do you think it wise to take her on while you are still human?"

Lucius frowned, looking down at his hands. "I've killed before."

"Yes, but Kali is a goddess made strong by feeding on the flesh of other immortals. Though I don't believe she would kill you, she could make your life more difficult if you cross her."

Lucius let out a sound of frustration, throwing himself back on his bed. "I wish I could remember all the things you told me about my past."

"What more do you want to know?"

Lucius sat up on his arms. "Did I enjoy stirring up crowds?"

Thoth laughed pleasantly. "Well, remember, I did not have the privilege of knowing you back then, but yes, you were notorious for inciting conflict. You enjoyed fighting wars. Not just the physicality they entailed, but you loved putting your mind to work solving conflicts—a grand scale of chess, if you will."

"So I relished in chaos so that I could bring order to it, to control it?"

His words seemed to take Thoth by surprise, and he paused thoughtfully. "Well, yes, I suppose that's true. Did you end up reading the book I lent you, the Egyptian myths?"

Lucius sighed. "You are worse than my old tutors. Yes, I read them, but I still find it difficult to connect emotions to the words. There are so many different accounts of things, and I find it hard to believe I once looked like a jackal." His eyes flitted up towards Thoth. "With all due respect, of course."

Thoth smiled at him, unoffended. "All things exist to be interpreted, and humans interpret things how they may. Sometimes their stories are passed down, sometimes they are trapped in artifacts that don't surface until much later, some stories are distorted with each retelling. It is good that you cannot connect to these tales, for they are only partly true—one man's view on what he has found."

Lucius sighed. "That doesn't make things any easier for me. The hieroglyphic images look nothing like the raven-haired woman in my dreams."

Thoth examined him carefully. "So that is what still consumes your mind."

Lucius looked away.

"For so long, I had you categorized as the perpetual Rebel, with David as the Lover, though the more I get to know you in your tabula rasa state, I think I have been mistaken. You really do cherish love above all else."

"Whatever do you mean?" Lucius said, his first reaction defense.

"I do not mean to offend you," Thoth explained gently, gazing at him over his wire rimmed glasses. "I enjoy categorizing things and I do enjoy our conversations. I only hope they continue when you have turned."

"Why wouldn't they?"

"I am only here through magical means," Thoth explained. "There is a caveat that allows me to visit you, since I am a god and you are currently human. Once you transform, however, it might be a bit difficult for me to reach you."

Lucius frowned. "It is hard to believe you are not really here, that you live across the ocean in a completely different land."

"Our world is very strange," Thoth agreed.

"Louis?" a high-pitched voice interrupted them.

"Until we meet again," Thoth said before he faded into nothingness.

Lucius looked up to see Angelique at the door, a vapid mouse dressed up in French silk and scented perfume. He tried to disguise the loathing she invoked in him, knowing that nothing about her was genuine; everything was a ploy to keep him as her puppet. He imagined setting her on fire in those moments, bringing a smile to his face that she assumed was delight in seeing her.

"I am absolutely exhausted," she declared, flopping down on his bed. "Did you finish your lessons?"

"Of course," he said, motioning towards his desk, where his books and ledgers were kept.

"Where is Kali?"

"I don't see why I still must have a guardian," Lucius said, taking the opportunity to complain. "I am a grown man and will be an immortal soon. I shouldn't have to be saddled by someone watching over me."

Angelique hopped to her feet, putting her hands on her hips. "Do you think when you are king that you will not have scores of guards and servants at your call? You will rarely have time alone. I suggest you get used to it now."

"The more I learn about this life, the more I detest the notion of becoming king."

Her mouth turned into a thin, angry line. "We have been preparing for this for years. You are meant to be a king, to rule over all. That is who you were in your past life—Hades, the king of the Underworld. You are destined for greatness—do not let fear prevent you from attaining it."

Lucius forced his lips to turn upwards.

She stood on her tiptoes to kiss his cheek, leaving behind a smear of pastel lip color. "I do like to see you smile," she told him. "Now get some rest, we have a long day ahead of us."

PARIS, 1789

LUCIUS SHOVED HIS HANDS IN HIS POCKETS as he walked, observing the humans around him beneath the rim of his hat. The alleys reverberated with the haggard coughing of men, women, and children as they huddled together. Though summer's heat reached the city, it did little to alleviate the ailments ransacking the poorest among them, most unable to afford even the stale, discounted bread sold at the market. Lucius meant every word he yelled over the raucous discord at his weekly meetings, as he lamented how atrocious it was to let Parisians starve to death in the streets…though he had to admit, it made things much easier for vampires.

He went unnoticed as he headed down the streets, sated by the dying old man he'd found earlier, grateful to have his stomach full before he joined the others. It amused him how the gatherings now served two purposes—to feed his inner drive to wreak havoc and to enact vengeance upon the vampiress who had ruined his mortal life. Her quest for power was so strong that he wasn't surprised to learn she still managed to become queen without him, taking a page out of his book to transform herself into Marie Antionette, the widely detested Queen of France. He encouraged this hate wherever he could, enjoying the rebellion that hung thick in the air, waiting for the right spark to ignite the pyre that would take the aristocracy down along with it. He regretted that he wasn't able to see her face when she discovered that he'd murdered his personal guard, Kali, as soon as he turned or her expression when she discovered he'd disappeared along with half her fortune. It was the reason he still lingered in France, even though she hunted him; he wanted very badly to see the look on her face when he helped burn the city down around her.

Genevieve noticed him as he turned the corner and smiled broadly as she motioned him inside the tavern. Madame LaBlanche's Den of Pleasures served only two types of patrons—the bourgeois with extraordinary tastes, and the insurgents who found a place to stay hidden where no noblemen would dare enter. Genevieve was the latter. The reincarnated god Genesha and an employee of the house, she was an integral piece of the burgeoning rebellion. Kali's death at Lucius's hands had brought her great joy, as she was furious that the death goddess struck down the rest of the Hindu gods to absorb their power. She hailed Lucius as a hero, ensuring not only his room and board at the den, but helping him secure money and property beyond the detection of Angelique. Tonight, she was dressed in her favorite silk, her long dark wig sweeping her waist as she motioned him past, her eyes checking behind him to make sure he hadn't been followed. "They're in the Orient Room," she told him when she was satisfied that he was alone.

He nodded, freeing his black waves from his hat. The patrons of Madame LeBlanche and their employees—women in men's clothing, men in women's clothing, and everything in between—paid him no mind as he walked through them, distracted by various stages of debauchery. Genevieve followed him closely as she filled him in on everything he'd missed. She was the only one who knew he was a vampire, often covering for him when meetings occurred in the daylight hours.

She adjusted his collar for him as he situated his hat, straightening his coat once more before he took a deep breath and strode in.

The men gathered at the table nodded in his direction as he found his seat behind a table teeming with wine bottles, half empty pitchers of beer, and cigarette stubs.

"We must secure proper ammunition," one of the men insisted, smashing down his fist and unsettling the glasses.

"I have told you all several times, they keep barrels of gunpowder in the Bastille," Lucius interrupted loudly.

"Glad you've finally joined us, Victor," a fair-haired man named Bertrand said dryly.

"You know what I say is true. It holds no more than five prisoners, and its stores of ammunition are vast." Lucius looked at the rest of the men. "It is waiting for us on a silver platter, with only a handful of guards to push through."

"He's right," a man named Christophe chimed in. "We have the numbers now. Our people are starving in the streets, furious at the tax increase—they will join us! We can overthrow the archaic fortress at any time. This may be our only chance to secure proper weaponry before the King tries to stop us."

"Then let us revolt—let us show them the fire of the sans-culottes!" another man yelled, raising up his glass.

Louis slinked towards the back of the room as it rose in clamor, until he was beside Genevieve, who had been listening intently behind the door. "You know they do not have the amount of ammo we require," she said under her breath.

"It doesn't matter," he said, matching her tone. "They need to see their own power, to feel what a mob can do. This will be what starts our revolution."

"Shall I tell the others?"

He nodded.

She disappeared as the meeting devolved, as it often did, into a shouting match lubricated with gluttonous imbibing at Lucius's expense. He slipped out of the room, confident Genevieve would spread the word quickly enough that everything would be in place by tomorrow morning. He found his room at the end of the hall, closing the door gently behind him before turning to face the stranger who was waiting in his room. "Can I help you?"

"You do not startle easily," the man observed.

"I know I can kill you in a heartbeat," Lucius explained, not unpleasantly, as he hung up his hat. "Now, please explain why you are trespassing in my room so I can rest. I have a busy day tomorrow."

"Ah, forgive me," the man stuck out his hand. He was well-dressed in a clerical sort of way, the ink smudging his fingers confirming his bookishness. Lucius realized he was a creature, but one unlike any he'd ever seen. "My name is Jonathan Harrow, and I work for Somnus & Mors. My employers have requested your immediate presence at our firm."

Lucius frowned. "I'm a little busy at the moment."

"Ah, yes, they had a feeling you would say that, so they told me to let you know you are a reincarnated god named Hades, with a vast accumulation of wealth that you entrusted to us. They need to speak with you regarding both your fortune and a vampiress who calls herself Angelique Delaroux."

Lucius stared at the man in surprise before collecting himself. "Ah yes, of course. Let me secure a carriage."

"That won't be necessary, sir; we have one waiting for you not far from the alley."

Lucius nodded, trying not to reveal how unsettled he was as he retrieved his hat. Although Mr. Harrow had figured out the hidden passageway Lucius used to move in and out of his room unnoticed, he guided him through it, popping out the back door to see that there was, in fact, a carriage awaiting his arrival. He appreciated the use of an older, shabby model; the creature had the foresight to understand the delicate nature of the times. Traveling through Paris in an open display of wealth was not the best move if one wanted to go unnoticed.

Mr. Harrow helped him board and they rode in silence, giving Lucius the opportunity to study him more closely. He appeared in every aspect a human, with fresh blood running through his veins, but his skin had a ghostly pallor. Although he looked quite young, his hair was a dusty sort of blonde that seemed silver, and he bore dark, oddly wide eyes that seemed out of place with a nose and mouth perfectly proportionate to his face.

"I am a Wraith," Harrow told him, noticing his observant stare. "I will let my employers explain things further, but I am an immortal, though I do not need blood to survive."

"Wraith is a Scottish term for ghost."

Mr. Harrow laughed. "They told me you were an educated man. I suppose, if you want to be specific, we are demons, since we come from Tartarus, which the humans now call Hell. However, it was pointed out that we are far more ghostly than our other supernatural friends, meaning we can travel through realms and through walls even though we are technically alive on earth. Wraith seemed to be a good term to describe these characteristics, and so it became."

Lucius nodded. "Are your employers Wraiths as well?"

"I have already told you more than I should have." Mr. Harrow offered him a smile as the carriage rolled to a stop. "Fortunately, we are here and my employers will answer all of your questions."

The coachman opened the door to what appeared to be any other Parisian street, though it was completely clear of street lamps and bodies, giving it an eerie feeling of abandonment. The office loomed above them, the street below bathed in shades of gray, black, and midnight blue.

"Only the supernatural can see this street, for it is situated in between reality and the outerrealms," Mr. Harrow explained as he opened the door marked Somnus & Mors in painted gold lettering.

Lucius entered the interior of the building, unsurprised to see that it was drenched in the cool, dreary shades that reminded him of a place that rested just beyond his conscious recollection. The front hall was long and lined with unremarkable doors, an indoor fountain spurting dark water at the apex. From the back of the office, two men appeared, moving so gracefully they appeared to be floating. They were well-dressed and trim, with natural silver hair gathered and tied at their necks and eyes as dark as Mr. Harrow's. He realized they were identical twins, the revelation stirring something in him that he could not quite explain. In fact, the entire experience was unsettling him, pulling forward the whispers that echoed in the blank, unknown space in his mind.

"Lord Hades, welcome," one of the twins said, unable to hold back his joy as he grasped Lucius's hand. "We have been searching for you for quite some time."

"Forgive me for not sharing your sentiment, but my past life memories are completely lost," Lucius explained politely.

"Ah, yes, we are aware," the other twin said with a sigh. "Please, right this way."

The two men led him down another hall that opened into a wide chamber bearing a double desk that spanned the length of the room. Behind it stood a fireplace with flames that appeared white rather than copper, another peculiar attribute that was distantly familiar. He took a seat in one of the black leather chairs nearby. "So, which one of you is which?" he asked.

The twin on the left chuckled. "I am Theodore Mors, but you once knew me as Thanatos, the god of death. This is my brother, Harold Somnus, the reincarnation of Hypnos, the god of sleep. And while we are at the introduction stage, I hope you are remembering that you are Hades, though you have been surrounded by magic that has prevented anyone from finding you. It was only recently removed."

"I'm sure I know the creature who is behind it," Lucius sighed.

Mors looked grim. "We believe the vampiress Angelique was the one who shielded you from others as well as your memories, though we do not know why. We do have an idea how to find out, but first, we must show you something."

Somnus rose from his chair to the cabinet sitting behind them. He waved his fingers across it, pulling out a ledger seemingly from nothing. He opened it at the table, flipping through a few pages before turning the book so Lucius could see what it held.

"These are your assets," Mors explained in response to Lucius's widening eyes. "You have a far greater history than Angelique has ever let on. A creature named Thoth once told you everything, but Angelique's power is strong. She has taken your memories and blocked Thoth from approaching you again."

Lucius frowned, the name sounding vaguely familiar. He began to flip through the ledger.

"We do not know your entire history, only ours—that you were King Hades of the Underworld, though we all knew you were far older than that. You left me in charge when you rose to Earth with a goddess named Isis, becoming the first immortal blood drinker ever created. You were eventually cast down into Tartarus, where you happened upon the repentant souls of other castaway gods. When you rose back up to our Underworld, you brought them with you, charging me with their care. You had acquired vast amounts of wealth during your time on earth, which we managed until the day the realms were destroyed. Since we were all bound by our common duty, my brother, the Wraiths, and I rose to Earth together and moved our operation to the Middleworld, where we are sitting right now.

"We have kept your assets, but we've taken on other supernatural clients as time went on. We've become an impressive bank in our own right, but our loyalty is to you, first and foremost. Anything you should ever need in any lifetime, we are at your service."

Lucius considered their words, looking over the impressive numbers again. A thought struck him. "What do you mean, the realms were destroyed?"

Mors sighed. "Unfortunately, we have no information except that something has swept through and destroyed everything besides the Earth and the Middleworld. We believe it is the reason why there are so many immortal creatures currently here. There is someone who we think can help give you more information on these matters, as well as more information on your true past. He is a blood drinker named David Hawthorne, residing in London."

Somnus handed him another sheet of paper, listing the name and additional information about his whereabouts. Lucius stared at the scripted letters and the sketch that had been drawn beside it. The name sounded familiar, but he couldn't recall why.

"He also happens to be blocked by magic, but we have a feeling you will be able to track him down. We can arrange for you to sail as soon as tomorrow," Mors informed him.

"That is not possible. I have matters to attend to here."

"That is the other thing we needed to tell you," Somnus said. "The vampiress Angelique is no longer masquerading as Queen Marie Antionette. She has swapped with a replacement and fled Paris, but not before she left your name with the authorities, blaming you for the ghastly murder of a nobleman. She also accused you of treasonous acts towards the king."

Lucius scoffed. "Which name?"

"Just the two, but we can't be certain they won't be able to find you by other means. We have it on good authority that she left several of her best demons to hunt you, in addition to the human soldiers sent by the king."

Lucius sighed. "What do you propose?"

"We think you should leave for England as soon as possible. You own several merchant ships that can be ready immediately for departure, or a train ticket can be arranged."

Lucius was quiet for a moment, considering everything they told him. "There is a woman named Genevieve who works at Madame LaBlanche's cathouse. Contact her immediately. She is a reincarnated god and ally who has been managing the assets I acquired in this life, including several properties and a steamship of my own under the name Victor Regis. She will fill you in on all the details." He wrote down a number on a slip of paper and handed it to Somnus. "I have a prior engagement tomorrow that I refuse to miss, but please purchase me a train ticket for the evening. And please give Genevieve the amounts listed on this paper, the top is for her personally, and the bottom amount is for her to give towards the Revolution, to distribute however she sees fit."

Mors and Somnus nodded in sync as they rose to their feet, both appearing pleased he'd easily moved from bewildered into his former commanding role.

"Mr. Harrow is at your disposal," Mors told him. "He will take care of anything you need to reach England."

"Excellent."

"Thank you, sir," Mors extended his hand. "It's good to have you back, sir."

Somnus smiled as he mirrored the movement.

Back at his suite, Lucius sat in quiet reflection as the hours passed. His body didn't need sleep anymore, but he still enjoyed moments of rest because they gave him time to think. The evening crept into morning and, by the time he emerged to greet the growing crowd outside, the sun was high in the sky.

The air was electric, as though lightning had struck in rapid succession, the swelter of summer morning thickened by the bodies who clustered the streets of Paris. Lucius hung in the shadows, watching the throng of bodies press forward, snowballing as it grew closer to the Bastille, pitchforks and shovels held high. He had anticipated the general excitement, but was pleasantly surprised to see how many regular Parisians promptly abandoned whatever they were doing to join the swelling group of protestors. He scanned the crowd, recognizing only a few loyal revolutionaries, the rest reacting out of pure frustration. He grinned as their shouting reverberated through the streets.

He adjusted his hat as he drew in closer, knowing that most were too distracted by the chaos to stop and wonder why he wore a full coat in the summer, or why he wore tinted glass over his eyes. He longed to be in the midst of the riot as they pounded relentlessly on the old wooden drawbridge of the archaic tower. He saw the handful of remaining prisoners hanging out their barred windows, cheering with the crowd as the guards let in a few representatives in hopes of compromise. Lucius shook his head with a smirk, knowing the crowd wouldn't be satisfied with anything less than blood sacrifice.

As he waited in the alley, he found himself wishing they'd brought torches, like a proper rebellion. Nothing seemed to stir up passion quite like fire. He was fixated on the wood gate, imagining it was kindling, when there was a sudden tingling warmth in his hands. He could feel the origin in his chest, as if his pumping heart ignited sparks of electricity that flowed throughout his body. He heard a loud pop in his ears and miraculously, the part of the fence he'd been staring at caught fire. He blinked in surprise, wondering if he had done it. The persistent tingling in his hands answered his question, provoking him to try again. This time it was a wagon situated not far from a lump of crowd, who cried out in alarm as the wagon burst into flames.

"Amazing," he breathed. Angelique never mentioned anything about vampires having supernatural gifts. It was either another thing she'd withheld as a method of control or it was something he'd carried over from his forgotten past. Either way, he was pleased.

He caught a few other structures on fire before deciding to conserve his energy, taking a look at his pocket watch to check the time. It was growing closer to one, which meant Christophe and an insurgent named Paul would soon be emerging from their fruitless negotiation. The watch burned a hole in his pants when he replaced it, a result of his scalding hands, letting him know that he needed to be careful with this new power. He found a nearby bucket of water, a low hiss releasing from the water as he submerged them, causing smoke to snake up and around him. Something about the dark water made him pause once it settled around his skin, hypnotizing him. A shadowy recollection pushed through the haziness of his mind, a woman sitting on his lap, staring with him into the water. Somehow, the water was hers, but they both belonged to him. He tried to grab at the faint images, but they drifted further away the harder he tried to pull them back. He let out a sound of frustration and a loud crow responded. He looked out to see that a group of them had collected over the crowd, waiting to see what would transpire.

"Mr. Hades," a man said breathlessly, as he rounded the corner of the alleyway. It was Mr. Harrow, dressed in rags as a disguise, his wide, dark eyes eerie in the daylight. "Everything has been taken care of, but we must leave now. Someone has given you up."

"Nonsense—" Lucius tried to protest, but suddenly he saw soldiers pushing through the crowd.

"Sir, I have to insist," Mr. Harrow said. "You are at a disadvantage in the sunlight. One accidental shove and you'll fall victim to the sun's rays."

Lucius grumbled, but agreed.

Mr. Harrow wasted no time, grabbing Lucius's hands firmly in his own. Lucius blinked and they were back at the offices of Somnus & Mors.

"Forgive my forwardness," Harrow said as he let go of his hands. Lucius noticed a pile of folded clothing and shoes on the table, proper attire for a gentleman to travel in. He was grateful to observe that the colors were dark, accented by violet. "I must change before we depart and I suggest you do the same," Harrow said. "We have a carriage waiting in the back. Our train departs in an hour. You will have a private box with shaded windows."

Lucius nodded as he pulled off his cloak and soiled linen shirt. He pretended not to notice Harrow's quick survey of his bare chest and his flustered expression as he turned away, heading to another room to get himself dressed. It only took a few moments before he resurfaced. "Are you ready, sir?"

Lucius gave him a curt nod as he adjusted his cravat. "Let us go to England."

THE ATLANTIC OCEAN, 1858
LIBRAEAN

LIBRAEAN OPENED AND CLOSED HIS FIST, stretching his sore writing hand. He watched the ink dry on the paper before looking up at Lucius, letting the story he just heard settle around the both of them. Lucius looked reflective, smoking one of his spiced cigarettes and watching the smoke swirl up to the ceiling. It was hard for Libraean to imagine how much life he had seen.

He was far from young himself, but his existence had been one of solitude and reflection. All the great moments of human history passed him by as he kept his nose buried in his work, the complete opposite of Lucius's turbulent reality. "And you still have no recollection of what happened to you from Tartarus to Hades?" he asked him.

Lucius shook his head, his eyes impassive. "I think we should give your hand a rest, regardless."

Libraean looked back down at Lucius's memoir, realizing only one page remained in the book. "Well, even without those millennia accounted for, your story is longer than David's," he commented. "I suppose it is high time I make you another book."

Lucius shrugged, a sideways smile lifting his lips. "Ah, well, maybe my story will end soon and you won't have to worry."

"I highly doubt that," Libraean snorted as he shut Lucius's book. "You seem to be utterly unkillable."

David breezed into the library where they sat, his sudden arrival unsettling the room. Libraean was undeniably startled, watching David try to fight the scathing look that Lucius's presence provoked. He felt a wave of guilt, as though he was somehow being disloyal to David by being in his brother's company, but he swiftly reminded himself how ridiculous that was. David had never been one to indulge in pettiness, there was no reason he would start now.

"I do hope I'm not interrupting," he said lightly.

Libraean showed him the book he had been working on. "Lucius was just helping me fill in some of the blank spots in his memoirs," he explained. "I've been updating the histories, trying to keep my mind busy during this long journey of ours."

"Ah," David nodded, sitting across from him in the chair next to Lucius. They both instinctively stiffened, the tension in the room becoming so thick it was almost palpable. Libraean shifted in his seat, wondering if it was even possible for the two brothers to co-exist in any semblance of harmony. "Which part were you writing about?"

"Oh, surely you don't want to hear all the deliciously sordid details of my life with Nephthys," Lucius cut in.

"Right, because I never heard you carrying on in Romania." David didn't miss a beat. "Rest assured, recollections of your escapades cease to give me pause, especially since she's shown time and again that she prefers me."

Libraean's heart rate increased, frantically wondering if he would be able to intervene between the two if a fight erupted. Where were the others—Cahira, Sandrine?

Lucius laughed, the sound bellowing through the room. "You were never one to throw barbs, brother. Something must have gotten under your skin."

"Perhaps it's the scent of your horrid cologne," David suggested. "If your intent was to repel Morrigan, you've certainly succeeded. I can barely breathe around you myself."

"Don't you have some dark hole to crawl into where you can lament your tragic existence, perhaps drown your sorrows in scotch and opium?"

"It's far more amusing to be the thorn in your side," David replied. "Besides, this excursion needs a true leader, not some lovesick pup wearing grown up clothes."

"David," Libraean gasped.

The fire in David's eyes suddenly went out, swiftly replaced by embarrassment. He licked his lips, fishing for a cigarette from his coat. "Forgive me, this journey has been wearing on me," he muttered.

Remarkably enough, Lucius didn't look angry, but rather amused. "No worries, brother," he said neutrally as he rose to his feet. "This lovesick pup is off to bed. The hour grows early, even for me."

Libraean peeked out the crack in the front doors to see that he was right, the skies were beginning to lighten, prophesying the dawn. When he turned back, Lucius had already left out the back, the door swinging shut with a clang. He turned back to David who seemed distraught as he pulled smoke from his cigarette. "You cannot allow him to get under your skin," he scolded. "We need him."

"I know," David sighed. "I haven't felt like myself since I came out of my last spell. My temper is uncomfortably short."

"You still don't remember where you went while you were unconscious?"

David shook his head. "I haven't a clue."

Libraean frowned. It seemed that his mourning paused only when it gave way to nagging worry, most often provoked by David. He looked down at Lucius's book, running his hand over the tight leather cover that had been etched in his own script. Just keep writing, he told himself.

"You look tired, Libraean. Can I walk you to your room?" David offered.

He nodded. "That would be nice."

Although the sun still had yet to rise, they avoided the open deck, though there was ample shade if anyone desired fresh air. Instead, they kept to the long, painted hallway that ran along the starboard side of the ship to their rooms. He had adjusted to the swaying, for it was a far smoother ride than in Cahira's clipper, but it was terribly loud and his shoes slipped on the tiled floor. He held onto David's arm for support, his pride long abandoned in favor of practicality.

"How have you been sleeping?" Libraean asked him as they walked.

"I've slept a few times since we began our journey, though I have been dreaming of my time with Morrigan in Ireland."

Libraean grew nervous. "Is that right?"

David gave him a weak smile. "Don't fret. Despite what I tell Lucius, I've accepted that things between us have ended. It's just never pleasant to relive the past when you know the outcome is not what you'd hoped for. I'm focused on reaching Africa to see what Anubis has to say about the realms. I'm also interested in this Discordia character you told me about, the one responsible for this mess. Have you found any mention of her in your texts?"

"No," Libraean admitted with a sigh. "Only that the Greeks called her Eris, the goddess of strife. Neither the Greeks nor the Romans worshiped her, simply considering her the personification of chaos. The Iliad describes her as being a sister to Ares, the god of war, and says she has a relentless wrath."

"Perhaps her wrath wouldn't be so relentless if she was more than a note in their texts," David speculated.

"The only story I've found that mentions her is the Trojan War, which details her part in it," Libraean continued. "Apparently, she was snubbed at the wedding of Peleus and Thetis, though the rest of the Olympians were invited. They claimed it was because of her troublemaking tendencies. So, she tossed a golden apple into the party with the inscription: To the Fairest One. It caused the three goddesses in attendance, Hera, Athena, and Aphrodite, to quarrel over who the apple was meant for. Zeus, at a loss, appointed poor Paris, the prince of Troy, to make the decision for him. Hera offered political power and Athena promised wisdom, but Aphrodite tempted him with Helen, the most beautiful woman in the world."

"And he chose Helen, therefore sealing in fate the Fall of Troy," David finished.

Libraean beamed up at him, his good blue eye sparkling with pride. "I never knew you had an interest in mythology."

"True. While I've always preferred poetry and art, I have been reading more historical accounts," he told him. "I suppose I can be grateful Lucius has such an extensive library."

"It is a good use of your time," Libraean approved.

"That story explains why Aphrodite, Athena, and Hera were her first victims," David told him. "It seems as if their constant neglect of her as a goddess was what led to her fury."

Libraean raised his eyebrows. "I never thought to put that together. Do we know for certain that she also killed Athena and Hera?"

"Well, I am only speculating, but it could be something worth investigating."

They reached his room. "Take care of yourself, David," Libraean told him as he hobbled into his starkly quiet, Jacob-less room. He was hit with a sharp pang of loneliness. Perhaps he would write a bit more before he retired. "Actually, David," he turned back towards him. "Do you have a few moments?"

David waited for him to continue.

"I was wondering if you could tell me your side of things, at the beginning."

"Oh," David looked surprised, but entered, settling into the soft upholstered chair near the desk. "What would you like to know?"

Libraean hurried to retrieve David's book from the shelf, an updated version of the decrepit volume left in the vaults which he had to put behind glass to preserve. Ironically enough, it was situated next to Lucius's scrolls. He settled behind his desk, turning to a fresh, unmarked sheet. "What can you tell me about the beginning?" he asked. "How was your life with Isis?"

David frowned as he considered his question. "Looking back, I know I loved Isis," he said. "I just wasn't sure what that meant. We were so painfully young then, with no direction on how to be."

"Of course," Libraean nodded. "You had no parents, no mentors to guide you."

"I thought both twins were beautiful, but I lusted for Morrigan immediately," he said, staring out the window. "This is difficult to speak about."

"You don't have to unless you want to," Librean promised him. "I only wanted to give you the chance to tell your side of things, since I offered the chance to them."

"Morrigan spoke about me?"

Libraean gave him a sad smile. "She wouldn't tell me what you wrote in your letters."

David looked wistful. "I was quite the artist, even then," he told him. "I drew her as I remembered her, naked in the river with water streaming down her skin. I even wrote poems to her on sheets of papyrus. They were painfully romantic, of course, how beautiful I thought she was, how her eyes reminded me of the sky. I admired her most, however, because she was free, untamed, and feral, so unlike her sister, Isis. So unlike me."

"You didn't feel free?"

David shook his head. "I was a god and the humans looked to me as their king. I had to be fair, right, and just. I had to lead them, to show them how to be. It was I who helped create them, therefore it was my duty to nurture them."

"Quite a lot of responsibility for a young god," Libraean sympathized.

"Lucius, on the other hand, didn't have a care in the world. He could do whatever he wanted, whenever he wanted. He even had a beautiful, determined wife who he could make love to every day if he wanted. But instead, he chose to neglect Nephthys. I suppose I wanted what he had—" His voice caught in his throat, as if his own words surprised him. He looked up worriedly. "I don't know where that came from, Libraean, please forgive me."

"You haven't been right lately," Libraean said quickly, not wanting to provoke another spell. "I shouldn't have asked you to talk. We can always resume at a later time, when things are less stressful." He rose to his feet.

"Perhaps you are right…" David murmured, looking quite distraught. "I must take my leave of you now."

"Of course," Libraean said, though he remained unsettled by the reaction, wringing his hands as he watched David walk out the door. Another time, he thought, as he looked on the page half filled with ink. Come to think of it, he'd become quite drained from all the interactions.

He reshelved the book beside the others and turned off the lamp. Then he shuffled towards his bed and put his worn, tired body to rest, imagining Jacob's arms around him.

PART THREE

GAIA STOOD IN FRONT OF HIM, a dozen horsehair brushes in her fists. "It's time to get up," she ordered.

He squinted in the morning light, something he was still having trouble getting used to, even in an ethereal realm. His head pounded right between his eyes, reminding him that he'd finished an entire bottle of wine before he'd passed out, tangled up in Gaia's limbs. Her hair was still pleasantly tousled, poorly covering the outline of her breasts under the sheer tunic she wore. He suddenly remembered the hours they'd spent rekindling their love, as well as the pleasant realization that, in this realm, he had the same youthful vigor that he had back then. He lifted up his blankets to confirm his suspicions; there was not one stitch of clothing on him.

"Can I have my clothes first?" he asked.

"Well, I would prefer if you didn't," she grinned. "But there are fresh clothes in the cabinets. I'll meet you outside."

David hurried to dress, exiting the old tree that served as her home to be met once again with blinding sunlight. He followed her to the nearby stream, light sparkling on its surface as it trickled along the stones.

She stood proudly next to an easel she'd created for him, every color of paint one could dream of spread out on the ground around her, nestled amongst numerous canvases and pieces of chalk. She seemed pleased by his expression, thrusting the brushes into his hands. "This is the second step in finding yourself again. Step one was last night." She smiled.

He laughed, selecting one and setting the rest down, the sensation of a brush in his hand just as distantly familiar as the feel of the sun. "I don't even know what to paint," he admitted. "What did I paint before?"

"The lovers," she said softly.

He stared at her. "How do you know that?"

"We are in the afterlife, my love. I've learned things here, remember?"

He looked back down at the jars of paint, remembering the shades he used on the walls of Lucius's home. He could see the image of the two intertwined bodies against the aging plaster, glowing orange in the sunset. And then it was as if he'd entered a trance, falling instantly into a rhythm of mixing, twirling, brushing, filling the canvases with paint. He was lost in each stroke, staining his fingers as he blended, the smell of paint sharp in his nostrils. Gaia sat beside him, but did not speak, bringing him more water, more canvas, more wine, as birds chirped around them and fish jumped in the stream.

Finally, as the sun began to dip behind the clouds, she grabbed his hand, jolting him out of his hypnosis to see dozens of paintings laid out before him on canvas, stone, and parchment. His entire life in paint. A painting of Gaia and him as children, running through a bustling Roman marketplace. An image of Lucius and him sailing under the night sky towards Greece. An image of Lucius in Morgana's arms as they stared at him in Wallachia. A painting of himself in the midst of war outside their crumbling castle. One of him thrusting his sword into the spine of a black dragon. A rendition of Lardone Manor. The tenements of London…and a painting of crows.

She put her hand on his shoulder. "You have lived a very long life, Davius. It's okay to let it go."

He pulled her close to him and kissed her head, reminded of how much he'd missed the smell of jasmine. "You were right when you said that my entire life is a series of decisions based on guilt." He sighed. "But I don't think creating more of it by abandoning the others I care about will solve my affliction."

She echoed the sigh as she nestled into his chest. "I was afraid you were going to say that."

He lifted up her head with his bent finger. "However, once things are finished, I will return. If you'll still have me, of course."

"Of course I will. We just have to figure out how to please the Watchers so they let you. Perhaps you can come to a compromise with them," she suggested.

David considered her words. "They want us all gone. They want me to stay here with you and put Lucius back in Tartarus. Dan and Cahira would have their own place, Libraean and Jacob would be together. But that would leave Anubis and Morrigan...and I might have accepted the truth of our affair, but I can't kill her, nor can I cast her into some horrid realm."

"Maybe you can offer an alternative. I would assume Morrigan wants to be with Lucius, maybe they can recreate the Underworld together. Then Anubis could be restored as guardian. Don't all three of them prefer it there anyway?"

"You do have a point."

"You can tell the Watchers that you won't kill anyone, but that you will convince them to leave Earth," Gaia said, "with the stipulation that they are allowed to recreate the Underworld."

David nodded. "They must also promise to get rid of Discordia. How do I talk to them?"

"That, I am not sure. They find me when they want to talk, but we can ask Aengus. He should be back at the house."

The two headed away from the stream towards the ancient oak, but neither the child nor the young man was anywhere to be found.

"He left behind his boat," Gaia murmured as she stared at the lake. "He does take his leave of this place often, so it is not cause for alarm. I suppose we can just take his boat to the Tower ourselves."

An uneasy feeling settled over David. "You should stay here," he told her. "I wouldn't want anything to happen to you."

Gaia put her hands on her hips. "In case you've forgotten, this is my realm. I am going with you. I just got you back after thousands of years, do you really think I'm going to let you go so easily?"

David smiled, grateful to see the old familiar spark in her eyes. "Alright, let us hurry though. It seems to be growing dark."

They slipped into the boat and David took up the oars, rowing them towards the place his son had shown him. The tall marble building soon appeared in the distance, reaching out of clouds that seemed pale orange next to the setting sun. Yet as they moved towards it, the boat abruptly stopped with a loud thunk. David quickly discovered they'd run into something that prevented their journey, as if a piece of glass separated the realms in two.

"We are trapped here," David realized quietly.

"How can that be?" Gaia sputtered. "This realm belongs to me."

"Technically, it belongs to them," he said disdainfully. "They wanted to trap me here with you."

Gaia's face fell. "But why?"

"I don't know," David admitted, leaning out of the boat to knock on the blockade, affirming its impenetrability. "There is only one way I know how to leave a realm. However, if I died, there is no telling when or how I would come back."

"You're not dying," Gaia scowled. "We will figure this out." She dove out of the boat and into the water, disappearing for several moments before she resurfaced, sputtering water as she gasped for air. "It goes down as far as I can," she told him as he helped her back into the boat.

"Perhaps we should head back." The sun had fully set now, its glow lingering on the unreachable building.

Gaia frowned, slicking back her wet hair. "When you and Nephthys died in Egypt, you ascended to a heavenly realm, correct?"

"Yes, but it was nothing like this one."

"But you created the first realm—you should be able to recreate one of your own here."

David shook his head sadly. "She created it for us. Isis created life, but Nephthys created realms. She was the one who designed the Underworld, Set only helped her build it. I never had those gifts."

"You could just stay?" she half-joked.

He pulled her into his chest. "It is a very enticing prison they've put me in," he admitted.

She drew away. "I think you are wrong," she said. "You were the original god of Light who walked the Earth until Nephthys created a realm for you both. If she created one that Lucius could bend, then you should be able to bend this one. You must at least try."

David frowned before he was struck with an idea. He paddled the boat back to the treehouse. "You must stay in your home no matter what happens," he told her once they were firmly back on shore. "I will come back for you when it is finished."

Worry overwhelmed her eyes. "I don't like this."

"Please trust me. If I think something might happen to you, then I won't be able to focus—you're not the only one who isn't quick to leave the other."

She nodded, giving him a firm kiss on his lips. "If anything happens, then call out to me," she told him. "I may not be the formidable Morrigan, but I will still murder for those I love."

David grabbed her face and kissed her again, harder this time, before putting his lips to her forehead, her closed eyes, her cheeks. "I will. Our story will not end like this."

"Look for Aengus, too," she told him as he pulled away. "He can handle himself, but I do worry."

"I will," he promised.

He withdrew before he lost his nerve, as she summoned vines and branches to weave into a solid wall, securing her inside. He hurried to the shore and fell to his knees. He extended his arms as he squeezed shut his eyes, envisioning the air around him swirling, stirring the slumbering storm in his chest until it was strong enough to radiate from his hands. He revisited the times in his life where his pain had been raw, settling on the day the Earth took Gaia from him, the day he realized Lucius's hatred… and the moment he knew Morrigan had made her choice. Gales of wind began to whip through both realms, regardless of their paltry barrier, creating full waves that crashed against the marble tower. He could sense their panic, but he focused on the tornado he'd created, strengthening it with each purposeful breath.

Finally, he felt a sharp tug, and he opened his eyes to see three angry angels looming above him. The one who called himself Michael had his sword pressed to David's throat, his foot on his chest. The angels' hair whipped around them as they struggled to stay planted, their feathery wings in complete disarray. "Call off the wind," Michael shouted, ugly veins popping out of his typically cherubic skin.

David realized his plan had worked. "You are the ones who trapped me," he replied, calmly meeting Michael's furious eyes.

Their glass ceiling collapsed, forcing the other angels under the marble table as glass pelted the floor. David raised his hand to deflect the shards away from where he lay. Fresh, angry squalls tunneled in, swirling around the chamber, knocking Michael off his feet.

"Please," the one named Uriel begged as he cowered to the ground, his arms over his head. "We will explain everything—just stop the wind!"

David took a deep, calming breath and let his world stop spinning. Gradually the wind responded, letting the upset angel feathers drift down to the marble floors and settle across the glittering glass. David stood as Michael scrambled to his feet, meeting him squarely with fists to his hips. "So, when I denied your request, you thought you would entrap me?"

"That was not our idea," Raphael snapped before Michael hushed him angrily, picking pieces of glass out of his wings.

"Then whose was it?" David pressed.

"You are not the only pagan god we approached," Michael informed him. "We have several agents working on our behalf. She thought you would be happier here with your wife. We were trying to be kind."

David crossed his arms. "You thought I would be distracted here," he corrected him, "so whoever you have working for you can kill the rest of them without me interfering."

"Regardless of what you think, our hands are tied. It is her magic that is keeping you here, not ours. Now if you'll excuse us, we have more pressing matters to attend to—"

David inhaled, and the settled feathers and debris began to rise again in the breeze.

"Do you not hear us?" Michael sputtered. "There is nothing we can do, threatening us with your windstorm will not solve anything—you are defying the Holy One Himself!"

David suddenly realized his way out. He thought of Gaia, knowing she'd be heartbroken when she learned what he'd done. I'll find a way to return, he promised. Then he took a deep breath and pulled all the emotions he'd just dismissed until the hall resumed its chaos.

The angels shrieked with fury at the raucous tornado, dissolving into their true selves, creatures that looked like swirls of feathers and eyes without discernable shape. They advanced to attack, but David fell backwards, shielding his eyes as he slipped through the floor, down below the clouds, and swirling in the wind before he hit the ground. Dazed, he tried to stand, but the earth trembled, cracking beneath him. He was struck with a vision of Lucius beside him, catching his golden eyes as the two of them fell, plummeting through layers of rock until the fire at its core grew so warm that David could no longer keep his eyes open. And then, everything went still.

🙰 The Master of Secrets 🙰

The Kingdom of Dahomey, 1858
Anubis

"My brother is dead."

Anubis looked up from his desk at the woman standing before him. He realized the sun had set hours ago and his office, situated in the far corner of the temple, was completely devoid of light. He removed his tinted glasses, tossing them down onto an open book as he stood to light one of the nearby lamps. He turned back to Helena to read her expression, grateful to learn she wasn't angry.

Though her skin was pale and her hair the color of the sun, she wore Dahomian style clothing, the fabric heavily draped over birthmarks that covered her entire left side. Though they crawled up the side of her face, giving the illusion that she had once been badly burned, she was still strikingly beautiful. Just as beautiful as he had known her to be in the Underworld, though he did wonder at times if his taste wasn't the most conventional. She carried a bottle of rum by the neck, her bare feet sweeping the dusty temple floor.

"Which brother?" he asked her.

"Both, actually," she said. "I received another message from Odin. Apparently, the wolf died protecting the witch on her journey here."

Anubis frowned. "And my family?"

"They are all still en route as planned," she assured him. "So will you be joining me?" She held up the bottle. "Loki and his detestable offspring are all dead. There should be a celebration."

Before he could say anything, she flopped down on his desk and took a long swig of the dark liquid.

He smiled, and sat down beside her.

"Thomas said you had a full day's work today." She pressed the bottle to his chest.

Anubis took a sip, enjoying the myriad of flavors on his tongue. She'd mixed it with hyena blood. "A young boy was stung by a scorpion today. As you can imagine, the entire family was frantic."

"Did you save him?"

"Of course," he said, passing the bottle back to her. "It's the least I can do while I'm here."

She chuckled. "Oh, how they would react if they ever found out how much their beloved Anubis hates being here."

He slid her a look. Only she knew how miserable he had been since his rebirth. After centuries of ruling the Underworld, content to remain in the Otherrealms while the other gods swept in and out of them, he had been rudely ousted from his home—a place he wasn't even sure existed anymore. He yearned to be back, the physical world a bit too hard and bright for his liking, even after the sun had long abandoned the sky. He missed the dead. "I had a purpose in the Underworld," he reminded her. "What can I do for them now except prevent them from dying for as long as I can? Once they die, they will be doomed to wander, and I am powerless to help."

"I know."

He snatched the bottle from between her thighs and took another swallow. He wasn't sure how long ago it had been since he first met Hel, the Norse Queen of the Dead, but it felt as if she'd been with him since the beginning. She bore witness to his trials and triumphs with the African kings, watching him fight any way he could against their tyrannical rule, against them selling humans to maintain their wealth and power. She knew him as a mortal shaman, the upcoming High Priest, and after he'd transformed, when the soul of Anubis roared to life.

Suddenly he saw their first meeting clearly, as he stood on the dreary shores of the Underworld dressed as Osiris, waiting for Mr. Aymen to cross the river to his realm. The old pagan had beamed immediately upon sight of him, though his jaw dropped when Anubis informed him that he would not have to suffer the twelve trials his ancestors once had, and that although he kept the old religion sacred, he could pass directly to the place where his soul would be weighed against the feather.

It was after he passed the test and ascended to his preferred heavenly realm that there was a sudden, loud pop, and down from the black skies dropped a woman unlike anyone he'd ever seen before.

He remembered being frozen in surprise, shifting back into his original form as he watched her rise to her feet and look around. Her entire left side was a decaying corpse, skeletal ribs popping out of her black, necrotic flesh, but her right side bore pale, supple skin, a bright blue eye, and soft waves of gold hair. Both her good eye and her rotten one settled on Anubis, her half-lipped mouth turning down into a frown.

"Where am I?" she demanded.

"The Underworld," he replied.

"This is not my realm."

He realized she was a goddess. "You have somehow crossed into Duat, the Egyptian Underworld, which is my realm. My name is Anubis. I am the one who sends your souls to your realm."

"Oh yes, the Guardian." She nodded with recognition. "But why am I in your realm?"

Anubis frowned. "I am not sure. The magic I put in place to keep the boundaries between netherworlds held firm for eons."

"This no longer seems to be the case."

Anubis scanned the shores for Thoth, locating his thin frame bent near the rocky banks. "We will figure it out," he promised her before calling out to his trusted friend and associate.

Thoth moved towards them in careful approach, his box of scales in one arm and a rolled piece of parchment in the other. Although the humans painted him with the head of an ibis, he preferred to look human when he wasn't working, letting the image fall away as he grew closer, revealing a narrow, gentle face, soft brown eyes, and the tiny spectacles he wore to complete his paperwork. He was a bit taller than stocky Anubis and quite slender, drifting along the shores with graceful and deliberate poise, rather like a cobra. "Hello," he greeted the strange woman without hesitation.

"My name is Hel," she offered, charmed, as most were, by his affable temperament. "I am the Queen of Helheim, an underworld of the Norseman."

"Hel has fallen into our realm by mistake," Anubis informed him. "Do you think there has been some sort of failure in our magic?"

"We can check the Records," Thoth suggested. "Follow me."

Anubis hesitated. "I have more souls to attend to this afternoon—is this something you can handle on your own?"

Thoth gave him a gentle smile. "I think you should be present, for you are the one who constructed the boundaries, therefore you are the only one who can fix them."

Anubis sighed, eager to get back to his work, even with the curious situation at hand. "I suppose they can linger for an hour." He raised his staff and brought it down with a thud, summoning a tall rectangular box made of shining gold. It opened immediately upon landing. He moved forward, motioning for Hel to follow.

"Do all Egyptian gods look like animals?" she asked as they grew closer to the metallic box.

"Some of us," Anubis replied, her comment reminding him to shift out of his own jackal guise as he shut the door behind them. He could see his reflection in her dead eye as she studied him, glinting like polished onyx inside its prison of decayed flesh. He saw his own eyes, radiant sky blue like his mother's, a stark contrast against his cool, sable skin and equally dark curls.

There was another loud pop as the golden box shifted, saving them hours of travel across the seemingly boundless realm, opening up right at the Underworld Palace. It had originally been built by his uncle Set at the dawn of civilization, but Anubis had since made adjustments. Even so, he rarely entered it, not one to rest when there was so much work to be done. He gifted the entire front part of the residence to Thoth upon his arrival, who in turn, used it to create a set of offices and libraries similar to the ones Nephthys used years ago.

Thoth led them out of the traveling box and into the front hall of the palace, which resembled an elaborate mailroom. It served as the direct line of communication with the old Records Hall, a living system that kept track of all the souls and their reincarnations. Mr. Aymen had decided to rest, so Thoth had made note of this preference and the date, placing the scroll into the compartment marked "R.H." and pressing the corresponding button, sending the scroll soaring down the tunnel to the Hall until further notice.

"Do you keep track of everything here?" Hel seemed mystified as she observed the hundreds of chambers and tiny tunnels that lined the cavernous hall.

"Yes," Thoth nodded, setting his box down on a nearby desk. "Every religion, every god, every soul, every reincarnation. Anubis is the being that greets them when they die, taking on whatever guise they need to see, whether it be the Angel of Death, the ferryman, or their ancestors. Then he sends them either to you, or one of the other death gods, or to whomever they wish to see. Some want to return to earth right away, some decide to rest. I make note of it all. Anubis's mother, Nephthys, created the Records Hall so that it would always keep track of things, even in her absence, so I work directly with that Hall to keep things in order."

"Thoth's work is imperative to the function of this place," Anubis added.

"Well, it was originally her design," Thoth said humbly. "I've simply taken over where she has left off."

Anubis frowned, suddenly realizing he'd forgotten to tell him about his mother. "She has made her way down here again with my Uncle Set. I keep meaning to visit, but I have been so busy."

Thoth's eyebrows raised in surprise. "You let him find her?"

Anubis slid a glance at Hel, who was intently observing their conversation. "You know they have always maintained a complicated relationship, even after she convinced us that she and Osiris were meant to be. I know my mother better than she thinks I do—I can assure you, she wanted to be found." He walked over to the adjunct library, running his fingers over the stacks of binders until he found the one marked "Norse." He brought it over to Thoth's desk. "Let's get back to the matter at hand, shall we?" he said as he opened it.

Hel leaned in to see what the binder contained, making a sound of amazement as she observed the shimmering letters that shuffled around as he flipped through them. He found the page labeled HEL, watching as the letters twisted and bent to spell out the word: CLOSED.

"That's strange," he remarked. "It says that your realm is closed."

"How can that be?"

"I have no idea," he murmured, flipping through the rest of the book. Each page he turned to gave the same message, from Valhalla to Niflheim. "It says they are all closed. But I know your religion still lives. I dispatched a man to Valhalla the other day."

Thoth caught his eye. "I do not like this," he said, his expression grave.

"Well, who can figure it out?" Hel demanded, growing visibly upset.

"I am going to have to visit my mother, though I don't believe she is too pleased with me at the moment. She is with the god we need to see, the original architect, my Uncle Set."

Thoth agreed with his assertion. "I will keep watch here until you return."

Anubis turned towards the increasingly agitated death goddess. "Will you be joining me?"

"Of course."

Anubis led her back out of the palace to the moving box, waiting until she was inside before shutting the door and drawing the Egyptian symbol for Set on the side with his finger. The box responded immediately to his magic, shuddering before it made its popping sound and jerked them downwards.

"Do you always take women to visit your mother the same day you meet them?" Hel teased, trying to establish her footing as the box continued to plummet.

Anubis let out a quick chuckle, surprised by her candor. "Well, I cannot say a woman has ever visited me at work, unless she was dead."

The box landed abruptly, but did not open.

Anubis went to pry at the doors, but found he could not. "That's strange…" he muttered, perplexed. He felt heat behind them as if they'd landed in the fiery realm of Tartarus, rather than the dark, watery Underworld his uncle had chosen to make his permanent home.

He dismantled the box with a few jolts of magic, jumping back in surprise as it revealed a raging inferno. He instinctively pulled Hel behind him, searching the landscape for any clues.

"Send us back!" Hel cried, alarmed by the black skeletal demons that began to approach them, impervious to its heat. He smacked his hands together and the box flew up around them, hurtling back up to his domain. "I don't understand," Anubis muttered, trying to gather himself together, "it took us to Tartarus."

"What is happening?" Hel demanded.

The box landed back on the shore, opening immediately to a frightened Thoth. "Anubis, half the realms have been destroyed, along with the gods and goddesses who dwell in them."

Anubis met Hel's mismatched eyes.

"My realm must have been destroyed too," Hel murmured from behind him.

"What are we to do?" Thoth asked, trying not to appear distraught.

Anubis was distressed. What could be so powerful that it was able to destroy the realms? "We have to warn Set and my mother—"

"It is a bit too late for that," interrupted one of the leathery black creatures they must have brought back from Tartarus, slithering out of the box and shifting into a woman with icy hair and fire in her eyes…

"Where did you go?" Helena's voice demanded, bringing Anubis back to the present.

Anubis blinked, his eyes settling on her human visage, wine-colored splotches where her dead flesh had been. "I was remembering when we first met," he replied. "When I tried to take you to meet them."

"Ah yes," she murmured, thoughtfully, "in their Underworld. I'm surprised they found each other in this life."

"Well, so did you and I," Anubis pointed out, then quieted, that memory laced with its own pain that he did not feel up to revisiting.

"Well, Xevioso is still not convinced of their benevolence. But I believe it's less a doubt of them than it is doubt of you. I don't think he'll ever forgive you after you took his place."

"I did not ask for any of it," Anubis pointed out gruffly. "He's lucky I turned him when I did or he would have been long deceased by now."

"Good evening," a gentle voice interrupted them. Thomas's long, narrow frame had appeared in the doorway to his office, his hands folded in front of his chest. "Do we know if they will be arriving shortly? Tonight, was the night they had planned to be here."

"They are back on track, but I don't think it will be tonight," Helena informed him. "They lost one at the beginning and another not too long after."

Thomas looked concerned. "Oh?"

Helena jumped off Anubis's desk. "Just the human and the wolf. All the ancients are fine. I should probably be going."

Thomas frowned. "Please don't feel you need to leave on my account."

"I better serve the cause when I'm traveling the astral plane and listening to the spirits. You two are better served by handling the rest. I will see you all soon enough." And she was gone.

"She seems in a better mood today," Thomas commented.

Anubis slid off his desk to retrieve several papers stacked on top of it. "These are to go straight to the French Ambassador."

Thomas nodded as he examined them. "Absolutely. I will tell Age immediately."

"Actually, I was hoping to send him away right when the others arrive tomorrow evening," Anubis said. "I do not want to deal with his temper when he realizes I have brought a ship full of white vampires to our land."

Thomas sighed. "That would probably be for the best."

Anubis recalled his first meeting with Thomas, when he was the Egyptian god Thoth, who appeared one day in the Underworld, walking along the shores as if he'd always been there. Anubis had approached him cautiously, assuming he belonged to another crop of humans, come to make his home in the Underworld like the other gods before him. He was surprised to learn that the humans had created him as the god of science and magic, tasked with assisting Anubis in the judgment of the dead. He was grateful to have help, the vast entirety of the realm was growing larger than he could keep up with. Thoth quickly became an irreplaceable presence and a valued friend. As with Hel, he was grateful to have found him again in his Earthly life.

"Goodnight." Thomas gave a bob of the head and bowed out of the temple door.

Anubis tucked the rest of his papers into his desk, and locked the drawer. He let out a deep exhale, wondering why Helena had left so abruptly. Usually when she was in the mood to drink, she was in the mood for other things. Theirs was a complicated enough relationship that he had learned long ago not to question nor try to predict what she wanted. After everything that had happened, he was just glad she'd found a way to still be near him.

He exited the temple to greet a night reverberating with choruses of insects. Though the sun had long abandoned the sky, the breeze was still warm, just the way he preferred it. They were entering the dry season, but he could taste humidity in the air, as if Earth decided to give them one more rainfall before covering them with dust. He knew the late hour kept the humans of the village away, offering him a cherished reprieve; he decided to walk down to the shoreline before he headed home, hoping to see the storm roll in from the distance.

Mama Mawu appeared next to him, keeping time with his footsteps, though hers did not appear in the sand.

"Hello," he greeted her. "I haven't seen you in a while."

"You will be meeting your real mother soon," she reminded him, peering up with her wise brown eyes set in a face full of wrinkles, "perhaps I am feeling a bit nostalgic."

Anubis nodded, finding her sentiment reflected his own state.

"Do you remember the day we watched the French roll in, all those years ago?" she asked.

"How could I forget?" he said softly, the vision of ships rolling along the jade-colored sky as clear in his mind as if it was yesterday. He realized what she was doing. Though his physical self found a cluster of stones to stretch his body out on, she was taking him back there, when the place they were standing on was called the Huada Kingdom, one hundred and fifty years ago.

HUADA KINGDOM, 1726

ANUBIS STOOD ON THE SHORES, his bare feet sinking into the sand, watching the ships boasting the colors of the French Company drift in with the waves. Each time the white men came, it gave him a new sense of dread, wondering how many African people would be sold to them this time. Today brought a stronger sense of foreboding, for he knew King Haffon had made arrangements for a group of Frenchman to settle in Savi, near his palace compound, in the hopes of improving relations between them while increasing productivity. The very thought of it made his blood boil, but he was forced to be patient, keeping his fury contained. Since his initiation as the upcoming High Priest, he was forced into the role of spiritual advisor to the king. It was a position he gravely detested, having to pretend he didn't mind the constant battles created to capture more prisoners and forced to turn a blind eye when he sold his own wives if their numbers were low.

"Let him win his wars and collect his slaves," Xevi had told him one day when he discovered him angrily pacing about their compound. He was the great-grandson of the High Priest who Mama Mawu replaced, later revealed to be Xevioso, the reincarnated god of thunder. He was up next to be High Priest himself before Anubis came in and took the role, and he never quite forgot about it. They were forced to share a convent and, despite any misgivings, they were expected to remain harmonious, working alongside each other until the day Anubis would take over. "It is better that he sells captives than take more of our people," he said.

"They are all human beings," Anubis shot back.

"Your job is to heal, comfort, and serve your people. You are their future High Priest. You cannot let your anger turn you away from your true calling."

Anubis had scowled, trying not to let the underlying animosity between them distract him from Xevi's words, for he knew, deep down, he was right. Yet he struggled to remain passive, a constant war inside him as each day passed. He could feel his restlessness beginning to reach its breaking point, which was usually the time when his mentor stepped in to talk him out of any action.

Mama Mawu was not only the Queen Mother of their village, but his adopted mother; she took him in after his own mother died from a snake bite. She had taken one look into his unusual sky-blue eyes and called a meeting of Elders, proclaiming him to be Anubis reincarnated, the god who came to save their people, as was told to her in a dream. She was met with plenty of resistance, particularly from Xevi's grandpa Papa Ode and a few female priestesses who had hoped their next elder would also be female. But Mama put her foot down, reminding them with her intense black eyes who she was and what she was capable of.

Although he had only been six years old at the time, he remembered the ceremony before his initiation, could remember the feel of his little heart hammering against his ribs and the worry that the congregation would be able to see it beating through his scrawny chest. He recalled the temple filled with bodies huddled alongside the walls watching him enter, shadowy figures amongst the animal lard candles and gruesome talismans. He could still see Papa's tall, barrel-chested figure in the far back, positioned directly in front of a shrine crowded with blood-stained statues and bones, one for each of the gods and their ancestors, the white of his eyes glowing against his leathery skin. He could still smell the freshly slaughtered animal offal and herbs, the stench of chicken blood as Mama sprinkled it on him, could hear the drums and voices as she cried out, "It is him! Our ancestors have spoken!" and the sounds of the room erupting into joyful dance.

"You still remember your initiation so clearly?" a low voice asked him.

He looked down to see Mama had joined him, right on cue, the tiny hair that managed to peek out of her bright head wrap now silver, laugh lines creasing her eyes. "I've asked you not to read my thoughts," he reminded her, not unpleasantly.

The wise woman smiled. "I know, but sometimes I can't help myself. You might be the future High Priest, but you are still my son."

Anubis watched the ocean push the boats closer. "Of course, I remember."

"I was met with such resistance then. They told me you were far too young to go through with the initiation. Papa wanted to have me removed from my position. But you died and were reborn, stronger than ever before."

Anubis sighed, remembering the three days of death he had endured, alone in a tent in the bush without food or water. He remembered the terror he felt as the sun fell and the screeching of hyenas began to echo in the distance. He had closed his eyes, centering his mind until he saw himself in a great hollow chamber, its ceilings too high to see, its walls in shades of gray. The only thing of note were the three doorways directly in front of him with doors made out of flat rock. He folded himself into a cross-legged position and waited.

After a while, he saw a thin snake appear in the dirt, only to disappear with a tiny flicker of its tongue. He wondered where it had run off to but was in no hurry to find it. For some reason he felt protected in the cool, damp chamber, out of the sun. He wasn't sure how long he'd been sitting in it, only that he felt no hunger or thirst and time seemed to pass quickly.

Finally, one of the rocks from the strange doors crumbled, and a young man with black eyes and strange silver hair came out, holding the snake he'd seen earlier. He dropped it to the ground where it writhed before rising up into the shape of a man who was so beautiful, he appeared female. A warm smile lit up his face as he took young Anubis by the hands. "Mawu and Lisa welcome you."

"Too young," the other man muttered from behind him, but tossed him a coin.

As soon as Anubis caught it, the tent he'd been sitting in opened, several priestesses hurrying to carry him out and bring him back to life with water and fruit. He remembered choking, bewildered to discover what happened.

"Don't go too far into your memories," Mama's voice warned him. "You will always feel their pull, for you are of the spirit world. But your place is here in this world, helping your people. That is why you came to us, the ancient Anubis incarnate."

Anubis scoffed. "I came to stand quietly and allow these white men to help themselves to the sons and daughters of this land?"

"You are fulfilling your destiny by aligning yourself with King Agaja of Dahomey. You must be patient—he will strike soon."

"Yes, but how many will die before then?" he pointed out. "And how many lives will be lost as he wages his war?"

Mama smiled sadly. "To save the humans, you must play their games.

Agaja will stop trading lives with the white men. We will deliver our people from their fear. Trust in the spirits, young one." She jabbed his chest with a narrow finger to make her point. "Now let us go. You have to join the court before they get here. Help your mama to her hut."

Anubis sighed, knowing there was no point in trying to argue with Mama. He took her arm and wrapped it around his, guiding her back up the beach towards their village. The sun was high and bright with no sign of rain, most of the villagers shirtless as they shopped at the open market. They nodded respectfully towards them as they passed. While Mama naturally commanded respect, most of them were aware of the rumors that swirled around Anubis, that he was an Ancient Egyptian god come to deliver them out of the dark days. Some doubted him, but most believed, patiently watching and waiting for the moment he'd reveal his true nature.

He guided Mama to her hut, planting a kiss on her dewy cheek as she shuffled into the cool shade of her abode.

The palace was not much farther up the road, but Anubis took a moment to wipe his brow with a rag before continuing onward. The palace guards barely glanced his way as they stepped aside so he could enter, opening the giant door set into the high walls so Anubis could enter the courtyard. The palace loomed ahead, set high above the ground, but the king had ordered his outer courtyard prepared. He rarely met visitors in his actual home, preferring to meet them outdoors, forcing the pale Europeans, not used to the harsh African sun, to stand in it while he sat in the shade, fanned by his servants. The King's arrival was not in the immediate future, but his servants were already frantic with preparation, worried things would not live up to his high standards, terrified they would be the ones sailing back with the Frenchmen.

Anubis found shade under a cluster of palm trees, giving himself a moment to think.

"You are early," a man commented from beside him. He looked up to see the appointed Captain Blanc, or Captain of the Whites, the sorry man responsible for all interactions between them. He looked apprehensive, sweat dripping from his forehead to his nose in fat droplets before he licked them nervously away from his lips. Anubis couldn't blame him; out of them all, his job was the hardest. If negotiations went sour, it was he who would take the fall, the last officer forced into self-sacrifice. He took a swig anxiously from his water bottle, offering it to Anubis, who gratefully accepted.

"I saw the ships rolling up onto shore," Anubis explained after he'd taken a long sip. "So, I decided to come early."

"Ah," the captain nodded. "What do you think of the king's idea to set up their compound so close?" he asked casually, leaning against the tree.

Anubis knew better than to reply honestly, for the king was as paranoid as he was greedy and one never knew when they were being set up. "It is a great idea," Anubis lied easily. "The better our relations with the French, the better for trade. We have already set up a fort for the Portuguese, it can only benefit us to expand."

The captain nodded, satisfied with his answer.

Suddenly, they heard the horn announcing the king's approach. Anubis was surprised, then immediately grateful he'd decided to come early. The servants all hurried into position, Anubis heading towards the makeshift throne to take his place.

He watched the king lumber over, dressed in his favorite shade of red, shielded by dozens of parasols held by his wives to protect him from the sun. Anubis fumed when he recognized a young girl from his congregation, one he had just seen playing freely in the dirt with her siblings the week before. He bit his lip to keep his face neutral, trying to temper his disgust and rage. If memory served, she was only twelve years old.

The king didn't even acknowledge his presence, falling sloppily into his seat. The sun had reached a blistering intensity and the king's servants began to fan him with giant palms salvaged from the outlying jungle. Its rays flickered on the gold and silver jewelry that lay across his globular stomach, glittering at hands he kept in plain sight. He wore the same bored expression he seemed to always have, staring ahead without uttering a word to anyone standing around him, his mouth set into a frown that left a deep crease between his eyebrows. Soon the guards opened the high doors, letting the parade of white men filter through.

Like usual, they were overdressed beyond the point of comfort in the blazing heat, sweat slick across each of their foreheads. Up close, their pale skin seemed as parched as their lips, deficient of pigment like their bland, starchy attire. They were lost amongst the bright greens, pinks, and teals that surrounded them, anemic outcasts in a land rich with color.

The man at the forefront offered a toothy smile as he removed his hat, exposing straight, straw colored hair. Although he attempted to appear pleasant, he looked tired, much like the rest of his group who were worn after the long months at sea. A younger man of mixed descent came up beside him, dressed in similar garb with a pair of wire glasses set on his long nose. He bowed towards the king, looking back up with kind, warm eyes. "It is an honor, Your Highness," he said in their language. "Monsieur Dupont is delighted to finally make your acquaintance."

The king gave a curt nod in reply, the captain stepping forward to take over.

"We welcome you all to the Kingdom of Hueda," he said in broken French before resuming his native tongue. "We have prepared your land for you as per our agreement, which you are welcome to explore before we make our final dealings."

"That would be wonderful, thank you," the light-skinned interpreter said after murmuring in his employer's ear.

"King Haffon invites you all to dine with him in his palace after you are settled. I am certain you are weary from your travels."

The French commander thanked him in his language before turning back to his officers.

Suddenly, Anubis noticed the flare of a woman's skirt from behind the men, shielded by a parasol of white lace. It shifted to the side as they all retreated, revealing the woman underneath. His breath caught in his throat. She had long hair the color of the sun, her skin clear until it reached her left side, where a crimson birthmark began at her hairline and seemed to end at her collarbones. However, she also wore a single glove on her left arm rolled all the way up to her sleeve, leading him to believe that her birthmark was larger than what could be seen. Though she looked wilted and her hair was damp with sweat, she was absolutely beautiful. Her eyes drifted upwards towards him and he realized the color matched his, a radiant, oceanic blue. Startled, he quickly looked away.

The captain positioned himself in front of him, blocking his view of her as she disappeared. "The king wants you in attendance before you retreat back to the convent," he told him. "He wants to know if these men are planning to deceive us. You must ask the spirits for him."

Anubis sighed, not looking forward to a night of forced pleasantries and pretending there wasn't an entire shack of humans sitting miserably in shackles, waiting to be shipped off to a hellish world that was not their own. He closed his eyes, picturing Mama's face. He played her words again in his mind; he had to continue to play the part to slowly win the war.

The dinner took longer than he had hoped, but he'd enjoyed the yam stew the chefs prepared, reminding him of the solitary benefit in working for the king. The table they sat behind was long enough to keep them comfortably separated from the French soldiers, but he saw her out of the corner of his eye, dining quietly next to the Commander, who he surmised was either her husband or her father. She picked at her stew, and when he caught another flash of her blue eyes he realized she was just as thrilled to be there as he was.

It was late in the evening when he returned to the convent, most of the recruits already in bed. His belly was full and his body was tired; he didn't even take the time to undress from his priestly robes and beads before he fell onto his cot. It hadn't been more than an hour before he was awakened by a noise at his open window. He bolted out of bed, grabbing the knife he kept by his bedside while hurrying to light his lamp. The warm light flooded the room just as a woman slid down from his window, landing on the ground with a gentle thud.

It was the French woman from before, but this time a playful smile replaced her pursed lips. "I was hoping I would not wake you," she said in his language.

"Why are you here?" he demanded in French, his heart racing in his throat. "You do not belong here."

She looked relieved that he spoke her tongue. "I didn't know how else to contact you without attracting unnecessary attention to us," she explained as she smoothed out her skirts, adjusting her long sweep of light-yellow hair. She was wearing a thinner dress than earlier, leaving her birthmarks completely exposed and confirming his theory that they went down the entire length of her body, dividing her neatly in half. "I am Helena Dupont. My detestable father brought me here as a last resort, his only unwed daughter who he has been trying to get rid of since I grew breasts. He thinks that if he leaves me here with the rest of the French settlers, one of them might eventually grow desperate enough to marry me."

Anubis blinked, surprised by the blatant admission. "This is a convent, a spiritual place. I do not live here alone," he dropped his voice to a whisper.

"We will just have to be quiet then," she shrugged with a smile. She looked around the room. "Do you have anything to drink?"

Anubis blinked again, still unable to reconcile having a strange white woman in his bedroom. "You really shouldn't be here."

Her eyes caught a bottle of spirits near his bedroom altar, which she moved towards.

"Don't—" He stopped her. "Those are for the spirits. There is rum to drink in the kitchen."

She nodded. "Alright then."

Anubis sighed, peeking out from behind the woven straw mat that separated his room from the hall, grateful his fellow priests were sound asleep. He motioned for her to follow him into their main eating room, a simple space with a low table and several cabinets that held cooking pots. He reached up to retrieve a bottle that was hidden on the top of them.

"So is that how you worship?" she asked him. "With gifts of rum?"

"It is one way," he said as he motioned for her to follow him back to his room. "Our religion is layered, one that has evolved over time."

He lifted the mat so she could enter first, letting it fall back behind him. Then he sat down on the floor, pouring the rum into a cup as her eyes swept across the room. He wondered for a moment what she thought of the various fetishes that covered his shrine, wondering if she could see the splatters of dried blood in the lamplight. She did not comment however, folding herself down across from him on the floor. He handed her the cup. "Now will you tell me what you are doing here?" he asked.

She took a sip, appearing to enjoy the taste. She didn't reply, studying him instead. "I have never seen a man with black skin and blue eyes."

"I have never seen a woman half-white, half-crimson," he retorted, then immediately wished he hadn't.

She didn't seem offended, lifting her arm as if to re-examine the dark splotches with a sigh. "The reason my father cannot find anyone to marry me."

"I shouldn't have said that, I'm sorry," Anubis muttered, embarrassed.

"I wouldn't treat me any differently," she shrugged, finishing her rum and motioning for him to refill her cup. "My father has come to exploit your people. We are your enemy, no matter what they pretend."

Anubis looked at her in surprise.

"The only good thing my father has ever done for me is allow me to be educated," she said, annoyed by his hesitation and grabbing the bottle for herself. "My tutor was born of a rich white father who also saw fit to educate his bastard son before he cast him off into the world. Fortunately, his African mother taught him the language and ways of her people, which he passed on to me. Over time, he has become my closest friend, the two of us sneaking away to listen to the abolitionists in the salons and learning about the atrocities of slave labor. I cannot tell you how many times I have funneled money out of my fathers' own pockets to give to their cause or to help freed slaves get established in society."

For the first time in a very long time, Anubis was speechless.

"Anyway," she said as she set the bottle down. "He eventually wants to meet you since he believes you are also on the side of liberation. But that is not why I am here." She started to move in closer to him. "I am here for purely selfish reasons." And before he could react, she was kissing him.

He broke away, jolted by her actions. "This is not right."

She smiled at him, the lamplight dancing in the darks of her eyes. For the first time, he noticed the corner of her left one was streaked with the same crimson stain as her scars. "I do not want anything from you," she told him in a soft voice. "I do not need a child, nor a husband, nor anything that women might require from this sort of thing. I just want you to touch me the way that you look at me."

Anubis took her face and kissed her, feeling her instantly respond by straddling him around her skirts. He had no real time for logical thought, swept up in the thrall of her rum soaked mouth and the sweetness of her hair as she grinded her body against him. It was only after they had finished, when they both lay naked and panting in the dirt, striped with shadows of lamplight that he sat up and stared at her. "I know you from somewhere," he said, confused by the sudden realization.

"You do?" she murmured sleepily, in no rush to get up from where she lay.

He pulled on his clothes and went to the shrine in his room, bringing its statues to life with the candles surrounding them. He heard her inhale with amazement as she rose to a seated position, pulling on her nightdress.

He could already feel the air thickening with spirits, the candle flames growing higher and flickering, throwing ghastly shapes at the walls.

He felt her edge closer to him, whispering, "You're not going to sacrifice me, are you?"

"No," he mumbled, beginning to grow lightheaded as his power rose. "But you must stay still no matter what you see."

She nodded solemnly, her wide eyes the last thing he saw before he entered his trance. He hoped she wouldn't flee, for the spirits might be able to see through her, but he had watched plenty of rituals in his youth and to witness one often proved too intense for the casual observer.

He didn't have much time to wonder, for soon he was in his hall, the long shadowy corridor made of stone walls that stretched to the ceiling. The spirits had already gathered, an old man with a crutch waiting patiently near the three doors at the end, another with a face neither man nor woman, holding a snake around his shoulders, and a crouching jackal who greeted him with cold black eyes. "Where do I know her from?"

"He's not ready," ejected the hostile old man in the corner.

"What am I not ready for?" he demanded. He could hear a whistling sound in the chamber, as though a cold wind had suddenly blown in and gotten trapped, swirling around him as he stood. The jackal beckoned him closer, letting him know it was something from his distant past, something he was just beginning to tap into.

"He's not ready," the old man repeated.

But the jackal still approached, staring at him until he bowed down to its level, staring it right in the eye.

"No," the old man's eyes blazed red with fury, shoving him away from the jackal and out of the spirit world.

His eyes snapped open back in his room, his vision focusing to see Helena staring at him from behind her knees. "Are you back?" she whispered.

"Yes," he sighed, realizing Legba had shoved him flat onto the ground. He sat up to observe the candles were low, fat pools of wax collected around them. Legba hadn't ousted him fast enough—Helena was a reincarnated goddess.

"What did you see?" she asked him carefully.

"Can I meet your friend tonight?" he asked, avoiding the question and rising to his feet.

"You mean to sneak into the French compound?" she said in surprise, though an intrigued grin crept across her face. "I can show you in the way I snuck out, but it's almost daylight. We have an hour at most before the village rises."

"It won't take long," Anubis promised her.

They artfully maneuvered their way out of the convent without arousing suspicion, hurrying past the church of snakes, down into the slumbering village. Beyond the shacks and huts were the palace high walls, the soldiers who kept guard at night already headed inwards as their shift ended. Anubis knew they only had a few moments before the day guards arrived. Helena led him to the newly established French end and once they hopped the wall, she pointed to her window. She lifted herself up easily, climbing through and landing with a soft grunt. He hoisted himself up to follow, landing in a room that was surprisingly clean and well-maintained for the short amount of time she'd been there.

They were both surprised to see her tutor already awaiting them, sitting patiently on the bed. It was the interpreter from before. He closed the book he was reading, removing his glasses to reveal kind brown eyes. "Hello, Anubis. Did you finally figure out that we are gods?"

A crack of thunder broke through his thoughts. He noticed Mama had left his side and he rose from his spot on the beach. Heat lightning cut through the agitated charcoal clouds, throwing flashes of light down on a group of figures walking up the shore. He squinted in confusion before realizing who they were. He hurried towards them as an uncharacteristic nervousness gripped him. In moments he would be meeting his true family, the ones who were tied to him since the dawn of time. The thought of it suddenly seemed overwhelming, his mind already unsettled by his vision.

He recognized David immediately, for he had not changed for centuries, and he assumed that the dark-haired man on the far other side of him was his twin, the infamous Lucius he'd heard so much about. He smiled when he saw his brother, Libraean, another unchanged creature from his distant past, the glasses that obscured his variant eyes picking up the flashes of light. He saw Cahira, the liminal being and sorceress, and Sandrine, the woman who'd made him immortal.

There was a figure further back, dressed in billowing fabric; the last one to drift up the shore, as if she was taking her time observing the new world she'd arrived in. Her body was different, taller and curvier than he remembered, but he knew without a shadow of a doubt that she was his mother.

Although she had kept distance behind them all as they approached, she was in front of him in an instant, as if she had been waiting for his recognition. She pulled him into her arms without any hesitation, as if it had been only hours since they'd last seen each other in bodies they recognized. He melted in her arms, finally complete in knowing that she was the one who birthed him, the magnitude of years between them meaning nothing as they stood in embrace, the rest gathering around them.

"Good evening," another voice said from behind him. Anubis realized Thomas had silently joined them. "My name is Thomas, Anubis's assistant. Allow me to escort you all to your residence. I'm sure you've had quite the journey."

Lucius reached forward with a smile and Anubis saw Thomas brighten. "I am so glad to see you again, young sir," he said, taking his hand in both of his.

"It's Lucius now," he told him pleasantly.

His mother pulled away from him but took his face in her hands, staring into his eyes as she searched them with hers. Though her skin was porcelain white against his own, the shades of bright blue that swarm in her irises exactly mirrored his own. "Hello, my son," she whispered.

He put his hands on hers. "Hello, mother."

He heard Cahira scoff as she brushed past them, marching up the sandy bank.

"She is angry with me," his mother explained. "We have a lot to catch up on."

David finally caught his eye, giving him a warm smile and a nod. "It is good to see you in person."

"Welcome back to Africa," Anubis said, taking Morrigan by the hand. "Come, let us guide you to your home."

THE KINGDOM OF DAHOMEY, 1858

THE RISING SUN STAYED HIDDEN BEHIND A WALL OF STORM CLOUDS, a few cracks of orange managing to peek out of the smoky overcast gloom. The ocean rolled and crashed with the increasing winds, the tide high and raucous as though a full moon shone above it. It seemed the land was responding to her gods returning to it, submitting to the power of their presence.

Anubis had opened his home to them for the duration of their stay, a spacious villa-style abode made of mudbrick, positioned to overlook the beach. It was hidden by towers of natural rocks, the back concealed by brush and palm trees. It was so far from the main ports and protected by the natural topography that its presence would remain undetected even if it didn't have the extra layer of magic surrounding its borders.

Thomas showed each guest their chambers, but Morrigan stayed with Anubis, not letting go of his hand until he led her into his open sitting room. Her eyes swept over his native-inspired pottery and animal bone art before they settled out the window. She took in the spectacular ocean view with a happy sigh, relishing in the occasional salt water spray that managed to reach its way through. "You have a beautiful home," she murmured as she left the window to sink into one of the couches. "I love that it's so close to the sea."

"It reminds me of the Underworld," he told her. "Rushing water and jagged rocks. Sometimes, I close my eyes and pretend I'm still there." Before he could finish the words, a memory came to him, as strong as the last one had been, dragging him out of the present moment and thrusting him back into an ancient world he often forgot.

He saw himself wandering the realms, a young god brimming with curiosity. It was around the time Osiris had grown distant from him, focused entirely on daily interactions with his human subjects with young Horus at his side. Isis had also grown detached, holing up in the palace and refusing visitors. His Uncle Set spent his days alternating between rage and sorrow, spending so much time hunting his lost wife that the Underworld fell into disarray. Osiris tried to keep up with managing both realms but was overwhelmed, eventually letting Anubis take over the Underworld. He'd fallen into the work with natural ease, finding comfort in its shadows, a contentment in working amongst the dead.

It was on a day like any other, as he guided the latest crop of souls to their places, that he heard a whisper trickle through the darkness, so faint he almost missed it. Suicide. He hurried to finish his task and followed the sound past the familiar hills and rivers, up into the stagnant space that held the souls trapped between the living and the dead. He felt instant hopelessness upon arrival, the air stale and unmoving, the sky perpetually gray, a giant unmoving pond that stretched out around him, interrupted only by a few bumps of rock.

He noticed a woman folded around the largest one, weeping, the lower half of her submerged. Tears poured down her cheeks, mixing with the blood that ran from her wrists before draining into the murky water below. Her pain was palpable, overwhelming the space. He staggered for a moment from its intensity, wondering if he should flee before he saw her face and a glimpse of azure blue. His chest seized with recognition, but he forced himself to remain calm, understanding the delicate nature of the Between Space and that she'd never met him before.

He let his jackal visage fall away so she could see his human face. "Hello," he said softly as he approached her. "Why are you so sad?"

She had grown thin and frail in her melancholy, nothing like the strong protectress he'd always imagined, her bones clearly visible through her lusterless almond skin.

"My children," she murmured. "I want my children."

Anubis knelt down to her level. "Have your children died?"

"No," she said, her face slick with tears. He tried not to look down at her gruesome wounds. "I made a horrible mistake and had to leave them behind to protect them. I have lived alone for so long without those I love...I can no longer bear it."

Anubis swallowed, trying to keep his own emotions steady. "What makes you believe death is better?"

"I was once the goddess of death," she whispered. "Death is my home, my comfort. I long to return."

"The Realm of the Dead is ruled over by Set," Anubis gently pointed out. "Are you willing to see him again?"

"He will not know it is me," she said. "He will think I am just another soul passing through."

"But what if he does recognize you?"

She looked at him, quiet for a moment while she studied his face. Was she beginning to see him, realize who he was to her?

"He still does not know why I left him," she finally said. "He might be furious with me for leaving, but I have nothing to fear." She let out a long sigh. "He will try to trap me there, however, but I can accept that."

"But what about your sister?" Anubis pressed. "You swore to protect her."

"We arranged everything before I left," she whispered as her tears began anew. "Osiris protects her now, and they watch over my children together. I am unneeded in any of their lives."

"How do you know?"

"My sons have never even met me," she explained. "They know her as their mother, as they should."

Anubis struggled to keep his emotions contained, swallowing hard. "Well, I cannot let you die," he told her. "Not yet."

She surprised him by reaching up to touch his face. "You are a very nice young man," she said with a weak smile, running her thumb along his cheek. "How do you know so much about me?"

Before he could help himself, he leaned forward to give her a hug, wondering how to tell her, when suddenly he heard her gasp, followed by an incredulous whisper.

"You are mine..."

He pulled away to see her face filled with wonderment.

"How is that possible?" she breathed, running her hands through his hair and around his face as she took him in with wide, adoring eyes. "It was not that long ago."

"You birthed gods," Anubis explained. "We grew into adulthood faster than humans. Though we do love her, we have long known Isis is not our true mother. Horus is content watching over Father, but I have always searched for you."

Nephthys let out a tiny sob, hugging him tightly. "Oh, sweet boy. You do not know how long I have waited to meet you." She pulled away suddenly, looking down at her wrists. "Though I suppose it is too late now."

"No," Anubis rose to his feet. "You are in the place between worlds and I have the authority to oust you from the Underworld. You will not sacrifice yourself to Set and live out your days in misery. I will not allow it."

He lifted her out of the mire. In an instant, they were back at the small clearing in distant woods where she'd tried to end her life. He shivered, the air much colder than in their homeland. He realized she'd hidden herself far away from the place from which they hailed.

Nephthys looked down to see that her wounds had healed and sighed at the revelation. "If I do not die, then what shall I make of this life? I once had a purpose—there is no purpose in hiding."

"Then create one," Anubis suggested. "Perhaps you are meant to become a different goddess. One that is earthbound, rather than a ruler of the dead. If it is purposeful work that you seek, that work can be found in any realm."

She stared at him, considering his words. "Perhaps you are right. How did you become so wise so quickly?" She beamed at him proudly, color coming back into her cheeks.

Anubis found himself smiling as well. "May I visit you again?" he asked.

"Of course." She knelt down to retrieve a box, opening it to reveal a collection of animal bones and dried herbs. She pulled out a delicate black feather and handed it to him. "When you want to visit me, use this. It is a crow feather."

"A crow?"

"I discovered them during my travels," she explained. "It is a beautiful onyx bird whose temperament reminds me of the raptors of home."

Anubis took the sleek, unusual feather and tucked it into his belt. "I will visit you as often as you let me," he promised.

Nephthys threw her arms around him, squeezing tightly. "I will never be too far from where you can reach me," she promised.

The memory faded, the present day Morrigan peering at him with the same eyes through a different face. "You were traveling through memory," she observed.

Anubis blinked, momentarily unnerved by how vivid and frequent his visions were becoming. "They are coming stronger than ever before."

Morrigan nodded. "You see like your father. It's more intense now because we are all together. What were you remembering?"

Anubis gave her a small, sad smile. "When we first met."

"Ah." She looked away, her eyes drifting back towards the open window. "I was so lost then."

"You have found your way," he said, rising to pour himself a glass of the tainted rum he kept nearby.

"Not so much," she admitted with a sigh. "Even after all these years, I'm still reconciling, even as the world around us falls apart."

"You have reincarnated quite a few times," Anubis pointed out as he slunk back into his chair. "This is my first time as an earthbound creature and I have my struggles. It is hard to bear so many lifetimes."

Morrigan smiled at him. "You have always been so wise and kind."

Anubis looked away, feeling uncharacteristically bashful. He took a quick sip of his drink.

"Though I should have your head for giving me up to Lucius," she added playfully.

He flinched, unaware that she knew.

"I know, I know. It was to protect me." She rose from the couch to stand back at the window, committing to her initial urge to stare out of it. "You were both right—it was Discordia all along who threatened us, and we were none the wiser."

"Well, her time of threatening us is over," Anubis declared, setting down his drink with emphasis. "She has no chance against us all."

"If we remain united."

"So, your reunion with Lucius in the Underworld wasn't quite as happy as he hoped?"

"No, it was," she sighed, a look of guilt flashing across her face. "It was perfect, actually. For the first time in our lives, we were committed to working through our antagonistic past, instead of me running and him following behind me, setting the world ablaze."

"What happened?"

"Discordia killed us both. We reincarnated separately and before he could find me again, I found David. He and I reunited instead, both of us completely unaware of the decision I'd made in the Underworld."

"Oh." Anubis winced.

"The worst part was that David and I found out together, and Lucius found out shortly after that, which painted me back into the corner I seem to be perpetually trapped in." She sighed again, deciding to resume her spot back on the couch.

"Then paint yourself out of it," he suggested.

"Do you believe Lucius has truly changed?" she asked him, searching his eyes. "He told me that you forgave him for all that transpired."

"I don't believe living creatures are capable of change," Anubis replied, honestly. "We are who we are. I think Lucius has always been a mix of darkness and light, but has let his rage take him to places many of us never see. I also believe David is capable of doing the same, even more so because he has never truly examined and confronted the darker part of himself."

Morrigan stared at him.

"Think about it. All of us—you, Lucius, Libraean, and I—have examined the shadows of who we are, whether we wanted to or not. We all felt our rage, waged our wars, made our mistakes. It made us strong. Isis, on the other hand, was so intent on being a beacon of light that it left her vulnerable to the darkness. David has that same quality about him—he runs solely on guilt and his own concept of morality. It is why he struggles to understand you and Lucius, why he falls into spells of discontent, why he is prone to anesthetize. He fits easily into the role of a hero—but only when Lucius plays the villain. But Lucius has faced his darkest parts and risen above them; he chooses to do right now because he wants to, not because he feels he has to. His existence in this life challenges David and causes him to question everything he has ever known about himself. It is up to them to resolve this dynamic between them, regardless of you being caught in the middle."

Morrigan gazed at him with adoring eyes. "I have to admit, the way your mind works reminds me of Lucius."

"Well, we are family." Anubis shrugged, her open adoration threatening to make him blush. "I honestly don't think they were supposed to separate like you and Isis did," he continued. "They have trouble existing in the same space without constant discord. You have been trapped in between them for so long because you can never resolve your own conflict, never make your own choice. Ultimately, it has always been up to you, but you are just like David in that way—you are controlled by guilt and what you think is the right thing to do. If you separate yourself from what you believe you should do, you will see what you ought to do."

Morrigan was speechless.

Anubis flushed, suddenly afraid he had crossed a line. "Please forgive me. I've had a lot of time to think in the Underworld."

"No, I'm grateful you can make things clearer for me," she assured him. "I'm not unintelligent, but my emotions tend to blind me, especially in this situation. I love them both."

"And here I thought my love life was complicated," Anubis joked as he rose from his chair to discard his empty glass.

Morrigan brightened. "You have someone in your life?"

Anubis fumbled, suddenly wishing he hadn't said anything. "Not quite…"

"Not quite?" Helena's voice tore through the room as she appeared in it, apprehending Morrigan with open disdain. "Did you really think I wouldn't discover you seducing another woman in your own home?"

Anubis felt his cheeks grow hot. "Helena, this is my mother."

Her eyes widened as she looked back at Morrigan, who rose up from the couch.

"You are the ghost of a goddess," Morrigan observed in wonder. "How can that be?"

"Unlike many gods, somehow Helena did not disappear completely after she died," Anubis explained. "She is an earthbound spirit who can travel the astral planes. That is how we were able to discover David and warn Cahira years ago, after you lit the way for us."

"We have to tell the others," Morrigan said suddenly. "There could be more gods alive out there—perhaps Dan is still alive." Without another word, she flew out of the room so fast, it seemed as though she had disappeared.

Helena looked after her. "Suddenly your temperament makes a lot more sense to me."

"They arrived a few hours ago," Anubis told her. "I was going to let them rest before summoning you here so we could all speak. Can I depend on you joining us?"

Helena groaned. "Isn't meeting your mother enough?"

Anubis chuckled. "I would also like you to meet my father, uncle, and brother, maybe even the woman who holds my aunt's soul."

"I am not a woman who appreciates family," she reminded him, her eyes settling on the open bottle of rum. "You were drinking without me, no less?"

"There is plenty left," he assured her. "I was also planning on heading to bed soon."

Helena gave him a look. "How romantic."

"Would you still want me if I was romantic?"

She didn't respond, brushing past him as she marched into his bedroom. "Leave the bottle."

🕸 THE SPACES BETWEEN 🕸

THE KINGDOM OF DAHOMEY, 1858
MORRIGAN

THE HALLS WERE QUIET AS SHE WAFTED THROUGH THEM, each guest sharing a collective exhaustion from the long journey at sea. She had yet to formally meet Anubis's friend, but she appreciated his foresight in putting the brothers at opposite ends of the house. Both their scents drifted through the air as she stood at the intersection of hallways where one of Anubis's altars had been arranged. She stopped and cursed, realizing she couldn't move confidently towards either one, choosing instead to examine the space that was carved into the treated mudbrick that constructed Anubis's home. A statue of a man with horns seated on a stone bench sat at the center of the niche, surrounded by candles and dried tobacco with an unopened bottle of rum situated behind him. Above the altar, a symbol was carved into the wall, reinforced with black paint so it stood out against the pale brick. It was magic she didn't recognize, but she could feel its power, transfixed by the statue that looked as though it had been sculpted centuries before.

"You don't need my help," a deep voice came from behind her.

She whipped around to see a young man leaning against the wall with dark eyes and wiry silver hair hidden underneath a straw hat. He held a pipe between his teeth that he lifted to speak. "You helped create the spirit world, it is yours to command," he said.

She was confused. "I didn't intend to summon you."

"Yet you cannot move past the crossroads."

Morrigan frowned, an old irritation she hadn't felt for days suddenly rising within her. There was only one thing she abhorred more than the sensation of being trapped, and that was a man she didn't know acting as if he knew better than her.

"Calm down, Mama Snake," the man chucked. "A lot has changed since you last been here. This is our land now, so you will have to be putting up with us."

Morrigan crossed her arms. "Who are you?"

"The humans call me Legba," the man lifted his hat to give her a short bow. "I stand at the crossroads between the living and the spirit world, similar to the job your son once held."

"How did you manage to survive the Purging?" she asked him.

"We are not gods in the way most humans think," he told her. "We are vodun, the intermediaries. The priests and the priestesses serve us and we serve them. As a human, your son was one of the most powerful bokor in our time, responsible for killing every corrupt king that took charge of her western kingdom even after a dead woman turned him into what you are."

"A bokor…"

"One who uses both the darkness and the light. Your son used his power to help his people, still does."

Morrigan felt a twinge of maternal pride before she refocused, starting to connect things in her mind. "We were told the astral plane is overcrowded and that only Heaven and Hell remain."

Legba laughed, his booming voice reverberating through the space around them. "Just like there is more than one up and more than one down, there is more than one middle. You should remember, you used to travel through them, hiding from your husbands."

Morrigan frowned, realizing he was right. "Do you know the chaos goddess Discordia and her actions against us?"

"I am the one who told Anubis."

"Has she tried to destroy your world too?"

Legba smiled, revealing tall teeth that seemed to overwhelm his skull. "The Holy Watchers do not pay us any mind. They gave her the ability to jump in and destroy realms, not the spaces in between them."

Morrigan considered his words. "Does this mean you remain neutral during this war?"

"I can't speak for us all." Legba shrugged. "We stay out of things, but we favor those birthed in our land, not the gods of those who murder and enslave our people."

Morrigan's thoughts returned to the matter at hand, gazing back down the hallway and wondering if she should head back to Anubis to ask for a room. She could just wait and tell the others when they woke.

Legba's booming laugh interrupted her thoughts again. "You still have to make a decision."

"You seem to have the answer—why don't you enlighten me," Morrigan said shortly, feeling her anger resurface.

Legba shook his finger. "I need payment if you want the answer."

The chamber suddenly filled with a hissing sound. Morrigan looked down to see several black asps materialized, rising up from out of the ground like sprouts. She stared at them in surprise, their smooth black bodies strangely familiar to her, until she realized with an incredulous laugh that they were hers—Lilith's snakes from a time before she'd ever heard a crow call. She looked back up to see Legba had promptly abandoned her, and she shook her head with a smile. The snakes gradually wiggled away when they discovered they were unneeded, one finding its way up the wall to wind itself around the spirit's statue.

"At the beginning, there was you and there was he," a voice boomed in her head.

She startled, whipping back around, but he had long retreated. She watched the remaining snake twist around the god's likeness, staring at her with shining black eyes as her small tongue flitted in and out of her mouth. Morrigan took a deep, steadying breath, and headed down the hallway to her left.

She kept her footsteps light as she moved down the long corridor until the scent of bonfires and spiced tea overwhelmed the brackish sea air. A dim light peeked out from underneath his door, causing her to hesitate. She braced herself, and gently pushed it open.

He was seated on the floor in the center of the room, cross-legged and surrounded by dozens of burning candles. Although the windows were open far enough to send the curtains flailing with wild abandon, the flames did not flicker, casting a steady glow across the serene expression on his face.

She was taken aback, unsure of what to say, when his eyes drifted open to greet her.

"Hello."

"Forgive me for disturbing you." She edged back towards the door.

"You never disturb me."

"What are you doing?"

"Attempting to stay calm." He gently chuckled. "Would you like to join me? It's a technique I learned long ago from a friend who lived amongst the Buddhists in Japan." His features looked soft in the candlelight, alluringly youthful without the tightness of his perpetual scowl or the heat of his simmering anger.

She bit the inside of her lip. "I wanted to speak with you, but I can come back tomorrow evening," she said quickly as she headed back out the door, but he had already risen to his feet, blocking her way.

"Please don't go."

She sighed, letting him shut the door behind her. She turned back to observe the room, discovering it was actually a suite, heavily accented in black, from the onyx statues and the charcoal pottery to the obsidian arrowheads nailed to the wall, as if Anubis had personalized it especially for Lucius in anticipation of his arrival.

She wondered absently what he'd put in her room, swallowing when she realized he hadn't shown her one. Her suspicions were confirmed when she noticed the display of avian skulls artfully arranged on the back wall, with a vase of white orchids on the table.

"You'll be proud to know I haven't had a drop of human blood since we arrived here," Lucius said as he waved his hands to extinguish the floor candles, moving towards a cabinet above the sink. "Thomas assured me they use the blood of predators in their rum." He produced a wide bottle similar to the one Anubis had enjoyed earlier, clouded glass with no label and dark, thick liquid sloshing around inside. "Would you like to try some with me?"

Morrigan's stomach suddenly responded with a growl, reminding her of how long it had been since she last ate. "The last time you and I sat around having drinks, you set a ballroom on fire."

Lucius laughed. "You make an excellent point," he said, looking at the bottle. Suddenly he brightened, setting it back down on the table. "I have a better idea."

"We shouldn't," Morrigan protested, knowing exactly what he was thinking. "No one in this land knows we are here."

"All the better then."

"We should keep it that way."

"I doubt anyone will notice."

"It will be high noon soon."

"Then make it rain."

She sighed, remembering what it was like to argue with him. They locked hands and in moments, they reached the savannah under an overcast sky, close to a herd of antelope who drank from the murky river that wound through the plains. She knew it wasn't the grazers he was interested in, but the beautiful pride of lions lingering nearby, who regarded them with cautious brown eyes. They were all female and Morrigan's attention settled on the oldest, who sighed with aching bones and battle wounds, exhausted from trying to keep up with her daughters but too stubborn to let them best her.

She felt Lucius slip away to search for the distant male. She stilled, patiently observing the lionesses as they honed in on their prey. She waited until the exact moment that they lunged, distracted, so she could attack hers. It seemed as though the old matriarch knew she was coming, for she didn't attempt to run, submissive as Morrigan dragged her away from the feeding frenzy. A rush of exhilaration seized her while she drained the old queen, ancient strength pummeling through her veins. Morrigan drank only what she needed, tenderly laying her to rest as she heard the distant, ferocious roar of a combative male echo in the distance.

Several feeding lionesses abandoned their food to investigate while others embarked on a search for their missing matron. Morrigan heard the hyenas creep in on the abandoned prey as she scanned the dark savannah, hoping Lucius was alright, when he startled her from behind. His eyes were wild with excitement, burning through the shadows, blood smeared on his lips and an angry gash still bleeding on his chest.

"The old boy put up quite a fight," he told her breathlessly.

They raced back to Anubis's house before the rest of the pride realized what had occurred, laughing like young lovers who had dodged their chaperones. Grateful the house still slept, Morrigan fell onto one of the leather hide couches with her appetite satisfied. She felt better than she had in months. A calm settled over her, replacing her dwindling adrenaline.

Lucius grabbed the rum bottle he'd left on the sink and two glasses, settling down on the couch next to her. They stared at each other for a moment before he reached up to tuck a lock of hair behind her ear. His touch sent a light shiver across her skin. "This is the longest I've seen you keep your hair this way," he remarked.

Morrigan realized he was right, becoming acutely aware of her tresses, long and loose around her shoulders.

He continued to admire her, his eyes sweeping over her face, lingering on her lips. "You look much better. One could assume it's the fresh blood, but I know seeing your son safe is what brought the light back into your eyes."

Morrigan smiled. "I may not have raised him, but he is my heart. Which brings me to why I'm here. I met his lover, a goddess who survived the Purging, and ran into one of his spirits, a type of god in this land."

Lucius looked surprised. "They were spared?"

"Apparently since they exist in a space similar to the astral plane, they were looked over. Discordia could not reach them."

"Interesting." Lucius considered her words. "What do the others think?"

"You're the first one I've told," she admitted, leaning over to pour herself a drink.

His eyebrows rose before his lips followed, turning into a half smile. "That is even more interesting."

"It's completely logical that I would come to you first," she said defensively. "You have a brilliant mind that is best used for solving puzzles."

"I see. So, you came rushing to my room in the middle of the day, while the rest of the house sleeps...to talk business?"

Morrigan stood up in exasperation. "Would you rather I go tell David?"

Lucius darkened, flying to his feet to block her. "Do not toy with me like that," he warned her.

"Then stop pretending like you don't know why I'm here."

He grabbed her face and kissed her roughly, the metallic taste of fresh lion's blood and cloves flooding her mouth as she hungrily kissed him back. Outside, the ocean waves lifted in response, crashing down so hard they reached the walls of the house with spray. He lifted her up so she could wrap her legs around him, staggering as he tried to make it to the bed before they were distracted by their rising passion. They fell together in a tangled heap, tearing at each other's clothes. Although they explored new bodies with impassioned hands, they fell into a natural rhythm. The surrounding candles sputtered to life as the ocean continued to steadily rise and fall, a clap of thunder sounding in the distance.

It was hours before Morrigan's eyes drifted open from their brief respite to see him gazing at her. "That is only mildly unnerving," she murmured sleepily.

He let out a soft chuckle. "Forgive me. You look absolutely enchanting when you sleep. Not a muscle in your face moves, like you're etched out of marble. It's strange…I can vividly recall what you looked like before and, although you're wearing a different body, you look very much the same."

"It's the eyes," she told him. "I recognized you in England by your eyes."

He swooped back down to kiss her, but before he had the chance to pounce on her again, she sat up, gently pushing him away. "The others will eventually look for us," she explained. "We still have problems to solve."

Lucius sighed in defeat, rolling onto his back for a brief moment before jumping out of bed.

"Where are you going?" she protested, sitting up on her elbows.

She blushed when he returned. He was completely unashamed about his lack of clothing, a lit cigarette hanging from his mouth and the half-empty bottle in his hand. He hopped back into bed, handing her the bottle. "There is something I need to tell you before we talk to the others. But it stays between you and I."

Morrigan frowned, pulling herself completely upright. "Of course."

"While you rested on our way to France, I was able to access my memories, the ones I tried to tell you about before the hydra attacked us." He took a hit from his cigarette, smashing it out on the table before taking back the bottle she hadn't touched. "I never had a taste for rum," he commented after he took a sip. "I have always preferred a strong red, but I believe in Africa, it's palm wine."

"Lucius."

He sighed. "Apparently, I was recruited by the Holy Watchers the first time I was sent to Tartarus. They pulled me out of there, promising that if I worked for them, I would no longer remain trapped. They also promised to reveal your location to me." He took another long swallow. "I believe my memories disappeared because I wanted them gone…because they were too painful."

Morrigan was quiet.

"No one has ever drunk enough of my blood to hear my secrets," he said softly. "No matter how many creatures I sired. I never offered more than a small sip from my wrist so that they would turn. You once trusted me enough to let me in, and I'm ready to offer you the same."

Morrigan reached up to caress his face, running her thumb along his jaw. "Only if you wish it."

"I want you to know everything; the good and the bad. It is only fair."

Morrigan was quiet, her mind drifting to her time in the Otherrealms, the time with David in Ireland. The only parts of her he didn't know. "There are some secrets best left unspoken," she gently pointed out.

He took her hand. "I know. But I want you to know mine."

Morrigan looked from his radiant ochre eyes, past his lips, and down to his throat, where his vein throbbed beneath the skin. Her heartbeat rose as she thought about the taste of his spicy blood, the flavors surpassing the taste of his mouth when she kissed him. She remembered the taste from the distant, hazy memories of the medieval world, when they tried to find each other in the violently passionate romps that often ended up on the castle floor. How wonderful it must be to drink it from a place of love and trust, rather than the confusion and anger that had devastated their past.

He seemed to sense her arousal and pulled her closer to him, one hand tangled in her hair while the other explored her body with his fingers. She kissed his neck, teasing him with her tongue before she bit. His blood was just as electrifying as she imagined it would be, a far more extraordinary pleasure than she imagined, and she nearly swooned before his memories began to filter in. Her mind was accosted by images of brown eyed twins and angel feathers, flooding waters and Heaven's golden gates. She watched Discordia try to deceive him, watched him mercilessly take her life. She saw the deceitful goddess return wearing her sister's face, witnessing her other attempts to seduce him. She watched her bring him to life on Earth, her tainted magic creating the dragon that would never leave him.

A low groan broke her concentration and she realized how fervently she'd been drinking. She forced herself to break away as her vision steadied, coming back to the present. It focused as he lay his head back against the wall, his eyes closed, his lips white. "I'm so sorry," she gasped frantically, feeling for his pulse and making sure he was still breathing. She exhaled when she saw his sideways smile.

"Don't apologize, Morrigan. Everything you do is intense," he whispered.

She tore at the veins in her wrist, pressing it up against his mouth. She watched the color come back into his face as he drank from her, fire resuming its place in his golden irises. From the corner of her eye, she caught the sun as it crawled back under the horizon in a blaze of vibrant color. She suddenly remembered the others.

Lucius gently broke away, lifting her mouth towards his for a kiss. "Thank you. I'm glad you still want to be here with me."

"I never knew you bore the pain of losing children," she said quietly, picturing the cherubic twins.

Lucius looked down. "Neither did I until recently."

"I seem to have walked in at the wrong time," a voice interrupted.

"What is the meaning of this?" Lucius snarled before Morrigan blocked his advance with her arm.

"This is Helena, Anubis's lover," she told him quickly. "She is the goddess spirit I was telling you about."

"I smelled the rum," Helena teased with a knowing smirk. "I won't stay long. I hear the secrets whispered in the astral place and the spaces in between, and they have been quite loud since you all came here." She turned to Lucius. "Discordia tricked you into giving her a child because she had a theory that a child born from the union between a life goddess and a death god would be supreme—and she was right. It took eons for someone like Cahira to be born, but she is the first goddess born of this Earth. She does not need a realm because this is her realm."

"A new type of god," Lucius commented, impressed.

"That isn't what I'm here to tell you," Helena continued. "Cahira does not hold Isis's soul as you thought, but there is one among you who does. Before you pulled the human girl out of the acacia tree and killed Discordia in the process, another piece of Isis's soul had been removed. It was stolen by a shaman who gifted it to an African cult; they then channeled it into a woman strong enough to bear it, the reincarnation of the goddess Medusa."

"Sandrine," Morrigan realized.

Helena nodded. "Cahira might be one powerful earth goddess, but it's because she is Lucius and Discordia's daughter. Sandrine is the one who has Isis's soul. If you are trying to reunite the ancient originals, she is the one you need to be concerned with. Discordia thinks Cahira is the one to consume for Isis's power, but in reality, she needs Sandrine."

Morrigan met Lucius's eyes before looking back at the spirit with bicolored flesh and flowing blonde hair. "Thank you," she told her.

Helena shrugged. "I'm helping you because I love your son…just don't tell him I said so."

"We need to find Sandrine," Morrigan said as Helena disappeared.

Lucius threw his shirt over his head, fumbling for his slacks. She followed suit, stepping into her dress as her mind took in everything that had just been revealed to her, including Lucius's memories. "So Cahira is an earth-made goddess, Sandrine has Isis's soul, and you have been quite literally painted as the God of men's archnemesis—are we still certain I'm the one being targeted here?"

Lucius came up behind her to button her dress. "I told you once before, there is a creature called Satan who resides in Tartarus now who acts as his nemesis, but he is just an ignorant demon. The humans have confused us in their theology. I have not spoken to any Watcher or anyone from Heaven's realm in thousands of years—they don't have a vendetta against me or they would have intervened in my life long ago."

"But why me?" Morrigan insisted as she ran her fingers through her hair. "I am not as powerful as Cahira. I threaten no one with my existence."

"You threaten Discordia."

Morrigan sighed, frustrated.

Lucius spun her around to plant a kiss on her head. "We'll figure it out," he promised. "As much as I enjoy avoiding my brother, it is high time we talk to the others."

Morrigan nodded, following him down the long, bending hallways towards the main rooms. She stopped abruptly as she remembered more of his story, grabbing his arm. "That was you in Ireland?"

He didn't have time to respond, for the moment they turned the corner, they were surprised by Libraean, who hurtled a burst of air towards Lucius, knocking him to the ground.

"What are you doing?" Morrigan cried out, positioning herself between them.

She had never seen Libraean look so angry, his normally serene face twisted up in passionate rage. David was right behind him, wearing a similar expression, but where Libraean's upset was blatantly driven by grief, David's was hardened by pure, unaltered hatred. His voice bristled with antagonism as he addressed her.

"You've been so busy salivating over him since he returned, you failed to remember what a monster he is." Wind picked up around the room, teasing the tapestries and sending papers to the ground.

Lucius quietly began to siphon his own power from where he sat behind her, patiently waiting for her to move out of the way.

"David, stop this," she warned him.

"Morrigan, move out of the way."

"Yes, Morrigan," Lucius said, his voice drenched in loathing. "Move out of the way."

Libraean realized the extent of his overreaction and removed himself from the crossfire with worried eyes. Morrigan looked frantically between both brothers, unnerved to see David irate beyond reason. Though she had stood between them more times than she could count, something didn't seem right. And as strongly as the thrashing sea beckoned to her to let it loose, this was not the time to let her own aggression get the best of her.

She tried again, calming herself before she spoke. "David, please tell me what is going on here."

"Don't petition me with your soft voice and batting eyelashes while you reek of my brother," he sneered.

Unwelcome memories suddenly slammed into her, jolting her away from reality and into the days of Celtic Ireland. When she discovered Daghda's affair, she stood in front of Lugh, peering up at him with gritted teeth and crossed arms. "You are going to tell me right now or I will kill them all myself."

The blonde warrior god sighed. Though he was taller than she was, rippled with the athletic build common to powerful warriors, she knew he was intimidated by her—all the gods were. It was she that could turn a battle into a success or a stormy failure, depending on how slighted she felt. In truth, she took each request for victory into careful consideration, thoughtfully choosing which side to bestow her blessing upon, but she never corrected it, allowing them all to think of her as an irrational harbinger of doom.

"I know of no affair," he repeated.

"I have looked into Aengus's eyes and I see Daghda reflected back at me," Morrigan insisted. She knew she was unreasonably incensed; she had always suspected infidelity and was not surprised by it, but she felt herself losing control. Her crows circled above her, agitated by the tumultuous waves of emotion radiating off their queen.

Lugh glanced at them nervously before meeting her eyes. "I can only tell you what I think. You been wed longer than some of us been alive. Daghda is old and worn, wanting to rule the kingdom and serve his people. You want war, you need adventure and conquest. I think for a time, when you were gone, she filled your place."

"No one can fill my place."

"Aye," Lugh smiled sadly. "But I think the old fool tried. Are you gonna be seeking your vengeance then?"

"Of course," Morrigan scoffed. "It is my right as a wife to strike down the woman who tried to take my husband from me."

"But can ya kill his son too?" Lugh pointed out. "What if Daghda finds out? He would never forgive you."

"Then I suppose I will have to kill him too," she replied before dissolving into her flock.

The present Morrigan blinked, trying to see past the vision of the young, blonde river goddess as she fell to her knees, her eyes wide and full of terror, so she could focus on what was unfolding before her.

"Please forgive me! 'Twas a foolish mistake, one that I will regret for the rest of my days!"

Morrigan bristled with hatred, fully prepared to unleash the fury intended for Daghda out onto his cowering lover. "You have no more days."

The present David pulled her out of the memory as he advanced forward, the wind now churning around them at whirlwind speed. His copper hair whipped around his head like flames, his teeth gnashed together as if he was wearing the mask of his brother at the height of his madness. She searched his eyes for any recognition, but they were unforgiving and blank, his mouth twisted into a sneer. "Morrigan," he repeated. "Get out of the way or I will tear you down."

His words were all she needed.

Snakes burst from the tiled floors as the building waves finally crashed against the house, filling it with seawater. Morrigan leapt forward, wrapping her hands around David's throat as she used the weight of her body to throw him to the ground. He managed to snap his own hands around her neck, the gales of wind now deafening, preventing anyone around them from intervening as the seawater swirled with the wind. Morrigan was trapped in a deadlock with her former lover, untethered fury pulsing through her limbs, rendering her unable to let go, even as black spots obscured her vision. Every emotion she'd fought to keep at bay the past year had unleashed itself, including the small part of her, buried deep inside, that wanted it to all be over, tired of struggling, wanting him to kill her.

"Enough!" A female voice shrieked, throwing her off him with a bolt of power, right into Lucius's waiting arms. He gripped her tightly as she tried to get away, only relaxing when she realized the rest had gathered around them and stopped, the wind slowed to a steady breeze. Cahira stood next to a coughing David and Libraean, the snakes Morrigan had inadvertently summoned twisting harmlessly around her feet as though calmed by the earth goddess. They all stared at her, surprised by her reaction. She looked up to see Anubis had taken his position beside her and Lucius, the presence of both of them soothing to her. The ocean waves crept back toward the shoreline as leftover droplets fell from the ceiling.

"You have snakes now?" Lucius whispered in her ear.

"You need to tell me right now why you have brought this chaos into my home." Anubis demanded of the three that stood opposite them. Although the air around them had settled, its energy shifted, a heavy presence like molasses edging inward. Morrigan could hear its whispers, smell the burning tobacco from Legba's pipe. Although Cahira had been the only one who could separate them, death had broken through to end it all, overpowering the life magic that had dominated the room. Its energy restored her, refocusing her mind and emotions as it settled around the three of them, protecting them from harm. She could tell Lucius sensed it as well, his own heart rate slowing as he helped her to her feet.

"I have no qualms against Lucius, but she would have killed David had I not intervened," Cahira replied coolly.

"David, what is the meaning of this?" Anubis redirected the question.

"He killed Jacob," Libraean said, his voice quivering.

"How do you know?"

"Why don't you ask him, Morrigan." David looked directly at her.

She looked up at Lucius, who still wore his familiar expression of contempt.

"She doesn't have to ask me anything because she knows me," he shot back. "Did you notice how easily she jumped to my defense? My, how things have changed."

"Jacob came to me in a vision," David continued to address Morrigan, undeterred by his taunting. "He told me Lucius fed on him during our trip across the Channel, knowing that he would soon die of fever. He couldn't resist feeding on something alive, even if it was someone we knew, someone we loved."

Morrigan scoffed. "That doesn't sound like something he would do."

David laughed incredulously. "That sounds exactly like something he would do! Lucius thinks only of himself—that fact hasn't changed for eons. How could you fall for this act of his? You are completely blinded by him."

"Enough," Anubis ordered. "There are ways to solve these things. But I will need you all to separate—this house might be protected from outside forces but dueling gods will surely draw unneeded attention."

Cahira put a gentle hand on David's arm. "We will sort this out," she told him and Libraean, who still looked terribly distraught though his anger had long since dissipated.

"I'll need you to come with me," Anubis told Morrigan gently. "They talk to you too," he added in reply to her confused look.

Lucius sighed, his hair disheveled from the wind. "I'll be in my room polishing off a bottle of rum," he decided. He pointed to Cahira, "Since you seem to be taking responsibility for them, it would be best to keep them the hell away from me." Then he surprised everyone, grabbing Morrigan's face and giving her a firm kiss on the mouth before he marched back from where he'd emerged.

She avoided looking at David, but she overheard him tell Cahira, "There is no need to watch over either of us. This evening has proven to be exceptionally difficult for Libraean, so I'll be keeping him company until this mess gets sorted out. We will wait to hear from you."

"Well, I guess I'll just wait here until you all resolve this," Cahira sighed as she flopped down on the soaked couch. "I have to wait for Sandrine regardless." David and Libraean disappeared wordlessly, heading back into the eastern part of the house.

Anubis looked at Cahira. "If you could, though—" he started to say.

"I will make sure no one dies tonight," she finished for him with a flash of her honey-colored eyes.

Anubis turned to Morrigan. "Are you ready?" he asked. She had trouble reading his expression, trapped somewhere between dismay and apprehension.

"Yes," she told him. He motioned for her to follow him outside. She licked her lips as she did so, the taste of cloves still lingering in her mouth.

THE MIDDLEWORLD

THE MOON DOMINATED THE SKY AS IT ASCENDED, burning rusted gold against cobalt. The air was thick and hot, filled with choruses of insects, seemingly locked in battle to see who could screech the loudest. Anubis led her down a sandy path that gradually turned to jungle, wide palms fanning out above them as brush overtook the dirt. When it appeared as if they could go no further, he paused to lift a curtain of vines, revealing a mudbrick wall covered in hand-painted designs. The scent of strange herbs and animal blood assaulted Morrigan before they even entered, whispers trickling through the air.

"What is this place?" she asked.

"This is where the spirits live," he explained. "The temple was built long before I was born and has been rebuilt several times, but always protected. Only the High Priests and Priestesses of each generation know its where-abouts. It's even hidden from the kings."

He moved forward to push open the door, but before they could enter, she heard rustling in the woods. Out of the brush, Libraean appeared.

"I left David…something does not seem right with him," he said. "I also want to see Jacob."

A sad, knowing smile accompanied Anubis's nod as he gestured them both inside.

Libraean surprised Morrigan by grabbing her hand, his skin callused and warm. He looked up at her over the rim of his glasses. "I shouldn't have lost my temper like that, dragging you back into the middle. You and Lucius have done so well at keeping tension at bay, and I stirred it all back up again. When David told me about Gabriel, I lost my head."

She squeezed his hand reassuringly, touched by his effort. "We will sort it out."

"Since you're here, would you mind illuminating the room?" Anubis asked him.

In an instant, hundreds of candles, old and new, threw their glow against the statues and fetishes formally hidden by shadows, distorting their features. Morrigan could now see what her senses had picked up—crimson stained the floor and painted the animal skulls that lined the walls. She recognized antelope and tiger skulls, their jaws cracked open in an eternal scream. There were raised platforms for each deity, gifts specific for each one draped over their statues or gathered at their feet. She recognized Legba, this statue more phallic than the other she'd seen, a half-drank bottle of rum beside him on a bed of dried tobacco leaves.

"You practice vodun," Libraean murmured as his eyes swept the room.

Anubis nodded as he rolled up his sleeves. For the first time, Morrigan noticed tiny scars interrupting the smooth plane of his dark umber skin. "I was a priest far before I was made immortal and remembered my true past," he explained. "The spirits speak to me now just the same as they did before.

It makes no difference to them." He grabbed Legba's rum and headed to a table where several tools had been laid out. When he'd retrieved a clean, glinting knife, he turned back around to face them. Again, he reminded her of Lucius, the same dance present in his widened pupils.

"I have to talk to Legba first," he explained. "Souls that have moved on can visit us, but to visit them, we must ask his permission. Though you could probably manage on your own," he said, winking at Morrigan, "I like to respect the old ways."

Morrigan nodded, stepping back to give him space. She sat on the floor behind him, assisting Libraean so he could follow suit. They both waited in silent reverence as Anubis knelt at the crux of his altars. The candlelight dimmed as he began to chant, the chamber reverberating with the low baritone of his voice as the heavy presence she'd felt earlier returned. The whispers floated about until they were directly in her ear, causing the hair on her arms to rise as if the world had been plunged into an early winter. Anubis's chanting grew louder as he sliced his palm, letting his blackened blood splatter Legba's edifice. He added a sprinkling of rum, the droplets agitating the candle fire with a hiss.

Libraean gripped her hand once more as the spirits of the dead filled the room, though she knew he could not see them. Dozens of faces studied her curiously, coming so close she could see inside their hollowed eyes. She realized they were trapped in the spaces between the realms, unhappy with their existence, recognizing she was the one who once helped such souls. Soon their moans and wails drowned out Anubis's voice and Morrigan felt pressed on all sides, their presence suffocating her.

There is nowhere for me to take you, she tried to tell them, but she couldn't speak, searching for Libraean's hand amidst the pressure. Instead, she grabbed another one, realizing it belonged to Legba, who pulled her up out of the swirling mire of spirits.

"Come, Mama Snake, you are needed elsewhere," he told her as he whisked her into the darkness. She shut her eyes instinctively against the wind as he sped her forward, opening them only when she felt his hand let her go.

She blinked, abruptly accosted by searing pain. She looked down to see she was sitting in a large copper bathtub. Her lower half throbbed, swirls of blood and afterbirth on the surface of the water. Incense drifted sleepily through the air as the sun streamed in through the window, drawing streaks across her face. Although she was in pain, she was wrapped in warm serenity.

She looked down to see two babies asleep on her chest, peaceful and still, their little heads sweet and warm as she took turns kissing them.

"Do you want me to help you to your bed?" her sister asked as she crouched down at the side of the pool, sweeping her long dark hair behind her.

"Not quite yet," Morrigan whispered, perfectly content to lay there with her babies for as long as she could.

Isis smiled, emptying a jug into the bath and releasing the scent of lilies and honey into the air. "Have you decided what you will call them?"

"Anubis," Morrigan said as she kissed the baby with a tuft of dark wispy hair, "and Horus." She kissed the one who looked hairless, white fuzz on his head.

"They are beautiful boys," Isis murmured, running her fingers over their little arms.

"I know you probably want to hold them, as they will soon be yours. I just cannot bear to let them go just yet."

"Take as much time as you need," Isis assured her. "I have surrounded this entire building with magic—not a mortal nor god will find us here."

Morrigan closed her eyes, focusing on the sensation of her little ones' skin on hers. Her heart screamed that they should remain there, for that is where they belonged, two souls created out of her own body, brought into the world through her pain. But her mind told her differently, pulling up tears from the depth of her soul and threatening to shatter her to pieces.

Isis came up behind her to put her cheek against hers. "Do not cry, sweet sister. You will see them again."

"You might have to bind me when you take them," she whispered sadly, though it felt good to have her own twin so close. "I do not think I can give them to you without a fight."

Isis turned her face and looked her in the eye. "Nephthys, this decision is still yours. You do not have to give them to me. We can find another way. Perhaps we can hide all of you from Set."

Morrigan shook her head miserably. "If I keep them, they will always be in danger, even when they are grown. He has to believe they are yours—it is what we decided. I cannot be selfish. I must do this for them."

"Then sit in this moment and enjoy this time with your sons," Isis said firmly. "Do not feel as though you are being rushed."

Morrigan gratefully obeyed, closing her eyes to listen to the sounds of their tiny breaths as she leaned back into the bath. A distant crow pierced the morning sky with its guttural croon. Confused, she opened her eyes, wondering how a crow had found its way into Egypt's skies. She looked down at her babies, holding them tighter as she sat upright, staring at Isis. "Who are you?" she demanded.

Isis smiled. "Do not worry, Morrigan. I am not Discordia. You are in the Middleworld, a place where she cannot reach. You created this memory as you arrived here; I only slipped in to play the part."

Morrigan continued to search her emerald eyes until she arrived at a realization. "You are David's lover."

"Well, technically so are you," she said pleasantly as she shifted back into her common visage, the curvaceous youth with freckled skin and blonde hair dusted with rose. "But yes, David knows me as Gaia, holder of one of the three pieces that make up your sister's soul."

"I came here to help Anubis and Libraean speak to Jacob's spirit," Morrigan suddenly remembered. "Why am I here?"

"It is more important that I speak to you," Gaia explained. "For I must tell you that David has been cast into Hell—Tartarus, if you will. I do not doubt his strength, but it has been weeks since he's resurfaced. I fear he may be trapped and need your help getting out."

Morrigan frowned, confused. "How can that be? David has been with us for the entirety of our trip."

Gaia shook her head. "His soul was summoned by the Holy Watchers right as he fell unconscious, bringing him to my realm in the Upperworld. Apparently their conversation did not fare well, for they promptly banished him to Hell. He has been trapped there ever since and Discordia has been wearing his face, acting like him as she collects power from all of you however she can."

Morrigan's heart thumped wildly as she started to rise, until she remembered the babies on her chest, which provoked her to pause.

"Time stays still here," Gaia assured her. "Do not worry about David at this moment. You must find a way to kill Discordia first, for it is only you who can succeed in doing so. Ending her life will help you save David's."

Morrigan struggled to maintain her composure. All this time, Discordia had been there, listening, observing. Sending her dreams to pull her away from Lucius. The babies stirred and she cradled them closer, their heads resting in the crook of her neck, taking another whiff of their hair as they nestled against her skin. Even though she knew it wasn't real, she didn't want to let them go.

"You will find the answers that you seek within you," Gaia told her.

"Why did I choose to come here when this is my most painful memory?"

"For many, the Middleworld acts as a limbo, where a soul becomes trapped in something they cannot get past. Perhaps your subconscious brought you here to show you something that you needed to see, that you could not see before." The color of her hair and eyes suddenly shifted, bringing back the image of her sister, Isis. She looked at her with sad, earnest eyes. "Though it pains me to tell you, it is time for you to go."

Morrigan felt the familiar rip within her heart as she thought of being separated from her babies. This is only a vision of what was, she reminded herself, though she began to sob. She knew it was time for her to move on. But as her sister reached out her hand to gently remove Anubis from her arms, she pulled him tighter, the water around her starting to bubble and churn.

Isis looked alarmed. "Nephthys, what is it?"

Morrigan met her sister's eyes. "Forgive me, sister, but they are coming with me."

"Now you understand," Isis said with a smile. "And so am I."

Her sister dissipated before her eyes, like particles of dust, finding their way into her lungs as she gasped. She shivered with the sudden influx of power, gathering the babies securely in her arms as the bath suddenly opened, swallowing her down into its depths.

Lucius

HE'D BARELY CLOSED THE DOOR TO HIS ROOMS BEHIND HIM when he heard a gentle knock. "It's open," he sighed, looking longingly towards the bedroom for the bottle of rum he'd come to retrieve.

"Sorry to disturb you," a pleasant voice said, entering the room as its owner followed.

Lucius brightened, the lingering anger from the recent upheaval dissipating quickly. "Thoth, what brings you to my area of the house?"

"It's Thomas now," he cheerfully corrected him. "I heard the commotion, but Anubis warned me not to intervene. I was planning, however, on checking in with you to see how you were faring, and I figured a well visit would be even more appropriate now."

"Ah yes, do come in." Lucius pulled out a chair for him. He ducked into his bedroom to grab the bottle of rum, trying not to think about Morrigan, though his entire room smelled of cedarwood and fallen leaves. He hurried to fetch two glasses, and took a seat across from his old friend. He paused to admire his new visage, the dark brown eyes behind wire glasses, his high cheekbones and stately nose. "This is a good look for you. Very similar to how you once appeared to me."

Thomas beamed. "I suppose it was in the stars. I have to tell you, I was so distraught once you became a blood drinker and I could no longer reach you. I'm not sure exactly what happened."

Lucius sighed. "The feeling is quite mutual. I have it on good authority that it was Angelique's doing."

"That would make sense." Thomas looked thoughtful. "In any case, I'm glad you all made it here safely. We heard about your trouble with the creature in the ocean. This business about the realms is just dreadful."

"Now if only we could reach a place of accord, we might be able to resolve it," Lucius muttered as he took a sip of rum.

"So that explains the commotion earlier. When you arrived, I was hoping to hear that you'd found the raven woman from your dreams, and all was well." Thomas took a tiny sip from his glass.

"Almost," Lucius sighed. "En route to France, one of the humans we were traveling with fell ill. He was the lover of Libraean—Horus reincarnated, if you remember the story—so naturally, it is a very touchy subject. On his deathbed, he told me he was holding the memories I was still missing from a former life and that I should drink from him to receive them. He wanted a swift release from his suffering, so I obliged. However, my brother and Libraean found out and are quite furious with me." He paused to swallow down the rest of his glass, then poured himself another. "Anubis and Morrigan are talking to the spirits to confirm."

"Oh my," Thomas murmured.

"Hopefully Jacob will confirm that I was following his wishes. He was once the angel Gabriel, you know."

Thomas's eyebrows raised with interest. "Well, I suppose you are stuck playing the waiting game."

"Your company could not come at a better time," Lucius said. "So tell me the story of how you came to be here. The last I saw you, you were some sort of spirit."

"Well, I cannot say my story is too pleasant of a tale," Thomas said.

"My father fell for my mother—one of his slaves—skillfully hiding the affair from his wife even after I was born. I enjoyed a special sort of privilege being his only son, but as my complexion lightened and my features appeared more consistent with his, he sent me away to another family to work as a tutor. That is where I met Helena, the daughter of a prominent French Captain who owned a lucrative slave trading operation. She was born with a port wine stain that covered the entire left side of her body, tarnishing her porcelain skin to the ruin of her desirability. As we know, that's all the high society humans see women as—a bargaining chip." He sighed, folding his hands on the table.

"She and I bonded immediately," he continued, "both of us trapped in the place between privilege and scorn, accepted by many, but outcasts just the same. It was one day, while we were studying geography outside in the sun, that she suddenly blanched, stammering that she knew me from long ago. She ran back to the house to pull out every old text she could find, finally finding one about the Ancient Egyptians. My memories were quite hazy at that point, but the more she spoke, the more certain I was that she was right. I had the innate ability to solve equations unlike anyone else, while she had been talking to spirits since she was a child. Eventually, she and I were drawn to the salons of France, where our minds were filled with enlightened thinking, quickly becoming swept up in the protests of the abolitionists."

Lucius nodded. "Oh yes, I found myself equally drawn to the salons, as you might remember. Though I did end up partaking in a more violent insurrection."

Thomas blinked. "I never thought to put that together. I knew you were headed to become king, but instead you escaped Angelique. Of course you were instrumental in her near beheading; I cannot believe I didn't see it."

Lucius shrugged. "We can speak of storming the Bastille later. You were telling me about yourself."

"Ah yes." Thomas leaned back in his chair. "Helena and my antics were never caught by her father, but eventually he brought us with him to Africa, to where we are now. Then it was known as the Kingdom of Whydah. Anubis was a human when we met him, the High Priest who served the king, but he and Helena discovered each other and he pieced together who we all were. You see, we died together in the Underworld, not long after you and Nephthys did."

"She goes by Morrigan now," Lucius explained. "She was the raven woman from my dreams as a child."

"Ah, that makes sense. It would make things easier if we all just kept our Egyptian names, wouldn't it?" Thomas smiled. "Not long after we figured all this out, Shokpana, the god of plagues, arrived on our shores, bringing with him a disease unlike anything we had ever seen. It wiped out the entire French settlement, infecting Helena and I, and trickling out onto the unsuspecting kingdom. It was madness, humans dying in droves.

"By this time, Anubis and Helena had become lovers and he broke into the compound to be at her side. He grew sick with us and for a moment, we believed all was lost. What we didn't know was that Shokpana, who went by the name Lesplaies at the time, brought Sandrine with him. She found Anubis and turned him so that he might live, causing his powers to heighten while restoring his memories. He found and turned me just in time, but Helena was not so lucky. But she did not cease to exist as we assumed would happen; instead, she found herself stationed in a place quite like the astral plane, where the African vodun live. It enables her to walk the middle realms, to eavesdrop where she can. She taught us how to travel on that plane ourselves, which was how I was able to visit you in the mid-eighteenth century and how Anubis finally reached Cahira. Though it proves much more difficult for us than her."

"Morrigan and I met Helena a little bit ago," Lucius told him. "She also told us that Sandrine has a piece of Isis's soul."

"Correct." Thomas nodded. "All the original gods are together at last."

"For now," Lucius sighed. He wondered how things were going with Anubis and Morrigan, and if they had contacted Jacob's spirit.

There was another knock at the door.

Lucius's heart leapt and his body followed suit, throwing open the door without hesitation. He scowled when he realized it was only Cahira. "Where is she?" he demanded.

"Calm yourself, Romeo, we need to talk first." Cahira breezed past him. She looked surprised to see Thomas seated at the table. "Oh, hello," she said awkwardly, her confident demeanor slightly deflating.

Thomas rose from his chair, staring at her with a strange look on his face.

"I don't know if you've had a chance to become acquainted, but this is Thomas, the reincarnated god Thoth," Lucius introduced him. "I have known him well in this life."

"Why are you staring at me like that?"

Thomas blinked, looking flustered. "Forgive me, I can see things that others can't, like the pieces of matter that make up a human's body—it's why I can solve equations so quickly," he hurriedly explained. "You—you have the same father as Anubis."

Cahira looked at him askance as Lucius scoffed.

"That is not possible," Lucius argued. "She was born out of the lineage started by Discordia and myself—there is no way David is her father. I refuse to believe it." He paused his outburst when he caught the look on Thomas's face. A shiver crawled down his back as he grew still. "Oh. You mean me."

"How is that even possible?" Cahira put her hands on her hips.

"Superfecundation is rare in animals and extremely rare in humans," Thomas explained, "but you weren't human then; you were gods. There were really no set laws at the beginning."

Lucius fell into his seat, stunned. "So we did have children together," he murmured, trying to wrap his mind around it. The urge to see her overwhelmed his body and he took a deep, steadying breath to remain still.

"Look, I'm sorry to interrupt this moment for you," Cahira broke in, "but they spoke to Jacob and he confirmed that you killed him."

"Yes, and?" Lucius raised his eyebrow. "Does David know?"

"We decided not to tell him yet—to protect both of you."

Lucius rose to his feet. "Fine. I need to talk to Morrigan."

Cahira blocked his path. "She isn't here right now," she told him carefully.

He didn't like the look on her face. "What do you mean she's not here?"

"I was told she left right after they spoke with Jacob."

"Yes, but the angel told them it was his idea, right? He asked me to end his suffering and returned my memories—did he tell them that?" Lucius felt his heartbeat climb in his chest. He smelled power rising that wasn't his, realizing Cahira was preparing for him to explode. Then it dawned on him that this was the reason they sent her—they anticipated an outburst because something was wrong. He sensed Thomas slowly backing away from them.

"He did tell them the truth," Cahira said, her voice taking on a slow and deliberate tone as she held him in the mirror of her eyes. "But she disappeared without telling us why, only insisting that no one come after her."

"You let her run away?" His anger grabbed hold of him with blazing fists as it pushed rationality out of his mind and replaced it with frantic possibilities. A part of him tried to fight it, knowing he'd succeeded at keeping it at bay thus far, but the other part of him screamed to stop wasting time—*I have to find her, she couldn't be far, I could follow her scent…*

There was a loud pop and every single candle in the room burst to life, surprising Cahira enough that he pushed past her. He darted through the hall, picking up speed until he was blocked by Anubis. He'd reached the point of franticness, barely able to search his eyes for answers. "Where is she?" he demanded.

Anubis looked crestfallen, though he tried to present a strong facade. Lucius tried to quiet his racing heart and the blood rushing in his ears so he could focus on his words.

"We don't know where she went," Anubis told him. "She took off while I was still in a trance. Helena said she left and wanted no one to follow her. Come, let's talk about this before we overreact—"

But then, in perhaps the worst timing conceivable, David appeared from behind him, wearing an angry scowl that revealed he had indeed discovered the truth about Jacob. But it was no matter, for Lucius could hear the calm part of him crying as it stumbled and fell, its pleas for peace stifled, while his rage stood above it as the proud victor, filling his eyes with a bright and blinding red before his entire world went black.

Lucius wrenched his eyes open to total darkness and a pounding headache. He felt pressure at his wrists, and realized he had been chained to the wall of what appeared to be an old cellar. He sat up as his eyes adjusted, discovering a single torch positioned far enough away that he couldn't use it to his advantage, but brightening the room so he could see a figure sitting smugly across the room. It was David.

"You can't deny the irony," he remarked. "As many times as you've set me up to die, now you're the one at my mercy."

"I only succeeded once, as did you," Lucius pointed out dryly. "I would say we are even."

"Ah, but you never really die, do you? This time will be different. After all these years of haunting my existence, you will finally be gone with no realm to return to."

"What happened?"

"As usual, you let your anger get the best of you." David leaned back in his chair. "You lunged at me, but before you or I could raise any power,

Cahira caused the Earth to tremble so violently, it threw us all off balance. A statue hit the back of your head and I grabbed you, flying you here before anyone else could intervene. There are some things that need to be resolved just between brothers."

Lucius surveyed the room, taking note of the dank mud that created the walls, and bits of crumbled brick and rat bones cluttering the corners. He felt the presence of deceased souls lingering nearby. "Where are we?"

David crossed his arms. "About a century ago, this was the site of King Haffon's palace. After the plague swept through the village, the Africans who survived buried who they could, mainly their own people. They threw the rest, French settlers and unclaimed African villagers, together into the palace and burned it to the ground. It is rumored that the gods were so angry over the entire affair that they didn't let the bodies burn, keeping them intact forever. Because of this, the souls could never move on, imprisoned in decrepit flesh that never fell away. It is rumored they rise from their graves at night, wandering the plains and feasting on the flesh of men."

Lucius raised an eyebrow.

"I don't know if that story is actually true, but we are proof that the spirit world does not obey the rational laws of man." David rose from his chair. "Nevertheless, I thought this would be a perfect place for you to meet your end. If you are not torn apart by the desperate souls trapped here, then you will rot here for the rest of your days. No one knows where this place is and no one will hear you scream. Morrigan has finally come to her senses and left you and when I find her to reconcile, I'll let her know you are gone for good. I highly doubt you will be missed."

Lucius narrowed his eyes. "If you want to keep playing David, love, you have to remember that he is the good brother and I am the bad one. He doesn't taunt, no matter how mad he is over something I've done. And I am the one who pines relentlessly for Morrigan, he just broods and flirts with death. You've gotten your script wrong."

"I had you all fooled for quite a while," David said as his eyes snapped back to red. "You have to admit it was an incredible ruse."

"I will give you that," Lucius said. "Where is she truly?"

"Oh, Morrigan leaving you again was quite real," Discordia informed him, still wearing David's body but revealing her mannerisms. "I had no part in that. As soon as she found out you killed the liminal's lover, she left without a word. It's been days and she still hasn't returned. That's how I'm certain no one will come looking for you as you rot away down here with no blood, no books, no fire, no wife—nothing but damp earth and misery." She smiled and sat back down in her chair, crossing one leg neatly over the other. "It's my guess that Morrigan finally made her decision. You had to know she'd eventually choose your brother. She always does, no matter how many times you try to fool yourself. I mean, look at me. I'm deliciously handsome, am I not? You'll never be good enough for her—why else would she completely abandon you without telling you where she was going?"

Lucius didn't respond. He knew she was just trying to provoke him, but her words still managed to sting. He'd been down here for days? He licked his lips, disappointed they no longer tasted like her.

"In fact, I found this earlier, hidden in your chambers." Discordia pulled out an old book that had been wedged behind her chair.

Lucius winced. He had stolen it from under Libraean's nose, trapped in conflict for weeks whether to read its contents.

"Apparently, you also doubt her, otherwise you wouldn't need to read what he added to her memoirs."

"I didn't read it," he growled.

"Then allow me to assist." Discordia flipped through the pages. "Ah, right here: 'She could no longer bear to be associated with Set, the detestable god of death, realizing that although he pleased her physically, she did not love him. Instead, she found herself drawn to the light, seeing freedom from bondage in Osiris's eyes. To her, he represented goodness, and his unwavering love for her meant that she was also good. For every note he wrote to her, pledging his devotions, he received one in return, where she poured out her heart to him in verse.' Did you know that bit? That she wrote to him as well? Surely you knew that."

Lucius was silent.

Discordia continued, thoroughly enjoying his discomfort. "'On the night she finally escaped from Set, she found refuge at their Earthly palace. After her sister had fallen asleep, she returned to the Nile where she met Osiris and taught him how to make the physical act of love. So strong was the love between them, that she became the first goddess to produce godly sons in her womb. Though the lovers were elated, they feared Set's retribution and hatched a plan to deceive him. The pregnant Nephthys went into exile, hiding away until her children were born.'"

"I know this story, love, you'll have to do better than that," Lucius finally spoke up, though a dismal feeling had crept into his chest.

"And yet, you still keep believing she won't run away…oh, now that is amusing." She snapped the book shut. "That is precisely what she just did."

Again, Lucius was silent.

"The most curious part of it all, is that I cast a spell long beforehand that would make reincarnated gods lose their memories. It was originally intended for Hera and Athena, should they make their way to Earth after I killed them. Yet when Morrigan and David rose to Earth, waking up to each other with no memories, they still fell in love. In fact, they fell in love again in Romania, and again in recent days. That is a love that transcends all time—the truest love of all. You have no part in any of it."

"Are you going to continue your blathering or can the corpses eat my flesh now?" Lucius asked, though he struggled not to succumb to his emotions.

Discordia smiled. "Though you present me with a face of stone, you know my words strike true. Tell David I said hello when you see him in Tartarus."

Lucius blinked. "You sent him there?"

"It was a happy accident," Discordia informed him. "The Watchers tried to convince him to kill you again, along with the others, but he refused."

"You plan to return and kill the rest of them with both of us gone," Lucius realized.

"I promised the African gods I would spare Anubis and Thoth, but I will absorb the rest of them. If I am going to be the only goddess left on Earth, then I should be all-powerful. Oh, and I suppose I can tell you now—I pretended to be Anubis's wife so I could steal some of his magic. I was so deeply inspired by the story of this place, that I decided to be the one to raise the dead and tear you apart. Now, if you'll excuse me, I'm off to kill your wife. Goodbye, Set, and good riddance to you. You have been a pain in my side for far too long."

Lucius snorted, causing her to whip around.

"What is so amusing?"

"I am not the pain in your side, Discordia. Morrigan is. You loathe her because you cannot be her, although you have spent your entire existence trying to do exactly that."

Discordia flinched ever so slightly behind David's frown.

"The only reason you hate me is because I won't use you as her substitute. I won't pretend along with you, no matter how clever your disguise. I know the difference between a real goddess and an imposter. Because that is what you are: a miserable fraud who has to scrape and claw her way into becoming something that can't even come close to Morrigan's magnificence. Even if you succeed in killing her, you will never, ever be the Great She."

She slammed him with the fire that rushed out of her fingers, but all it did was heat his skin enough to melt the chains from his wrists. "Damn you," she sneered as he smiled triumphantly.

She turned, focusing her energy on the ground instead. It trembled in response, and soon rotten fingers and decrepit arms clawed their way up through the dirt. She gave him one last victorious smile before abandoning him to the resulting chaos. Lucius soon found himself boxed in by dozens of reanimated corpses wearing nothing but bits of putrid skin and moldering linen as they reached for him out of their bed of dirt.

He noticed someone else standing in the doorway, shocked to see it was Libraean, who stared at the scene unfolding before him with wide eyes.

"Discordia has been masquerading as David," he called to him as he began to pool together his powers of fire, the nearby torch growing in flame. "Tell the others and when they don't believe me, have Thomas look at him."

"We already know—let me help you," Libraean called back, though he seemed frozen by shock, unprepared for the nightmarish visual assaulting his senses.

"Open the portal to Tartarus," Lucius said as one of the undead finally pulled itself free. It lunged, and he snapped its neck hard enough that the force removed its head. Lucius threw it against the wall with a resounding splat, but its jaws continued to open and shut after it landed in the dirt, its rotten tongue lapping the air in fruitless fervor. "Open the portal and get out of here as fast as you can."

Libraean stayed frozen as he took in the implication of what was just said.

Cahira streaked into the room, also stopping dead in her tracks. "What the he—"

"These are undead; you cannot control them like you can animals," Lucius informed her, growing more frustrated with the interruptions as he narrowly avoided another corpse that lurched in his direction. "I'm taking them with me to Tartarus—I believe David is trapped there. I will also look for your wolf. Now help Libraean open the portal and get the hell out of here so I don't take you both down too!"

Cahira nodded, her expression shifting between hopeful and worried as she grabbed Libraean's hand, pushing her power into his palms as he closed his eyes in concentration. Lucius ripped the head off another creature, catching Cahira's attention with his eyes. "Tell Morrigan—" His voice caught in his throat. "Just tell her I still love her."

Before Cahira could respond, he let go of every emotion he had been holding in—from the refreshed agony of losing the twins to the thought of Morrigan leaving him again—letting his anger extend from the tips of his fingertips, embodying the dragon in human flesh, until the entire chamber was consumed again by flame, taking the reanimated corpses down with him.

CHAPTER EIGHT

❧ The Hangbe Warrior ❧

Africa,
Sandrine

S HE SAW THE BUZZARDS CIRCLING ABOVE, but was not afraid like the others. She heard a few weeping nearby, moaning for their mothers, but she knew better than to indulge in such things. She had to save her strength. There was no one coming to rescue them—they had to save themselves or die.

She thought about the day her mother and father handed her over to the future queen, recalling the burns on her skin left from struggling against the men who dragged her from her home. She turned cold the moment they threw her in the cage with the other girls, refusing to show any weakness while they cried. Eventually, the girls talked amongst each other, but she kept to herself. She knew the true reason they were there. Queen Hangbe worshiped the old gods, and her cult hunted for a girl strong enough to bear the spirit of the Great Egyptian Goddess. Most would not survive the process, and those who did would either inherit the goddess's power or be deemed strong enough to become one of the queen's personal guards. Her mother had warned her the moment she woke up to her first blood. She knew that Sandrine—Ekhorose, as she was known then—was exactly the sort of girl Hangbe was looking for.

"I don't need borrowed power. I am strong enough on my own," young Sandrine informed the queen when she visited her cell after the process.

She didn't care that her body now shook with power; she was still incensed by the way they tied her to the floor, holding her down as the soul of Isis entered her body and found a resting place beside her own soul. Although she could hear the small whisper of the ancient goddess, learning she was far from overbearing or cruel, Sandrine knew she didn't belong there.

Queen Hangbe was undeterred, beaming down at her as she dabbed her sweaty skin with a moistened cloth. "You will be my first in command and preside over my army. You will have power over the others, whether you approve or not. I think you will decide to use the Goddess's Gifts. She chose to give them to you." Then the queen stood, offering Sandrine one last smile before she withdrew, her bright robes sweeping the dusty floor behind her.

I will prove otherwise, Sandrine thought as she drifted off to sleep. Throughout the training that immediately followed, Sandrine never once needed her extra power, and this current time was no different. She would pass this trial like the others before it.

She allowed herself a few more moments to rest under the poor shade of the dust storm, trying to gather enough saliva in her mouth to swallow. The act split her parched lips, but the sharp pain was nothing compared to the ache of her dehydrated muscles, which screamed as she climbed to her feet. She paused to adjust before moving forward, keeping her movements slight and her breathing steady, lest she faint like the girls behind her.

It was not the physical suffering that bothered her—she'd long learned life was nothing but suffering—it was the sounds the others made, and the haunting knowledge that she was physically unable to help them, lest she fall victim to the sun's hellacious rays herself. She ignored their weeping and focused on her feet, ripped and raw from the harsh desert floor. One step at a time. Step, step, step. Step into the dust, lift your foot, watch the wind take it away. Step, step, step, the steps won't let you faint.

She couldn't recall how many steps she took, her vision nothing more than black fluttering patches. But miraculously, she reached the bushes that bordered the village and promptly collapsed. When she awoke, she was inside the compound, aloe vera salve applied to her peeling, sunburnt skin and her blistered feet wrapped in gauze. She shivered with pain, unable to clearly see the woman who squeezed drops of water into her mouth. It was after several days of convalescence that she realized it was once again the queen.

Hangbe was dressed in billowing robes of white, her head wrapped in a matching scarf, pulling at her temples. "Some may think my methods are cruel," she offered. "But I know what lies outside our village. I not only want to see who can withstand suffering, but how quickly you can heal. I am surprised you have not once used the powers gifted to you."

Sandrine panicked, wondering if she'd failed.

The queen seemed to read her mind. "You and three other girls have withstood the trials. The rest have died. You will finish your healing and join the other warriors. Though you have not used your gifted powers, I still want you as commander. You are undoubtedly strong without them."

Sandrine let the memory fade. She sighed, her eyes sweeping the empty shell that was once their training center. Roofless, with only three dilapidated walls remaining upright in the dirt, it was merely a ghost, but she could still hear the grunts and groans of women fighting. She could even smell the sweat and spilled blood, and taste the fresh stew slopped into their bowls. The queen always served the leanest cuts of meat, insisting it was better to grow the muscles and strengthen the bones. It was a great pleasure for many of the women, but Sandrine's great pleasure had always been the fight.

Was it that long ago that she had transformed her body into a perfect warrior, standing at the head of a ruthless army with the hope of a new world booming in her chest? Her gaze moved across the plain to the capital. Abomey dozed to the sound of buzzing insects and the distant chattering of hyenas, a false sense of security behind the tall mud wall and five foot ditches filled with prickly acacia branches. It was how the kings maintained their rule—terrifying their subjects into blind obedience, preying on their desire to be protected from the outside terrors. But no one was safe from sacrifice; the kings cared nothing of human life beyond their own.

I have killed too many kings, Anubis had written to her. They tell me he is different, that the kingdom will transform from one drenched in blood money to one that survives off her natural bounty. He created farms to harvest the oil, but he has filled them with slaves. He signed the treaties, but he makes secret pacts with other kings. He promises to stop the sacrifices, but has a harem of ahosi that includes your warriors, and his throne is made of human skulls.

He knows I lurk in the shadows, protected by things he cannot see. He fears me so much that his militia exceeds far beyond any other king before me. No military has ever worried me. I kill the kings just the same. Yet he keeps his ahosi on the front line, sending them into all of his battles. Many of the women do not want to join his army, but they are forced— girls as young as thirteen. They all must disavow men, for in his eyes, they are married to him. When the white men come, he has the ahosi put on theatrical fights to entertain them, scaling giant walls barbed with Acacia, miming hand to hand combat while the crowd cheers them and judges their performances. It is unclear if the winners or the losers are sent to the bedrooms of the guests, but if one of these unions happen to be fruitful, they are swiftly sentenced to death.

It is for this reason that I think his death should be yours.

Most of his letters she'd burned, but this one she'd kept, folded neatly into a small pocket in her boot. It had long since disintegrated, but it became a symbol of her mission. She never questioned how the letters found her, no matter where she ended up, instead relying on the last surviving piece of her human life, given to her by the poor young man she once forced into becoming a creature like her.

She remembered his eyes, bulging out of a narrow face as he searched hers frantically, struggling to scoop air into laboring lungs. His ebony skin had been riddled by pustulous sores, his organs struggling to function, his teeth chattering although he was hot to the touch. "Are you my real mother?" he whispered, delirious, trying to reach out to touch her face.

"Not exactly," she told him, cradling his head in her lap. "But you are dying, Anubis. You have been kept half-alive by the blood of an immortal creature who wants to steal your power. But I can turn you into a being like me to take away your fever."

The young man moaned. "My wife…"

Sandrine recalled the emaciated Frenchwoman she'd found, barely alive in his arms. "It is too late for her."

"Thomas…he is a god," he gasped.

She had assumed then that he'd reached the point of delirium. "You can save him yourself if you let me save you now. I have to get you off this ship before he returns."

He had closed his eyes then, his hand resting on her arm. "Please."

She'd sunken her teeth into his neck, but it was unlike any human she'd ever fed from. His blood was fresh but ancient, like an aged wine, bursting with secrets that threatened to overwhelm her own mind. She saw his life in Egypt, the mother who looked like the soul who lived inside her, the spirits, the dark realms. She heard the angry echoes of the vodun gods she knew from childhood, drawing in to stop her. She let him go, forcing him to pull blood from her neck as she carried him out of the ship and into a nearby cave. She had no time to watch him turn, worried that he'd have no guidance, but an old woman spirit with rich eyes put a hand on her shoulder. "Kill the one who caused this. I will take care of my son," she promised.

After that moment, it seemed Anubis and Sandrine were tied together forever, two gods who had reincarnated into a larger purpose—to walk the fine line between the wars waged in the spiritual realms and the atrocities created by humanity.

Over time, she observed many reincarnated gods abandoning their human lives completely, remembering their godly ones the strongest, but even decades after Angelique turned her, Sandrine felt tied to her humanity. She wondered if it was because her life as Medusa was fleeting, or that her soul was tied to an older one she had no memory of. Or perhaps, it was what she told Cahira years ago—she came back exactly how and when she needed to, so she could help the humans who depended on her.

In any case, she found the blood of treacherous men to taste the sweetest, and she had been on Lucius's ship without indulgence for much too long.

She scaled the wall with little effort, slipping around the guards that patrolled the gates. A few torches burned along its borders, but the village was dark, the royal palace not far ahead. Soldiers moved listlessly between the fields and huts, armed with their long knives, some men, some women, all dressed in the colors of the king. She avoided them all as she reached the thick mud bricks of his palace walls, and heard the low rumbling laughter of night guards as they waited for their shift to end. A single woman soldier stood staring out into the distance as if she could sense something.

Sandrine slipped up behind her, silencing her with her hand before she could scream. "I am looking for Iziegbe," she whispered in her ear. "My name is Ekhorose, and I once served Queen Hangbe." She ignored the shiver down her back that saying her original name caused.

The woman nodded, and Sandrine gradually released her grip.

The soldier motioned to follow her, taking Sandrine down a long corridor into a room illuminated by dozens of candles. A group of women wrapped in silk lounged amongst pillows, apprehending them with frightened eyes. Being in close proximity with so many humans brought saliva to Sandrine's mouth, but she pushed aside her hunger.

A petite woman sat in the middle, noticeably older than the rest. Her face was locked in awe as she rose, her skirts a vivid pink, and her hair cropped tightly around lined but soft features. "Are you her?" she whispered.

Sandrine nodded.

Iziegbe took her immediately by the hand, guiding her into another room with hundreds of brightly colored fabrics hanging on the walls. It reeked of scented oils, lavish pieces of jewelry spread out on display.

Sandrine scowled with recognition. "No," she said. "I will meet him as I am."

"They will kill you unless they think you are one of his wives," Iziegbe insisted.

Sandrine grabbed her by the back of her neck, letting the candlelight hit her face so she could clearly see her radiant eyes and glinting, pointed teeth. "Child, I am not afraid of men."

Iziegbe nodded quickly, her frantic eyes wide. "Follow the smaller hall through the doorway," she stammered. "He is sleeping, but the warriors surround him."

Sandrine released her, and she ran back to the others.

Sandrine pulled out the thin knife she kept in her boot near Anubis's letter. There were only two male guards who lunged for her as she pried open the door, but she snapped both of their necks easily. Their bodies crumpled to the ground as the women guards rose to their feet. They did not lunge, however, backing away from the king's bed instead.

King Ghezo sputtered obscenities as he watched them quietly leave the room.

He turned his venom towards Sandrine. "You are not him!" he spat. He looked like a sad old man wearing nothing but his undergarments, wiry gray hair twisting around his birdcage chest. It was a far cry from the image his statues and paintings boasted, where he stood regal, draped in expensive fabrics and jewels with a gaudy crown positioned atop his head.

"No, I am not him." Sandrine smiled.

"I tried to end the trade, but it has been a ruling principle of my people—a source of glory and wealth! I cannot end it just because white men tell me so. The songs of my people celebrate our victories, the mother lulls the child to sleep with notes of triumph over an enemy reduced to slavery—"

"I am not a white man," Sandrine said dryly. "I am a goddess and an original Hangbe Warrior. I have come to kill you as a service to the women and children enslaved and massacred, I care nothing about your politics."

"If you kill me, my son will only follow in my footsteps!"

"Then Anubis will kill him. We will continue to hunt corrupt kings for the rest of days. We are immortal, but kings are not." Then in one swift movement, she slid her knife right into the soft part of his eye, up into his brain. He fell to his knees, stunned, as snakes crawled out from her curls.

As soon as he saw them, he petrified, the stone capturing his look of stupefied horror. She wiggled her knife out of his socket, satisfied that even if someone managed to melt her curse, he was left with a brain too useless to live. Her knife was still wet with his blood and brain matter, and she slid her tongue across it, savoring the taste. Yes, she thought with a smile. The more corrupt the man, the sweeter the taste.

One of the women guards crept back in, looking down at the floor where he cowered. "I will tell Glele it is done," she said with a nod.

Sandrine grabbed her arm, staring straight into her dark eyes. "If the next king does not live up to what he promises, tell Anubis to find me again."

The warrior nodded, shifting her arm so that her hand wrapped around Sandrine's, a gesture of camaraderie. "Thank you for your help."

Sandrine dipped her head in solemn reply before bolting out the way she came, letting the palace slowly awaken to chaos. She leapt back over the wall, landing far from the trench, and paused to delicately tuck her blade back into her boot. Then she took a deep breath, and headed back to Anubis's home.

Her path was swiftly blocked by a man she hadn't sensed approaching, causing her to jump back and brace for attack.

"My name is Xevioso," he said in a deep, graveling voice. "I am a blood drinker, the reincarnation of the god of thunder. You killed one of ours for their war. You are brave to come back here."

"Shokpana deserved to die," Sandrine said calmly. "Besides, it was Anubis who summoned me here."

Xervioso scoffed, rattling his beaded necklaces. "He is an imposter here as well. His soul is Egyptian."

"He has spent his entire life, human and immortal, here," she argued.

"It does not matter. You might be born with African blood, but you are one of them—your soul is Egyptian and Greek. You sailed here with Europeans. We are not the same."

"Does that mean you are against us in our spiritual war? Even though Anubis and I directly offer our aid and guidance to the Dahomian people?"

"The white man's God does not intervene, he allows. The Ancient Ones do not intervene beyond death. But the African gods are one with the humans and their spirits—we guide, protect, and help them. We do not interfere in the affairs of other gods. Why should we? We exist because our people call it to be so. They take us to different lands, hide us under different names. They keep us alive, therefore we keep them alive. They come first above all else. You must decide which sort of god you wish to be. Anubis has made his choice."

"So you do not care what happens to them in death?" Sandrine asked. "Because that is what we are attempting to resolve. If there are no godly realms, there is no place for souls to rest."

"We concern ourselves with life."

"But death is a part of life," Sandrine argued. "You would have them be trapped in the Middleworlds, never able to find peace?"

"I don't expect you to understand our ways," he said, crossing his arms. "Even as a human, you were more concerned with the physical world than the spirit world."

"Well, I'm not going anywhere until my task is completed. You're welcome for killing your diabolical king."

Xevioso shook his head. "It doesn't matter how many human kings you kill, they will continue to replace them."

"Yes, but one day, it will end. And you will have Anubis and I to thank for it." She turned away, swiftly ending their conversation.

He didn't follow, retreating into the night as she continued on towards Anubis's home.

She sensed something wasn't right the moment she saw the cluster of palm trees that kept the house hidden from view. The magic surrounding it had been dismantled, and the sea was furious, although there was no wind. She broke into a sprint towards the house, throwing the door open to see the interior had been upended by volatile air and water, the floor still slick and water dripping from the ceiling.

Anubis stood at the window, staring at the violent ocean as each wave brought it closer to where the house began.

"What happened?" she asked. "Where's Cahira?"

Anubis turned to look at her, studying her face. Although worry tensed his jaw, she was reminded how handsome his features were, youthful even with the ancient blood coursing through his veins. It was remarkable how much he looked like Morrigan, though they wore totally different bodies, separated by miles of ocean. "Did you kill him?" he asked.

"Of course, I did," Sandrine replied, coolly. "Although it doesn't seem to matter to the African gods."

Anubis snorted, but seemed pleased by her response. "Good," he said as he headed into the room closest to the decimated room they stood in.

"What are you doing?" she asked as she followed him. It was an office,

Spartan compared to the rest of the house, only a mahogany desk and a cabinet inside four bare walls.

"I have to relocate again," he sighed as he opened one of the drawers. He gathered a few papers, folding them before tucking them into his pockets. "The safest place for me now is the temple. Glele knows where I live. If he decides he doesn't want to risk me staying here, he will send his soldiers."

"What about the others?"

Anubis sighed. "There was an altercation and everyone scattered. My mother left with no explanation, and Cahira and Libraean are out searching for the others. They both have enough power to find us. The temple is comfortable enough that we can wait until we receive word," Anubis explained. "If Glele does not attack my home, then we can return."

Sandrine nodded. "What would you like me to do?"

Anubis gave her a half-smile. "You can do whatever you want, Hangbe General. You can enjoy your victory however you'd like—I do think you've earned it."

"I will celebrate when Angelique is dead," Sandrine told him. "Though apparently, I must decide what sort of goddess I should be."

Anubis's soft blue eyes met hers. "Ah, you've been talking to Xevioso. He must have gotten back already. He does not like me very much, nor does he approve of my loyalty to the other gods, despite me saving his life." He took a seat on top of his desk, folding his arms across his chest.

"As a human, I never questioned the concept of the vodun, but after I learned about my past and the other gods, I was surprised to discover how many of them resided in the Middleworld, acting as spirits. They are quite content to stay out of the affairs of others, an entirely autonomous existence centered around the humans that need them. It was strange to me at first, for I have worked peaceably along other gods for eons without question. But eventually, I came to the conclusion that they have lived that way for thousands of years—and who am I to change them? I might have blood ties to them and the people I now serve, but I am Anubis, the guardian of the Underworld, and that is who I will be, regardless of what body I inhabit. If there is no Underworld to tend to, then I will help where I can on Earth until I die. I think you saw that in me, long ago, when you turned me into a blood drinker."

Sandrine nodded. "An old woman whispered in my ear who you were. When I saw you, I knew she was right."

A look of sadness flashed over his eyes, though his lips turned up into a smile. "The woman who raised me, Mama Mawu. She died right before the plague came to us." He looked thoughtful for a moment, his eyes drifting out the window like Morrigan often did. "Perhaps we can make a new class of gods," he suggested, "ones that both intervene in the lives of humans and in the affairs of the gods."

Sandrine smiled. "Perhaps you are on to something there."

"Oh, hello, Sandrine," Thomas's soft, melodious voice interrupted. "Has our latest problem been resolved?"

"The human one," she replied.

"Oh, wonderful," Thomas said before turning to Anubis. "We cannot go to the temple. Helena says it is filled with guards. Apparently, there was a massive fire at the old plague burial site and people are panicked. Fortunately, this means you are not being hunted."

"But for how long?" Anubis's brows furrowed as he put his hands on his hips, contemplating their next move.

"We should wait here," Cahira said as she strode into the room. Relief washed over Sandrine, glad to see she was still alive.

The liminal crept up sadly behind her, Anubis appearing just as relieved to see him. He went up to give him a gentle hug before holding his shoulders as he stared at him. "Where did you go?"

Libraean sighed. Sandrine was struck by his appearance next to Anubis, his weathered skin still accumulating wrinkles, his white hair growing thinner with time. How strange it must be to have immortal blood flowing through your veins, but to feel yourself age regardless. Although his one eye stayed clouded and unmoving, the one that matched Anubis's held the knowledge of a thousand worlds. "First, is David here?" he asked.

Anubis shook his head. "He was irate even before I arrived."

"That is because he was Discordia in disguise," Libraean sighed. "We have all been made the fool."

Sandrine's eyes widened, taken by surprise. It was quickly replaced by anger. "Angelique was here the entire time?"

"Yes," Libraean told her as Anubis helped him to a chair that hadn't been ruined by the flood. "I lost you all when we contacted the spirits, but I found Gabriel. He revealed it all to me—that he forced Lucius to drink from him because he wanted to die, that Jesus needed him, and that he held Lucius's lost memories over his head so he would do it. He told me that the creatures who have overthrown Heaven, the Holy Watchers, are the ones who contracted Discordia to destroy us all. They tried to enlist David to assist, but when he refused, they cast him into hell, allowing Discordia to take over his body."

"Then that is where Morrigan must be—hunting Discordia," Anubis realized. "We need to find her immediately. Where is Lucius?"

"He has gone into Hell to retrieve David and Dan," Cahira told him in an uncharacteristically soft voice.

Anubis looked taken aback. "He has?"

Libraean confirmed his question with a nod. "I think we should wait here until they all return."

"I don't feel particularly at ease with my mother out there alone," Anubis looked out to the tumultuous sea. His eyes traveled back towards Libraean. "Our mother."

"I can go out and look for her," Cahira offered, addressing Anubis. "After all, she is my mother too. But before I do, there is something Thomas and I need to tell you about your father."

ANUBIS

THE TEMPESTUOUS WIND HAD MADE VIOLENCE OF THE SEA, but Anubis walked down the shore unaffected, his bare feet sinking into the sand. The squalls that whipped around him roared in his ears, but it was no match for the thoughts crowding his mind. He tried not to think, for he knew all was handled, but the emotion trapped in his throat begged for release.

Before he realized where he was going, his legs instinctively carried him to a grotto, one he hadn't entered for many years. The steady drip of water was a welcome reprieve from the billowing wind, but the scent of cool, dank earth and stale sea water brought him back to the time when he was human.

He could almost see her silhouette against the candlelight, almost feel her heated breath on his skin. He squeezed his eyes shut, bracing himself for yet another intrusive memory that refused to stay buried. Soon the revolting stench of burning flesh bit his nose, tortured screams filling his ears. Too tired to resist, he slipped to the ground, succumbing to the obstinate pull of memory.

It was the moment he turned.

He hadn't realized he'd died, for it wasn't unusual for him to visit the spirit world unintentionally. But when his eyes opened to see the three doors and gray walls, he felt disoriented and confused, as if it had been a mistake. The feeling was compounded by the presence of Mama Mawu, who wore a youthful facade of fresh, unlined skin and supple lips as she looked down at him with love in her eyes.

"Why are you here?" Anubis was groggy, unable to lift his head off the stone floor she knelt upon.

"Be still, we only have moments," Mama told him. "Your body is dying, but your soul will remain."

Her words confused him until he remembered the plague, the raging fever that had gripped him, burning out his consciousness as he lay helplessly in the French compound among the sick and dying. "Helena," he remembered, bolting upright.

"It is too late for her," Mama told him sadly. "You must listen to me, child. When you wake up, you will no longer be human. You will be like the adze, a creature who needs blood to survive."

His jackal crept forward from the shadows, a welcome familiarity as it settled down next to Mama, its eyes aglow.

"I don't understand…" Anubis murmured. "Are you dead?"

"Shokpana's sickness took me long before the woman blood drinker killed you and gave you her blood," she replied. "Now hear me. When you rise, you will feel a hunger grip you unlike any other. Find an animal to eat so you can control yourself. Return to the village and save as many of our people as you can. There is madness there. King Agaja's army has swept through, thinking the kingdom weak with death. But the sickness created monsters, which drew the attention of wicked spirits. The humans are being forced to fight them all. You must save them."

"Wicked spirits?"

"Trust in me, child," Mama said. "You will see when you rise. Now it is time for you to know who you truly are and what you have left behind."

The jackal crept closer with no Legba to stop him.

"You will have your answers." She rose to her feet, stepping backwards with a sad smile. "Until we meet again."

Anubis tried to move forward to kiss her cheek, but the eyes of the jackal grabbed his attention, shining hematite stones penetrating his own. He gasped as he saw the pyramids of Egypt, heard the shriek of a kite, smelled the rushing black rivers of the Underworld. Every memory he'd ever lost came rushing back to him, assaulting his mind as he staggered, trying to make sense of it all. The jackal's howl echoed in his mind, finally succeeding in bringing him to his knees. And then the hunger hit, jolting him back to consciousness.

The craving burned every part of his body, demanding submission. His mind wanted to piece together all that had transpired but the thirst was stronger, lifting him out of the sand and catapulting him forward to the plains. He was shocked at how fast he moved, arriving at his destination in a matter of minutes with little exertion. Although it was night, everything around him seemed vivid, as if it had been infused with moonlight though the sky above held only distant stars. He found the herd of antelopes before they had a chance to sense him and he lunged clumsily, hearing Mama's words as he sunk his teeth into one of the poor beasts, sucking it dry and chucking it aside before chasing after another. The thirst did not quench until the last animal fell to the dirt, Anubis heaving for breath as the leftover blood dripped down his chin.

Then he remembered Helena.

He raced back towards the village, away from his carnage, realizing he'd become like David, like Lucius, like his mother once was. He was one of them—a blood drinking immortal, his past restored and at war with his human present. He was Anubis, the god of the Underworld, but he was also Helena's husband, and he was just as frantic now to find her as when he stumbled his way to her chambers, dying in his fevered human shell. He heard screaming and the laughter of hyenas before he saw billowing smoke, the entire village ablaze.

He saw glimpses of Agaja's warriors fighting what looked like beasts obscured by the thick smoke, but he rushed past them all into the French compound. Fire had yet to climb over its walls, but he had to fight through swarms of flies to reach her chambers, the smell of waste and decaying flesh souring the air. Even with heightened senses, he struggled to distinguish between which bodies carelessly thrown across the floor were dead and which were still alive. Skin both light and dark, French and African, all thrown together, dying in a heap of misery. The lack of human dignity made him sick but he pushed on, finding the door to her room still bolted shut. He used his weight to push it open, revealing her laying still on her bed, a slip of arm hanging out of the blanket, her hand already stiff. A dark liquid had dripped through the mattress and pooled on the floor. He rushed to her side regardless, and gathered her lifeless body into his arms.

The groan that escaped his lips sounded otherworldly, laced with a heart-shattering pain that transcended his immortality. He held her to his chest as his body shook, unable to reconcile his sorrow. Mama was right—he was too late. He tried not to picture her on the day they married, how the candlelit grotto brought warmth to her ghostly visage in lacey stays, since she'd refused to wear anything that looked like a formal gown. She'd let her light hair fall loose around her shoulders, twisting around layers of his beaded necklaces.

"We are not following my traditions or yours," had been her first stipulation when he asked her to be his wife. "No witnesses, no spirits, no recitations. Just you and I."

He had agreed, letting her plan it all, delighted to see the grotto she found and filled with flowers and candles. It brought a smile to his face that did not leave as they spoke promises to each other, nor when they made love afterwards on the damp, wax speckled floor.

He didn't want to let go of her now, but he heard a groan behind him and remembered Mama's instruction. He laid down the disease-ravaged body that had once held his wife's soul, draping her blanket back over her and kissing where it lay over her eyes.

He went to the heap of blankets across the room to find Thomas, emaciated with painful sores riddling his skin, remembering him now as his dear friend, Thoth. Anubis bit his neck immediately, before his mind started to wonder how he felt hunger where he once felt disgust, letting him fall back before cutting his own wrists as he'd seen others do, dripping blackened blood into his friend's open mouth.

Anubis fell back to gather his bearings. He wondered how long it would take, but the crackling sound of an approaching fire let him know they couldn't chance a lengthy wait. He lifted the still unconscious Thomas onto his shoulders, refusing to look back at Helena's corpse, and hurdled himself out the window of the compound.

The fire raged around the palace, slowly melting the mudbrick and going wild when it reached the straw rooftops. Anubis broke into a run, searching for a place where they could find refuge. He saw the convent still intact and hurried inside. The interior was dark and lifeless, untouched by the outside calamity. He laid Thomas gently down on the ground, and rose to begin searching to see if any priests survived.

"Leave this place," a haggard voice tried to sound intimidating, but failed.

Anubis saw Xevi's scrawny frame, barely able to stand. His hollowed face was covered in sores, sweat coursing down his skin. He held a knife loosely in his hand.

"Xevi, it's Anubis," he told him gently. "I've come back to save those I can."

"I do not need you to save me," Xevi insisted, though he swayed where he stood. Sickly yellow surrounded his dark eyes.

Anubis rushed to help him to the ground. "Reveal to me the wicked souls who fight us," he said.

"Can you not hear their laughter?" Xevi said through chattering lips, though his skin burned to the touch. "They are hyenas, possessed by magic to attack both the living and the dead."

Anubis frowned. "The dead?"

"The dead have risen to attack the living," Xevi said, closing his eyes. "The hyenas came to make sure no one is left alive, so the dead can rise again as mindless creatures, able to be controlled by dark magic. Someone has cursed this land." He erupted, spewing blood and froth onto the dirt.

The sight of it stirred Anubis, the hunger pangs from earlier creeping back into the forefront of his mind. Did it ever cease? he wondered as his eyes drifted towards Xevi's exposed neck, hearing the sweet song of blood in his veins.

"I will stop them," Anubis promised, although he'd begun to salivate, his eyes fixed on the throbbing vein in his neck. "But first, I must save you."

Before Xevi could protest, Anubis clamped down on his neck, releasing his fevered blood into his mouth. Xevi barely stirred. He drank deep before he returned the favor, splattering his immortal blood into the open mouth of his fellow priest.

No sooner had he pulled back than he was interrupted by the largest hyena he had ever seen hurtling into the room. Anubis immediately ducked out of the way, his newly developed speed causing the beast to slam against the wall. It shook off the blow, allowing him time to observe its manic black eyes and gore-splattered fur as it licked blood off jagged teeth. It lunged again but Anubis was quicker, pouncing to land on top of its back. He grabbed its grotesque, cackling head and pulled until he heard a sick, juicy pop. Anubis jumped off, throwing the freshly severed head aside as its body crumpled to the floor. He paused to catch his breath, watching the bleeding lump shrink back to its normal size. Someone enchanted the animals, he realized.

He startled as another beast came stampeding through the door, but this time, he saw Thomas, fully revived, with his teeth in the beast's neck. It fell, skidding across the floor as it tried to thrash him off. Finally, it stilled, letting Thomas take his fill before he broke away with a satisfied slurp. He stood, wiping hyena blood from his lips. "Hello," he panted.

"Forgive me, it was the only way I could save you," Anubis explained hurriedly. "I will tell you everything, but first we must save what is left of the village. Someone has unleashed a curse upon us."

"Where is Helena?"

Anubis found he couldn't say the words. Fortunately, the crestfallen look upon Thomas's face let him know he didn't need to.

"You villain!" Xevi interrupted, taking them by surprise as he threw Anubis to the floor.

"Please forgive me," Anubis said, shielding himself from Xevi's blows. "It was the only way to save you."

"I wanted to die!" Xevi growled. "I wanted to take my place with the other gods in the spirit world. You have made me a demon!"

Thomas grabbed his wrist midswing. "This is not the time," he said firmly. "Our village is in ruins. We must stop the walking corpses and beasts before they spread to the rest of the continent."

Xevi still shook with rage, but he nodded. The three withdrew from the convent and were immediately met with sparring bodies. Xevi did not stay near them for long, disappearing into the mass of fighting limbs. Anubis squinted into the smoke, observing the reanimated corpses in a languid shuffle. One of the creatures paused to tear a limb from a dying warrior, chewing the flesh from his bones as the dying man screamed. The possessed beasts finished off the rest.

"You can control them," Thomas's voice came from beside him. "Your power is magnified now. Guide them into the blazing palace!"

Anubis didn't have to question if he was right. He shut his eyes, picturing his life before humanity. He saw the jackal in his mind—his jackal—its amber eyes glowing and rows of pointed teeth turned up into a snarl. He heard the whispers and groans of the dead filling the air with sludge, slowing down the world with their presence. He watched as a shadow of dread crawled over every face around him—human, immortal, creature—for nothing in this world was absolved of death. It was forever constant, and it was his. He pulled the reanimated corpses towards him, attracting them with the aubergine light that now surrounded him, fulfilling their desire to be guided home.

Anubis focused on the building inferno and pushed them towards its open mouth. They lumbered over willingly, trailed by the hexed hyenas, who didn't even scream as their fur caught fire. Anubis relaxed only after the last one was swallowed by flame.

"They cannot truly die that way," a voice said, breaking through his thoughts. Legba had heard his call, standing next to him in his young man visage, his hair still coiled silver around his ears.

"Where were you?" Anubis demanded.

"We were blocked," he replied. "Shokpana turned his back on us all, bringing plague back to our homeland as revenge. The sickness takes their souls, but their bodies never rot. Won't catch fire neither. They will be trapped under the earth til you call them again. Shokpana is a blood drinker now. He works for a group that wants to absorb all gods' powers. He tried to create a death army and intended to use your power to guide them. But Medusa killed him, right after she saved you."

"Why did she leave?"

"She killed one of ours," another voice explained. Anubis turned to see the spirit form of Okanu, the god of dreams, dressed in shimmering white robes. His pristine dress was terribly out of place amongst the devastated village. "She is no longer welcome here."

"After all Shokpana did, you punish her?" Anubis sputtered.

"You should not question our ways," Xevi spoke up from beside him.

Anubis blinked. "You see the spirits now, too?"

"Of course," Xevi huffed. "You are not the only one with powers—I have always spoken to them. They just chose you over me."

"Tell him the rest."

Anubis's heart seized. He turned to see an apparition, none other than Helena. Although she had never been much for affection, he rushed towards her, pulling her into his arms. "Forgive me for not saving you."

She gently drew away. "We will talk, but first Legba must tell you the truth."

Legba scowled. "It does not involve us."

"It involves him," she shot back.

"I want no part," Legba asserted and with a pop, he disappeared. Okanu followed suit, leaving Xevi the last one standing.

"I want no part of your struggle, either," he said with a sneer. "I will be helping make sure the living stay that way." Then he too disappeared.

Thomas approached from the shadows, up to where Helena stood. "Oh, my dear friend," he said sadly.

"You both are immortal," Helena observed.

"I could not get to you in time," Anubis told her, "or you would be, too."

"I can do more for us in the Middleworld," she assured him. "I can travel through what is left of the realms and eavesdrop when I need to." She turned towards Anubis. "There are other blood drinkers besides the one who turned you and the Ancient Ones you left behind."

"David." Anubis nodded. "And my brother, Libraean."

"There are others who have cropped up as a force against you, who are destroying the realms, and who seek to destroy your Egyptian family. You need to find David and warn him."

Anubis heard crashing and turned to see the last of the structures crumble in the flames. The entire village was lost. "We need somewhere to go until the humans can rebuild. There we can figure out how to contact him."

"I know a place," she said.

The memory faded, leaving him in darkness. Anubis rose to his feet, startled to see Helena standing where he once married her, so long ago. They no longer needed candles, two dead things walking around the land of the living.

"You really have been trapped in memory," she commented softly. "You were lost in a trance for hours."

"Since they arrived, I seem to be pulled back towards my former life," he admitted. He fell back down onto the rock he'd been sitting on. The thin stream that once wound through the grotto had split in two, its soothing trickle amplified within the dome of rocks.

She followed suit, sitting between his legs so he could rest his chin on the top of her head as he hugged her. "Did you know Lucius was my father?"

"I actually did not," she replied. "Apparently there are some secrets even I cannot uncover."

"What do you remember most? Your life as the goddess Hel or your brief life as a human?"

"So you are not only nostalgic, you are speculative," she remarked.

"I think I am finished with my human life," he told her.

"Honey, you have been finished with this life since you got here," she laughed.

"I am serious."

She turned to face him, squinting as she studied his eyes. "When this is over, we will find a place to store your body. Then I will take your soul."

Anubis was surprised. "Is it that easy?"

"I've always known how to bring you to the Middleworld," she said. "I simply waited for you to be ready. You put your people first, and I respect that about you. But I did make a deal with Legba long ago that your soul will belong to me."

Anubis struggled to find words, touched by the gesture. He'd long accepted her sarcasm and aloofness, they were qualities he liked about her. But this felt like something quite different. He cleared his throat. "Where will we store my body, then?"

She stood and smiled. "When this is done, I will show you."

CHAPTER NINE

❧ THE ANCIENT ONES ❧

THE NETHERREALMS
LUCIUS

LUCIUS CRACKED OPEN AN EYE.

He lay under a tree, its empty black branches cutting jagged lines across the burnt orange sky, sulfur and smoke filling the air. He sighed, recognizing the dismal realm even without the tormented wails carried along the noxious wind. Back again. He stood, and brushed off his trousers. Charred skulls and torsos surrounded him on all sides, seeming to stretch on infinitely. Many housed ugly brown mushrooms, some with spindly black trees growing out of their spines. He shook his head, annoyed by the mess. "When I ruled down here, it was a beautiful landscape of volcanic mountains and lava," he informed one of the nearby demons who had come to investigate his arrival. "Now it's a complete disaster."

The demon, a spidery looking creature with human eyeballs and bat wings, sniffed him once before cowering in fear.

"I'm looking for someone, an old pagan weather god with curly reddish hair and green eyes," he told the creature. "Do you know where I can find him?"

The demon looked relieved to learn Lucius wasn't planning on killing or eating it, and replied by scuttling through a break in the field of bones. Lucius followed as the sky shifted, a mountain gorge appearing before them. He looked up to see the giants that created it, tied together by chains wound so tightly they could not move. He couldn't believe they were still alive, their labored breaths and eruptions of discontentment audible as he walked through the valley their figures made. He knew them as the Titans, giants cast down by the Olympian gods as they rose in power, long after Lucius left and before he masqueraded as Hades. So large were the Titans, that those who didn't end up tied together for eternity, found themselves stuck in whatever place they landed. Oceanus became the great Lake of Agony, where souls eternally drowned; Cronus's rib cage became a prison for murderers; and Hyperion's fiery jaws were the place where rapists burned.

Lucius pulled his gaze away, wondering where the imp led him. After some time, they reached the end, where a large sphere of wind swirled and spun, crackles of lightning flickering through its agitated clouds. The demon looked up at him as if waiting for payment, but after seeing the look in his eyes, it hurried away.

Lucius marched up to the tornado and inhaled, pressing forward with flattened palms until he created space between squalls. He fell into it blindly, stumbling only for a moment before he found himself in an old cemetery, similar to the one David left behind in England. The wind outside the space howled, but inside was still. The ground beneath his feet felt more mud than grass, and the gravestones were mossy and crumbling. The trees were dead, as were the brown plants that pushed up through the inhospitable earth. The atmosphere suffocated, thick with despair.

He found David lying in the mud, half-sunken and oblivious to Lucius's presence. His skin bore a sickly shade of gray, and his clothing moldered around his body as if he'd been decaying in the ground for months. He stared listlessly up at the only sign of life—a dozen quiet crows who circled, but never swooped down.

Lucius let out an exasperated sigh. Of course this was his torment—trapped, rotting away in his own muck, lamenting her. He crouched down to meet him at eye level. "Are you going to keep feeling sorry for yourself, or are you going to come with me?"

David's eyes drifted towards him and landed without a flash of recognition. "I'm just resting," he said in a detached voice.

Lucius rolled his eyes. "Come. You and I both know you don't belong down here." He grabbed David's arm, and began hoisting him to his feet.

David looked bewildered as he complied, staring at the desolate graveyard with saucer eyes. "Where am I?"

"Hell."

David stared at him blankly until recognition softened the confusion wrinkling his forehead. "Lucius?"

"There you are." Lucius gave him a stiff pat on the back, sending globs of mud away from his mildewy clothing. "Now I just have to figure out a way to get you out of here."

David frowned, staring off into the horizon at the swirling shades of gray that created the sky. "Where is she?"

Lucius tried not to let his agitation surface. "On Earth somewhere, I believe. You'll see her soon enough."

David turned back to face him, something different in his eyes. "I've always thought it was you who was at fault. For eons, I believed the story affirmed by historians—Set, the destructive, wicked god of the Underworld, murdered his twin brother, Osiris, the good and the just, out of jealousy. I thought I was rescuing Nephthys from your clutches, thought I was doing right by running away with her to Ireland." He sighed, running his fingers through his hair. "But it's all wrong. I was the jealous one. I viewed my life with Isis as a prison, a box of what the world expected of me as their king. You were free to roam the Earth fighting wars, causing mayhem— not bound by expectations. Even your wife was beautiful, passionate, and strong… Although it has taken millennia to clearly see what I should have seen all along, I think a part of me has always known my entire existence was based upon a lie. I am not a hero, nor am I a leader. I am just a jealous brother who stole your entire life away from you. Lucius, please understand how deeply s—"

"Oh no," Lucius cut him off sharply. "Absolutely not. I came down here to rescue you, and I'll be damned if you suddenly see the error of your ways and come out on top. For once in your cursed life, let me be the damned hero!"

David blinked. "You came here to rescue me?"

"Yes. Now stop talking before anyone realizes we're down here." Lucius grabbed his arm, and pulled him back up the hill to the hole he'd created in the wind. No sooner had they stepped through it, back into the world of stifling air and burning skies, did a giant, demonic wolf block their view.

"No," Lucius snapped before it spoke. "You tell him I'm not interested in talking. This soul does not belong down here and I am getting rid of him."

"Lucius, wait, is that Dan?"

The wolf scowled down at them, its red eyes glaring above rows of fangs. "My name is Fenrir. I've come here to bring Lucius to the Master."

"Technically, I am your master. Your father and I made a deal," Lucius reminded the giant beast. "So, you must reply truthfully to what I ask you: is the soul once bound to you here?"

"Baldr?" the wolf sneered. "I have been rid of him since we entered this realm. He is not here."

Lucius nodded, disheartened for Cahira. She wasn't going to take the revelation well. "Fenrir, I need you to escort my brother to the Asphodel Wasteland so he can find his way back."

The wolf growled. "Master is not going to be pleased with me."

"Oh, let me handle that obnoxious fool. You just take this one where he needs to go."

"You're not coming with me?" David looked confused.

"I'm dead, David. You are only visiting," Lucius explained impatiently. "I'm surprised they let you stay down here as long as you have been. I can't even begin to tell you how poorly this place is managed now. Now go. I'll distract King Demon, and you find your way back to the rest of them. It's not a difficult endeavor; once you reach the old meadows, you'll see the portal. Tell Cahira I'm sorry I couldn't send her lover back with you." He started back down the Hall of Giants.

"Lucius," he tried to stop him.

"Go, David."

"You're a bastard for murdering me."

"That's more like it."

"But you didn't have to come down here to rescue me. It means a lot that you did."

Lucius finally paused his stride. He looked back at David and shrugged. "Well, you know I enjoy any opportunity to make you look bad."

And before David could say another word, he marched down the great hall, leaving the giant wolf and his brother behind.

The Kingdom of Dahomey, 1858
Morrigan

THE SAVANNA WAS HAUNTINGLY BEAUTIFUL AT DUSK, the moon burning a gold disc into the sky as it rose above the horizon. A warm breeze drifted across her skin, its very scent wild and untamed, holding a hint of promise.

He stood against an acacia tree with his hips forward and his arms crossed, looking more like the alluring Lucius than her quiet, contemplative David as he stared at her with hungry eyes.

"I wondered if you'd know to find me out here," she said, letting a smile glide across her lips.

"I knew you would run when you learned of my brother's lies," David said. "It seemed logical you'd go to the place where the moon shines the brightest."

"Is it you who has been sending me dreams of Ireland?"

"Perhaps."

Morrigan drew closer as the breeze picked up around them. "I'd forgotten those days," she said dreamily, reaching her hand up behind his head. He smiled before she closed her eyes and pressed her lips against his, knowing she was kissing a stranger.

When he opened his eyes, he immediately jumped back, taking in his new surroundings with alarm. "Where did you take us?"

Morrigan smiled, standing serenely in the bleached sand as a thin black snake wove around her bare feet, her crows circling above. She saw her image reflected in the pupils of his eyes—a blend of every goddess she'd portrayed—tall and regal, wearing billowing black with hair that matched, her arms and tattoos exposed, blue eyes rimmed with smudged kohl, her hand clutching an obsidian staff that ended in a python's head. One of the crows landed on her shoulder, settling his wings as he apprehended David with a resounding squawk. Beside her stood a wolf with fur as black as the rest of her familiars, all patiently waiting for direction from their queen. "You can stop pretending to be David now."

Discordia shifted back into her blonde-haired, red-eyed physique, her ruby lips pursed with annoyance. She looked out of place in the morose, ethereal realm Morrigan brought her to, a blinding sore against the peaceful grayscale. "It took you long enough to realize it was me," she huffed. "I can always count on you to be distracted."

Morrigan apprehended her calmly. "I'm not distracted now."

Discordia cast a disapproving look at the gradient silver sky and the black waters that crashed against the sand. In the distance, sharp black mountains cut through smoky white fog. The air sighed around them. "Where is this place?" she repeated in disgust.

"It took me a moment to remember," Morrigan began as she gazed across the waters, "but I once created the realms. Isis created the life that dies upon the Earth, but I created the spaces where death is reborn. We are in the Middleworld, the place between the realms. A place you cannot harm."

Discordia scoffed, though her eyes betrayed her concern. "I always find a way. I'll consume your powers soon enough and then it will be mine."

"I have thought much about the events in my life," Morrigan continued as if she hadn't heard her, "wondering why you've been such a persistent annoyance throughout my life, and I've come to a conclusion. At the beginning of time, there was heka and chaos. Until one day, the two merged and birthed a pair of twins: the Great She. All was well until the day one of the twins fell in love, which birthed chaos as a separate entity. Chaos might have broken away, but it was nothing without heka. It was forced to feed off others to survive. Chaos wanted so badly to be a goddess in her own right, but she couldn't, even though she walked in their footsteps and made love to their husbands. She began murdering other goddesses and absorbing their power, but in doing so, she simply became pieces of them sewn together—not the real deity she longed to become."

Morrigan turned to her, watching her face twitch and twist at her words. "Finally, she decided to kill every god and goddess so she could be the only goddess standing, giving her all the power and prestige she craved. But it will not work, Discordia. Even if you kill us all, you will still remain a sad, empty shell filled with the stolen souls of others."

"You know nothing of what you speak," Discordia snapped. She shifted into the image of Isis, Morrigan's twin staring back at her with violent green eyes. "I am the one with heka now, and when I take the rest from Cahira, I will be the most powerful goddess on Earth."

"My sister was far more brilliant than you give her credit for. Cahira does not have Isis's heka. It is safely hidden away. And even if you did manage to find it and steal it, it won't help you." The crow on her shoulder let out a squawk of agreement.

"You will still be alone. You can surround yourself with minions, you can make deals and raise demons, you can steal the power of others. But you will never have true devotion, never feel the love and loyalty of family."

Discordia gave her a smug look. "I've made love to both David and Lucius in so many different ways, Lilith. Your words do not upset me."

Morrigan shook her head, offering her a sad smile. "You had to trick them to do it. You could have had your own life, your own realm even. You could have found your own lover, bore your own children. But you chose to take over my sister's life and mine—and you failed. You cannot fake true love, nor can you pretend your way into having another person's life, no matter how appealing it might be."

Discordia's face twisted horribly as she spoke, shifting through different faces before slipping into Gaia's form.

Morrigan laughed. "She's actually the one that sent me to you."

With a furious screech, Discordia opened her palms, letting the fire she'd stolen from Lucius fly freely from her hands.

Morrigan barely flinched, dropping her staff to extend her own hands. In an instant, she felt them all around her—David's wind, Lucius's fire, Isis's heka—blended with her waters and the spiritual powers of her sons. The pulsating, black energy gifted to her blocked Discordia's stolen fire, driving it backwards. She sputtered, dismayed as she tried to push harder, shifting into her many forms as she tried to match the strength radiating from Morrigan. The crows began to circle and caw, creating a cyclone above them, riddled with flashes of lightning that threatened to strike at her command.

"Show yourself," Morrigan demanded as she inched closer, watching the chaos goddess falter and fade, unable to bring forth strength that was her own.

Discordia screeched with frustration as she submitted to her preferred avatar, her white-blonde hair whipping around her face as she struggled to keep Morrigan from advancing.

"No, the real one," Morrigan ordered as she pulled power from the depths of her soul. She heard her sister's wild battle cry reverberating in her mind as she worked through her, slamming Discordia to the ground.

The stream of power was broken as the imposter goddess crumbled. She balled herself up in fear, shaking as Morrigan stood in wait. The magic Morrigan had invoked twitched around her like electricity, snaking around her form, waiting to strike.

Discordia gingerly uncoiled, pulling herself to her feet. She was a mirror image of Morrigan now, tears streaking down her face as she stared at her with manic eyes a piercing shade of blue. "I hate you," she screamed.

Morrigan marched up to her double without hesitation. She thrust her fist into her chest and cracked her ribs in one solid movement, capturing Discordia's fearful eyes with her own as she ripped the still-beating heart from her chest. She stared in shock and horror as Morrigan promptly sank her teeth into it, releasing the blood of a hundred stolen lives.

Chaos let out a defeated whimper before she crumpled to the ground, splitting into dozens of snakes. They slithered to Morrigan's feet, up her legs and into her skin, her body seamlessly absorbing what was meant to be hers. The heart she held transformed as well, coiling around her fingers before finding a place on her arm, turning itself into another tattoo.

Morrigan blinked, and she was back on Earth.

She wiped her bloodied lips with the back of her hand, feeling her sister's spirit humming around her, flickering like fireflies. Although her heart was still pumping from exhilaration, she felt warm and complete, as though she'd been wandering lost for days and finally finding the path home. She looked down to see David resting peacefully in the grass, his body freed of Discordia's spirit. She knelt by his side, tenderly brushing back a lock of rusted hair. His eyes opened, his pupils shrinking as they focused on her face.

He immediately smiled. "Hello."

"Hello," she echoed.

"This was how we first met in Ireland," David remembered. "Except our roles were reversed."

"I remember."

He suddenly looked bewildered, sitting upright as if remembering where he was. "Did Lucius make it?"

Morrigan frowned. "What do you mean?"

David pulled himself to his feet, searching all around them. "He—he pulled me out of Tartarus."

Morrigan's heart gave a thump as she stood. "Tartarus? I just killed Discordia; she had your body hostage. Your spirit just returned."

"That explains why they imprisoned me," David realized, his energy frantic. "Where is everyone? We need to get back to the others—"

Morrigan grabbed him by both arms, halting his movement. "David," she said sharply, "where is Lucius?"

She realized she didn't even need to hear the words—she could see the answer reflected in his somber eyes.

"He is in Tartarus," he told her gently.

Although her body was humming with borrowed power, her mind had trouble comprehending his words.

"He was there to rescue me. Morrigan, I didn't believe him, but he told me he was dead..."

Her knees buckled. She knew she was falling away from reality, but she felt David's strong arms lifting her up, holding her tightly as he sped her across the plains. She slipped away as she heard the sound of the ocean when they arrived, grateful to be back at Anubis's home.

DAVID

THE PATH TO THE HOUSE WAS RADIANT WITH TORCHLIGHT, illuminating their path forward. The equally aglow windows let him know everyone awaited their return. He didn't stop to question how he knew the way to Anubis's house, nor did he wish to indulge in the morbid reflection of having his body possessed. Instead, he was consumed by the present, worry heightening his senses as he raced Morrigan through the front gates.

A rumbling storm brewed as they ran through, and Anubis flew out of the house to fetch Morrigan out of his arms. Libraean emerged from behind and spun David around to face him, patting his face and shoulders, while searching his eyes.

"It's you," he breathed in relief.

David drew his old friend into an embrace, grateful to see him again. "Morrigan has killed Discordia," he told him and Anubis, "and Lucius sacrificed himself to pull me out of Tartarus—when I told Morrigan, she collapsed. Her body is engorged with extra power right now, so please be careful."

Anubis looked up at the crackling, electric clouds. "I see. Let's get inside."

David followed them through the door, only to have his path blocked by Cahira, her expression prematurely hardened as if bracing for bad news. "Tell me," she said through lips that barely moved.

David took her hands, and met her eyes. "We spoke directly to Fenrir," he told her gently. "Dan is not there."

Without a word, she pulled away from him and marched out the door. He looked to Sandrine, who nodded to confirm they should not follow. He quietly acquiesced, instead turning back to Morrigan. She'd found her legs and now stood unblinking in front of the fireplace, the flames reflected in dilated pupils. He noticed her eyes had changed color, now shades of blue and green, swirling together like the tropical ocean. He realized with a start that she held Isis's power, finally able to see it buzzing around her like lightning in a heat storm. She caught him staring at her.

"I am going to retrieve Lucius from Tartarus," she said.

"No," David said immediately, vividly recalling the grim world he'd just been trapped in. "I cannot let you go to that horrible place, Morrigan. It is unlike anything we have ever witnessed."

He braced himself for her anger, but she surprised him with calm resolve. "Let us speak alone," she said.

David nodded and followed her outside. The sky broke into a drizzle as a loud clap of thunder struck overhead, vibrating the ground beneath their feet.

Morrigan stopped to stand before him, unbothered by the mist dampening her hair. Her light eyes burned, her face locked in calm resolve. "David, I have to."

"Perhaps we can bring him back here," he pleaded.

"I am not afraid of the Netherworld, David. I am its mistress." She folded her arms in front of her. Then she added softly, "Please don't think it easy for me to speak about him to you, but I cannot—I will not—leave him down there. Even if that means I must die myself."

David frowned. "I don't want to imagine what Discordia said to you in my body, in my voice. I'm quite sure she used anything she could find in my head to upset you."

"She sent me dreams of Ireland." Morrigan smiled sadly.

"Ah." David looked down at the damp earth then back up towards the sky, blinking away the raindrops. The thought of Gaia weaved through his mind. "I won't stand before you and tell you that my love for you was not deep, nor will I lie and tell you I don't love you still. You were my first, my real true love."

Morrigan looked away.

He grabbed her hands so that her eyes found his. "But for a very long time, I have been plagued by guilt for taking you away from Lucius. I do not regret what happened, but every decision I have ever made since that moment has been because of guilt. The only way I can ever resolve it is if I finally let you go."

Morrigan was quiet.

"I think guilt also binds you to me. You regretted leaving him, which is why you had to convince yourself you hated him, why you had to create an entirely different world where he did not exist so you could live happily with me. Even then, you let slip that you still longed for him. I chose to ignore it—I was blinded by my own stubbornness."

He pulled the vision forward, sharing it with her: the two Celtic deities in ancient times, standing inside their stone palace, the hollow chamber echoing their sadness.

"Please do not go," David pleaded as Daghda, his long, auburn beard overwhelmed with gray, striking evidence that the old god had aged. "You were gone for so long, I thought you'd never return. I was weak when she approached me. I was a damn fool. Please forgive me—it was not love or lust, it was sorrow."

Morrigan stared back coldly, choosing to look like her true self instead of hiding behind her maiden aspect, her own hair streaked with white. "I do not need your apologies, nor do I want you to beg me to stay. You made a choice and I am honoring that choice. You should know by now I am not one who can simply ignore a slight made against me."

He grabbed her arm in desperation, but the act only provoked her rage. She spun and kicked him, sending him sailing into his throne. She began to run but he hoisted himself to his feet, throwing his arms around her. Outside, clouds blackened the sun, the wind beginning to howl as a chorus of crows screeched their protestations. They dove into the chamber, but she held them back.

David grabbed her face, kissing her cheeks desperately. "Please forgive me, Morrigan. My wife. I have loved you for so very long, how could you doubt that I still do?"

"I do forgive you," she growled, undeterred by his affections. "But you know better than to expect me to stay. If you love me as you say you do, then you will let me go. I have kept this from you, but there has been a voice calling to me that I have ignored. If you are allowed to find solace in others, then I should be allowed to find him."

He released her, his heart shattered. "There it is. That is the reason you never felt like you were truly mine."

Her eyes narrowed. "You will not blame me for your own transgressions," she warned him. "I never once lay with another man whilst with you."

"I know," he said miserably. "I just cannot stand to think of life without you."

"Then find me in another." She turned on her heel and marched out of the throne room, her crows trailing behind her.

The memory faded as David stared into eyes that never changed. It unnerved him to revisit their most heartbreaking memory, reminding him of his agony when he found out she'd abandoned him on Earth to return to the Upperealms. How he abandoned the Tuatha de Danann, moving mountains so he could follow her.

"I did forgive you," the present Morrigan pointed out, though she appeared equally grieved by the memory. "When you found me in the Upperrealms, I'd had time to contemplate, remembering our ancient past and how I was just as capable of betrayal myself. We both decided to move past it."

"I know," he said. "But still."

"David," she said suddenly. "There is more to the story than I ever told you… The woman you slept with bore you a son."

"I know," he told her, thinking of Gaia and Aengus. "I had a feeling you might have known."

"Back then I was so swept up in furious jealousy, all I wanted to do was run. I thought you'd find out about the child and reunite on your own. You followed me to the Upperealms, but by then, I was so distracted by Lucius being free and rising to Earth with my sister—it was the farthest thing from my mind. I should have told you before you died."

David studied her. "Did you kill him?"

"No," she promised, her light eyes earnest. "As much as I hated that pathetic excuse for a goddess, I saw myself in her eyes. I didn't want her to feel the pain of losing a child."

David let out his breath. She still looked worried, and a small part of him still wanted to comfort her, though he knew it was no longer his place. "I'm glad I found out about him the way I did," he told her honestly. "It's not your fault we are constantly piecing together lost memories or that there is always some crisis to solve. We haven't had much time to breathe, let alone revisit old wounds. I don't hold it against you, Morrigan. I promise."

"Thank you," she whispered, her eyes glistening.

"Can I…"

She didn't let him finish, moving forward so he could hold her one last time. He buried his face in her wet hair, reminded of the last time they were forced to violently part, when she drove a knife into his stomach. He closed his eyes, letting the rest of his senses appreciate her as he did back then. "My favorite memories will forever be the ones where we lived away from it all, just us, in an enchanted realm made of grassy knolls and silver moonlight," he said softly. "But…it will never be just us, no matter how many ways we repeat this cycle. He is eternally my shadow."

Morrigan pulled back, reaching up to touch his face. "I will always care for you, David, please know that," she said with soft eyes. "Until the end of my days."

He put his hand on hers, pressing it into his cheek. "I know you do, and I feel the same. And I do love you enough to let you go, to let you be happy with the one who you never stopped loving. The one who is supposed to have your heart."

Tears streamed freely down her face. "Thank you," she whispered.

He grabbed her hands in his, squeezing them as he leaned forward so their foreheads could rest against each other. They remained still for a moment, breathing each other's air, listening to the song of each other's blood running through their veins.

"Come," he finally said as he pulled away. "Let us go save our shadow."

She nodded, wiping her tears away with renewed determination. David turned to see Anubis and Libraean standing in the doorway.

"Is everything alright?" Anubis asked.

"Yes," David nodded. "We need to open a portal." He reached for Morrigan's hand and together they walked back into the house.

CAHIRA

SHE IGNORED THE ACCUMULATING STORM as she headed into the wild brush, stopping only to pull the knife from her boot to assist in cutting away a path. She heard a pack of hyenas cackling in the distance, the closest thing to the howling of wolves she could cling to as she marched farther and farther from civilization. The sweltering African jungle had its own beauty, but she missed the smell of evergreens, though she tried to appreciate the dense leaves and humming insects, the humid air, and the sensation that the majestic animals forged out of its red dust were near. She continued to chop until her arm got tired. She switched hands, alternating between arms as she hacked, chopped, and slashed her way forward. The sound was rhythmic and satisfying, distracting her from the hollow feeling that had settled in her bones.

She stopped once she heard rushing water, mystified to discover she'd found a waterfall. The pause in movement allowed the ache in her limbs to roar to life, and she tucked her knife back into her boot. She found a nearby rock to rest and watched the steady cascade of water splash into the tiny stream below, the wildlife around her humming and buzzing, unconcerned with the sweeping winds and electricity overhead.

She imagined a cave behind the waterfall and remembered herself as a child, healing from the wound in her side, wondering if the wolf she'd forced to be her companion was really going to come back for her or if she'd have to make the long journey alone. She pictured him climbing up the rocks to cheerfully reveal the rabbit he'd brought to feed her, remembering the overwhelming feeling of being loved. How the feeling frightened her, so she turned it off, although her physical self refused to leave his side. She recalled the emptiness that took her over when she was forced to. Even then, it was nothing compared to what she felt now.

Cahira wanted to cry but she was numb, feeling as though someone had cut open her chest, swirled their hands around her insides, and pulled out the tiny fragments of emotion she had left. Oh, how she wanted them back, cursing herself for abandoning them when he was still around. She should have appreciated them—appreciated each moment they spent together. How nothing was demanded of her, she simply was. And he loved her for it. She was a fool to think that being a supernatural being in a physical world made her impervious to death, that she would be spared from its sting. But the one whose life she had taken for granted was gone, and there was nothing that anyone could do. It was final, the door slammed shut, the Earth claiming her prize.

Cahira squeezed her eyes shut. She pretended he was sitting next to her, that they were back in their forest and she could feel his warmth again. She recalled the scent of pine and snow, the memory cutting through the scent of wild jungle and parched grass, crickets replacing tree frogs. "Please forgive me," she whispered to no one as a tear finally made its way from the corner of her eye.

"There's no need for that," a voice replied.

Her eyes popped open and she scrambled to her feet, staring in disbelief at the apparition next to her. "How do I know you are real and not Discordia?" she immediately asked.

Dan's visage gave her a sideways smile as he stared down at her with dark blue, adoring eyes. "Don't worry, your mother killed me proper. It's me."

Cahira continued to stare as her eyes took in the rugged outline of his face, his long, matted silver hair, the matching crowns capping his teeth, and the tattoos etched across his body. He'd chosen to appear to her the way she remembered him.

"Are you a ghost then?" she whispered. She realized she was trembling.

"Something like that. My spirit lives in the Middleworld now."

"Why didn't you come to me earlier?"

"Well, I never truly died before," he explained. "So I had no idea that dying takes your memories away. I'm only conscious of them now because a spirit named Helena found me and told me, reminding me that I left you and it was time to return. But even then, I had to wait for you to summon me first."

Cahira grew quiet, struggling to believe what she was seeing was real. She could have fallen asleep from exhaustion, her consciousness given way to dreams. Then she remembered that godly apparitions were corporeal, naturally able to bend the realms where human spirits could not. "Can I touch you?" she whispered.

He pulled her into his chest. Every fiber of her being surrendered to the sensation of comfort, sighing with relief as she took in his piney scent and relished the warmth of his touch. She knew it wasn't real, but for that moment, she would pretend it was. "I was going to bring you back," she murmured into his chest.

He kissed her head, heated lips to her skin. "I was surprised to learn you hadn't, but Helena explained you were trying to be patient. I have been at peace since I died. I reunited with Odin, the All-Father."

She lifted her head. "Isn't he your real father?"

He nodded. "We were wrong to assume Discordia killed all the gods. There are a great number of them who found ways to hide, many by making their homes in the Middleworld. Odin split his soul into four pieces long before she could find him. He put his spirit inside two crows, Hunin and Munin, who told me where to find David and who told David about Morrigan. He also put himself into two wolves, Freki...and Geri."

"Our Geri?" Cahira said with surprise before murmuring, "I have always known something was off with her. That would explain why she is immortal."

He nodded.

Cahira grew quiet again, enjoying the sensation of being nestled against him. "I do love you," she said finally, enjoying how the words felt on her tongue. "I wish I would have said it to you a hundred times."

"I know," he murmured, his chest vibrating against her ear. "I didn't know it then, but I know it now. I am so sorry I had to leave you."

"How long can you stay?" she asked, suddenly remembering the others.

"As long as you'd like. Though I think right now you are needed else-where." He looked up at the lightning-streaked sky.

She followed his eyes. "You're not wrong," she admitted with a sigh.

"Have you forgiven Morrigan yet?" he asked. "She did take down Angelique for us all."

"How did you know I was angry with her?"

"Because I know you." His chest rumbled with laughter.

Cahira thought for a moment, realizing the rage she had been holding on to had long melted away, unable to maintain its momentum. "I've forgiven her," she told him.

"Good," Dan nodded. "I knew you would be upset with us, but I hoped you wouldn't take it out on her. I bear the painful memories of her fighting the Wolf to protect you. A woman who chooses to mother a child that is not hers and defends her with her very life offers the sort of love that transcends all else."

Cahira felt a jab in her chest. "I should go back and help her."

"Before you do, I want to tell you one last story. This one is about a little soul so powerful, she brought the Morrigan to life just by listening to her sing. The goddess became her mother, protecting her until she met a ferocious wolf who the little soul bent to her will. Yet even after she released him from servitude, the wolf made a vow to himself to protect her, even beyond death. Even as the little girl grew physically stronger, she forgot the power inside. That she could move mountains with her mind, bend the realms as she desires, and bring gods to life with her will."

Cahira stared. "Are you saying what I think you're saying?"

Dan gave her a shrug, though he couldn't hold back his smile. "I've never been a patron god before. I think it might be fun to try it out."

Without another word, she threw her arms around his neck and kissed him, tasting minty pine as a burst of cold air tostled her hair until her braid came loose, flowing freely behind her with his hair still attached to it. His lips were soft behind his rugged beard, scratching her own lips in a pleas-ant way as his arms wrapped around her, pressing her up against his broad chest. She was lost for a moment before she pulled away, surprised by the sensations that consumed her. She realized no words needed to be said, no spells needed cast, that just the simple kiss had brought him back to her.

"So that's what it's like kissing you," she whispered, fighting against the gentle sway of dizziness.

He looked equally bewildered, but chuckled. "I won't mind if we make that a habit."

Cahira stared at him, drinking in his kind, sapphire eyes and wild silver hair. "So you are now my patron god," she said in wonder. She touched his face again to confirm it, running her fingers through his beard. He was truly corporeal, bound to her like her mother once was. "Will you be coming with me then?"

"This part of the war is not mine to fight," he told her. "So I will busy myself by preparing for our journey home. You and I belong in the mountains." He kissed her once more, any hesitation that used to plague their relationship gone. "I will be waiting when you return."

Still dazed, Cahira nodded, backing away from him with shaky legs. "Is this real?" she asked him again.

A laugh tumbled out of his chest. "I've never once seen you doubt your own power. Don't start now."

She grinned. "I can't argue with that."

"I promise I will be here when you return," he repeated, recognizing her hesitancy.

She gave a firm nod and wrenched herself away before she lost her nerve, running out of the jungle and back through the path she'd made towards the house. The outer torches were lit, fighting against the turbulent weather that still had yet to settle, though the ocean had finally calmed. She noticed Sandrine was waiting for her right outside, leaned up against the wall, an indiscernible shadow save for the outline of her hair.

"Did you find what you were looking for?"

"Not the way I thought I wanted, but yes," Cahira stammered, hoping she wouldn't see her reddening cheeks. "Where is everyone?"

"Waiting inside," she replied. "But before you go in, I must speak with you. There is something I need to confess. The first time Lesplaies and I came here, there was a reason he was able to unleash the plague without me knowing. It's because I was distracted. The reason that Queen Hangbe chose me as leader of her warriors is because she forced me to endure a possession. The spirit was a piece of Isis's soul, trapped in the branch of her acacia tree, stolen from Egypt and brought here. I was the only one strong enough to bear it. I never once used her power; in fact, I pretended as though it didn't exist. It was my way to rebel against what was done to me. When I came back to Africa as a vampire, I left Lesplaies to travel to Egypt, where I put Isis's power back into the old acacia that still will not die."

Cahira was stunned. "That was over a hundred years ago—the power would have long leaked out of its roots."

Sandrine nodded. "It's the reason I am making this choice. I left a piece of Isis's power unattended, letting Lesplaies murder hundreds with his plague. For that, I am responsible. I will be staying here in Africa. I plan to keep an eye on the power that I unleashed and ensure it never gets into the wrong hands, as it did with Discordia. It's my way of making amends to the deaths I caused."

"His plague was not your fault."

Sandrine sighed. "I've never quite connected to my life as a goddess, Cahira. I feel drawn to my human life first—my life as an African warrior. This is where I belong, helping the humans I am connected to in my own homeland. I lent myself to your godly cause, but Morrigan has taken down Angelique for good. The discord with the Watchers does not involve me. I think it is best that I move on. Please forgive me for not telling you."

Cahira nodded, though her sorrow had returned. "I hold nothing against you, but my heart is heavy that we must part. We have been together for a very long time."

Sandrine's stoney exterior melted to reveal a vulnerability she rarely trusted with another. "You are the closest I have ever had to family," she admitted. "But, like you, I am a lone wolf. We were once connected by a common cause—to rid the world of Angelique and her demons. Now we are free to resume our natural ways."

"I understand." Cahira nodded. "I will miss you though."

Sandrine grabbed her arm in the old style of handshake, meeting her eyes. "And I will miss you. If you ever need me again, you must promise that you will find me."

Cahira clenched her jaw against her rising emotion, offering instead a firm nod.

Then Sandrine was gone, with no further word, no further action, her figure enveloped instantly by the darkness.

Cahira let out a deep exhale. Although she fought the steady foreboding tremble that persists when loved ones part, she knew Sandrine was right. To beg her to stay would be asking her to sacrifice her true nature. And to Cahira, that was the antithesis of love.

She headed back into Anubis's house with slow and heavy steps. The torch light flickered in the wind as she approached.

Morrigan, Anubis, David, Libraean, and Thomas stood in the main room, and as soon as David saw her enter, he immediately rose to his feet. "We need to open a portal to Tartarus," he said without greeting.

"Since the beginning of this trip, I wanted to do exactly that and no one wanted to hear it," she said, half in jest.

"I am sorry I tried to persuade you not to save Dan," Morrigan broke in. "Especially since I have decided to retrieve Lucius from the very same place." She looked different, a peculiar energy flickering around her, bringing flecks of emerald into her eyes. Cahira picked up whispers as she drew closer and, with a start, she realized the same spirits who once guided her path to David were now running through Morrigan's veins.

Morrigan smiled, as if knowing exactly what she was thinking.

Cahira resumed focus on their conversation. "You do not need to apologize," she told her. "You were right. Dan chose to die to save my life, and it was right for me to honor that choice. I no longer hold any resentment towards you for your decision to do what I could not."

Morrigan did not speak, but a trace smile appeared on her lips, the swirling sky blue and sea greens of her eyes full of emotion.

Cahira moved to the front of the fireplace to address them all. "I have spent the last few months disconnected from the spirit world, so focused on my own desires that I could not see what was plainly in front of me. All of us knew we should be together to restore the realms, and that is true. Morrigan, Anubis, and Thomas are death gods—you three can open the portal to Tartarus to retrieve Lucius. As far as the rest of us," she looked between David and Libraean, "I have a plan. It's time to put this all behind us."

MORRIGAN

HER WORLD WAS DRENCHED IN COLOR, swirling and vibrating as what was left of her family spoke amongst each other. She still held Isis's hand, the falcon and the crow standing in quiet observation, though no one else could see it.

"I think I finally understand love," Isis murmured from beside her.

Well, please enlighten me, because I have yet to understand it, Morrigan replied in her mind.

"It is not chaos, as Discordia proclaimed. It is the opposite—what keeps the world in a state of ma'at, balancing all the pain and hatred."

Love can be painful.

"Lust perhaps, but love itself is beautiful. It is what I felt for you when you told me of your affair with Osiris, and when you asked me to watch over your children. It is what enables David to let you go. It is what makes Libraean care for David, what helped Cahira come up with a way to save the realms. What pushed young Anubis to prevent you from taking your own life. What has kept Lucius alive for so long. Anything Discordia has thrown at us, love has defeated it."

Morrigan raised an eyebrow, feeling both surprised and moved. *You turned out to be quite the romantic after all.*

Isis laughed. "I have been existing silently beside you for quite awhile now. I see what you cannot."

Morrigan smiled, though sadness wove its way around her heart as she gazed at her. *You were smart to split your soul to prevent Discordia from being all powerful, but it pains me that you will never exist whole.*

"You should know better than to say never."

"Morrigan," David's voice interrupted. "Are you ready?"

She was grateful to observe eyes that resumed their softness when he looked at her. Even if they could no longer be lovers, the world felt better when they were at peace.

"Allow me one last thing," she said. Then she went to Cahira, taking her by the hands. Morrigan was pleased she didn't recoil, enjoying the warmth of her hands against the coolness of her skin. "I have something for you."

Cahira nodded as if she already knew.

Morrigan suddenly saw her sister and herself running in the fields, Heka and Lilith painfully young and blissfully unaware of what would soon befall them. Little Morrigan hurried to keep up with her sister, but she'd already transformed into a black kite, her wings spread out as she soared and dove in the clear blue expanse dotted with clouds. Morrigan followed suit, the two weaving together as they cut through the skies in a spiraling dance, wild, happy, and free.

The vision ended to reveal Cahira's face staring back at her, two tears neatly streaming down her face. Isis's apparition had vanished.

"Thank you," Cahira whispered. She learned forward and she kissed Morrigan's cheek.

Morrigan smiled, assured her sister was finally at peace.

"You are now the Earth's protector," Anubis told Cahira from beside her. "While the rest of us have ties to other realms, the Earth is yours, blessed by Isis." He gestured to the rest of the gods who had gathered around her. "And we will all protect you."

Cahira nodded, her strong facade crumbling with emotion.

Morrigan seized the opportunity to embrace her. "I deeply regret how things turned out for us in this life, but I cannot think of a better vessel for my sister's soul. I am honored to have helped raise you."

Cahira did not speak, but squeezed her back tightly in reply.

Morrigan gradually pulled away, echoes of her sister's voice and young Cahira's laughter in her mind. "I am ready now," she told Anubis. He nodded and, as they headed out the door, she found David's eyes.

His jaw trembled but stayed tight, battling tears she knew threatened to spill from his soulful eyes. "In another life," he said softly.

Morrigan swallowed. "We do tend to find each other," she agreed. Though her insides screamed, she forced one last playful smile, and darted after her son. She pictured Lucius's face, forcing herself to remember why she made her decision.

Anubis slipped his hand around hers as they headed back towards the temple, Thomas trailing behind. He lifted the draped leaves so they could enter, revealing Helena waiting for them inside.

Though he spoke quietly, Anubis's deep voice resounded throughout the chamber. "The only way to send a creature to Tartarus is to kill them, but even then, they must be an abominable being. I can open the portal, but after that, I am at a loss."

"I am an abominable creature," Morrigan told him quietly. "I killed David's lover in Ireland, long ago."

"You were a goddess enacting vengeance on one who disrespected you," Helena spoke up. "That is not an atrocious act. Besides, you spared her son."

Morrigan looked up at her, realizing that as a spirit, Helena had access to all knowledge. Pangs of regret descended upon her as she pictured Boann's face, horrified to learn she'd spend her eternity as a river. "I have killed more humans than can be counted," Morrigan insisted.

"You only killed one in this lifetime, and he threatened you," Helena argued.

Morrigan blinked, taken aback. She was right. "Then what should we do?"

"If I may," Thomas gently interrupted. "There might be another way."

"Do tell." Morrigan turned towards him.

"I have often wondered, when considering your history in Egypt—how was Set banished to Tartarus?"

Morrigan looked to Anubis, but he shook his head. "Tartarus already existed before I took him there. I did not create it."

Morrigan grew quiet, sweeping away the cobwebs that cluttered her mind to her days as Nephthys. Then it hit her. "Because I created it to send him there."

Thomas nodded, warmth in his brown eyes. "You are the creator of realms. If you want to go to Tartarus, send yourself there."

She clasped his hands. "Thank you," she whispered. Then she turned toward her son, and took his arm. "I am ready."

The air around them grew thick and hot as they sat in the temple, like the sweltering jungle right before a monsoon. Although hundreds of candles smoldered all around them, she could not see, her son's glowing blue eyes the only thing visible in the darkness as he chanted. She heard the distant beat of drums keeping time with her own heart as she relaxed into an ancient world she had long forgotten, the place where her soul had been born. Her son was now the jackal, the god Thoth standing beside him, working together to pull Nephthys out of hiding. The drumbeats soon shifted into the chanting of Egyptian priests, the incense smoke biting the air as Anubis traced symbols on her forehead and eyes with oil. He stood back as violent purple flickered around his skin like heat lightning, raising his power until it trickled out of his fingertips. It fell to the ground in a circle, where the souls of the chanting priests sprang up, strips of linen hanging from their necrotic, mummified flesh. They bowed to Morrigan, singing her praises with rotting mouths as the ground opened at her feet. The heat of the room intensified, but she was kept cool, her own manifestation of power—black shadows—swirling around her for protection. The priests were soon joined by other nameless souls, drawn to the one who once cared for them, preparing to carry her home.

She closed her eyes, thinking of David, Cahira, and the precious Earth she was leaving behind. Then she saw his face, his adoring golden eyes, and she let herself go, suddenly weightless.

The souls guided her as she floated down through the barriers between realms, their frayed spaces bending easily to her presence. But what met her as she landed was not the shadowy realm she remembered, but a blast of raging fire and scalding heat. Intensely bright and suffocating, she shut her eyes against it as the souls pulled her through the worst until they reached a calm space to lay her down. Then they lingered, as if hoping she'd give them a resting place better than where they currently stood. She quickly envisioned the Underworld that she remembered—the one that she and Lucius had created, with its towering Records Hall, the obsidian mountains, and indigo pools. She waited until it was perfectly clear in her mind before she whispered, Go. And it was suddenly so. When she opened her eyes, they had all disappeared.

What met her instead were the empty eyes of an overgrown crow skull, which cocked its head to the side as it examined her with intrigue. She sat up to observe her surroundings, the world around her painted in shades of rust and burnt orange. A reddish haze snaked through a cemetery formed out of mushrooming human bones. The crow skeleton cocked its head to the other side and decided to move on, tugging bits of rotten flesh from some of the remains. One batted the crow away with its bony arm, its putrefying eyes still rolling around in its sockets.

Morrigan noticed some wore clothing from a century prior, their leftover skin pockmarked from disease. They didn't match others splayed out in shambles, so old they grew fungi out of their crevices. "You do not belong down here," she realized as she rose to her feet, startling the dead crow who flapped at the stale air.

The living skeletons began to lift themselves out of their plots, groaning as she heard their voices loud in her mind: We don't belong here, please… we just want to rest.

Go, she commanded as she thought of her Underworld once more. Their gruesome physical husks fell immediately into dust, leaving behind ethereal human apparitions who floated peacefully and disappeared into the caliginous space above them. She smiled, satisfied, although the crow was not, and she gathered up her black skirts to leave the field of bones. She caught the attention of a few leathery demons that had been scuttling around in search of food, who now stared at her with open curiosity. They bowed as she walked past, their bones cracking and popping with movement as they squeaked like overgrown rats with wings. She marched past them through the Hall of Titans, who groaned and grumbled, the sound reverberating through the passageway. Every demon she passed immediately gave her a deep bow, even the horrible wolf that flew up to her before realizing who she was. She gave him a hateful sneer, remembering when he tore her apart on Earth a century ago. He retreated as quickly as he'd approached.

She eventually reached Phlegethon, once a winding river and now a lake of fire that covered the Elysian Plains, the place in Hades where souls could rest in peace. She pooled a white mist together to surround her in a watery veil, protecting her from the heat as she stood at its banks, gathering it up in a great, swirling ball. Then she pushed the fallen rocks back where they belonged, and trapped the flow of lava in its original place so the plains were free.

Satisfied, she turned to see dozens of demons gathered around her in awe. She ignored them, intent on finishing her work, correcting the places that once belonged to other realms with careful sweeps of her arms. She passed by the old Asphodel Meadows, a dank, sunless space where the disembodied spirits once wept and wailed, now overcrowded with the souls she'd sent there. She showed them the cleared Plains in her mind, and dozens headed back that way, revealing a towering mountain range made of rock and bone. She blinked when part of it moved, recognizing the bulky shape she'd mistakenly assumed was stationary.

"Cerberus," she said in disbelief. He immediately shrunk down to her size, wagging his tail as he ran to her, all three heads panting happily, pink tongues hanging out of their mouths. "You're still alive," she said in wonder as she ran her fingers through his fur. "Is he here?"

Cerberus abruptly grew back into his giant proportion, bowing his three heads so she could use one to climb onto his back.

"That is very kind of you, thank you," she said as she seated herself between his massive shoulder blades. She held onto his fur as he lifted her up, taking her past the deepest places of torment and lakes of trapped bodies, straight into the mountain range itself. He dropped her off at the mouth of a cave, gesturing inside with his heads. She patted him again, advancing into the darkness until she finally reached the cold world she remembered.

She saw him from the back, standing shirtless with his hands on his hips, admiring the palace he was in the process of rebuilding. Hades's towering obsidian palace was nearly complete as demons carried the fragmented chunks of stone forward, the sounds of clanking tools echoing throughout the empty hills. In the distance was a deep crater that once held the River Styx, its waters trapped by the mountains she'd just walked through. She could see sweat dripping down the muscular curvature of his back as she crept closer, running fingers through hair he'd apparently decided to keep short, even in the Netherworld.

But when he sensed her, immediately whipping around to see if his senses were betraying him, he looked like a mix of all of them—Set, Lucifer, Lucius, and Louis—a blend of all his faces possessing the same brilliant gold eyes.

He froze, staring in utter disbelief.

As much as she felt like throwing her arms around him, she marched up to him instead, shoving him as hard as she could and knocking him to the ground. "How could you kill yourself without telling me?" she demanded.

He scowled, jumping back to his feet. "You were the one who left me, remember?"

"What are you talking about?" She glared at him, hands on her hips.

"When you came back from contacting Jacob, Anubis and Cahira told me you'd left," he told her. "We didn't hear from you for days."

"I was gone that long?" She frowned, looking away as she tried to piece things together.

"Morrigan, why are you here?" he asked softly, emotion thick in his voice.

"Because you are here!" she said in exasperation.

"Please don't shove me again," he said as he put his hands up in defense. "I thought you'd run off again, upset that I killed Jacob, perhaps upset from the things I showed you about myself..." He trailed off, unnerved by his own admission.

"So you let yourself die? That is absolutely ridiculous."

"I assumed you'd finally made your decision," he added quietly.

"I did make my decision!" Her anger rose again, followed by a rumble as a boulder crashed to the ground from the mountains, releasing a gush of water that filled the empty River Styx. The force of the water loosened the rock that had been blocking the lake, joining the two as it had been before. "I have chosen you a dozen times over."

"Throughout our long history, you have always chosen him in the end," Lucius pointed out. "You may enjoy me for a moment, but you always go back. And I cannot chase you anymore. I know I love you completely, but if you're happier with him, then you should be with him. How can I proclaim my love for you, but not allow you to be happy?"

Morrigan was stunned.

"That being said, I have no desire to live on Earth without you and I'm quite certain I could not physically handle witnessing your reconciliation with David. I can make do here, like I've always done."

"You are the decision I should have always made," she insisted. "I had hoped you saw that in me."

He softened as he searched her eyes. "Please forgive me, I should have trusted you." He crept closer with the careful approach one uses with a wild animal. "I wanted to, but there was too much noise in the background, preying on the nagging voice that tells me otherwise."

Morrigan sighed. "I know I must earn your trust again. But perhaps we can both stop running from each other until then?"

"I can do that," he agreed. His lips turned up in a sideways smile. "In any case, I did feel bad leaving David down here. He's far too delicate for this realm."

She matched his grin with a roll of her eyes. "I did figure out that part on my own. Also, you were right from the beginning—the Holy Watchers didn't want any gods to live, but they were targeting me specifically because I am the one who created the realms. They wanted you gone, not only because you helped me build them—even inspiring me to create Tartarus and the Upperrealms—but because you protect me at all costs. Even when I don't want you to. There was no getting rid of me unless they first got rid of you."

Lucius gazed at her with adoration. "I do love your mind."

"As mad as I am that you came here without me," she continued, "you knew this was what we had to do—it was our part in saving the realms. To come back here and rebuild them all. You just wanted it to be my choice to make…and I made it."

"Can I please hold you now?"

She smiled, and he pulled her tightly against him. She sighed with relief, grateful to be back where she belonged.

He rested his face against her hair. "All I ever really wanted was for you to want to be here," he murmured.

"I think all I ever wanted was the choice," she said against the warmth of his chest. "I realized that as furious as you make me, I don't want to live in a world without you."

"And my brother?"

Morrigan lifted her head to meet his eyes. "He has chosen to let me—let us go. I think it's high time we all moved on."

"Then you must promise me that if you need to return to Earth, you do so," he told her. "I might have finally made peace with my place in the Netherrealms, but I don't ever want you to feel trapped and restless again. I will do my best to trust you. Besides, you've discovered you're a liminal deity now, like David. Somehow you can both move between the realms without much effort. There must be a reason why."

"Thank you." She smiled. "But I do think I'll be down here for quite a bit of time." She took his hands from behind her back and guided them so they rested on the low part of her stomach. "I seem to have picked up a pair of twins along the way."

Lucius blinked several times in shock, his mind racing behind his eyes to understand what she just told him, before tears beaded their corners. "Is it true?" he whispered.

She grazed his lips with hers. "They were peacefully awaiting you in the Middleworld and recognized me immediately. I'm thinking we should call them by the names they once had—Ashera and Abi."

Lucius grabbed her face, covering her with kisses and squeezing her joyfully before hoisting her up in the air. Tears freely streamed down his cheeks, his face lit up with the happiest expression she had ever seen on his face, his eyes like radiant stars in the night sky.

"Come," he said, kissing her again as he carried her up the steps towards Hades's palace. "We have a lot of rebuilding to do."

David

THE WATCHERS STARED AT HIM COLDLY from behind their human facades. The atmosphere was tight and still, a far cry from the pleasant ethereal realm he'd once visited. All three of them stood with their arms crossed in front of them, Michael's lips pressed into a hateful line.

"I am not here for war," David told them, "but to offer you an accord. We have successfully avoided all of your attempts to stifle us. The goddess Discordia is now dead, her minions purposelessly roaming Earth until they are found and killed by Cahira. Lucius and Morrigan are rebuilding the Underworld, and will soon be joined by the other death gods hiding in the Middleworld. You have lost."

"Did you come here to gloat?"

"Not in the slightest. But we cannot let go of what you have done. You murdered the Council that Anubis created to protect the realms, and you have done anything but. It would only be fair that we destroy your realm like you did ours. But we know your Holy One is loved by many, and Jesus has persuaded us that He is not to blame—His sycophants are.

"You can stay here in the Kingdom of Heaven, but you must stop interfering in the affairs of the other gods. In turn, we will leave you in peace. You will no longer act as the Council—Cahira, Morrigan, Lucius and myself will take our rightful place, with Anubis and Libraean standing in for Lucius and Morrigan while they are in the Underworld. You can have your own Council here, but you will reinstate Gabriel. He will keep an eye on you to make sure you are following the new rules. I wouldn't attempt to get rid of him, for Jesus has agreed to this plan and plans on protecting his trusted friend."

Micheal's scowl did not move. "Is that all?"

"Almost." David smiled back. "You can keep your Kingdom, but I will be taking back control of the Upperrealms. They were not even yours to begin with. I will take Gaia's Forest and you will let any other gods who ascend have whatever else is available. Libraean will be in charge of it all—he is a remarkable record keeper and you are lucky to have him guide you. As far as the humans are concerned, you can continue to have your religions and your rules, but you will cease your torment of those who do not choose to believe in your ways. You may quarrel amongst each other, but you will leave those who practice the old ways alone."

"Is that all?" Michael repeated coldly.

"Yes," David said as he headed out of the Tower. "And God help you if you cross us again."

No one moved to stop him, but the realm shuddered as the Tower that was once firmly planted in the atmospheric island promptly disappeared from sight, taking the clouds and fog with them. David turned to see Libraean and Jacob, both restored to their younger selves. Strikingly blonde and handsome, Libraean's clear blue eyes rivaled Morrigan's; they were completely restored with his death, a gift finally given to him, as well as the one that allowed him to finally join his true love. Tears amassed in his eyes now as Jacob, then he, gave David a warm embrace.

"You must visit," Libraean told him.

"I will," David promised.

"You are welcome any time in Jesus's realm, as well," Jacob said.

"Thank you." David smiled. In his peripheral vision, he saw the outline of two others on shore waiting for him.

Libraean gave him one final squeeze. "Go. Please be happy for once."

David tried not to show the struggle to leave his oldest friend, but the gentle beckoning of Gaia and his son soothed him as it pulled. He moved to join them, not having to look back to know the men who played his fathers had disappeared. He was fully convinced they would handle the heavenly affairs.

Gaia squeezed David so tightly he thought he might stop breathing, as his grown son beamed at him, his hands at his waist.

"Welcome back," he said.

"Thank you," David said breathlessly.

Gaia released him from her grasp, only to take his face in her hands and smother it with kisses.

"Let him breathe." Aengus laughed.

"Okay, okay." Gaia finally took a step back. The grin on her face refused to fade, her cheeks flushed a rosy pink. "Did you learn that Aengus is not my actual son?"

"You are just as much his mother as Boann, but yes," David told her. "How did you find each other?"

"When Boann found out she'd spend the rest of her immortal life as a river, she sent out a petition for Danu to watch over his soul," Gaia explained. "Danu honored her promise and, right before Discordia ended her life, she sent him to me."

"I'm glad to finally know you," David told his son. "I regret I never had the opportunity in life."

"Well, we have an eternity to do so." Aengus smiled, looking very much like young Davius from Ancient Rome.

"You are staying, right?" Gaia asked, suddenly concerned.

David cupped her shoulder. "There is more to be done on Earth, enough that I must stay planted there. Things are resolved for now, but that doesn't mean the balance won't tip again. However, I did finally realize, after all that time of thinking my physical body was failing me, that I am a realm traveler, meant to move freely between them, not force myself to stay in one place. I believe I am supposed to spend my time where I want, and return when I'm needed."

"What about the others?"

"Morrigan and Lucius are restoring the Netherrealms," he told her.

"Unbeknownst to us, Sandrine and Anubis worked out a plan for her to take over his position in Africa, where she hopes to find and guide those who have inherited the remnants of Isis's heka. Anubis has resumed his work as guardian of the dead in the Middleworld with Helena. Thomas has offered to take up residence at Lardone Manor, joined by Dan and Cahira when they are not off hunting the rest of Angelique's demons and recruiting lost gods to come back with them. We have decided to open the house to all reincarnated gods, until everything is back in order. Apparently, Lucius foresaw all of this happening, including his own death, and instructed his lawyers to entrust his entire estate to us."

Gaia looked surprised, but satisfied by his response. "Then everything is as it should be."

"Yes, I think it is." David looked up to see that Aengus had disappeared.

"He likes to be on his own," Gaia told him as she slipped her hand in his. "He knows we need our time."

He beamed down at her. "Let's go home."

With that, the two lovers walked along the shore, hand in hand under the sunset, its rays throwing gold and copper along their freckled skin, brightening their auburn hair.

Epilogue

D AVID STOOD, WIPING THE LEAVES AND BRUSH FROM HIS PANT LEGS as he searched around the forest floor for his hat. He retrieved it from a tree branch, situating it atop his head, though the weather was calm and warm with the onset of summer. When he visited Earth, he enjoyed dressing the part.

As soon as he exited the forest, he saw the manor ahead, each one of its windows filled with gaslight, the stained glass of the third story fully restored to its former glory. His chest warmed at the sight of it, fully operational and filled with creatures he cared deeply for, but he was in no hurry.

The wind picked up around him as he headed into the cemetery, the sight of the Lardone crypt reminding him of how much he missed Libraean. He smiled when he thought of him alongside Gabriel in the Upperrealms, assured that when business slowed—or when their yearlong honeymoon was over—and he was ready for a visit, he would find him.

He approached the southern cemetery, heading straight towards the Angel of Death gravestone, awkward amongst the dilapidated slabs. He put his hand on the torch and pushed, causing the ground to shift and reveal a hidden opening. He descended quickly, on the off chance someone else otherworldly had caught wind of his presence.

The door sealed as he walked down the long, winding staircase of jutted stone steps, torches lighting his way.

Lucius waited for him at the bottom, sipping a goblet of wine, the chessboard still arranged from the last time they played. He was in his favorite form, a cross between Lucius and Louis, wearing a casual Victorian ensemble with his short black curls brushed away from his forehead.

"How did you know I'd be down to visit?" David asked him, hanging his hat on one of the hooks.

"Call it brotherly intuition," Lucius shrugged. "Hurry, it's your move."

David sat across from him, studying his face before his eyes moved down to the board. "You look tired."

"I am tired," he replied, brows furrowed as he studied David's play. He swept his rook upwards.

"How is she?" David asked as casually as he could, moving his knight out of the way.

"She craves nothing but black licorice," he told him. "I don't understand it, either. She was a vampire longer than she ever was a human—I can't even think about human food."

David was thoughtful. "Perhaps it's because the children are human?"

"Whatever the reason," Lucius swiftly castled the king, "I've had to keep it in stock. She's more tempestuous than I've ever seen, and I'm not in the place where I want to encourage her moodiness."

David felt a whisper of sadness but didn't reveal it, noticing Lucius had left his queen exposed.

"And how is your family up north?" Lucius asked him.

"Good," David replied, grateful for the change in subject. He smiled when he thought of Gaia and Aengus on their trip to Ireland. Over time, he'd realized the two of them needed their own time just as much as he and Gaia did, and when Aengus was summoned for diplomatic measures, he urged Gaia to join him. "I'm interested to see what they uncover on their trip."

"Ah, yes. The humans," Lucius nodded. "Have you been to the manor yet? Tell my granddaughter her mother is upset she's only come to visit once."

"I will tell her. I'm headed there now, I just wanted to finish our game." David inched towards Lucius's exposed queen with his bishop.

"Well then. Allow me to make it easy for you," Lucius said, putting David's king into checkmate.

David blinked, surprised he hadn't seen the move coming.

Lucius laughed. "Perhaps you shouldn't be so focused on my queen."

David felt his face flush as he rose from the table. "One day I'll beat you at this damned game," he said, reaching for his hat.

Lucius leaned back in his seat, folding one leg over the other. "I'll be here."

The two stared at each other for a moment before David offered him a tight nod.

"Goodnight, Lucius."

"Goodnight, David."

Acknowledgements

Where can I even begin? There have been so many people near and dear to me who have helped bring this trilogy into fruition. From the very beginning, there were voices who helped push me to publish something I knew in my heart should be read, but wasn't sure exactly how it would happen. Andrew and Lauren, thank you for being those early voices.

As the novels progressed and Quill & Crow Publishing House grew, the supportive voices changed, and I would like to deeply thank Marie, William, Alma, and Lucas, for seeing something in me and in this trilogy that was worth fighting for. None of this would have been possible without your support. I would also like to express my deepest thanks to my editorial team at Q&C including Kayla, for catching the typos that somehow survived six rounds of edits, and Tiffany for suggesting the perfect tweaks to ensure Revelations would shine. I'd also like to thank Lucas for having a brilliant mind best used for solving puzzles, who helped me fill in the blank spots where I could not see.

The support of the indie community has also been a big part of this book's completion. I am honored to be part of a growing initiative that is changing the face of publishing. Authors supporting authors is a beautiful thing.

And lastly, my family. Whether we are tied by blood, by love, by Bill, or by corvid creed, you all have helped these books come about. Your support is cherished, always.

Discover more from this author at
www.quillandcrowpublishinghouse.com

www.ingramcontent.com/pod-product-compliance
Lightning Source LLC
Chambersburg PA
CBHW050829190726
48286CB00007B/2012